The Righteous Arrows

The Righteous Arrows

by Brian J. Morra

© Copyright 2024 Brian J. Morra

ISBN 979-8-88824-280-3

All rights reserved. No part of this publication may be reproduced, stored in a retrieval system, or transmitted in any form or by any means—electronic, mechanical, photocopy, recording, or any other—except for brief quotations in printed reviews, without the prior written permission of the author.

This is a work of fiction. The characters are both actual and fictitious. With the exception of verified historical events and persons, all incidents, descriptions, dialogue and opinions expressed are the products of the author's imagination and are not to be construed as real.

Published by

◄ köehlerbooks™

3705 Shore Drive
Virginia Beach, VA 23455
800-435-4811
www.koehlerbooks.com

THE RIGHTEOUS ARROWS

A NOVEL OF RETRIBUTION

BRIAN J. MORRA

VIRGINIA BEACH
CAPE CHARLES

For Tracy

*Through our great good fortune, in our youth,
our hearts were touched by fire.*

—Oliver Wendell Holmes, Jr.
(future associate justice of the United States Supreme Court and former captain,
United States Volunteers on Memorial Day, May 30, 1884)

PRINCIPAL CHARACTERS

The Americans

Captain Kevin Cattani: US Air Force Intelligence Officer

The Red-haired Major: Retired US Air Force Intelligence Officer and current senior CIA Officer in the Special Activities Division

Captain Sandy Jackson: US Air Force nurse and medical student at Georgetown University

Lydia Morelli: Civilian nuclear weapons analyst, Defense Intelligence Agency

Major Mike Hosenko: US Air Force Intelligence Officer

General Douglas Flannery: US Air Force, Commander-in-Chief US Air Forces Europe and Allied Air Forces, Europe

Brigadier General Leonard Palumbo (later Major General): US Air Force, Deputy Chief of Staff for Intelligence, US Air Forces Europe (Ramstein AB, West Germany), and later Chief of Air Force Intelligence

Colonel John LaRoche: US Air Force Intelligence Officer

Mr. Rand Bottoms: the civilian Deputy Director of the Defense Intelligence Agency

Dr. Robert Gillis: Deputy Director of Central Intelligence

Mike "B": CIA officer and in charge of the secret war in Afghanistan

"Brad": CIA Special Activities Division officer

"Phil": CIA Special Activities Division officer

Ronald Reagan: President of the United States (1981–1989)

The Soviets
General-Major Ivan Ivanovich Levchenko: GRU Intelligence Officer, Air Defense Forces of the Soviet Union. He also is known as Vanya (Russian diminutive) and Ivanko (Ukrainian diminutive)

Boyka Levchenka: Musician and wife of Colonel Levchenko (Ukrainian)

Oxana Koghuta: Boyka's married sister (Ukrainian)

Oleksandr Koghut: Oxana's husband (Ukrainian)

Major Anatoli Zhukov: GRU Intelligence Officer

Lieutenant Colonel Vasily Zaitsev: Commander of the GRU 22nd Special Forces (SPETSNAZ) Brigade, Asadabad, Afghanistan

Lieutenant Colonel Mikhail Grishin: GRU officer and Ivan Levchenko's long-time nemesis

Colonel Gennadiy Sidorov: Commander of the 15th GRU Special Forces (Spetsnaz) Brigade, Jalalabad, Afghanistan

General-Lieutenant Victor Dubynin: Commander of the Soviet 40th Army, Afghanistan

General of the Army Pyotr Ivashutin: Director of the GRU (Soviet Military Intelligence)

Marshal of the Soviet Union Sergey Ahkromeyeev: Chief of the General Staff of the USSR

Yuri Andropov: Former Director of the KGB, General Secretary of the Communist Party of the Soviet Union (November 1982–February 1984)

Konstantin Chernenko: General Secretary of the Communist Party of the Soviet Union (February 1984–March 1985)

Mikhail Gorbachev: General Secretary of the Communist Party of the Soviet Union (March 1985–December 1992)

The Communist Afghans
Babrak Karmal: President of Afghanistan (December 1979–1986)

Anahita Samar: a medical doctor, a member of Karmal's government, and a political advocate for the rights of Afghan women

The Rebel Afghans
Jalaluddin Haqqani: Pashtu leader and senior member of the Haqqani clan, a leading group of Islamic rebels in the Northwest Frontier region of Pakistan

Ahmed Shah Massoud: Tadjik leader, "the Lion of the Panjshir," the most acclaimed Afghan warlord in the fight against the Soviets

FOREWORD

No less a figure than the last Soviet President, Nobel Peace Prize winner Mikhail Gorbachev, characterized the first half of the 1980s as perhaps the most dangerous time in human history. In fact, it was a time when the United States and the Soviet Union flirted perilously with nuclear Armageddon. In the autumn of 1983, provocative American policies combined with extreme Soviet paranoia nearly led to a global nuclear war. The crisis reached its climax with the Able Archer exercise in November 1983. Then, in the spring of 1984, the Kremlin conducted a massive nuclear war exercise, mere months after the two superpowers nearly stumbled into war. The Soviet exercise demonstrated that we were not yet out of the woods and distrust remained dangerously high both in Washington and Moscow.

When Gorbachev came to power in 1985, he had to deal with the nuclear balance of power and the final foreign adventure of the Soviet Union, the brutal Soviet War in Afghanistan. After initially increasing the Soviet military presence, he concluded that the Afghanistan War was a conflict the USSR would not win and could not afford to sustain. By 1986, Gorbachev had decided to withdraw Soviet forces from that ill-fated adventure and to pursue nuclear arms talks with the United States.

Ironically, around the same time Gorbachev concluded he needed to get out of the Afghanistan conflict, the United States decided to provide the Afghan Mujahedin rebels with advanced weapons with which to fight the Soviets, including the CIA-supplied Stinger anti-aircraft missiles—called by the Afghan fighters the "righteous arrows of retribution." In upping the stakes in Afghanistan, Washington was motivated by various factors, including revenge for the Kremlin's support of Communist forces against America and its allies during the Vietnam War. Many think the CIA covert war in Afghanistan was among the Agency's finest hours and I agree, but it did not come without cost.

The CIA's support of the resistance in Afghanistan clearly hastened the collapse of the USSR. Arms transfers to Afghan rebel fighters in the 1980s also inadvertently helped to create the conditions for the rise of radical Sunni Muslim forces. Despite conspiracy theories to the contrary, Washington never provided support to Usama bin Laden in Afghanistan. Nonetheless, he rose to prominence during the Soviet War, and later he used Afghanistan as his base of operations while planning the 9/11 attacks on the United States.

The Righteous Arrows reacquaints readers with the two protagonists from *The Able Archers*—me as a young man and the Soviet officer Ivan Levchenko. In *The Righteous Arrows,* Ivan Levchenko is a highly successful Soviet military intelligence officer, recently promoted to one-star general. In Afghanistan, he experiences the horrors of combat for the first time. The two of us are on opposite sides in the Soviet War in Afghanistan and meet as adversaries, not as the peacemakers of *The Able Archers.*

The Red-haired Major, who was introduced in *The Able Archers,* is a major figure in *The Righteous Arrows* where we find him at the peak of his singular powers. Speaking of that old warrior, he recently visited me in my office at the headquarters of the Office of the Director of National Intelligence. We chatted about world events and reminisced about departed friends, a sad tally that seems to lengthen every week. He was in high spirits, but he looked terribly unwell. I realized immediately that this was not a social call; it was a farewell visit. As we parted, he embraced me weakly with his once-powerful arms. I felt him sob as he whispered, "I'm so proud of you, Kevin. Promise me that you'll keep fighting after I'm gone. Promise me, old friend."

How could I refuse? The Red-haired Major is the one person I could never bear to disappoint.

Dr. Kevin Cattani, General, United States Air Force (retired)
Director of National Intelligence
McLean, Virginia
28 November 2025

PART ONE

A Man of Certitude and Violence

I can't think that slowly. If I did, I'd be dead.

—**Michael J. Hritsik, Colonel, United States Air Force**

CHAPTER ONE

A VISIT FROM THE RED-HAIRED MAJOR

Captain Kevin Cattani, US Air Force Intelligence
Ramstein Air Base, Federal Republic of Germany (West Germany)

14 April 1984

Ever since I was a kid, I have wanted to be a spook, or if you prefer, an intelligence officer, a spy, an international man of mystery. This started for me as a fantastic dream—a means of escape for someone desperately seeking a way out of a boring existence in a dead-end town. I never actually thought such a silly pipedream would come true.

Was I driven by patriotism? A thirst for adventure? A chance to see the world? Or simply the need for a steady paycheck? The answer is probably "all of the above." I certainly had an aversion to totalitarian regimes, whether their underlying political philosophy was communism, fascism, or any other "ism." Russian culture fascinated me, but I was disgusted by what the Communist Party had done to Russia and its satellite countries within the USSR and the Warsaw Pact. Playing even a minor part in the great game of geopolitics seemed like a better use of my time than almost anything else I could envision doing, short of being an international rock star or a professional athlete.

I suppose one could say that I have gotten what I asked for. Given my experiences over the last several years, a wiser man might be reconsidering his career choice. But being a spook is a vocation, not a career, so is it a choice? Some spooks are like missionaries who go out in the world intent on doing good works. In fact, some of the best spooks I know are the children of actual Christian missionaries. They are native speakers of the languages of the countries where they once lived and have an intuitive feel for the cultures. Other spooks are like princelings who travel to the far reaches of the empire to do the bidding of their betters even if they question the wisdom of the orders they are given. The worst spooks are functionaries who do not have a true vocation. I have no idea why they are in the spook business in the first place, and I have no tolerance for them. I am no functionary. Am I a missionary or a princeling? I am a bit too cynical to be a genuine missionary and lack the radical idealism of the missionary. I grew up in sketchy financial circumstances and that makes it hard for me to think of myself as a princeling. Nonetheless, if I am not a zealous missionary or a miserable functionary, then by a process of elimination, I must be a princeling. We princelings are the true enforcers of the national will. Genuine princelings believe they are superior to their superiors and often question the wisdom of their orders, even while carrying out those orders with skill and determination. Princelings are ambitious and position themselves to become princes someday.

My first boss in the spook business was a princeling and was a major influence on my development as a proper spook. A model man of action and known to all as "the Red-haired Major," he is the most preeminent spook I have ever met. Adept in all aspects of the intelligence discipline, his forte is most definitely the hardest skill of them all: dealing with and—if necessary—killing bad people.

The Red-haired Major is from a Scottish family that settled in

Newburyport, Massachusetts in the late 1600s. He has never talked about his family with me, other than an occasional reference to a wife who has her own business in Tokyo or to a cherished ancestor who fought in Washington's Continental Army. He has an extremely high opinion of himself and is not averse to sharing it with anyone he meets. A graduate of Harvard College, he is the opposite of the privileged, upper-class man one associates with old Harvard. The best way to imagine his appearance is to think of Paul Bunyan as he is depicted in books for young readers, preferably wrestling with Babe the Blue Ox. He is massive in every way—physically, mentally, and in personality. I think of him as the somewhat unhinged older brother I never had, and I love him more than a brother, which—for the record—I do not have. I have a blood brother in the Red-haired Major.

I first saw the Red-haired Major in action in Cambodia in 1980. Back then, he and I were part of a special CIA operation designed to determine if a genocide had occurred inside Cambodia. The communist Khmer Rouge were suspected of mass killings, and they ruled Cambodia until the North Vietnamese Army kicked them out of power. Were the Khmer Rouge capable of killing millions of their own citizens? The rumors of their brutal reeducation and extermination camps were viewed by many intelligence authorities around the world as rather too outlandish to believe. After all, the Khmer Rouge could not be as bad as the Nazi SS, right? Awful stories circulated but there was scant evidence to support the reports of mass murder.

The night before our little CIA-led team was to enter Western Cambodia, we camped in a tiny village in Thailand within shouting distance of the murky Cambodian border. As we ate a meager supper, the Red-haired Major drank scotch and regaled me and the rest of the guys with stories of his exploits, disappointments, and wounds from the Vietnam War. Once he tired of telling his tales, he abruptly stopped and told me to check the team's weapons cache and then take the first watch.

As I got to my feet to carry out my boss' order, I looked around the firepit at the faces of the other guys on the team. They sat in silence, impassively staring at the flames. What were they thinking on the eve of such a dangerous mission? The leader of our team was a former Army Special Forces officer who had transferred over to the CIA's Special Activities Division at the end of the American involvement in the Vietnam War. This Agency man—a Lakota Native American from the high plains—had the ominous name "Sixkiller."

The CIA guys called my boss the red-haired "maniac." The name fit. To my chagrin, my boss was unsure of me, and I was overanxious to prove myself to him. He was probably the oldest major in the United States Air Force, having been passed over for promotion innumerable times. I was a first lieutenant, and the Red-haired Major seemed like a mythical god of war to me. I was eager to measure up to his high expectations.

I walked over to our weapons cache and nearly stumbled. The Thai beer I'd consumed, preserved with an ample amount of formaldehyde, had me reeling a bit. My boss saw my unsteadiness and shook his head. I watched him close his eyes and slip off to sleep immediately.

I found the team's weapons stacked against a rickety little shed within sight of the firepit and I got to work. I examined the weapons methodically because I did not want to be responsible for any fuck ups in the morning. My meticulous work was made almost unbearable by the stench from an open sewer just feet away from me.

After checking each one thoroughly, I started to place the guns one by one inside the shack. As I handled an M16, I heard a noise coming from the dense trees that bordered the clearing where the team was bedded down. I heard it again—a faint rustling of leaves. I grabbed the rifle tightly and silently chambered a round. Who the hell would be out here in the boonies at midnight?

I switched off the safety and made sure the rifle was in semiautomatic mode as I stared intently at the tree line, which was partly illuminated by a lightbulb strung precariously from the eaves of the storage building. I saw nothing moving in the woods.

Craning my neck around the corner of the shack, I could see the Red-haired Major and the rest of the team sleeping soundly near the firepit. Should I wake up my boss and risk looking like an idiot rookie crying wolf for no reason? No. I started to breathe heavily, and I could feel a red snake of anxiety creep up my spine. The lousy beer I had consumed came back up on me, searing my esophagus with a fiery, foul taste. I started to take measured breaths—a deep breath in followed by a long exhale like the Red-haired Major had taught me.

If there were bad guys in the bush, I knew they probably could not see me. I knelt in the shadows behind a fidgety pile of scrap lumber. I leveled my gun's barrel on top of the sturdiest part of the stack of wood, staring intently at the woods. The dim light of the half-moon high above the jungle and the weak lightbulb dangling from the shack provided the only illumination. I strained my eyes and thought I saw foliage being shifted aside, like someone was forcing their way through the thick vegetation. Christ.

Suddenly, a small man cradling an AK-47 stepped out from the woods, walking in a cautious, measured crouch. Two others followed closely behind him, walking in the same careful manner, their heads turning slowly from side to side. It was eerie how silently they walked—like spectral executioners. I struggled to see if they wore the telltale Khmer Rouge red and white checkered scarves around their necks. One of the men half-turned toward me and I glimpsed a scarf wrapped around his neck, but I couldn't make out the color. He murmured something and cocked his head toward my little shack. Did he see me? I guess not because the three continued their slow march.

I crouched lower behind the haphazard lumber pile. I could feel the blood pounding through my neck and head so hard that it hurt. The scene was surreal. My mind was telling me not to believe what I plainly saw. My thighs were screaming with pain as I maintained my crouch. I told myself to shut out the pain and concentrate on my breathing.

I aimed at the lead guy. Should I shoot? What if these dudes turned out to be the guides who were scheduled to join us in the morning? It would be a royal fuck up for me to shoot our own goddamn guides. No. We were briefed that our Cambodian guides were expected at 0500, not at midnight. The men creeping from the bush could not be our guides. They had to be bad guys—Khmer Rouge assassins who'd slipped across the porous border to ambush us. My brain filled with red fog. I had to concentrate and use fear to focus my mind and not freeze.

The lead guy paused, chambered a round, and nodded at his companions. I heard them chamber rounds, too, and they began to level their guns at my teammates sleeping by the fire—including, of course, the Red-haired Major.

I took aim at the lead guy's torso, fired two rounds, swung around to the second guy in line, and did the same. Bad guy number three turned toward my muzzle flash and started to shoot in my direction, but I beat him to the trigger and drilled one round into his chest. The three men were on the ground but not dead because they were moaning and struggling to return fire. I was still aiming at guy number three, and I fired two rounds at him and shot at the others in reverse order. Suddenly, the Red-haired Major was standing beside me. He grabbed an M16 from the remaining stack of weapons, selected full-automatic mode, and poured rounds into the three unfortunates writhing in the dirt.

Then, he strode quietly to the three bloody bodies, his rifle in firing position. He put two rounds into each man's head, turned around, looked at me, and grinned. "Good shooting, kid! I wasn't sure you had it in you, but you're a fucking killer, you gorgeous bastard!"

He reached down and grabbed a red and white checkered scarf from the neck of one of the dead Khmer Rouge fighters. Throwing back his bearded face, he tied the gory scarf around his own neck and roared like a bloodied Scotsman at the Battle of Culloden. I was transfixed by his display of martial savagery. The Red-haired Major grinned at me and said, "Always remember to put rounds in their heads to make sure they're dead!" He nodded at me like a classroom teacher, making certain his student understood the lesson. He walked over to me and enveloped me in a massive bear hug, squeezing me so hard that I started to throw up. I bent over and puked up the formaldehyde-infused beer and rice with mystery meat I'd consumed earlier onto his shoes. I gasped and he relaxed his huge arms and let go of me.

Hooting in delight, he said, "That's right, kid. Get it all out. You won't want that shit in your system tomorrow when we go into Cambodia, anyway! We may have a real fight on our hands over there." He waved the rifle over his head and bellowed, "All clear, boys! Cattani got the motherfuckers!"

I stood up straight and watched as the rest of our small team grabbed weapons and instinctively formed a defensive perimeter. They seemed a bit sheepish, like they were embarrassed to have been surprised by the attack and mortified to have been saved by the rookie on the team. Our team leader, Sixkiller, strolled over and patted me gently on the back. He whispered, "Well done. Good job." It was the greatest compliment I'd received in my entire life. Then, he sauntered away to confer with the Red-haired Major, his deputy on this mission, walking so unhurriedly it amazed me. How could he be so calm?

I felt exhausted and my head was pounding like I had a New Year's Day hangover, but I ejected the magazine from my M16 and slammed a fresh one into place. I didn't want to be caught napping if there was another Khmer Rouge hit squad out there.

The Red-haired Major would still give me shit after that night, but from that point on I was "his boy." We were bonded for life. To steal a phrase from Humphrey Bogart's character in the finale of the movie *Casablanca*, it "was the beginning of a beautiful friendship." The Red-haired Major and I do not have that much in common, but we were both on our college track and field teams. He put the shot and threw the hammer for Harvard College, and I ran long-distance races and cross-country at William and Mary. We couldn't be more different physically. The older man looks like an ancient Scottish king. He stands about six foot four inches and must weigh more than two hundred and fifty pounds. He is almost twenty years older than I am, so we never competed against each other in college. Our respective athletic disciplines say as much about our personalities as our body types. I have the steady demeanor of the long-distance runner and he has the explosive character of an athlete whose events last mere seconds.

Ramstein Air Base, where I am stationed now, is one of the major nerve centers of the Cold War. Located in southwestern Germany, Ramstein is home to the headquarters of the United States Air Forces in Europe and NATO's Allied Air Command. General Doug Flannery is the commander of both. Flannery "asked" me to go with him to Germany last fall when he got promoted to four-star general. He was my commander in Japan for a couple of years. Only an idiot would turn down a four-star's offer to go with him to his new command. Come to think of it, the Red-haired Major might have said no and he's certainly no idiot. I will admit there were times during the harsh German winter we just experienced that I regretted coming to Germany. On the other hand, the snowy weather forced me to rest and recover from the injuries I sustained in East Germany in November of last year, courtesy of Soviet military intelligence.

At last, it is early spring here in Western Germany and the scents on the evening air hint of warmer weather to come. I'm in my quarters at Ramstein, a one-bedroom apartment with just enough room for my toys—a road racing bicycle, a Fender Stratocaster with a Princeton amp, and my stereo. I still run but I'm more passionate about cycling these days and I've played guitar since I was thirteen, so I always manage to have one with me wherever I am in the world.

I have a window cracked open to let in the mild early evening air as I sip a glass of scotch while listening to the new album *Reckoning* by my favorite band, REM. There is a knock at my door. I'm not expecting anyone right now, and I'm annoyed. I hate to be disturbed by unexpected interruptions. I open the door to find a surprise visitor filling all the available space.

"Did you miss me, kid?" It's my old boss, the Red-haired Major.

"Jesus, boss! What are you doing in Germany?"

He looks at the glass in my hand. "Invite me in, pour me a drink, and I'll tell you." His massive frame brushes past me and he plops down in my favorite chair in the tiny living area. He looks around my quarters, sniffs the air, and asks, "What the hell is that crap you're listening to?"

"It's a band from Georgia—REM."

"Sounds like the singer is being tortured with a coat hanger. Turn that crap down and get me a scotch. I can't understand anything that guy is saying—not that I give a shit." He shakes his head in disgust.

I turn down the stereo's volume to the lowest level—with apologies to Michael Stipe and company. There's a nearly full bottle of Glenlivet on the sideboard and I get him a drink.

Unlike me, the Red-haired Major is built like a Soviet tank—a hulking, powerful brute of a man. His degree is in history, and he is fluent in Russian, German, Mandarin, and Vietnamese—he's a man of many skills. He also is sporting a major-league beard.

"It's great to see you. What brings you here?"

He gulps the scotch and sighs. "Ah, that's better. Oh, I'm on my way to Berlin. I needed to stop here at Ramstein to change planes, and I thought I'd check in on my boy. By the way, thanks for saving the world from nuclear holocaust last fall. Good work! Those few of us who know about it say, 'thank you.'" He grins through his beard and takes another drink.

I raise my glass toward him. "You're welcome. I enjoy saving the world from time to time. What's with the beard?"

The Red-haired Major's face is largely obscured by his beard—like the one he had when we were together in Cambodia a few years ago. "I'm retired. I mean I retired from the Air Force last year, around the same time those dipshits at NATO were on the verge of exterminating humanity during the Able Archer bullshit. I'm working for the Agency full time now—with my Special Activities bubbas. Langley went and made me a goddamn GS-15—what do you think of that?" He smiles so hard his eyes contract and nearly disappear into his bearded face.

"Congratulations. It's about time you got a promotion. What will you be doing in Berlin?"

"I can't say exactly, but I'll be meeting with the station chief to discuss a few ideas I have for a new job and then I'll head back to Langley. You remember Sixkiller, don't you? He was our head honcho back in Cambodia. Now he's the station chief in Berlin. Can you believe it?"

I will never forget Sixkiller. He saved my life twice in Cambodia. "I remember he was a great fighter—Sixkiller. He's in Berlin?"

The Red-haired Major nods vigorously. "Yeah, the SOB learned to speak German and is in Berlin now. He's a good shit, not like some of those assholes at Langley. I'm sick to death of those pinhead analysts and political backstabbers and I gotta get the fuck out of there." He shakes his head in exasperation at the thought of the suits back at CIA headquarters in Virginia. He's only happy in the field where his considerable skills can be utilized.

"Well, I hope it works out for you." I drain my drink while he points at his now empty glass, ordering me to refill it. I grab the Glenlivet and pour him another.

He takes a sip and asks with concern in his voice, "Are you recovered from that beating you took in East Germany?" He gives me a sympathetic look but continues talking before I can answer him. "I bet you miss being in the action now that you're in a staff job, eh?"

"I'm better, thanks. And I think I had enough excitement last fall to last me a while."

"Well, the GRU really beat the crap out of you." He nods knowingly and changes the subject abruptly. "Are you banging anybody?"

I roll my eyes and shake my head. "Jesus, boss." He's as subtle as ever. "I'm seeing a nurse that I originally met back in Japan—at Yokota Air Base. Her name is Sandy Jackson and she's stationed at the medical center at Landstuhl. She lives on base here at Ramstein."

"Good." He strokes his chin and muses. "So, she would be Chief Jackson's daughter? He told me his daughter is a nurse stationed at that big-ass Landstuhl Medical Center."

How does he know Sandy's father, Chief Master Sergeant Charles Jackson? I guess it shouldn't surprise me that he does. Sandy's father was assigned to the US Military Liaison Mission in Potsdam, East Germany, during last fall's Able Archer nuclear crisis. He rescued me from a GRU black site where the Russians had beat the living shit out of me.

He continues. "Now, Chief Jackson is a real warrior. You must know him from Potsdam. I bet his daughter is a pistol. I hope you can handle her!"

Somehow, it's reassuring to me that he knows Sandy's father. "Sandy's applying to med school and the Air Force medical education program. She's smart, pretty, and tough. The jury is still out on whether I can handle her."

He grins and nods his approval. "I bet she's a babe—half Black and half Japanese. I know both of her parents and they're a great-looking couple. Good on ya! I hope she's treating you right." He raises his glass in a toast to my good judgment in women.

"Thanks. Well, Sandy doesn't like me doing operational things. Since you know her father, you know that he's done some hairy shit over the years."

"Well, if she wanted a wimp, she shouldn't have picked you." He grabs the bottle and refills his own glass. "Anyway, I wouldn't want you to develop DSB. You're still a young man."

"DSB?"

"You mean you haven't heard of deadly semen buildup? That shit can kill you." The Red-haired Major nods with a very serious look on his face and mutters, "DSB, my friend—don't let it get out of control."

I shake my head and reply, "Right—DSB. That's not an actual medical condition, is it?"

He shrugs his enormous shoulders and takes another gulp. "It's real enough."

"Okay." I check the time on my watch. "Hey, Sandy will be here in a few minutes. You can judge her for yourself."

The Red-haired Major scoffs, "Hell no. I don't want to hang out with a couple of moony-eyed kids. Besides, I'm on tonight's C-130 flight to Berlin. I just wanted to check in and make sure you're holding it together after all the shit you've been through." He finishes his drink, stands up, and says, "Why don't you get out of the Air Force and transfer to CIA now that I'm there? You told me years ago that you only joined the Air Force because your CIA class was delayed a year. Wasn't your plan to do four or five years and then move to the Agency? Now's your chance."

He's right. That was my grand plan when I joined the Air Force. "I don't know, boss. I'm doing well in the military, and I can always transfer at some point."

He squints hard. "How old are you now?"

"Twenty-eight."

He shakes his big, bearded head. "You'll never have the opportunities in the Air Force that you could have at the Agency. You don't wear wings and it's a pilot's Air Force." He looks hard into my eyes. "Kevin, I know you have issues with your father, but you've already proven yourself to your old man, haven't you? He was never an officer, and you are. I doubt he ever saved the planet from nuclear annihilation either. What else do you have to prove?"

"This isn't about him."

The older man scoffs, "Bullshit. All right then, it's about you. And *you* come from Bumfuck, Virginia, where you went to a one-room schoolhouse where you were the only 'student' with a full set of teeth. Then, by some miracle you managed to graduate from William and Mary. It ain't Harvard but everyone knows it's a tough school. Then, you got through the CIA selection process for career trainees but were told you had to wait a year to get a class. So, by another fucking miracle you got yourself into Air Force officers training school even though you didn't know the difference between an F-15 and a toaster oven. Look at you now; you're a decorated young captain with three meritorious service medals and two Air Force commendation medals. I ask you, what the fuck do you have to prove?"

I smile. "Well, I don't have an Air Force Cross like you do."

He shakes his huge, bearded head. "You don't want one. You have to get killed or be half-past dead to get an Air Force Cross."

Belatedly—the scotch must be slowing me down—it occurs to me that he just summarized my life story in a paragraph. I'm not sure whether to be insulted or impressed. I reply, "Let's see what happens with Sandy's med school thing. If she goes to Georgetown Med School, I can explore all my options in Washington, including the Agency."

The big man guffaws, "'Explore my options,' he says. Jesus! Shit, you could run the Special Activities Division! Hell, with your background and talent, you could run the entire fucking clandestine service someday. You're a great analyst, too. You could be the director of the DI! I'd pay to fucking see that one! Kevin Cattani in charge of all the pussy analysts in CIA. You'd shake up those assholes but good. Plus, the Agency needs another movie star-handsome, brilliant badass. After all, I'm not going to live forever!"

"You should have been a used car salesman, sir," I reply as I stand and shake his hand. "Thanks for stopping by. It means a lot to me." For some reason, I feel a powerful emotion and I start to tear up. I guess I've missed him more than I realized, and I've also had two large glasses of scotch.

"Don't get all mushy on me, Kevin. For a mother fucking killer, you're awfully sentimental sometimes." He looks at me with no glint of humor in his eyes. Then, a smile slowly pierces his beard, and he cackles wildly at my expense.

"Fuck you, sir. I still appreciate you coming by."

"That's more like it!" He hoots loudly and gives me a crushing bear hug. "I'll be keeping an eye on you, wherever I end up. Don't get yourself into any trouble here in Germany and for God's sake don't go back to the other side of the goddamn Berlin Wall. It's easy to find trouble in East Germany. But you already know that don't you?"

CHAPTER TWO

SANDY JACKSON

Captain Kevin Cattani, US Air Force Intelligence
Ramstein Air Base, Federal Republic of Germany (West Germany)

14 April 1984

Sandy will be arriving soon, so I put away the Glenlivet and wash the glasses the Red-haired Major and I used and tidy up my place. I am fastidious, but Sandy is a terror about order and cleanliness. She grew up an only child in an Air Force family. Her career Air Force father and Japanese mother must have run a very tight ship.

Chief Master Sergeant Charles Jackson, Sandy's father, served three combat tours in Vietnam, two of them as a pararescue jumper. PJs are the guys that jump or rappel from aircraft to save downed pilots and administer first aid, usually under preposterously dangerous conditions. Sandy told me one night that her father's third tour in Vietnam was a particularly dangerous one with a special operations unit that operated in Cambodia and Laos. I wonder if that's how he met the Red-haired Major. Chief Jackson helped save me from Soviet captivity in East Germany last fall and provided me medical aid (his PJ experience at work). The guy is a goddamn hero. I wish he were *my* father. He grew up in Mobile, Alabama, and enlisted in the Air Force as soon as he finished high school.

Sandy's mother is named Keiko, and she is of Ainu background. The Ainu are the native inhabitants of the northernmost reaches of the Japanese archipelago, making Keiko a member of a minority group in Japan—a culture that cherishes conformity and racial purity. In the States, Keiko is pigeonholed as an "oriental" military wife and in Japan, she is looked down on as an Ainu woman who is married to a foreigner—a "gaijin." She's a lovely woman who humors me by speaking English around me. When I attempt to speak Japanese, she giggles and tells me that I sound like a sumo wrestler, which should tell you all you need to know about my sparkling Japanese elocution.

Sandy and I met in the Philippines when I was in the hospital after the mission in Cambodia. We began dating at Yokota Air Base, which is in the far western suburbs of Tokyo. She was a nurse at Yokota, and I was chief of intelligence analysis at the headquarters of United States Forces, Japan. I fell in love with her quickly, but she was tentative in her feelings toward me.

Sandy is a rare beauty, with skin the color of creamed cocoa, doe eyes of light blue that contrast strikingly with her skin tone, and an exotic air of enigmatic complexity. She's very smart and earned her nursing degree at the University of Virginia. She's unfailingly blunt, while I'm relentlessly guarded and careful about what I say and who I say it to—except when my anger gets the better of me. We have fun together, but she never quite lets me in no matter how hard I try.

She broke things off with me just before she was to transfer to the Landstuhl Medical Center near Ramstein here in West Germany. Why did we break up?

I had one of my PTSD nightmares the last night we were together in Japan. Sandy was freaked out by the episode and told me to get help from a mental health professional. She even gave me the name of a doctor at the Yokota hospital that she respected. I told her I couldn't see a shrink because I'd lose my security clearances. Exasperated with me, she left me and moved to her assignment in Germany shortly thereafter. I didn't see her again until last November when I was admitted to the hospital in Landstuhl.

Unlike me, Sandy saw the world as a child. As an Air Force brat, she lived in California, Hawaii, northern Virginia, Japan, Florida, and Germany. I envy her experience, which was so much more expansive than my own.

My bad relationship with my father motivated me to leave home. We had violent confrontations and were like aliens born on different planets. He's ruled by emotion and rarely thinks before he speaks. I'm rational and studious, traits that he views as fatal defects in a grown man. I had to get away from him, and I also wanted to show him I could be more successful than he'd ever been. When I first decided to go into the Air Force, I knew I had to become an officer because my father had been an enlisted guy. Anger is corrosive rocket fuel and I have a tank full of it. Early in my Air Force career a good friend asked me, "Where does your drive come from? I'm ambitious, but you're so driven it's goddamn scary sometimes."

Sandy arrives at my door right on time, walks in, hugs me, and kisses me hard. Pulling away from me, she frowns and says, "You smell like scotch. Have you been drinking without me?"

"I had a visitor, and we drank a little while we talked."

Sandy steps back and raises an eyebrow. "Who?"

"You remember me talking about my first boss—the Red-haired Major?"

Rolling her eyes, she says, "Oh, great. The wild child with no name. Don't the CIA guys call him the red-haired maniac?"

"Well, yeah."

"What did he want? And why the hell is he in Germany?"

"He checked in to see how I'm doing. He wanted to make sure I've recovered from last fall's craziness."

"Okay . . . he's not dragging you off on some covert mission, is he?"

"No. He's flying to Berlin tonight. He's going to meet with the CIA station chief and talk about a new job or mission or something. He didn't share much."

Sandy takes a seat and I pour her a healthy draught of scotch. I go to the kitchen to get myself a beer and she calls out to me, "So, he didn't share much. Gee, that sounds familiar. No wonder you guys are so close. He's the one who almost got you killed in Cambodia—right?"

"That's right." I go back to the small sitting area and sit down across from her.

Sandy sighs and settles into my favorite chair—what is it with everybody sitting in my chair tonight? She looks at my beer. "Good. No more scotch for you tonight. You can have beer with supper, but I expect you to be able to perform for me tonight, so no more scotch—understood?"

"Yes, ma'am, Captain Jackson—understood!" I put my bottle of Bitburger beer on the table and lean over and kiss her deeply. The tangy taste of scotch is strong on her tongue.

She pulls away from me and laughs. "I'm glad you caught up with the man with no name tonight. You need more friends, you know."

I pick her up from the chair, stand, and sway back and forth, cradling her in my arms. "Who needs friends when I've got you?"

She laughs again and says, "Wow, you're stronger than you look! I feel like a little girl with you holding me like this." She looks up at me with those exotic, erotic eyes and kisses me. Then she pulls away and giggles. "Just don't forget to bring my scotch into the bedroom, Captain Cattani. You know how it puts me in the mood."

CHAPTER THREE

THE OTHER SIDE OF THE BERLIN WALL

Captain Kevin Cattani, US Air Force Intelligence
Ramstein Air Base, Federal Republic of Germany (West Germany)

15 April 1984

I have a meeting with the senior Air Force intelligence officer in Europe first thing this morning. I grab a cup of black coffee as his aide waves me into the general's expansive but dimly lit office.

"Ah, it's my most intelligent intelligence officer. How are you feeling these days—fully recovered from your injuries?" Brigadier General Lenny Palumbo, the head of Air Force Intelligence for the European theater, smiles and invites me to take a seat across from him. He leans back in his blue leather desk chair, tilts his head, squints at me, and waits for my response.

"Yes sir, I'm fine. Working regular day shifts help. The doctor tells me that getting adequate sleep helps with healing." I hate the early morning schedule that I am supposed to be working as Palumbo's primary current intelligence briefer. The longer I can avoid crazy hours, the better. I suspect that General Palumbo sees through my thinly veiled ploy to avoid going to work at 2:00 a.m. every night.

He doesn't respond immediately and devotes a moment or two to appraising me with his always active eyes before saying, "So, you feel fit and ready for duty?"

Fit and ready for duty? "Yes, sir. Although, I suppose it depends on the type of duty."

In his typical, rapid-fire manner he says, "I need to talk with you about a new tasking." He raises his chin like he's issuing a challenge. "After this new op, we can discuss moving you wherever you want to go. I know your nurse—Captain Jackson—applied for the Air Force to send her to medical school. You want to be with her wherever she ends up in school—right?"

How does General Palumbo know that Sandy applied for the Air Force's medical school program? "Sir, sure. How do you know about her application—if you don't mind me asking?" I hear the brittle uncertainty in my voice, and I hate it.

Palumbo shrugs. "She asked me to endorse it for her. So, I did. I think she got General Flannery to endorse her application, too. She's very impressive. I was glad to do it."

No shit? Wow. "Well, thank you for doing that. I appreciate it."

"Okay, let's talk turkey. You gotta keep this very close hold, okay? This one comes straight from Defense Intelligence Agency Headquarters—right from the director himself. The DIA director thinks his people have located the Soviets' covert war-time nuclear command-and-control bunker in East Germany. It's in a PRA. We've never been able to get inside one of these bunkers. DIA wants inside."

That sounds stupidly dangerous to me. "That's awfully risky, sir—breaking into a covert facility inside a PRA. We aren't supposed to go into PRAs—that's the whole point of the Soviets calling them permanently restricted areas."

The general waves away my concerns. "We need to assess the Soviets' current nuclear readiness. DIA needs to be able to tell President Reagan if Moscow is still on high alert, especially now that General Secretary Andropov has died. Extraordinary times call for extraordinary measures and all that."

I'm stunned—astounded. He wants me to go back into East Germany—on the wrong side of the Berlin Wall—with a military liaison mission team to break into a top-secret Soviet nuclear command bunker? Inside a PRA? If we get caught, the Soviets will shoot us, and they'll be within their rights to do so. Shit, just last night the Red-haired Major warned me about going back to East Germany.

General Palumbo continues. "And you're going to take a DIA analyst in with you. That's another reason I want *you* on the mission. I think that you and the DIA analyst will make an ideal team. The analyst has all the book smarts about the Soviets' nuclear command and control in this theater and you have invaluable real-world experience. Understood?"

This still sounds reckless to me. I'm confused, too. "Is this DIA analyst in the military? Army?"

Palumbo shrugs. "You'll be in and out before the Russians know it. The MLM and the Army Special Forces in Berlin will supply a security team. You won't have any trouble. Oh, and the DIA analyst is a civilian. She was an Army intelligence officer for a few years, but she's a DIA civilian analyst now."

What the . . .? "*She*, sir? The analyst is a woman?"

Palumbo nods at me with a glint in his eye. The general stares at me over his reading glasses. "The DIA director says that she is the best nuclear command-and-control analyst he has. She'll be able to read all the Russian technical nuclear lingo once you get in the bunker."

Sending me and a civilian woman on a mission like this makes no sense, unless you are a civilian official sitting in a safe cubicle at Defense Intelligence Agency headquarters in Washington, DC.

Palumbo is finished with me. "Okay. She'll be at your office at 1500 today to meet you. Good luck."

"Yes, sir. And thanks again for helping Sandy with her application."

I cannot believe this crazy mission. I'm also upset that Sandy asked both General Palumbo and General Flannery—the top Air Force officer in NATO—to endorse her application without telling me first. They're both in my chain of command and I see them almost every day.

Later, I am engrossed in reading a National Security Agency report about the Soviets' recent nuclear war exercise when I hear a gentle knock on the plastic molding of my cubicle. I glance at my watch and see that it's 1500. The DIA analyst is right on time. I look up to see a tall woman wearing a well-fitting, expensive-looking blue suit. My first thought is *how can she afford that suit on a government salary?* My second thought is that she is dazzling with long strawberry-blonde hair, high cheekbones, and graceful limbs like a dancer's. She's easily the most beautiful intelligence analyst I've ever seen.

I stand up and extend my hand. "Hi, I'm Kevin Cattani."

She nods and smiles uncertainly and takes my hand. Her hand feels delicate and strong at the same time. "Lydia Morelli."

I grab a chair for her from the adjacent cubicle. Lydia sits down and scoots close to me, smiles, and gives me an expectant look.

"Welcome to Ramstein. You have an Italian last name like I have." Christ, why did I say that? An Italian name? Really? Her looks are making me nervous.

"Yeah, my father's family is originally from Calabria. They've been in upstate New York for several generations."

I smile and respond, "The Cattanis are from Trentino—at the foot of the Dolomite Mountains. And Lydia—that's a lovely Russian name." I soften my normally stern face to let her know that I'm simply interested in her background and not a creep, although I must sound like a babbling idiot.

"My mother is Russian. Her parents are from Smolensk."

That's a volatile combination—southern Italian and Russian.

Must've made for an interesting household to grow up in. "Have you been to Germany before?" I'm really nonplussed by her beauty. I expected a woman . . . but not someone who looks like this. I have a weakness for beautiful women.

"Yes, I have—when I was in the Army. I spent some time in the Russian language program at Garmisch."

That is impressive. The Army only sends their very best to Garmisch.

Once we start talking shop, it becomes clear that Ms. Morelli's knowledge of Soviet theater nuclear systems and doctrine far exceeds mine. An hour of conversation convinces me that she's a first-rate analyst and an excellent communicator—precise and concise in her delivery. I understand why DIA has confidence in her. She also seems acutely aware that her looks are both an asset and a potential liability.

As I outline what little I know about our upcoming mission, her face remains impassive. By the time I finish, however, she frowns and expresses severe misgivings. "I'm not operational. I've never been operational. Don't you think I'm the wrong person to go breaking into a covert nuclear facility? I mean, I love the idea of getting access to this place, but what if we get caught?"

I try to reassure her, but I don't sound very convincing, given that I share her apprehensions. "Well, the MLM will send a security team to back us up." I pause. Lydia doesn't look swayed. I admit, "I did tell General Palumbo that this op seems very risky."

She looks distraught and folds her elegant hands in her lap. That worried look on her face makes her look even more beautiful. We sit silently for a few seconds.

I break the uncomfortable stillness. "Look, we'll just have to make the best of it. We'll have time to prepare with the MLM guys. They're used to doing crazy stuff like this." But not this crazy, I muse to myself. "The MLM team will bail us out if things go south."

She nods, but it's clear to me that her anxiety is undiminished.

Evening

As the sun sets over the German countryside, Sandy and I have dinner in the nearby town of Landstuhl at a lively spot perched high on a hill next to the local castle. The sky is clear, and we sit at an outside table with a marvelous view of the valley below us. As we eat, we discuss Sandy's medical school plans.

"I saw General Palumbo today and he told me that you asked him to endorse your application. You also sent it to General Flannery for endorsement?" I don't mean for my questions to sound accusatory, but instantly I know that they do.

Sandy's sloe eyes narrow and she visibly bristles. "Yes, I did. Was I supposed to ask your permission?" She wraps her long fingers around the stem of her wine glass and takes a sip. Her hands are graceful, like Lydia Morelli's.

Oops. "No, no, of course not. I didn't mean . . ."

She replies, "I didn't do anything I shouldn't have done. Look, I should hear later this month whether I got into any med schools. I still have Georgetown as my number one choice."

"You'll get in. How could they possibly turn you down? I'm more worried about your Air Force application. God knows what criteria the Air Staff use in their decision-making."

We eat silently for a few minutes and drink more of the Mosel Riesling I ordered. Sandy is so lovely that there are times when I just sit quietly and look at her. There also are times that I wonder if I'm a victim of the "Florence Nightingale" syndrome—falling for the nurse that tended to me in the hospital.

Sandy perks up as she eats, and her face relaxes. She looks stunning in the golden glow of the outdoor lights. She asks, "What did you and Palumbo talk about? He must've wanted to discuss more with you than my med school applications. Why did he want to see you?"

I need to tread lightly, given the sensitivity of the mission that

Palumbo presented to me. "Well, he wants me to go to Berlin and do something with the military liaison mission. I can't say much about it. I'll be gone a few days."

She puts down her knife and fork and asks indignantly, "What? What the hell? The MLM? Haven't you been through enough? It's bad enough that my own father is still working for the MLM in Potsdam. Why do you have to go? It's not fair after all you've been through—after all that *we've* been through! You're still recovering from being injured last November, for Christ's sake!"

I take a sip of wine and sit back in my chair. "It'll be okay. Oh, General Palumbo told me that he'll help me get assigned close to you—wherever you go to school. Georgetown would be ideal, of course."

Sandy sits back in her chair and folds her arms. Glaring at me, she exclaims, "The MLM? The fucking MLM? After the Russians nearly killed you last fall! Are you insane? That's completely and totally ridiculous. What about us? Christ!" Her eyes narrow, and she holds her knife and fork vertically—like a prison inmate who is about to demand better food. "If I get in, I'll be at Georgetown Medical School for years. You can serve on the Air Staff, or go to . . . what's the name of the Pentagon's intelligence agency?"

"Defense Intelligence Agency."

"Yes, DIA. You can go to DIA, or CIA. All those guys at the Agency love you. You won't have any trouble getting great jobs in DC. There's nothing for you to worry about!" She lowers her utensils and looks triumphantly at me, her face breaking out in a broad smile.

I feel like my mother is lecturing me. "Yes, it makes sense. I just don't know. Washington is so far away from where things actually happen."

She's firm with me. "You need to get your head straight, mister. What do you want? Do you want to marry me? Do you want us to be together while I'm in med school? What do you want?"

Did she just ask me to marry her? "Yes, I want to marry you. Yes, I want to be with you while you're in med school."

She sighs deeply and takes time to answer. "Okay. Let's not get ahead of ourselves." She takes a sip of wine and gives me a skeptical, sideways look. "What's this mission that Palumbo wants you to do with the MLM?"

"What? Oh, he, uh, wants me to go to Berlin to help them with something. I can't really . . . you know . . . I can't discuss it."

She takes another sip of wine. "You better not be going back into East Germany. Those crazy Russian bastards will try to kill you again."

Later that night in bed, I feel Sandy shaking me. She's yelling at me to wake up.

Slowly, I shake myself out of a deep sleep and look at the bedside clock, which reads 3:00 a.m. "Okay, I'm awake. I guess I woke you up?"

She turns on a bedside light. "Yes, you were moaning, and you stopped breathing and then you moaned louder and caught your breath. I thought you were having a heart attack or something."

I sit up and shake my head. "Nightmare. A bad one."

She puts her hand on my shoulder. "You want to talk about it? You *need* to talk to me. You keep having these nightmares."

I'm dazed. I'm cold and I want to go back to sleep if I can. What can I tell her? "I'd like to tell you, but you know I'm not supposed to."

"Christ! If you won't go to a shrink, then you need to talk to me. Who else are you going to talk to?" She's insistent and she's wide awake now.

Nobody. I talk to nobody. That's what we do. I stutter. "Re . . . uh, remember, when I told you about going to Cambodia with the Red-haired Major?"

"Yes. I remember. Tell me what happened. Tell me your dream."

I reach for my glass of water. My mouth is dry, and I need to collect my thoughts. "Remember our last night back at Yokota?"

She shrugs. "Yes, but you didn't tell me much. I told you to go get help at the hospital and you wouldn't do it. I walked out and I didn't think I'd see you again. That's what I remember."

Yeah, I remember that part, too. "Well, I . . . we went into Cambodia a couple of times. I'll tell you what happened. But you can never tell anyone else. Understand?"

Map 1: Cambodia

CHAPTER FOUR

AT WAR WITH THE RED-HAIRED MAJOR

Captain Kevin Cattani, US Air Force Intelligence
Ramstein Air Base, Federal Republic of Germany (West Germany)

16 April 1984

Sandy sits up in bed and looks at me expectantly, demandingly. "Go on. Tell me."

I'm still half-asleep and I don't want to have this conversation. "The Red-haired Major and I flew to Thailand where we hooked up with a team led by a CIA officer named Sixkiller. The Red-haired Major was the CIA guy's deputy for the mission."

Sandy smirks. "The CIA guy's name was *Sixkiller*—for real?"

I sit up on the edge of the bed. "Yes, he's a Lakota Indian and he's the station chief in Berlin now. Shit, forget I said that part about Berlin. It was a Title 50 mission—led by CIA. The military guys: me, the Red-haired Major, and four Army Special Forces guys were chopped to CIA, and we operated under their authority."

Sandy interrupts. "What is Title 50? I've never heard of that before."

There I go again—assuming people know what I'm talking about. "Right. Title 50 is the US code under which the CIA operates. We—the military and the Department of Defense—operate under Title 10 authorities. The CIA can do things the military can't legally do. CIA can direct the military to supply men and equipment to them to conduct Title 50 operations."

Sandy muses for a minute. "So, you guys are basically temps who are sent to CIA to conduct operations that the military can't legally perform on its own—is that right?"

Temps? "Yes, that's it, essentially."

Sandy seems satisfied. "Okay, go ahead."

"You remember hearing about the Khmer Rouge? The Cambodian killing fields? The Khmer Rouge took power and killed a lot of their own citizens after the end of the Vietnam War—maybe a couple of million people were killed."

"Two million people? For real?"

Yeah, not many people outside of Asia know about this genocide, which is shameful. "Our job was to go into Cambodia and see if we could find evidence—concrete evidence—of a holocaust."

She looks a little confused. "I thought . . . I remember reading that the North Vietnamese invaded Cambodia and got rid of the Khmer Rouge. Wasn't the country safe after the Vietnamese went in?"

"The North Vietnamese were disgusted by Pol Pot's genocidal policies. They invaded Cambodia on Christmas Day 1978 and took the capital of Phnom Penh, toppling the Khmer Rouge's bloody regime. After the Vietnamese invasion, a lot of the Khmer Rouge officials fled to western Cambodia, near the Thai border. It wasn't safe in that part of Cambodia."

"Did you find what you were looking for?"

"Eventually. I can't describe how horrible it was."

Sandy puts her arm over my shoulder. Her touch elicits a deep emotion in me, and my chest starts to heave, and I drop my head and sob.

She reaches down and holds my hand. "We can stop. Look, it's getting light out now. We both need to get up and get ready for work."

"No. I need to finish. If I don't do it now, then I never will. We interviewed villagers and took hundreds, maybe thousands of photographs of mass graves. We got all the information we needed—everything we came for. Our team leader—Sixkiller—briefed us that our Cambodian guides had learned the Khmer Rouge were planning to ambush us. Sixkiller said, 'We are going to set up a counter-ambush. We can't outrun them so we're going to beat them. These bastards are used to killing unarmed women and children. They won't be able to handle us.'

"We humped as fast as we could to a river, where Sixkiller had us set up an ambush. The Red-haired Major directed preparations. We dug slit trenches on the far side of the river in tiered rows and mined an ancient bridge, which was the only way to cross the river for some distance. We set up a phony camp on the near side of the river to make it look like we were idiotic enough to spend the night there. Basically, the plan was to wait for the Khmer Rouge guys to approach our fake camp and then hit them from our trenches high across the river.

"Our guides finally reported that there was a large body of fighters heading our way—as many as a hundred fighters. We only had twelve guys, including the four Cambodian guides, but we had the benefit of surprise, and we had the high ground. We held our fire until the Red-haired Major started shooting. The tremendous noise from the weapons made my senses shut down. I just kept up a steady series of short bursts aiming wherever I saw movement. A squad of bad guys charged the bridge trying to get across the river. The Red-haired Major ordered a Green Beret to blow the bridge. It took a few minutes to detonate and more Khmer Rouge guys tried to rush across it. As they got midway across the bridge, the bridge exploded, blasting them to pieces.

"Several of them managed to get across the bridge prior to the detonation. I shot at least two and the Red-haired Major jumped out of his trench and tumbled down the hill to where the wounded Khmer Rouge had fallen. We gave him covering fire while he pulled his .45 pistol and shot each of them in the head. Then, he clambered back up the hill to his trench. His entire movement took less than two minutes."

Sandy gasps, "Kevin, were you terrified? It sure sounds terrifying."

"Yes, I was terrified. The weirdest part was that I could barely turn my head. I don't know why, but my neck was stuck in one place. I knew at the time that it was fucked up, but I couldn't do anything about it. Isn't that strange?"

Sandy rubs my neck as if to soothe the memory.

"The Red-haired Major crawled over to my trench, yelling at me to get up to the top of the hill and to establish a new firing position. In a few minutes, we all were on the top of the hill. One of our Cambodian guides was on the ground with his left kneecap blown off and his right lower leg covered in blood. I picked him up and carried him on my back. We moved across the ridge while Sixkiller and the Red-haired Major took a quick inventory of injuries. Once the wounded were ready to move, we humped off the ridge toward the exfil site. There was no panic, it almost seemed like we were on a training exercise and not running for our lives. When we finally got to the helicopter LZ, we set up a defensive perimeter as two choppers attempted to land. Once they were on the ground, we loaded our film canisters and other evidence onto the choppers. Air Force para-rescue jumpers dismounted from the helicopters to help the wounded.

"It looked like we'd get out safely when the tree line erupted in gunfire. The Khmer Rouge had caught up with us. When the firing started, I was carrying the Cambodian guide with the blown-apart knee toward one of the choppers. A bullet hit him in the butt and forced both of us to fall face first into the dirt. My nose broke from the impact and bled heavily. The PJ near me returned fire and helped me to my feet. I struggled to get to the chopper in front of me. The

Red-haired Major lifted me into the helicopter, while a PJ laid the wounded guy down on the deck. We took off immediately. The chopper was raked by automatic weapons fire. One of the PJs was hit in the arm by shrapnel. Something sounded wrong and we listed hard to the port side. We barely cleared the trees and turned west. The pilot struggled to keep control and nurse the busted-up chopper across the border into Thailand. The copilot warned us that we were going to have a hard landing.

"He was right, and we went down hard. I felt a tremendous shock to my spinal column. I either passed out or I was knocked out. I don't remember much after that. I was in and out of consciousness until I was loaded on a medevac flight to Clark Air Base where I met you for the first time. As you'll remember when you treated me at Clark, my back was a mess. I had a concussion. The mission was a success. None of our guys were killed."

Sandy hugs me hard. "My God, Kevin. What a story. You poor guys. I'm so sorry you had to go through all that. It's horrible. No wonder you have nightmares. What you've been through . . . I had no idea."

She tries to kiss me, but I look at her sternly. I'm pissed off that she insisted I tell her my story.

She hugs me and pulls me close to her with her head on my shoulder. "Thank you for telling me, baby. I hope you never have to go through anything remotely like that again. I'm so sorry." She looks up at me and starts to kiss me. This time, I let her.

Map 2: East and West Berlin

CHAPTER FIVE

A DEADLY DAY IN THE WOODS

Captain Kevin Cattani, US Air Force Intelligence
West Berlin, Federal Republic of Germany and
A Permanently Restricted Area (PRA) in the German Democratic
Republic
16–17 April 1984

16 April 1984

I am on a C-130 flying to Berlin with the DIA analyst, Lydia Morelli. I am still reeling from my late-night conversation with Sandy. It feels like a turning point of some kind. I don't feel great about it. In fact, I've got a queasy stomach from lack of sleep and anxiety and the rocking motion of the big transport plane isn't helping. We're in jump seats and the cabin is so noisy that conversation is just about impossible and I'm grateful for it since I don't feel like talking to anyone. Lydia has her duffel bag on the seat in between us and she has her eyes closed. I wish I could sleep since I got very little rest last night.

The aircrews who conduct these flights high above the Iron

Curtain are known as the "Berlin for Lunch Bunch." Traversing the three Berlin air corridors the Soviets permit the western allies to use, these Air Force transport planes also are configured for collecting electronic and photographic intelligence. They fly passengers like me across the waist of East Germany to the city of West Berlin, collecting intelligence along the way. Wall-encircled West Berlin is a little island of freedom in a bleak sea of repression.

As soon as we land, I call Sandy from flight operations to let her know I'm safely in Berlin. She's worried about this new escapade of mine and blows me a kiss for luck over the phone.

In the afternoon, Lydia and I attend a briefing at the American Military Liaison Mission headquarters in West Berlin given by an almost comically huge Army Green Beret lieutenant colonel. He's got a lazy western drawl—my guess is that he's from Oklahoma.

This guy could pass for a veteran NFL offensive lineman. "Okay, how y'all doin'? Doin' okay? All right, well this is an important mission." He points at a map with his massive left hand. "Your target is a Soviet wartime mode nuclear command-and-control bunker. The bad guys conduct exercises in this puppy several times per year. They just finished a big one and there should be good gouge to collect. She'll be unoccupied when y'all go in, but this beauty is located inside a Soviet PRA. They conduct regular patrols around the PRA, both mounted and dismounted, so you gotta have your eyes on!" The colonel makes rings around his eyes with his thumbs and index figures to make sure we get the message. What a tool.

"Questions?" The ten or so people in the room remain silent. The big colonel looks around the room. "No questions. Okay, y'all must be real quick studies." He chuckles. Even his laugh has a cowboy drawl. I wonder if he can even speak Russian. "All right. Listen up, here are your EEIs." An EEI is an essential element of intelligence, or the information we are supposed to glean from the bunker.

The Army officer holds up a brawny index finger. "Number one: determine what you can about their current nuclear alert status and the big exercise they just stood down. Since that Able Archer goat rope a few months ago, we don't think the Soviets have backed off their nuclear alert, but y'all will tell us for sure."

He holds up two fingers with his palm turned toward his face, a very obscene gesture here in Germany. I wonder if he knows that. "Number two: find out what the Russians know of our collection capabilities—our intel collection flights, satellite tracks, MLM activities, and anything else you think is of value. They should have status boards readily visible in the bunker that you can photograph."

He turns his palm back toward us and holds up three meaty fingers. "Number three: determine how often they update the facility's security and status boards. Do they update monthly? Weekly? Quarterly? Anything you can find out about their SOPs will help."

Then he goes over security procedures we'll be using for this crazy op. He concludes by saying, "There'll be time tonight to get smart on all the intel we have on the site. You better study hard and fast since we are going tomorrow morning."

We are going tomorrow morning! We get one whole night to prep? This is bullshit. I look around the room to see if anyone else is reacting like me. All the MLM guys look cool. Maybe I'm overreacting?

I raise my hand. "Sir, why are we going tomorrow with such . . . with such minimal prep for the mission?"

A huge harrumph erupts from deep in his belly. "Shit, son, you got a whole night to get ready. How long you need? We ain't planning D-Day here!"

Is this guy for real? "Sir, I have minimal operational experience in East Germany. The whole plan just seems risky."

The cowboy colonel walks over to my seat and leans over so that his coffee and cigarette breath is all over my face. "Young captain, if I say it's safe to do this mission; it's safe to do this mission! You'll have plenty of backup. Now, you and the lady need to get smart on the target tonight and be ready to mount up at zero dark thirty."

Arguing with this Green Beret is useless. All I can do is nod. "Yes, sir. We'll do our homework."

Morelli has said nothing, but I can sense that she is extremely anxious. As Lydia and I walk out of the briefing room into the hallway, I hear a familiar voice calling my name.

"Cattani! What the fuck are you doing back here?" Air Force Colonel John LaRoche walks down the long hallway toward me, his bulky upper body bypasses my outstretched hand, and he gives me a bear hug.

Struggling for breath, I gasp, "Hi Colonel, how've you been?"

"Fine. Tell me why you're here." His substantial jaw thrusts out toward my Adam's apple.

Lydia looks at us both with a nervous smile and brushes strands of blond hair away from her face with her long fingers. The hands of a pianist.

LaRoche looks at Lydia for the first time. "Wow, where'd *you* come from? Is she your girlfriend, Cattani? I thought you were seeing Chief Jackson's little girl."

Leave it to LaRoche to say the most inappropriate thing possible. He and the Red-haired Major must be distant cousins or something. They both have a flair for embarrassing me.

"Sir, this is Lydia Morelli. She's a DIA nuclear analyst. And yes, I'm still seeing Sandy Jackson."

He gives Lydia the once over, taking her in from head to toe. He turns to me. "Why are you here? I want the two of you in my office now." LaRoche turns sharply on his heel and strides back down the hallway.

Lydia protests to his retreating back, "Sir, we have a lot of work to do tonight. I don't think we have time for a visit."

LaRoche turns around and looks at her curiously—like she's an exotic bird. "My office. Now."

LaRoche motions for us to sit down and closes the door with a loud thud. "Now, tell me why you're here."

Morelli and I look at each other anxiously. I respond, "Sir, we're here on a DIA-directed mission. I don't know if we can discuss it with you."

Colonel LaRoche thrusts his jaw out again. "Bullshit. If you don't tell me, then I'll make that Green Beret light colonel tell me." He leans across his desk, menacingly. "Don't forget who rescued you from the GRU last fall."

I remember. "All right, sir. This op is being led by the MLM's ground team, which is why you and your air team aren't aware of it. Before I start, I gotta tell you I don't like this mission. It feels like a train wreck to me."

LaRoche nods, relaxes his jaw, and says, "Tell me about it."

He listens closely as I run through what I know about the mission. Morelli adds color here and there.

We conclude and the colonel puts his head in his hands. "Christ, Cattani. Jesus fucking Christ. This is a bad idea." He rubs a hand through his thinning, sandy hair. "I'll make sure one of my own guys is on your security detail. You know we normally do our tours unarmed. Do you have a weapon? For tomorrow?"

"Sir, I was hoping one of the Special Forces guys would give me a .45 or something in the morning."

LaRoche's eyes are swimming in his head. He puts his right foot up on his desk and rolls up his pants leg to reveal a holstered .38 revolver around his ankle. He unbuckles it and hands it to me. "Put this on. Now. I'll get you a .45, too. You'll need personal protection if you're going into a PRA on the other side of the Wall. Jesus."

17 April 1984

Lydia is mute as we load up the vehicles in the early morning darkness. We're wearing BDUs—battle dress uniform—and the two of us climb in the back of the first vehicle. It is very cramped since we both have long legs. The security team is in the second vehicle and will follow closely behind us.

I need to know how she is doing. "Lydia, are you ready for this?"

She tosses her long hair in the darkness and laughs tensely. "I guess I must be ready because we're going. I don't know. I wish we'd had more time to prepare and more than two hours of sleep. I know what I want to collect once we get inside the bunker—but Christ . . . what if we get caught? That Green Beret colonel seems to think this is going to be a cake walk."

Yeah, but LaRoche doesn't. And I trust Colonel LaRoche's judgment more than a Green Beret lieutenant colonel I don't know.

I see her turn to face me briefly in the darkness of the backseat of the vehicle. "Kevin, you don't like this, do you? I mean, you don't think we're ready."

I breathe a deep sigh. "Well, no. I mean . . . I think we know the target, but I don't like the fact that we haven't rehearsed anything with the MLM team. It all seems reckless to me, but I'm probably just being a pussy. No offense."

She laughs nervously. "Well, Captain, I hope you know how to handle a gun. I'm not carrying one."

Everyone in the car is silent as we arrive at the entrance to the Gleinicke Bridge—the span that leads to East Germany. Here is the point of no return. The Soviet guards on the bridge are in no hurry to wave us through. One soldier takes our credentials to the guard shack to have them checked. I shake my leg tensely while I wait for him to meander back to the car. In the end, we are ushered through the Soviet security gate with no incident.

On the other end of the bridge lies East Germany—riddled with the notorious East German STASI secret police and the potentially ruthless Soviet GRU. I bet both spy agencies will be interested in why two MLM vehicles are crossing the Gleinicke Bridge early this spring morning.

Somewhere deep in the forest awaits a secret nuclear command-and-control bunker within a Soviet permanently restricted area. I'm supposed to break into it with an inexperienced DIA analyst along for the ride. What could possibly go wrong?

Our driver is an Army Special Forces sergeant. As soon as we clear the Soviet checkpoint on the far end of the bridge, the sergeant demonstrates the driving skills he will use to elude the inevitable STASI tails. I peer out the window fretfully, searching for GRU and STASI vehicles and hoping we don't lose our backup team that will keep us safe once we get to the PRA. If things go to shit in the bunker, I'll want backup close by to bail us out. I am certain that our escorts have a planned rendezvous point somewhere along the way.

I lose track of time as the driver makes a series of evasive maneuvers. Despite the stress I feel, fatigue gets the better of me and I fall asleep for a few minutes. As soon as we leave the paved road and dive onto a forest track, I get jostled so hard that I wake up and I fall over into Lydia who is holding on to a window strap with every ounce of strength in her right arm.

In a silly attempt to make light of the situation, I ask, "You don't get carsick, do you?"

She stares straight ahead and replies, "I'm too terrified to throw up." Her teeth are chattering as our vehicle flies over huge ruts in the forest road. "Is this really necessary? I'll be completely exhausted by the time we get to the site!"

I try to nod in agreement, but the g-forces throwing us around the back seat prevent any normal movements. Finally, our driver slows down. He and the guy sitting next to him are craning their necks around looking for something. The security vehicle? We lost it shortly after the Gleinicke Bridge crossing. We drive on a narrow woodland path for a while until the driver turns abruptly into a small glade, barely illuminated by the slowly rising sun.

I'm relieved to see that the security detail has arrived before us. They are busy setting up high-powered binoculars and checking their weapons. We must be close to the bunker. I start feeling sick to my stomach and the old, familiar precombat redness creeps up my neck and into my brain. I breathe deeply to get control of myself.

Two officers approach our car from the four-man security team. One is a Green Beret captain, and the other is an Air Force major. The major must be LaRoche's guy from his air team and he takes charge. He has intensely blue eyes that seem to penetrate everything. He inquires in an affable tone of voice—a tone that to my mind is incongruous with the situation, "How are you two feeling this morning?" It isn't an idle question. He wants an answer.

Lydia speaks first. "That ride wore me out. I feel sick. I just want to get in and out as quickly as we can."

I can't think of anything to say that won't reveal my anxiety and I simply give him a thumbs up.

This Air Force major has a serene confidence about him. "My name is Mike Hosenko. We'll have the site under surveillance while you go in. Go in fast, gather what you came for, and get out as quickly as possible. We don't want to give the Soviets any indication that we've been here. The bunker door is probably padlocked. You'll need these bolt cutters." He hands me the tool. "We have a new Russian lock we can install once you get out. Any questions?"

Lydia and I shake our heads. It occurs to me that if we replace the padlock with a new one, then the Russians will know that *someone* broke into the bunker, but I keep my mouth shut.

"All right, we're going to do a weapons check and then you need to move out. Get in and out as fast as possible. Take photos. I know you both read Russian, but don't worry about taking down notes.

Use the cameras."

Lydia and I leave the clearing through a small opening in the trees—not a path exactly, but an opening large enough for us. This leads to a grassy mound. That's our target. Approaching the grass-covered site, I find it's much larger than I'd imagined. I walk around to the opposite side where the entrance is located with Lydia close behind me. I crouch down and use the bolt cutters to cut the shackle in two and then sever a heavy chain secured to it. I drop the broken lock and chain on the ground. I'll stuff them inside once I get the door opened.

Pulling the door ajar requires more effort than I'd expected, but finally it swings open with a loud creak. Sounds like the Soviets haven't bothered to lubricate the hinges in a while. Once inside, our flashlights illuminate a spiral staircase. I search for a master light switch before allowing the heavy door to swing shut. I throw a switch and weak overhead lights come on and barely illuminate the stairs. I guess I failed to find the master switch; it appears to be an auxiliary light. Well, it doesn't matter. There's enough light for us to do what we need to do, and I don't want to waste time hunting for the main switch.

We try to be quiet but make a lot of noise as we go down the staircase into the operations center. Lydia follows me with tentative steps into the main chamber, which smells so strongly of mildew that we both put our hands to our noses involuntarily. My heart rate is sky high. At the front of the big room is a large, clear map display, which covers European NATO—from Turkey to Iceland. Overlaying the display are the orbital paths of the United States' classified intelligence satellites. Each satellite track is annotated with the time of day that the satellite is over East Germany. Lydia pulls out a camera and starts to take photos at a furious pace.

While Lydia takes photos, I search for documents—binders that detail operational procedures and contain war time modes and codes. It's not likely that such precious documents will be left lying around, of course. Where would I store sensitive documents? They must be in a safe or a locked cabinet.

Lydia continues to take photos and I tell her I'm going to hunt for safes. She nods almost imperceptibly in the gloom, and I head toward the rear of the chamber where I find storage cabinets. I check the doors and all of them are locked—no surprise. The bolt cutters will make quick work of their flimsy locks. Where are the safes? They must be back here somewhere. At the far end of the cabinets, I find what I'm looking for. Two squat safes. How the hell will I get these open? They have spin dial locks, so my bolt cutters won't work. I squat down to check out the locks on the safes and as I do, I hear a loud crashing noise. It's the bunker door shutting closed!

Instinctively, I crouch lower and remain silent. I feel for the .45 in the holster at my side and I unsnap the holster cover as quietly as possible. I chamber a round silently. Lydia is still somewhere at the front of the bunker—I can't see her from where I am, but she's up there alone and unarmed. Abruptly, I hear heavy footsteps on the metal staircase. How many people? Two sets of footfalls. Loud and heavy. The men make jingling sounds as they thud down the stairs—they sound like troops with a full combat load.

From my concealed location I can make out the shapes of two men. They're standing by the map display in the dimly lit room. I hear a rifle bolt drawn back. Shit! My heart is beating wildly, and I see red, red, red. Where is Lydia? The two soldiers are talking but I can't make out what they're saying from the back of the room. I can't see their faces, just dim shapes.

One of them yells out in Russian, "Intruders! Show yourselves!"

I crouch lower. Where is Lydia? Where is our security detail?

Something very heavy crashes to the floor. There's a rapid burst of automatic gunfire. The sound is absolutely deafening in this confined space. As the echo from the gunshots dissipates, the same guy yells again. "Intruders! Show yourselves or I will fire again!"

I inch forward on my hands and knees. There are several rows of ascending theater-style seats that separate the back of the facility from the map display. I crawl along the side of the rows of seats toward the front of the room. I'm armed with a pistol, and they've got fully automatic assault rifles. It won't be a fair fight.

There's another burst of gunfire that shatters glass, which I can see flying around in the yellow-brown light. I hear a whimper. Lydia? It must be her, of course. Is she wounded?

Silently, I make my way to the front row of theater seats and peer around them to see the two Soviet infantrymen. They have their assault rifles in firing position and are facing away from me toward the wall that runs perpendicular to the map display. Do they see Lydia? They'd be shooting if they did. Is she already hurt? The dim light in this man-made cave is throwing long shadows that should help me stay hidden. I see the soldiers' shapes well enough, however. That's my only advantage since I'm seriously outgunned. The two are separated from each other by about ten feet and are advancing slowly toward the only part of the bunker where Lydia can be hiding. Boom! They both fire another short burst.

Goddamn it. They're going to kill her. I position myself and steady the .45 on a chair arm. I notice that I still have the bolt cutters in my left hand, and I hurl them across the floor toward the two soldiers. The heavy tool clatters loudly and they both turn around to find the source of this unexpected noise. I shoot the guy on the right full in the chest. His comrade reacts quickly and draws his weapon down on me, or where he thinks I am. I fire three shots and one must've hit him in the right rib cage since he grabs that spot with his left hand. I roll across the floor and lie prone. I fire three more rounds and I think one shot hits guy number two, but I can't be sure.

Meanwhile, the other soldier, who is now lying prone, points his rifle at me and squeezes off a burst, which narrowly misses my right shoulder. I fire three rounds rapidly at him and at least one of my shots is good because I hear him cry out.

In my head, I hear the Red-haired Major telling me to kill them. Make sure they're dead. Both guys are lying on their stomachs. They're not wearing helmets, just garrison caps. I roll across the floor and try to shoot both in the head from close range. The .45 jams. Christ! I reach down and grab LaRoche's .38 from my ankle holster. I get up on one knee to try to get a better shooting angle and I fire two rounds at each of them. I'm so close that I think all my shots hit the targets.

Rising to my feet, I scream, "Lydia! Where are you? We have to get the fuck out of here!"

She crawls out from behind heavy shelves that I haven't noticed before in the murky light, rises to her feet and asks, "Is it safe?"

"Yes, come toward my voice."

Now, I can see that she's bleeding from her head—shattered glass must have struck her. I hope that's the extent of her injuries. She freezes when she sees the soldiers lying on the floor.

Gingerly, I hop around the bodies toward her. Are they dead? The smell of death is heavy in the confined space—gunpowder, blood, and human shit. I grab Lydia by the arm and guide her around the two bodies. I push her toward the stairs, and we fly up the spiral staircase. She's clutching her camera. Smart woman. Should I go back for the bolt cutters? No time.

Once we exit the bunker and get outside, I see Major Hosenko at the tree line waving at us to run toward him. We stagger over there, and he quickly appraises Lydia's injuries. "I think she's okay. How are you?"

"I'm okay, but I left the bolt cutters in the bunker—the broken lock, too."

Major Hosenko waves and two of the MLM guys run over to help us. Hosenko is highly agitated—no wonder. "I'll go back to the bunker. Those bastards came out of nowhere and we didn't have time to intercept them or warn you. Just two inside?"

"Just the two."

"KIA?"

"I think so. My .45 jammed and I had to shoot them with the .38." I pantomime shooting myself in the head.

"All right. I'll get your bolt cutters and lock it back up. You get her to the vehicle ASAP! You need to get the hell out of Dodge immediately. I'll follow with the security vehicle. Now, get out of here before the Soviets find us because they'll be coming!"

CHAPTER SIX

JET LAG

Captain Kevin Cattani, US Air Force Intelligence
West Berlin, Federal Republic of Germany

17 April 1984

Lydia hobbles across the clearing to where the vehicles are parked, firmly refusing any assistance. When she reaches the door of our vehicle, a Green Beret sergeant stops her and examines her wounds. She protests but he just smiles and uses a damp towel to clean the blood from her face, neck, and arms. Garish threads of blood streak her long hair. The sergeant pulls bits of glass from her hair. Satisfied with his work, he hands her a ball cap to put on. She tucks up her hair with one hand and puts the cap on with the other, strands of hair fall out of the cap to the nape of her neck.

I gaze back toward the path that leads to the bunker. The Green Beret captain notices and says, "Don't worry about Major Hosenko. He'll be fine. We need to get you out of here ASAP. Are you okay? Any wounds?"

I hadn't thought about whether I might be hurt; I feel fine, physically. He points at my left hand, which is covered in blood. I shrug sheepishly, "I guess I cut my hand at some point; maybe on the bolt cutter when I threw it."

He nods, hands me a towel so I can clean the blood from my hand. Once I wipe my hand, I see there's a nasty slice below my thumb. The Army captain gives me a bandage and helps secure it around the wound. Then he looks at our driver and orders, "Okay, mount up. You need to get them back to Berlin ASAP."

Lydia and I fall in the back seat, and she leans against the side window and closes her eyes. The ride out of the forest is even worse than the drive into it. Lydia and I bounce around the back seat like laundry tossing in a clothes dryer as we plow our way through the East German woods. I find myself frantically searching each forest path we pass looking for Soviet patrols. Once we leave the forest and get on a paved road, I calm down a bit, my head bouncing against the window in time to the wild turns being made by our driver. I feel sick to my stomach as we slow down and stop at the Soviet checkpoint on the Gleinicke Bridge. The bridge is our gateway to West Berlin and its grimy freedom. I crane my neck around the driver to see if the guards are doing anything out of the ordinary. Activity around the checkpoint looks normal. Nonetheless, I start hyperventilating to such an extent that Lydia reaches over to me and holds my right hand.

I'm surprised by her gesture and grateful. I look at her, smile, and try to slow down my breathing. "I guess I'm pretty winded."

She nods and pulls hard down hard on her hat. She smiles faintly, "I can't imagine why. Why can't they just wave us through?" Her voice is desperate, almost frantic. She squeezes my hand hard. "Can't they hurry up?"

I tilt my head toward the Soviet checkpoint. "They have their procedures. We want to be calm and not give the guards a reason to start asking questions."

Lydia nods in agreement. She looks terribly pale.

Our vehicle idles at the closed gate, and we wait. Finally, a Soviet guard saunters toward us. He leans down against our driver's door and the two men chat nonchalantly. Apparently, they are acquainted, and they exchange small talk. Lydia tightens her grip on my hand. The waiting is driving her crazy. At last, the guard gets down to business and enquires. "Who do you have in the back?"

Our driver responds, "The same two we took in early this morning. I've got to get them back to Berlin so they can have a nice dinner and not miss their bedtime." He's trying to keep the banter casual as he hands the guard our credentials.

The Russian holds our papers up to the sky as if that will improve his ability to read them and laughs heartily. "I understand! Okay, their credentials look to be in order. But I'll need to look in the back." He's in no hurry—it must be a slow day on the bridge. He taps on my window. I roll it down and the Soviet soldier peers inside. He glances at me and then focuses his attention on Morelli. "What? I didn't know you had a woman in here!" He double-checks Lydia's ID card, as if to confirm that she is, in fact, a woman. He looks at me and asks, "She doesn't look well—is she sick?"

Fortunately, our driver is fast on his feet. "She flew in yesterday from America and has jet lag. She's just dozing back there. She's fine."

The Russian is skeptical. "Hmm. Jet lag? Is she in the Army?"

I answer him this time. "She's got jet lag, like the sergeant said."

The guard looks at my face intently—with a sudden annoyance. "I don't know you. Are you new to the Liaison Mission?"

"No. I'm from Ramstein. We had a routine meeting today at Potsdam House. I'm not in the MLM, but I have clearance to pass over the bridge, as you can see from my credentials."

He gives me a once-over and squints like he doesn't believe me. "Routine?"

Lydia shoots me an anxious look.

The guard walks away and takes our credentials to the guard shack. Through its filthy window, I can see men gesticulating. Are they arguing? Have they discovered something wrong with our papers? Has the incident in the bunker been reported? If the officer of the guard has been informed, then we will be detained and questioned, or worse.

I just killed two young men. My entire body feels wrong, like none of my organs work properly. I have killed before, but it never gets easier. I yawn and then can't stop yawning. The uneasy wait is agonizingly long. Finally, the guard returns and hands our papers and IDs to our driver. "All right, you're free to go."

Our driver gives the guard a mock salute and drives rapidly through the open gate. He doesn't slow down until we are back at the MLM facility in West Berlin.

17 April 1984

No one at the MLM knows the mission was a fiasco. Once the facts are known, the roof will blow off the building. We didn't merely violate a Soviet restricted area; I killed two of their soldiers. The Russian leadership is almost certain to make this a major international incident. If they do—and they have every right to—it will cause an earthquake in Washington. I will be grilled and second-guessed, and I probably will receive disciplinary action. I killed two Soviet soldiers, for Christ's sake. Any doubts I voiced about the wisdom of this mission beforehand will be forgotten.

Lydia and I are ushered into the same room where the Green Beret lieutenant colonel briefed us yesterday. He is seated at the conference table with a younger Army officer. The burly cowboy colonel takes one look at Lydia and his face falls. Anyone can see that Lydia has been through hell. Her appearance is the first clue that the mission may not have been a resounding success.

He asks her if she is injured, and she responds. "Yes, sir. I don't know how badly. I think I'm bleeding in several places."

The colonel glares at me and yells. "Captain, what the hell happened out there?"

I feel like punching him in the mouth. "Sir, before we debrief, Ms.

Morelli requires medical attention. We don't know how badly she's hurt, and she must be seen immediately."

The colonel tells the other Army officer to escort Lydia to the facility's clinic.

Once she is gone, I demand, "Sir, I want Colonel LaRoche brought in for the debrief." I smile to soften my request, although I feel like gouging out this dipshit's eyes.

"This ain't LaRoche's business and he isn't going to join the debrief." The cowboy colonel drawls. He is very angry, and he hasn't even heard my story yet.

Really? "Colonel, with respect, I am an Air Force officer and Colonel LaRoche is the senior Air Force officer at the MLM. I want him in the debrief."

He doesn't answer immediately. He lights a cigarette and drawls with somewhat less hostility, "Captain, what the hell happened out there?"

"Sir, I will be happy to tell you once Colonel LaRoche is in the room."

His face twists into a contemptuous frown but lifts his massive frame from his chair. He looks like he's going to slap me across the face but pauses and mutters, "Fuck me in the heart." He stamps out his cigarette with more force than is required. "I'll see if LaRoche is in." He wags a long finger at me. "Don't go anyplace."

"Yes, sir." Where the hell would I go? I don't really care how he treats me if he gets LaRoche in the room. I know LaRoche well from last fall's nuclear crisis and I trust him.

Minutes later, Colonel John LaRoche walks into the conference room with the massive Green Beret in tow. LaRoche is a good seven inches shorter than the Army officer but he's just as broad and looks even more menacing. He sits down across from me with a look of grave concern on his face. I know from experience that LaRoche has a titanic temper, but for now he speaks very calmly—even softly. "Kevin, tell me what happened. Don't leave out any details, even if you think that they're insignificant."

I relate the entire story very carefully, trying not to leave out any particulars. LaRoche takes notes without asking questions while the Green Beret fumes. It's apparent that LaRoche wants me to relay the story while it's fresh in my mind without being hindered by interruptions.

After about thirty minutes, Lydia joins us. LaRoche looks at her with the same curious expression that he had on his face when he met her last night—like she's an exotic bird. She sits next to me and LaRoche asks, "Miss Morelli, how are you feeling?"

Lydia regards him indirectly, staring at the wall. "I'm okay, considering that I was nearly shot to death by two Soviet soldiers. Kevin got me out of the bunker in one piece, thank God. I guess I'm okay."

We debrief for another hour, with Lydia adding her perspective. A lot of time is spent retracing the same ground, which is annoying, although perfectly reasonable under the circumstances. As we conclude, LaRoche and the Army light colonel leave the room to confer privately. Lydia and I don't talk while they are gone. We're both emotionally out of gas and lost in our own thoughts. For a passing second, she looks at me and slowly shakes her head.

After a lengthy interval, the senior officers return and sit down at the conference table. LaRoche declares, "We want to get you out of Berlin as quickly as possible. We'll put you on the flight to Ramstein tonight. I'll go with you. As you undoubtedly know, we're all in for a big shitstorm. You'll probably have to go to DC to debrief."

The Green Beret cowboy looks like his best horse just died. He leans across the table until he's right up in my face and glares at me with deadly intention. "Captain, this was a simple mission and you fucked it up royal—royal! I knew we never should've sent a zoomie on a mission like this. You fucking lost your cool and now we have the mother of all shit storms blowing in our faces."

I don't like people getting in my face. "Sir, with all due respect, fuck you! You're the dipshit that planned this fucked-up fiasco! We walked right into an ambush thanks to you and we're lucky to be alive."

The Army officer lunges across the table, grasping for my throat. He's huge and the table buckles under his weight. I get up and kick my chair out of the way, ready to fight. Colonel LaRoche grabs the man's legs around his thighs and uses his own immense strength to restrain him. I sense someone standing behind me, and I'm about to throw an elbow but back off when I see that it's Lydia who's simply trying to get out of the line of fire. Jesus, what a fucked up mess.

LaRoche yells at me. "Get the hell out of here and take the woman with you! That's an order."

He doesn't need to tell me twice. I grab Lydia by the hand and half-drag her out of the room and don't slow down until we are at the building's entrance. I can feel Lydia trembling as she squeezes my hand.

An hour later, we are on the C-130 flight to Ramstein. Major Hosenko sits in the jump seat next to me and asks me as he settles in, "How's your hand? I heard you cut it."

My hand is the least of my worries. I just got into a fight with a superior officer. I reply quickly because we won't be able to talk once we get airborne due to the noisy engines. "It's fine. I didn't realize it was bleeding until we got to the vehicles. Morelli took the worst of it."

He looks at me with those spooky blue eyes. "It's going to be okay. You didn't do anything wrong. This mission had 'fuck-up' written all over it."

This makes me feel a little better about the horrific events of the morning, but I still suspect I'm in career-ending trouble. "Did you find the bolt cutters?"

Hosenko gives me a crooked smile and nods his head. "Yeah, I got 'em and the lock and chain you cut. Your two guys were KIA. You were right." He stares at me intently.

I know it took balls for him to go back into that bunker alone. I imagine he shot the Soviet troops again to make sure they weren't a threat to him. I feel sorry for those poor kids. They were just conscripts from the provinces doing their job. What a crappy way to die. But they could've killed Morelli and me. The fault is with this mission, which was fucked up beyond all recognition from the start.

Lydia is sitting immediately to my left with her eyes closed. Her beautiful face is contorted while she sleeps or attempts to. Why? With pain? With nightmares? We'll both have nightmares about today for a long time. Clearly, this mission was more than she bargained for when she agreed to leave the safety of her DIA cubicle in Washington and travel to Germany. I worry about what will happen when we get to Ramstein, but I know there's no point. It's gonna be what it's gonna be. My head feels like an anvil being pounded by Thor's hammer. It may well be on the chopping block in a few hours.

CHAPTER SEVEN

THAT SOUNDS RECKLESS

*Captain Kevin Cattani, US Air Force,
Ramstein Air Base, Federal Republic of Germany (West Germany)*

17 April 1984

General Palumbo's normal rapid-fire delivery has accelerated to Gatling gun-like speed. We are gathered in a secure compartmented information facility (SCIF) near his office at Ramstein Air Base to debrief him on this morning's debacle in East Germany. I'm on the hot seat, certainly more than anyone else in the stuffy room, including Lydia Morelli, Major Hosenko, and Colonel LaRoche.

Due to the sensitivity of the mission, the group gathered to hear my side of the story is small: General Palumbo, his deputy, and the colonel who leads the Air Force Office of Special Investigations (OSI) for all of Europe. The OSI is like the Air Force's FBI, and it handles internal and external counterintelligence actions.

Palumbo peppers me with questions, his deputy listens intently, and the OSI colonel scribbles notes furiously in a vain attempt to keep up with the general's frantic pace. I relate the sequence of events as completely as I can.

When Palumbo is finished asking me questions, the OSI officer takes over. "Captain, there's a lot to dig into here. My first question and the most important question is why did you have to *kill* the two Soviet troops? Wasn't there some way to neutralize them without killing them? The Soviets will play this up for propaganda value all over the world! After all, you were trespassing in a PRA, and you were in a covert nuclear command-and-control bunker of all places. Of course, they had a right to defend themselves and their facility!"

Well, that's a moronic take on things. I work hard to control my anger. "Colonel, I was conducting an officially sanctioned DIA mission in East Germany. Those two soldiers fired their weapons first and did so indiscriminately. They nearly killed my colleague." I nod in Lydia's direction. "I neutralized the threat the only way I could. You need to understand, and it may sound corny to you, but it was us or them. But you've probably never been in that type of situation, have you, Colonel?" My snarky comment elicits a silent rebuke from LaRoche, who's directly across the conference table from me.

While the OSI colonel stews trying to compose a response, Palumbo interjects, "All right, guys. Let's lower the thermostat. I want to hear what the senior officer who was on the scene has to say. Major Hosenko, what's your take?"

Mike Hosenko doesn't clear his throat and he doesn't pause even one beat before answering in a calm, even voice that brooks no caviling. "General, Captain Cattani did what he had to do. I think this mission was ill-advised from the start and far too risky in conception. He made the best of it." Hosenko turns to the OSI colonel and pierces him with those blue eyes. "Colonel, this mission gleaned valuable intelligence. We know far more about the Soviet nuclear posture in Europe than we did yesterday. Things did go sideways when those two Russians showed up. Captain Cattani had no choice but to put them down to save himself and Ms. Morelli. He acted without hesitation, which is more than most would do in his place. My guess is that there will be *no* international incident. I spent four years as an attaché in the US Embassy in Moscow. The Russians won't publicize the fact that we got into their covert nuclear bunker and killed two of their guys. There won't be a propaganda bonanza because they won't be able to stand the embarrassment. What's more likely is that they will retaliate against the MLM. They will demand retribution. Our guys need to be ready for it."

Everyone is silent, even Colonel John LaRoche, which is rather remarkable. I look at Major Hosenko and he is staring Zen-like at General Palumbo with those blue eyes. It's spooky. I've never seen anything like it. The Red-haired Major would have lost his mind in this meeting. Hosenko is *running* the meeting.

Palumbo looks at Hosenko with an odd tilt to his head. "Major, what's your story? Are you Ukrainian? 'Cause, your name sounds Ukrainian."

The major smiles and brings his right hand to his chest in a gesture that is theatrical without seeming so. "My parents emigrated from Ukraine to western Pennsylvania. My father was a coal miner. We spoke Ukrainian at home. I went to Virginia Tech on an Air Force ROTC scholarship and majored in aerospace engineering. After I was commissioned the Air Force allowed me to stay at Tech to get my master's degree, also in aerospace engineering. I went to pilot training and became an F-111 pilot. I flew seventy-five combat missions over North Vietnam—mostly over Hanoi. When I came back to the States, I had a retina detach in flight. I was grounded and I asked to be transferred to Air Force Intelligence. I volunteered to be an attaché in Moscow, went through intensive Russian language training, and spent four years in Moscow. After Moscow, I volunteered for the MLM and here I am."

No one speaks after hearing this verbal resume. Frankly, it leaves me breathless. Lydia and I exchange a quick glance.

Finally, Palumbo responds. "Okay, Major. Thanks for that. And thanks for taking charge at the site." He looks at the OSI guy. "Does the OSI have any other questions?"

The OSI colonel looks startled, like he's waking up from a nap. "No. No, General, no additional questions at this point. But there is the question of Captain Cattani's clearances. It's probably prudent to revoke them, at least for the time being."

Palumbo shakes his head. "What are you proposing? This entire episode will be made into a special access program. Captain Cattani will require his clearances to participate in any investigation. On top of that, he didn't do anything wrong. Why would you revoke his clearances?"

"Well, General Palumbo, this entire matter is highly irregular, and I think the young man needs to be put on ice while I brief my superiors and we see how things play out." Mr. OSI finishes his statement with a self-satisfied smirk.

Palumbo is fuming. "Colonel, you are way out of line. First, this is now a SAP program and you will not brief anyone, including your superiors. They are not cleared for this matter. Second, Kevin was nearly killed today performing a mission mandated by the director of the Defense Intelligence Agency. And you want to revoke his clearances? Are you in your right mind? Maybe I should revoke your clearances, Colonel!"

The OSI colonel raises his eyebrows but wisely doesn't respond to Palumbo's outburst.

Palumbo asks Lydia, "How are you feeling, young lady? Are you ready to travel?"

"Yes, sir. I think so. I am feeling much better. I'm ready to get out of Germany. Thank you."

The general looks at me. "Kevin, both of you need to go to Washington to brief the DIA director. He won't have a lot of strap hangers in the meeting—that much he promised me. Tell him the whole story. Major Hosenko will go with you."

Now, it's Hosenko who looks startled. "General, I don't think it's necessary for me to go with them. I've got a lot of work to attend to with the MLM and we know the Soviets will be out for revenge. No, I think my place is in Berlin."

Hosenko has balls—I'll give him that. He delivers his rebuttal in that same preternaturally calm voice. Palumbo doesn't buy it. "Major, you need to go to Washington. I'm not allowing a company-grade officer, no matter how accomplished he may be, to dive into that snake pit alone. I admire your dedication to the MLM, and no one values them more than I do, but I want you at DIA when these two young people brief the director. Clear?"

Mike Hosenko never hesitates. He seems to process everything faster than anyone else and answers almost before the general finishes. "That is crystal clear, General. Understood."

General Palumbo stands up, signaling to everyone that the meeting is adjourned. Hosenko shoots up from his chair and Palumbo shakes his hand. Lydia bows slightly to the General and is the first one out the door. Colonel LaRoche, the OSI colonel, and Hosenko follow. I'm about to go when Palumbo puts his right hand on my shoulder. He motions for me to sit down. We sit in silence for a couple of minutes.

I hear the vault door open and General Doug Flannery, the four-star commander of all NATO air forces in Europe, walks in with a bemused smile on his face. "Hello, babes. How are you doing?"

General Flannery started calling me "babes" when we served together in Japan. I know it is a term of endearment, even flattering, but it is embarrassing when he uses it in front of people like General Palumbo.

General Palumbo and I stand at attention. "I'm well, sir. How are you and Mrs. Flannery?"

The commanding general laughs and sits down across from me. "She's aces, babes. You know how much she likes Germany."

Palumbo and I take our seats.

Flannery looks at me with kind eyes and asks, "Are you okay?

That was a hell of a thing you went through in East Germany, based on what I've been told." He leans toward me and asks, "Did you kill two Soviet soldiers, Kevin?"

"Yes, sir."

The two generals share a glance. Flannery looks worried and asks, "Lenny, how is Moscow going to respond? It's a big deal losing a couple of men."

Palumbo says, "No doubt, sir. Our Soviet experts believe the Kremlin will keep this under wraps. Tensions are already high, and they have a new leader—Chernenko, who may not be in charge of things. Our analysts think that this incident is such an embarrassment for Moscow that they won't want to publicize it. Hell, sir, they may not even tell Chernenko about it."

Flannery muses for a moment and asks me, "Kevin, what do you think?"

Great. I love it when Flannery asks me to comment on my boss' assessments. It puts me in a no-win situation. "Sir, I think General Palumbo has it exactly right."

Flannery nods. "Lenny, you need to tell me how best to explain this incident up the NATO chain. I assume the fact that it happened will be protected in a special access program."

"Yes, General Flannery. We will establish a SAP. Very few people can know about this. And Kevin will have to go to Washington to brief the director of DIA. ASAP."

Flannery rubs his eyes tiredly and asks, "Will DIA want to investigate? Are they likely to give Kevin a hard time?"

"Sir, it's possible. I will do what I can to smooth the way with the DIA director." Palumbo looks worried. If he's worried, I should be terrified. "Also, I may need your help to keep the OSI from making trouble. They can't recommend criminal charges against Kevin—the Soviets would have to do that—but the OSI has the power to revoke his clearances."

That information surprises Flannery. "They do? Well, that's

nonsense. It would destroy Kevin's career."

"Yes, General, I told the OSI colonel to stand down. I hope he listens to me."

"Okay, Lenny, I will talk to him." Flannery smiles at me. "This will be okay, babes."

Palumbo looks at me kindly. "Kevin, you can't come back here after the trip to Washington. I mean you can come back for your things and to clear out your quarters, but you need to leave Germany. I'm worried about the reach of the GRU."

I'm stunned. "But sir, I've only been here since last fall. Where will I go? And Sandy is here. General Flannery asked me to come here from Japan." Christ, I'm babbling in front of two general officers.

"Look, Kevin, I'll get you a job on the Air Staff at the Pentagon," Flannery says gently. "They'll be happy to have you. Did your Sandy apply for medical school anywhere in DC?"

Oh, that's right—the general endorsed her application to the Air Force-funded medical program, but he has no idea where she applied to go to medical school. "Georgetown. She applied to Georgetown, and it's her first choice."

Flannery says, "Then, I'll pray she gets into Georgetown. You must understand why you need to get out of here, don't you?"

I know it's the logical thing to do. "Yes, sir." It's logical but it still sucks.

"We want you to be safe; you know that," Palumbo says with a sigh.

"Yes, sir. When will I—the team—leave for DC?"

Flannery looks at Palumbo for the answer. "Tonight. You'll leave tonight on a C-5 that will take you straight to Andrews. You'll probably meet with the DIA director tomorrow."

That's fast. Everything's happening so fast.

Flannery stands up and we follow suit. He says, "Babes, it's going to be okay. You and the DIA lady survived this deal and that's the most important thing. I'll be seeing you in Washington once you get settled. I fly back there once a quarter to report in, whether I want to or not." He grins and says, "You deserve a break from Germany, don't you think?"

Flannery puts an arm around my shoulder, and the three of us walk out of the SCIF together.

Back at my quarters, I shower, change, and pack a bag for the trip to DC. At the last minute, I decide to take my winter uniform overcoat. It will be cold in the hold of the C-5. Those planes are built to haul cargo and there are no creature comforts.

Before I go to the airfield, I drive to the Landstuhl Medical Center. I need to talk to Sandy and bring her up to speed on what's happening—to the extent that I can.

Sandy giggles with joy when she sees me standing at the nurses' station. I manage a wan smile. Immediately, she senses something is very wrong. She kisses me and gives me a long hug. "You're back early from Berlin. Are you okay? You don't seem okay."

"Baby, I'm all right now." I squeeze her harder. "Can we talk in a more private area?"

She nods and leads me to the end of the hall where there is a small sitting area for patients' families. It's deserted.

"What's going on?" Her voice is apprehensive and taut.

"I just got back from Berlin and now I have to go to DC tonight."

She straightens up and her luminous eyes register alarm. "DC? Now? Tonight? What the hell is going on? Are you in trouble?"

"No! Of course not. Well, maybe a little. Things didn't go well with the MLM."

A look of startled concern crosses her face, and she asks, "You mean you've already done your mission? It's over, already?"

"I didn't know when we were conducting the mission until I got to Berlin. We had last night to prepare and left at zero dark thirty this morning."

"Why was it so rushed? That sounds reckless."

"Yeah, that's a good word for it."

"Well, what the hell happened? Did anybody get hurt? Did you get hurt?"

"I just cut my hand." I raise my hand and show her my bandage.

"Is it serious?"

"No, it's really nothing. But the mission got complicated. The DIA analyst got hurt a bit worse than me, but she'll be okay. She's flying back to DC tonight on the same flight."

Sandy slumps in her seat. "My God. Are you sure you're okay?"

"Yes, I'm sure." I can't bring myself to tell her what Palumbo told me. But I know that I can't avoid it. "I met with General Palumbo this afternoon. He told me . . . he told me that I have to leave Germany. Leave for good, I mean."

Sandy gasps and claps her hand to her mouth. "Leave? Where are you going?"

"I can come back after this trip to get my things. He and General Flannery want me to go to Washington—to the Air Staff at the Pentagon. They think Germany isn't safe for me anymore."

Sandy gasps. "It isn't safe? Why isn't it safe? And he's the one who ordered you to do the mission with the MLM. And now it isn't safe for you to be at Ramstein? You're scaring me!"

I don't know what to say. I feel awful and my head is pounding. We sit in silence for a few minutes.

Sandy is trying hard not to cry while she processes everything. "Look, I have work to do. I have patients to check on. When will you get back from DC?"

I don't know. That hadn't even occurred to me—when I might return. "I guess I'll be back in a couple of days. I'm not sure. It depends on how many debriefings I have to do in Washington."

She stands up and sighs. "Call me when you get in tonight or tomorrow or whenever the hell the plane lands. Are you flying to Andrews?"

I feel totally deflated. "Yes, Andrews. Look, you must get accepted at Georgetown med school now. Since I'm going to be assigned to the Pentagon, I mean."

Sandy shakes her head. "Oh, Kevin. Be careful in Washington. My dad has always said it's a snake pit. Oh baby, what happened to you out there? I know you can't tell me, and I know it was bad." She stands and straightens her nurse's uniform. "Okay then, stand up and I'll kiss you goodbye for now."

CHAPTER EIGHT

VAYA CON DIOS

Captain Kevin Cattani, US Air Force Intelligence
Defense Intelligence Agency, Bolling Air Force Base, Washington, DC

17 April 1984

It's nearly midnight when we depart Ramstein. Thank goodness the Air Force loadmasters have installed a few rows of airline-style seats on the cargo deck of our C-5, which means we don't have to sit on jump seats during the long flight to Andrews Air Force Base in Maryland. As soon as we get to our cruising altitude, I move to an empty row of seats, wrap my winter coat around me and lie down across several seats. I go to sleep in the near-freezing conditions and don't wake up until we begin our descent into the suburbs of Washington, DC.

18 April 1984

It's about 2:00 a.m. Washington time when we land and an Air Force OSI team meets us planeside at Andrews Air Force Base. They hustle us into vehicles and drive us down the Suitland Parkway to Bolling Air Force Base, which is located along the Potomac River in southeast Washington, DC.

The base no longer has a flying mission and its old hangars have been converted into warehouses and office buildings. The Defense Intelligence Agency's analysis center and headquarters are located at Bolling in a new, gunmetal-gray multistory building. The OSI driver points out the building to us in the pre-dawn gloom. That's where we will meet with the director of DIA.

The three of us—Hosenko, Morelli, and I—are dropped off at the Distinguished Visitors quarters. Somebody is looking out for us—I haven't stayed in DV quarters since I traveled with General Flannery around the Pacific.

Another OSI officer is waiting in the small lobby to ensure we are checked in and shown to our rooms. I'm hungry and I ask him about getting breakfast. The OSI guy shrugs. "There're no twenty-four-hour options. The officers' club opens for breakfast at 0700. I'm afraid that's your only option. It's a short walk from the DV quarters, where we're putting you for your security."

Security from whom? I doubt the good citizens of the Anacostia section of DC are a threat to us. What's he talking about?

I decide not to get into it with him and the three of us trudge to our respective rooms in an exhausted daze. Even though I slept most of the flight, I'm still tired. I eat a package of crackers from my room's minibar, undress, and crawl into bed. I'd like to call Sandy and let her know I've arrived in DC, but I am unable to get an overseas phone connection from my room.

I wake up shortly after 7:00 a.m. I shower, put on a uniform, and walk over to the nearby officers' club. I've never been to Bolling before, and I discover that its club is one of the nicest I've seen anywhere in the world. Breakfast is served in the elegant main dining room. Somehow, I'm not surprised to see that Major Hosenko is already seated at a table and is eating a bowl of oatmeal with fruit.

He smiles as I approach his table. "Did you get your beauty rest, Kevin?"

I don't want to tell him that I need all the rest I can get before I start having nightmares about the bunker incident. Once they start, I won't be getting much sleep at all. "Yes, sir. I feel almost normal this morning."

Hosenko chuckles, "They have a great buffet here, but I always order oatmeal, so I don't overdo it."

I order an omelet and start power-drinking black coffee. I notice that Hosenko is drinking tea, as Ukrainians will do at breakfast time.

He looks at me after taking a sip. "You know, Kevin, you can call me Mike, especially when it's just the two of us."

I'm not accustomed to calling superior officers by their first names, but what the hell. "Okay. Will do."

He smiles his crooked little smile and looks at me with those piercing blue eyes. "I went to school at Virginia Tech—near where you grew up. It sure is pretty country where you come from, but I bet you never really fit in with the kids you grew up around. Am I right?"

I suppose so, but I'm not sure what he's driving at. "Yes, I guess that's true."

He continues. "I grew up speaking Ukrainian, and there were a lot of Russian and Ukrainian families living all around us in western PA. I bet there weren't too many kids where you grew up in southwest Virginia who wanted to learn Russian and leave home to do the sort of stuff that we do." He looks directly at me, and those eyes of his are boring holes in my face.

"Yes, Mike, that's true."

Abruptly, Hosenko puts down his napkin and stands up. "Well, I'm going to take a walk. I guess we won't see the director until this afternoon at the earliest. See you later."

I am back in my room unpacking when an OSI officer knocks on my door and tells me that we're scheduled to see the DIA director at 0800 tomorrow morning. I feel like my execution has been postponed.

Since I have down time, I decide to go for a long run around the base. It's a lovely spring day in Washington and the air is fresh and pleasantly warm. I have an invigorating run along the Potomac River, where there's a cool breeze coming off the water that complements the warmth of the springtime sun. It's so lovely that I forget about East Germany and dead Russians for a while.

As I warm down in front of the DV quarters, I see Mike Hosenko sitting on a bench reading in the shade of a cherry tree laden with blossoms. I walk over to him, although I am uncertain whether to disturb his reverie. "Hi, Mike. How was your walk?"

He looks up from his book and shakes his head like he's struggling to return from a distant place. "Can you believe this weather, Kevin? This is one of the best times of the year to be in Washington."

I glance more closely at the book he's reading and silently translate the Cyrillic title. It's a Soviet technical book on cybernetic warfare—jeez—the Russian vocabulary needed to read such a book is way beyond me. Mike seems to be reading the weighty tome like it's a trashy beach novel.

Lydia is on my mind, and I want his opinion about her state of mind. "Hey, Mike, how do you think Lydia is doing?"

He closes the book and muses for a moment before answering, which is unusual for him. "She's a mess. She's trying to process what happened in the bunker and she's doing it alone. It makes me think of the aircrews I flew with in Vietnam. You know, guys coming back from a mission where they got shot at—seriously shot at—for the first time. After a mission like that your brain is all jumbled up. She doesn't have anyone to help her unscramble it. At least in Vietnam, guys would commiserate at the O club after a tough mission. Here, it's different. She's completely on her own."

Well, I believe he's nailed it. I say, "It's surreal to be back here in the States where everything is 'normal' when we were just in a situation completely disconnected from normal. I think it's a good thing that the OSI won't allow us to leave the base. If I were out in the real world right now the juxtaposition of normalcy with what we just experienced would drive me off the deep end. Does that make sense?"

Mike stares at me with those eyes. "Yes, it makes complete sense to me. It'll be smart for you to get back to Ramstein as quickly as possible. But Lydia—she's already home. She'll go back to her apartment and her regular job and everything that's 'normal' with no help. It's going to be tough as hell for her."

I get up from the bench, stretch my arms above my head, and say, "Well, I'll see you later. Good luck with the light reading."

He laughs and gives me a perfunctory wave. Back in my temporary quarters, I delay taking a shower for a bit. I sit in an easy chair and start to read today's *Washington Post*. I've just turned to the editorials when someone knocks on my door. I put down the paper and go to the door, expecting to see an OSI officer. Instead, I see Lydia with a nervous smile on her face.

"Hello, Lydia. What can I do for you? Do you want to come in?"

She moves halfway across the threshold, holding the door partly open. "Hi, Kevin. Hey, I was wondering if you want to go to dinner tonight at the O Club. I feel like a prisoner here and I need to do something fun. Did you know that the OSI won't let me leave the base to go to my apartment in Alexandria? I've got nothing clean to wear." She makes a face like she's smelling something awful. "One of the OSI guys is going to drive me to the BX so I can buy some extra clothes and makeup. Can you believe it?"

Dinner with Lydia? We aren't permitted to leave the base and the officers club is the only option. It makes sense. "It sucks they won't let you pick up things from your own place. I think dinner would be nice. What time do you want to walk over to the club?"

She seems relieved that I accepted her invitation. "I'll come by at six thirty and we can go to the bar and get a drink first—okay?"

"That sounds fine, Lydia. See you then."

I close my door. Was that weird? Asking me to dinner? Probably not. She's walking a knife's edge with her emotions. And we're treated like prisoners by the OSI here.

She is beautiful—even in the state she's in.

18 April 1984

Lydia arrives promptly at my door at 6:30 p.m. She's wearing a dress that accentuates her large breasts without being ostentatiously revealing. That's a tough balancing act, but she's pulled it off.

We leave my room and I see an OSI guy pacing on the grassy knoll adjacent to the parking lot, guarding or observing our rooms—probably both—and he almost falls over when he sees her. Lydia and I walk under delicate, blossoming cherry trees that line the pathway to the club. It's a perfect spring evening. It reminds me of soft nights in Williamsburg, where I went to college.

As I open the main club door for Lydia, I chuckle to myself.

Lydia isn't supposed to hear my private laugh, but she does. "What's so funny?"

I blush slightly. "I was just thinking that I doubt the patrons of the Bolling Officers' Club are ready for a sight like you tonight."

I'm still holding the door for her, and she gives me a quizzical look. "What do you mean? And you know, now that you mention it, you haven't said a thing about how I look, Captain Cattani."

I stutter, "You look amazing."

"Oh, yeah? Well, I'm not used to fishing for compliments, Kevin!" Taking my arm, she guides me into the club.

She glides into the club's lounge like a ballerina, dragging me by the arm. When we reach the bar, the bartender's eyes go wide. He looks up and down her tall, lithe frame so obviously that it's comical.

She orders. "I'll have a vodka on the rocks with soda, a splash of tonic, and two limes. What are you drinking, Captain Cattani? It's on me."

"Okay, I'll have a McCallan neat. Let's make it the eighteen-year-old, seeing as you're buying, Ms. Morelli."

"All righty, then. Good choice. Bartender, make his drink a double. He deserves it."

I follow her to a high-top table, and we sit down. Her dress rides up her right thigh as she crosses her legs. "You know Kevin, I could drink a pitcher of these vodka drinks tonight." She adjusts her dress to show even more of her thigh.

I raise my glass to toast her. "Yes, but then you'd have a headache like after a Led Zeppelin show when we brief the DIA director in the morning."

She winks at me. "I'll have a headache when we brief the director tomorrow whether I get drunk tonight or not."

As I expected, Lydia is attracting a lot of attention. Every guy that walks in the lounge does a double take. One older dude at the bar can't keep his eyes off her and stares to the point that he's making me uncomfortable. None of this attention seems to faze Lydia in the least. It's her world and men are welcome to look as much as they like.

She smiles devilishly at me. "I'm ready for another round! How about you, Captain Cattani?"

"Not right now. I want wine with dinner, and this will hold me until then. You know that you can call me Kevin, right?"

She tosses her long hair and laughs rather loudly. "Yeah, but where's the fun in that? Besides, I just like the way that Captain Cattani rolls off my tongue, so to speak. It sounds like a character in a Fellini movie!"

Lydia gets her second drink, causing a commotion amongst the patrons at the bar. She says something amusing to her admirers and sashays back to our table like a triumphant empress. A man who has been standing at the bar walks over to our table. Lydia sees him, cuts her eyes toward me, and grimaces.

The man stands on the side of our table, turns his back to me and says, "Hello, Lydia. You look spectacular tonight."

"Thank you, sir. Let me introduce you to Captain Kevin Cattani."

Rudely, the man keeps his back turned and says, "I'm not interested in meeting one of your friends. I want to talk to you." I can't see his face, but I can tell from his languid delivery that he's rather drunk.

Lydia looks panicked but collects herself. "Now, Mr. Bottoms, don't be bad-mannered. Kevin and I just got here from Germany this morning. Kevin, this is Rand Bottoms. He's a very senior civilian at DIA."

Mr. Bottoms turns to face me, and says, "I am *the* senior civilian at DIA. I'm the deputy director."

Oh, yeah. Good for you, fuckface. I respond firmly, "Pleased to meet you." I don't bother to extend my hand since he didn't.

Lydia interjects, "Well, Kevin and I are going to the dining room now. It was great to see you, Mr. Bottoms." She gets up, grabs her drink, and nods goodbye to Bottoms. She grabs my arm, and we walk away from the clearly annoyed DIA man.

He calls after us, "I will see you in the morning. I hope you're ready."

As Lydia and I sit down at our table, I say, "That was fun, Lydia. We should've invited old Rand to have dinner with us."

"Oh Kevin, he's an insufferable douchebag and he hits on me whenever he sees me. Everybody at DIA knows that he's a lush and a womanizer. He disgusts me."

We have a good bottle of wine at dinner—a huge, ripe Napa cabernet. She talks throughout the meal about her days in the Army, her job at DIA, her parents, and her apartment. She's hyper and seems extremely fragile to me. I say very little. I just want a good meal, some nice wine, and a good night's rest. Lydia is another story, however. She seems intent on eating and drinking everything in sight.

As we finish the main course, Lydia exclaims, "I want dessert—cheesecake! Do you want dessert? And I want an after-dinner drink, too. How about you?"

I'm buzzed from the combination of scotch and the wine, and I really don't need an after-dinner drink. "No, I think I'll just watch you indulge yourself. I'll be doing the briefing in the morning, remember?"

She feigns dismay. "Ugh. All right, fine. I'll spoil myself—just keep flirting with me!"

Flirting with her? What's she talking about? Have I been flirting with her? I don't think so. "Lydia, if you want to think I'm flirting with you, then go ahead."

"Look, Captain Cattani, I'm an expert at men flirting with me, and you're definitely flirting with me. I admire the way you do it, too. You're so nonchalant about it. It's like you're not *actively* flirting, but you are. Don't worry. I like your style of flirting without flirting. It's extremely sexy."

I don't have an answer for that one. Lydia is riding tonight on high emotion. It's a natural posttrauma condition. I get it. The way she's eating and drinking are a manifestation of her response to our near-death experience in the East German bunker. She wants to consume life.

She savors every bite of her dessert and each sip of her Cognac. She stares at me as she rolls the liqueur around in her mouth like it's the most savory and satisfying thing she's ever tasted. Who's flirting now?

Lydia is rather tipsy on our short walk back to our quarters. She trips on a curb and falls into my arms. She laughs a too-loud laugh and says, "Thanks. Thanks for saving me again. Are you always going to be around to save me?"

"Well, I'll be here until tomorrow night anyway. I'm hoping to get a hop back to Germany as soon as I can. Then you'll be able to go back to your apartment in Alexandria and back to your normal life."

She scoffs and pouts. "That sounds *so* boring! Why would you say something mean like that?" Suddenly, she looks like she's about to cry. I remember what Mike Hosenko told me earlier today about how people process traumatic events. Lydia is as fragile as Murano glass. I'm empathetic but I'm also exhausted emotionally myself.

I need to get some rest to be ready for the DIA director's inquisition tomorrow morning. I don't want to play games with Lydia. "It's been a long couple of days. We're both exhausted."

We're at her door now and the OSI officer guarding the place is nowhere to be seen. Where is that guy? He's got to be lurking nearby.

She notices that he's gone, too. "Well, well, well, Captain Cattani, the coast is clear." She opens her door and walks inside. "Let's hope you're not *too* exhausted." She motions for me to join her inside her room.

I hesitate and remain on the sidewalk. Lydia smiles and gestures for me to join her again. She stumbles backward. Wow, she's very drunk. Reluctantly, I step inside, and the door closes behind me. I want to go to my room and get some sleep. I don't need her unsubtle, seductive bullshit.

"Come closer, Kevin. Come on. I don't want to be alone. I'm a wreck since the bunker thing. Hold me."

I know she's a mess and I feel for her. I don't move but she does, and she wraps her arms around me and kisses me hard on the mouth. I can taste the cognac on her tongue and feel her large, soft breasts press up against my chest. She wriggles her hips against me.

She pulls her mouth away from mine and shoves her hips forward. "Why, Captain Cattani, that's a *very impressive* hard-on you have there."

I pull away from her and she falls backward and sits down with a plop on the bed. She laughs her too-loud laugh again. "Kevin, I'm ready for you." She hikes up her dress to show me her thighs and spreads her knees apart. She's not wearing panties.

"Lydia, you're gorgeous *and* you're completely drunk. You're out of control."

She laughs loudly. "Now, be a good boy and come to bed. I know all about your girlfriend—the nurse. She's what? She's half-Korean and half-black. I mean, c'mon Kevin—really? When you could have me—a Russian-Italian goddess? Think of the beautiful babies we'll make together!"

I was feeling sorry for her, but she crossed a line with her racist insult about Sandy and I snap back to my senses. "She's half-Japanese, actually—not Korean." I turn around and walk to the door. "You're drunk and we have an early wake-up in the morning!"

I grab the doorknob and one of her stiletto heels hits me squarely in the back of my head. Her aim is impressively accurate, especially given her inebriated state. "You motherfucker!" she screams. "You're turning me down? Nobody fucking turns me down! Ever!"

I open the door, step out on the sidewalk, and close it shut. I hear her second shoe bounce against the back of the door. Turning to go to my room, I collide with the OSI guy who is "guarding" Lydia's room.

We're both startled. Then he asks, "Trouble in paradise?"

He's a big dude and looms over me. I'm deciding whether to punch him in the throat or kick him in the balls when I restrain myself from doing either. I just mutter, "Fuck you!" I walk down the sidewalk toward my own door.

He starts to follow me and yells, "Listen, asshole, we're out here all night protecting your sorry ass!"

I get to my door and insert the key. I turn around to face him. "You do not want to follow me. Back off. The last thing I need is protection from the goddamn OSI!" I open the door and yell, "Vaya con Dios, motherfucker!" I have no idea why I said that, but it's the only thing that came to mind in the moment.

My room is dark, and I leave it that way. I sit down on the bed and pound myself in the head three times—hard—fuck, fuck, fuck! What a royal mess. Sleep is impossible when I'm revved up. Should I get a drink from the minibar to calm down? No. That'll ensure I'll have a headache in the morning. To make matters worse, I haven't been able to get Sandy on the phone today either.

Lydia will be a pissed-off, hungover mess tomorrow morning. But I won't be. She's probably taking the right approach. Why not get drunk and fuck the night before your hanging?

CHAPTER NINE

NO GOOD DEED GOES UNPUNISHED

Captain Kevin Cattani, US Air Force Intelligence
Defense Intelligence Agency, Bolling Air Force Base, Washington, DC

19 April 1984

I have a rough night and am up before dawn. After I shower and dress, I write down the key points I want to make when I brief the DIA director this morning. While I'm working, an OSI officer knocks on my door. He doesn't wait for me to open it, but simply yells through the closed door, "We leave in ten."

I go out to the parking lot, where I find Mike Hosenko seated in an idling van.

"Good morning, Mike."

He gives me that blue-eyed stare and smiles. "Did you have a good night? Are you ready for the big show?"

I shake my head. "I didn't sleep well, but I'm ready."

Lydia arrives about five minutes later. She gets in the van and sits down wordlessly in the seat directly in front of me.

As the senior officer of our little team, Mike feels responsible for

Lydia and me. He taps her on the shoulder. "Are you good to go?"

Lydia bristles visibly at Mike's touch. "I'll be fine. You don't need to worry about me. Okay?"

"Okay." He replies but it's obvious that Lydia is making Mike nervous. He's assessing each of us. "What's with you two this morning?" Neither of us answers immediately.

The OSI driver puts the van in gear, and the vehicle lurches forward.

Lydia hunches her shoulders and sighs, "Major, I will do what I need to do. I can't speak for him. His solipsism is boundless. He'll have to tell you what's on his mind."

Solipsism, eh? Technically, I don't think solipsism can be boundless. You either hold to the theory or you don't. I guess she drunkenly dusted off her dictionary last night seeking an inventive way to insult me. Mike grunts in response.

We remain quiet until we arrive at the DIA headquarters complex, which is so new that the official opening won't be held until next month. The main entrance doors still have blue construction tape on them.

We clamber out of the van and go through the security checkpoint. An Army major greets us in the lobby and escorts us upstairs to the director's suite. He takes us to a small anteroom, where we sit down. Mike asks for hot tea from a young administrative assistant. I pull the notes I prepared earlier this morning from the inside pocket of my uniform and review them. Lydia stares at the floor. The minutes drag by as we wait. There's no nervous banter among us, which is unusual while waiting for a meeting as important as this one. Finally, a Navy lieutenant appears and guides us into the director's small SCIF. I get very light-headed when I stand up. I steady myself against the wall. Mike notices and mouths "You okay?" I look at the floor to get my equilibrium and nod.

As we enter the SCIF, I'm surprised to see that there are two people seated against the far wall. One is an Army JAG officer, and the other is a civilian woman who sits behind a tiny table with a court recorder's typewriter. Mike and I exchange worried glances. The Army lawyer is here for a deposition, not a debrief.

We take seats around the small conference table and wait for the senior people to arrive. I pull out my notes and place them on the table in front of me.

After a few minutes, the same Navy lieutenant opens the vault door and the DIA director and a civilian walk in together. The director is a tall, lean Army three-star general, and he greets us with a wry smile and handshakes. The civilian is the same asshole who hit on Lydia last night—Rand Bottoms. He wears very preppy, horn-rimmed eyeglasses, a blazer, khakis, a rep tie, and penny loafers. He's a perfect specimen of the civilian national security professional species, native to the Washington capital region. The DIA director introduces himself and Bottoms, who is the deputy director of the agency, while Hosenko responds by introducing himself, Lydia, and me.

Bottoms sneers. "We know who you are." He gives me a particularly hostile look.

The DIA director clears his throat and says to Lydia, "I'm so pleased to finally make your acquaintance, Ms. Morelli. I want to thank you for volunteering for this difficult mission. I understand you suffered some injuries."

Lydia looks like her dog just died and she's ready to crawl into bed to nurse her hangover, but she rallies and responds. "Thank you, sir. I had cuts from flying glass—I lost some blood but nothing serious."

He looks at me and nods a greeting. "Well, Captain—Cattani is it? Is that Italian?"

"Yes, sir, although my strain of the Cattani family came to America by way of Luxembourg."

"Luxembourg is so quaint—lovely." He clears his throat and gets down to business. "Well, I suppose this mission didn't go precisely to plan, eh?"

Shrugging, I reply, "No, sir—not precisely. I must ask you why there is a JAG officer in the room."

Rand Bottoms doesn't wait for his boss to respond. "They are here to make an official record of the proceedings. One may be needed in future."

I see that my buddy Rand has a propensity for speaking BBC English with a slight Virginia drawl. What a dick. I am about to respond with something impolitic when suddenly, the vault door opens again with a loud *whoosh*. The two DIA men exchange surprised looks, and the director asks his deputy, "Are you expecting someone?"

"No, sir." Bottoms shifts nervously in his seat. "No one."

There's a bit of a ruckus at the door. The cause quickly becomes apparent—it's the Red-haired Major and he barges into the SCIF with the grace of a rabid grizzly bear. "Good morning, everybody! I'm sorry to be a few minutes late." He grins like a demon on cocaine.

Clearly annoyed, Rand Bottoms demands, "Who the hell are you and what are you doing in my director's meeting?"

My old boss sits down heavily before answering with a maniacal grin. "I'm here for the DCI, of course."

Good old Rand's face turns very red. He has the complexion and eyes of a man who eats and drinks too much. "This is a DIA director-level meeting, and you're not welcome here."

"Yeah, well, Mr. William Casey wants me here. Heard of him? He's the director of Central Intelligence and everyone in this room works for him, last time I checked. So, if he wants me here, I'm staying." He looks at Bottoms with a ferocious grin and points to the end of the table where the legal team is seated. "What's with the JAG and court stenographer? Is this a formal hearing? A deposition?"

Bottoms angrily replies, "It's none of your business how we conduct our investigations."

"Oh yeah? Well Mr. Casey made it my business. Unless this is a formal hearing under the Uniform Code of Military Justice, then I demand that the lawyer and the recorder leave the room." The

Red-haired Major leans across the table forebodingly and sneers at Bottoms. "You don't have the authority to hold a deposition. This is an intelligence community matter, bucko!"

A bit ruffled, the DIA director responds, "I didn't realize they'd be here either. I see no need for them." The general looks at the JAG officer and the recorder and says gently, "You may leave now."

Bottoms starts to argue with his boss, but the Army officer shushes him. The legal people gather their things and leave the SCIF as hastily as they can. They both look relieved to be going.

The DIA director waits until the SCIF door closes with a pronounced, vacuum-seal-like *thump* and says, "I simply want to know what happened in East Germany. This isn't a witch hunt. As you know, the Soviet nuclear alert didn't end with the conclusion of Able Archer 83 last November. In fact, in late March and during the first part of this month, the Soviet Union conducted the largest integrated nuclear war exercise we've ever seen—ever seen in the entirety of the Cold War. Did you know that they recently concluded a naval exercise that involved twenty-three nuclear ballistic missile subs that conducted mock nuclear launches on targets in the United States and NATO? We've never seen anything on that scale before. Obviously, this information cannot leave this room. It's based on highly sensitive special intelligence sources." He pauses to see the effect his words have had on us. "You must appreciate the urgency of the mission in this context."

Mike Hosenko can't contain himself any longer and jumps in with no preliminaries. "General, despite that context, this mission was ill-advised. The mission wasn't rehearsed adequately. There should have been much more preparation before undertaking something so challenging."

The Army general sits up straight. He must be nearly six foot five and he appears every inch of it even while seated. "Major, this mission was urgent. I believed we had a unique opportunity to gain important intelligence on the Soviets' theater nuclear posture. We need to know if they are preparing to attack us, as they were last November."

I can tell that Mike relishes this kind of sparring. "No doubt, sir. I completely understand the motivation behind the mission. But something like this demands precise preparation and we didn't have it."

Bottoms shakes his head in obvious disgust and retorts, "Major, there *was* adequate time for proper preparation. The problem, it seems to me, is that we had a cowboy on the scene who took it upon himself to kill two Soviet Army soldiers." The civilian glares at me. "Captain, you have created a major problem for this agency, this government, and for President Ronald Reagan. Do you have any idea how much damage your trigger-happy behavior has caused?"

So, this is how it's going to be. I guess I don't need my notes. I am presumed guilty. I look at the Red-haired Major and his eyes are dancing in his head. He's enjoying this and that gives me the freedom to play it my way. Fuck, this isn't a debriefing; it's an inquisition. "Mr. Bottoms, I take the use of lethal force very seriously. Had there been another way to handle the incident, then I would have done something different. Those Soviet soldiers fired first. They were shooting at Ms. Morelli and were going to kill her and then kill me. They fired multiple volleys before I fired my first shots. I did the only thing I could do to save our lives. And Major Hosenko is right, we had minimal time to prepare and no rehearsal at all with the MLM security team." That old familiar hot feeling creeps up my neck and my head starts pounding. I need to control my breathing, so I don't completely lose my temper. I can feel myself losing control.

Undeterred, the angry preppy Bottoms says, "Captain, it's clear to me that you are a man of certitude and violence. That's a catastrophic combination in our business. In this case, it was . . . catastrophic."

I steal another glance at the Red-haired Major. He rolls his eyes at me, grins, and says, "Hey, wait a second. I want to write that one down—a man of certitude and violence. I kinda like that. Wow! That one's a keeper. Good on ya, whoever the hell you are!"

Bottoms face is completely crimson now. "Who the hell am I? Who the hell are you?"

The DIA director interjects, "Let's dial it down. We're all on the same team. I have seen the preliminary reports from the mission. It looks like we got at least some of the intelligence we were seeking. It was bad luck that the patrol came along when they did. I would've expected the security team to take action to divert the patrol, but that didn't happen."

Hosenko grimaces in reaction to the criticism.

Bottoms sees an opening and now directs his unhinged ire at Mike. "Major, you failed to secure the area, leading to the enemy entering the bunker, and then *you* entered the bunker after this captain and Ms. Morelli got out. Why didn't you clean up the scene? You should have removed the bodies and swept the entire bunker so that the Soviets would never discern that we had been in the facility. Why wasn't that done?"

Christ! Is this Bottoms as idiotic as he appears? Clean up the scene? Clearly, he's never been in a situation remotely like this one. Mike Hosenko is literally biting his tongue.

The Red-haired Major shakes his head at Bottom's obvious stupidity, and he says, "Hey, bucko, they were in a goddamn PRA. There were Soviet patrols all over the area. I have conducted plenty of dangerous missions, but this one takes the cake for lack of preparation. As for 'sweeping' the scene after the fact—it was impossible under the circumstances and the risk to the entire team was simply too great. We're lucky Cattani and this young woman weren't killed. You're lucky they weren't killed, Mr. Deputy Director!"

Bottoms remains smugly convinced that we totally fucked up everything and that he is blameless. "Well, there's going to be hell to pay for this. Mark my words. You may have gotten the JAG excused but this doesn't end here, and it doesn't end well for you." The preppy civilian glares at me when he says that.

Mike Hosenko has had enough. "With all due respect, the only hell will be paid by the MLM. The Soviets will retaliate, but they will take revenge against us, or our French or British partners. They will *never* publicize this event. President Reagan has nothing to worry about. The MLM teams will pay the price. There will be no political fallout."

The DIA director. who has allowed the freewheeling dialogue, now retakes control of the meeting. "I think Major Hosenko is correct on both counts. The MLM will bear the burden and Moscow will not use this incident for propaganda purposes." The General turns to the Red-haired Major. "You may tell Mr. Casey that this matter is classified as a special access program and that there will be no repercussions on the team that conducted the mission. I don't believe the team did anything wrong, given the circumstances." Bottoms looks like his head is about to explode. I would pay a month's salary to see that asshole's brains all over the wall. In fact, I'd be happy to make it happen.

The director turns to Lydia. "Ms. Morelli, you will take charge of the analysis of the intelligence collected on the mission. If you need anything—any assistance—then, let me know, personally. This was a difficult mission. We're not in a shooting war with the Soviets, but it is still a war. There will be casualties." He pauses and says, "Thank you." The DIA director stands up, ending the meeting. We all stand at attention as he departs.

Rand Bottoms hangs back and lets the door close behind his boss. He wants the last word, and he glares at me. "You're not out of the woods, my young friend. I will not let this matter drop."

I respond, "Listen, I am not your friend and—" I am interrupted by the Red-haired Major putting his lumberjack's arm around my shoulder.

"It's okay, Kevin. I got this." He smiles malevolently at Bottoms who recoils and steps back a good three feet. "Look, Bottoms. I've dealt with pussies like you my entire career. You fuck with Kevin Cattani, and you are fucking with me, and you really don't want to do that. You will drop this, or I will drop you. I hope that's clear enough for you—you fucking microprick."

Bottoms' looks horrified. No one speaks to him like that, and the Red-haired Major scares him. He turns away and exits without another word.

My old boss squeezes my shoulder very hard. "Kid, I will need to keep an eye on that Bottoms guy. He won't let this go easily, but neither will I."

We walk silently behind our escort and exit the building. The four of us stand on the sidewalk in the morning sunshine. I am stunned by what I just experienced. The Red-haired Major, of course, is not at a loss for words. "Well, that was a hoot. We need to do this more often. And I got a new best friend out of the deal. That dopey-ass Rand is on my radar screen now, and that is not a pleasant place to be."

I shake my head over the absurdity of the entire situation. "Thanks for being here, boss, and for getting the JAG officer and stenographer kicked out of the meeting."

Mike looks at the Red-haired Major admiringly with his laser-blue eyes and says, "Sir, I don't know who you are, but I'm glad you were here. Did the DCI really send you to this meeting? How did he even know about it?"

The older man tosses his head back and laughs. "I guess you'll never know for sure. I doubt the DIA director will have the balls to call Mr. Casey and ask. If his dipshit deputy makes trouble, I'll find a way to fuck him up. Anyway, I'm glad I could help. As for knowing about the meeting, there's very little that happens to my boy Cattani that I don't know about." He grabs me around the shoulder and digs his elbow into my ribs. It's embarrassing, especially in front of Lydia, who looks simply bewildered by the events of this morning. I guess I look that way, too.

The big man has the final word. "Okay, gang, I gotta get back to the mothership before someone notices that I'm missing. Kevin, didn't I warn you about getting into trouble in East Germany? Next time you better listen to your old boss!" With that, the Red-haired Major strides into the brilliant spring sunshine.

The OSI van is waiting for us, and we board in silence. Mike is pensive. Lydia's face is drawn and expressionless. I feel a bit faint until I get seated.

I break the silence as we drive away. "Well, what do you think, Mike?"

Instead of responding immediately, Mike leans forward and puts a hand on Lydia's shoulder. Lydia doesn't flinch at his touch this time. "This will blow over soon if that civilian deputy allows it. It'll be overtaken by some new crisis next week, or even later today. But Mr. Bottoms seems to hold a grudge, so be careful. And, someday, somebody at the MLM will get hurt by the Soviets and who knows if they'll pay any attention here in Washington when that happens. That's just the way things go."

Lydia replies, "I think it's bullshit—total bullshit. I almost got killed over there and my own civilian leadership blames me and Kevin. Total bullshit. Bottoms is a dangerous prick, too. Dangerous." She stares out the side window and I can see that her face is very flushed.

Mike leans back into his seat and says, "You know the old saying, 'no good deed goes unpunished.' You have to be careful when you're asked to volunteer. Weigh the risks and the rewards before you agree to something like this in the future."

This whole episode makes me sick. I can't believe that Bottoms ambushed us in the meeting by bringing in a JAG officer. Who the hell can you trust in this business? Things might have really gone to shit if the Red-haired Major hadn't shown up uninvited. Mike is right. No good deed goes unpunished—no kidding. A wave of anxiety overwhelms me as I think about returning to Germany only to pack up and fly back here to Washington. After today's experience,

I never want to see DC again. I have no guarantee that Rand Bottoms won't come after me in the future. I would prefer to keep an ocean between me and bottom feeders like that guy.

We unload in front of the DV quarters, where each of us will go our separate ways. Lydia doesn't talk to either of us. She disappears quickly into her room. I stand on the sidewalk in front of mine and Mike Hosenko walks over to shake my hand. "Kevin, are you headed back to Germany, or are you going to visit your folks in Virginia?"

I shake his hand. "Germany. My relationship with my family—especially with my father—is not great. In fact, my father and I are . . . well, I guess you could say that we hate each other. And I'd have to give advance notice about a visit. I'm hoping to fly to Ramstein tonight to see my girlfriend, pack up, and get a flight back here ASAP. How about you, Mike?"

I get the blue-eyed stare. "My father is sick—very sick. I'm flying to Pittsburgh this afternoon. I'll be back home with my parents tonight. Now that I think about it, I haven't been back there in a couple of years." He pauses as if to ponder what's kept him away from home for so long. "What's with Lydia?"

How can I answer that question? "She had a lot to drink last night, and we had an argument. I guess she's still mad at me."

He pierces me with his penetrating stare. "Hmm. Well, she's the prettiest intelligence analyst I've ever seen. That's for sure."

I sigh deeply and try to smile. "Mike, travel safely. Look me up when you are back in Washington." He starts to turn away and I ask him a question I've been thinking about since I met him. "Hey, tell my why a Ukrainian-American joins the Air Force, becomes a fighter pilot, and then an intelligence officer focused on the Soviet Union?"

Mike stops in his tracks. I hope I haven't offended him. We don't know each other very well, after all. He doesn't seem perturbed with me when he responds, "I've always wanted to fly. The Vietnam War gave me the chance to fly in combat. It was good training."

Good training? "Mike, you flew a bunch of combat missions over

Hanoi. That's war, not training."

He fixes me with his blue lasers. "Well, I mean training for the big war—the one with the Russians. I am in the Air Force to kill Russians, or at least be prepared for it."

No shit? "So, you want to hurt the Soviet Union—to help the United States or to free Ukraine from the Soviets?"

He looks up at the cloudless sky and thinks about his answer for a few seconds. "Both. I'm an American first and foremost. But if I can help Ukraine too, then I think that's a good use of my life."

"I am glad you're on our side, Mike."

He laughs, waves, and heads toward his room.

Later, an OSI driver meets me in the parking lot and tells me that he'll take me to Andrews. "I'm driving Ms. Morelli to Alexandria first. I'll drop her and then take you up to Andrews. Okay?"

No, it's not okay. I don't want to share a ride with Lydia. There's no sense in being petty, however, and the OSI guys have more important things to do than chauffeur us around separately. "Yeah, that'll be fine. I'm ready to go whenever you are."

"Okay, I'll get Ms. Morelli."

A few minutes later, Lydia climbs into the van and sits next to me. I say, "Hello" and she mumbles, "Hi." We don't talk during the drive across the Potomac River to Alexandria, Virginia. The driver stops in front of a small apartment building and Lydia gathers her things.

I feel like I have to say something, even if it's not well received. "Lydia, I wish you the best and hope you'll be okay."

She doesn't look at me and snaps. "Why wouldn't I be, okay?" She starts to climb out of the van and turns back to look at me. She says in a gentler tone, "Good luck getting back to Germany." And with that, she walks to her apartment with the OSI guy following her, carrying her bags.

At Andrews, I manage to call Sandy and let her know I'm on my way without sharing any other details about my whirlwind trip to Washington. Eventually, I get on a C-5 that is headed to Ramstein by way of Lakenheath Air Base in England.

My journey to Germany turns into an odyssey. We refuel in England and the C-5 copilot tells me that he's been ordered to stop at Zaragoza, Spain, on the way to Ramstein. This lengthy journey gives me too much time to think about how unsettled my life has become and I keep going over my future options. I'm depressed about moving to Washington. The meeting at DIA was an eye opener about how things work in "the swamp." There's also no adrenaline rush in pushing paper around in a stuffy cubicle in the Pentagon. And, of course, there's no guarantee that Sandy will be able to join me in DC.

Maybe I should resign my commission and leave the Air Force and go work for the CIA like the Red-haired Major recommended. If the Air Force pushes me into a desk job, then why should I stay? The Red-haired Major would be happy to have me work for him again. And after all, I've always wanted to be a spook, not a bureaucrat like that pathetic Rand Bottoms at DIA. Maybe this is a time for me to let go and allow my emotions to tell me what direction to take.

PART TWO

THE BLACK TULIPS

> If we sent in our troops, the situation in your country would not improve. On the contrary, it would get worse. Our troops would have to struggle not only with an external aggressor, but with a part of your own people.
>
> —*Soviet Prime Minister Alexei Kosygin*
> *(speaking to the president of Afghanistan, Nur Taraki, prior to the Soviet invasion of Afghanistan in December 1979).*

CHAPTER TEN

A BUNKER IN THE WOODS

General-Major Ivan Levchenko, GRU, Soviet Air Defense Forces Moscow, Russia, USSR and German Democratic Republic (East Germany)

23 April 1984

Two dead soldiers. In a matter-of-fact voice, the briefer states that yesterday afternoon two Soviet troops were discovered dead inside a covert nuclear command-and-control bunker in East Germany—our only such facility in East Germany. This is astounding news. Who killed them? And why?

The briefer—a military intelligence colonel—continues. "The dead men were discovered when a maintenance team found that a new lock had been placed on the door to the bunker. To gain entry, the maintainers had to break the lock. I don't have to tell you the implications of this discovery. This could be an indication that the nuclear war crisis is entering a new and even more dangerous chapter. Operation RYaN is still viable."

Operation RYaN is the largest intelligence program ever

conducted by the Soviet intelligence services. RYaN stands for *nuclear rocket attack*, implying a "surprise" attack by the United States. The RYaN program is designed to ferret out indications that the West is planning a nuclear first strike on the USSR. Most of my colleagues think it is an absurd notion, but the program was created by the men at the top, so it continues. Despite the skepticism, it is fair to say that the RYaN premise nearly became reality last fall during the Able Archer crisis.

My boss is the head of the GRU, meaning he is the most senior military intelligence officer in the Soviet Union, a supremely powerful position. He's an older man with arthritis and he rises from his chair with difficulty to face the twenty-odd intelligence officers in the conference room. "Comrades, as the briefing shows, RYaN is still operable. This incident in East Germany represents a dangerous escalation in tensions with the West. Is it a continuation of NATO's nuclear war preparations? Is this a new phase? I welcome opinions." General of the Army Pyotr Ivashutin—the legendary "Peter the Great"—was appointed head of the GRU by Leonid Brezhnev in the early 1960s. He's a Hero of the Soviet Union and a survivor of many bitter clashes with the KGB. Ivashutin had a personal feud with the late Yuri Andropov, the long-time KGB chieftain and most recently the general secretary of the Communist Party of the Soviet Union. Their bitter clash reverberated throughout both intelligence services, making cooperation difficult on projects like Operation RYaN, the massive collection effort designed to find indications of a Western nuclear first strike. A highly decorated veteran of the Great Patriotic War, Ivashutin is the personification of the Russian bear—a massive, tough brown bear.

Oh, what the hell, I'm the most junior general officer in the room, so I'll speak up. "Comrade General, it is my view that this is an isolated case. It appears to be the handiwork of the Western MLM." I turn my eyes to the briefer and ask, "Do we have any information on who might have conducted this intrusion?" Although this incident is disturbing, I don't want the GRU leadership to jump to the conclusion that we are facing imminent nuclear war.

The GRU colonel clears his throat heavily—he must be a smoker. "In this instance our evidence points squarely at the Americans. The autopsies show that each man was shot by both .45 and .38 caliber rounds. To my knowledge, only the Americans carry sidearms with such ammunition. I think we may safely rule out the French and the British in this instance."

The Americans? This briefer annoys me with his incremental disclosures. I ask, "Colonel, do you have other critical evidence to disclose, or are we to play a guessing game with you all morning?"

My comment elicits chuckles around the table. The briefer is flustered but answers, "Sir, the blood of a third person was discovered in the bunker. Intruders broke the lock on the outer door and installed a new one of Soviet origin in its place. Tracks from two vehicles were discovered. Our patrol pursued one of the enemy vehicles for a time but lost it in the maze of trails in the forest. That is all we know at this point."

Really—that is all? "Did anyone interview the guards at the checkpoint on the Gleinicke Bridge? The Westerners must return to West Berlin via the bridge. Did the guards note a vehicle returning to the west with an injured passenger, perhaps?"

The colonel's neck turns a shade of crimson. "General, I am not aware that the guards on the bridge were interviewed. I will see to it."

I can only shake my head at such incomprehensible incompetence.

General Ivashutin asks me directly, "Ivan Ivanovich, do you have anything else to add? More recommendations for the team in East Germany, perhaps?"

At this point, I may as well jump all the way into the deep end of the pool. "Comrade General, it is my view that this information—the fact that this incident occurred at all—must be considered a state secret and treated accordingly by every officer in this room. In addition, the GRU must interview the Gleinicke Bridge guards, as well as any patrols that were in the Permanently Restricted Area on that day. We need to know who from the American MLM went in and out of East Germany on the day of the incident. This is the most crucial information."

The beleaguered colonel nods.

Ivashutin walks over to where I'm sitting and hovers over me. I start to rise, but he motions for me to stay seated. "Levchenko, if this was perpetrated by the American MLM, then what is their next move? You're the expert on the Americans. Tell me why you believe that this terrible incident—the murder of two Soviet soldiers—is an isolated case and is not related to Operation RYaN?"

I fidget with my uniform coat before I respond. "General, it is prudent to look at the incident from all sides to ensure we don't miss something—but I believe that this is likely an isolated incident. If the Americans were planning an imminent nuclear strike, and this intrusion into the bunker was a part of the plan, then I think their strike would've occurred by now." I look around Ivashutin at the briefer. "Colonel, approximately how many days ago did this incident occur?"

The briefer, who has just taken his seat, stands again. "Sir, it was on the seventeenth of April."

Why didn't he disclose that information already? "Comrades, it is my opinion—since today is the twenty-third of April—that if an American strike were planned and this intrusion were a precursor to it, then they would not wait nearly a week before launching their nuclear missiles."

My comments stir up a great deal of discussion and excited gesturing. General Ivashutin quells the rumblings in the room. "Comrade General Levchenko, I will discuss this matter further with the General Staff. In the meantime, prepare to go to East Germany. I want you to personally investigate this incident and report back to me, promptly."

I begin to protest; however, the general glares at me and I keep my mouth shut. An event in East Germany like this one has nothing whatsoever to do with my job as chief of intelligence for the Moscow Air Defense District. That's what I get for jumping into the deep end of the pool and letting my mouth run. I am my own worst enemy at times. My wife, Boyka, won't be happy about me going to Germany.

Boyka is playing her violin when I get home. I follow the magnificent sound she makes into her music studio. "My, that's quite a piece, Boyka! I don't recognize it, but it sounds extremely difficult. Who is the composer?"

She smiles and drops the instrument from her shoulder. "It is difficult, but I love it. The composer is Korean—Isang Yun—and he lives in West Germany. I met him when we lived in Frankfurt, and I bought several of his scores—not that the Soviets will ever let me perform them. They're challenging pieces and great exercise for the fingers and the mind."

I kiss her radiant face. "You sound wonderful." I take her hands in mine and gaze into her eyes. "My love, I must travel to East Germany for a few days. I shouldn't be away long."

She pouts like a schoolgirl and then her eyes flash with anxiety. "Don't tell me that the Americans and the Kremlin are on the verge of blowing up the world again."

"No, no. Nothing so dramatic this time. Just an incident that General Ivashutin wants me to investigate. It's probably nothing."

She's unconvinced and somewhat alarmed. "East Germany? That's not remotely in your area of responsibility, is it?"

Of course, she's correct. "No, but once one becomes a general officer . . . one's responsibilities are not limited to the current job."

She shakes her long blond hair, stands, and puts her hands on my shoulders. Staring directly into my eyes, she says, "I see. Well, if you must go away, how about a drink, mon cher general?" Boyka is from Kiev, capital of the Ukrainian Socialist Republic, and she has the hauntingly beautiful Nordic blue eyes of the original Viking rulers of that refined city. We're both in our midforties now, and she remains the most beautiful woman I've ever met.

After more than twenty years of marriage, I remain amazed that this dazzling woman is my wife. I'm an average looking guy, of average height and build. There's nothing remarkable about my appearance and everything is remarkable about hers.

We share a deep kiss and have a loving, quiet evening at home, which always makes it difficult to leave her.

24 April 1984

Joining me on the flight to East Germany this afternoon is a certain Major Anatoly Zhukov—a promising young officer on my staff who is fluent in German. I may use him to keep the East German STASI occupied and off my back. He bears the name of the most famous marshal of the Great Patriotic War. That officer, the truly great and justifiably renowned Marshal Zhukov, was the young man's great uncle.

Zhukov proves to be an excellent traveling companion, full of interesting stories about the political and social elites of Moscow. He's much better connected to the Communist Party higher-ups than I am, owing to his distinguished family pedigree. He's a tall, athletic young man with classically handsome Russian looks—and he is extremely self-assured. Among other things, he tells me he is engaged to the daughter of a powerful member of the Communist Party's Central Committee. Young Zhukov is going places.

25 April 1984

Major Zhukov and I have breakfast in our rather dismal East Berlin hotel (is there any other kind?) with a local STASI commander and a newly-assigned-to-Germany GRU lieutenant colonel by the name of Mikhail Grishin. I have known Grishin for years—he worked for me in the Soviet Military Liaison Mission in Frankfurt, West Germany, until I became fed up with his antics, which included attempting to seduce my wife. Unfortunately for me, Grishin despises me, and he is even better connected than Major Zhukov since his father is one of the most powerful men on the Communist Party's Central Committee.

Mikhail Grishin is a Communist Party "princeling" from birth—one of Russia's new socialist aristocrats—and he never lets one forget about his superior status. Grishin believes that a Crimean peasant like me is not worthy of being married to a beauty like Boyka. Therefore, attempting to seduce Boyka was not only exciting, but it was also a princeling's duty and a public good. Grishin and I are of the same medium height and build, but I am much fitter, and I was captain of the boxing team at the Kiev Air Force Academy. I would love to get him in the ring for a few rounds.

Between bites of greasy sausage and potatoes, Grishin briefs us on the paltry results of the interviews he has conducted related to the bunker incident. The evidence indicates that an American MLM team conducted the mission. But why? And why kill two Soviet soldiers? Why take that risk in this time of fraught relations between the superpowers?

I need to get rid of the intolerable Grishin and the STASI officer as expeditiously as possible. I conclude breakfast by saying, "Gentlemen, I want to thank you for your assistance. Major Zhukov will go with you to your offices presently to review the transcripts of your interviews, while I go into the countryside to talk to the patrol's commanding officer and the guards from the Gleinicke bridge checkpoint."

The German and Grishin exchange annoyed glances and it is the latter who speaks. "But General Levchenko, surely you will want us present when you conduct your interviews? We have the most insight into the events. Personally, I am convinced the Americans conducted this mission with the intention of provoking us—and our German allies—into some kind of military response. The fact that they executed the two soldiers is damning. We are owed justice, are we not, General? The Soviet people demand it."

As I said, Lieutenant Colonel Mikhail Grishin is well connected with the Moscow elites. Apart from that fact, he and Zhukov have little in common. Grishin is an ambitious bully—a self-aggrandizing schemer. Smiling, I reply, "Thank you for your assessment, Colonel Grishin. The Americans must have had a strong reason to undertake such a risky mission. Provocations go both ways, you know. After all, we just concluded the largest nuclear exercise in Soviet history."

Grishin scowls, "Surely, you are not comparing our peaceful exercise with the deliberate actions of the Americans—actions that resulted in the murder of two of our men! There are times when I wonder where your loyalties lie, General. You seem too sympathetic to the Americans."

Grishin thinks he can bully me even though I outrank him. "Colonel, I do not condone what the Americans have done, nor do I absolve them of guilt. I don't require lectures from junior officers about loyalty either. I know who I serve, and I serve the Soviet Union. Major Zhukov will be my eyes and ears, learning all he can from you and our friends in the STASI. In the interest of an independent view, I will undertake my own investigation, not to supersede your work but to augment it." I rise from the table. Grishin seethes. I can understand that they don't want a general from Moscow nosing around without them present, but this is my investigation, and I will handle it my way. I pity poor Zhukov for having to babysit them! But rank has its privileges, which Zhukov no doubt understands better than most.

I'm most interested in hearing from the guards at the Gleinicke Bridge, who were not interviewed immediately—which I still find incredible. Grishin should be sacked for negligence, powerful connections or not. The guards would have seen and spoken to the MLM team on its return trip over the bridge to West Berlin. I have arranged for the interviews to be conducted at a GRU facility near Potsdam, East Germany, not far from the Gleinicke Bridge.

My first interviewee is a very young Army officer—a senior lieutenant who led the mounted patrol that pursued one of the MLM vehicles from the site of the incident. The lieutenant is an earnest kid who is embarrassed that he failed to stop the Americans.

I try to put him at ease. "Don't worry about it, comrade. Those Americans are highly trained special forces troops who are experts at evading pursuit. They do it literally every day in East Germany. After all, how often have you attempted to pursue an American MLM team? It wasn't a fair contest, young man."

The young officer runs his right hand through his hair, nervously. "General Levchenko, we tracked them briefly and then they vanished into the forest like spirits. They simply disappeared, sir."

I smile, reassuringly. "Yes. Was there only one vehicle? How many men were on board the vehicle?"

"We pursued one vehicle. It was a big one and we don't know how many men were on board. Later, we determined that there must have been two vehicles parked in the clearing."

That seems to confirm that there were two vehicles. "I see, Lieutenant. Did you speak to the guards at the Gleinicke bridge to determine what they saw?"

"No, sir. The bridge—the guards on the bridge—are outside of my jurisdiction. They also are not in my chain of command, and I had no reason to talk to them."

Typical Soviet Army nonsense. "Outside of my jurisdiction." I don't blame this young man. It is how he's been trained. It is the institution's fault. "It's okay, comrade. I understand. Tell me, where are you from?"

The lieutenant looks confused. "Sir? Why . . . I am from a small town near Volgograd. You would not have heard of it; it's quite small."

I smile to put him at ease. "I see. And the men in the bunker—the dead men—they were under your command?"

This question makes him uneasy. "Yes, sir. They were troops in my platoon. Recent conscripts, you see."

New conscripts. Poor bastards. "Did you know them? Where were they from?"

"General? I didn't know them, and I don't know where they were from. Sorry, sir." He looks at me with a pained and befuddled expression.

"Did you notice that I asked you where you are from?" The young man nods. "It only takes a minute. In the future, you should get to know your men." He nods vigorously. "Were these men steady? Would they have fired their weapons indiscreetly?"

The young man is downcast and looks at the floor as he answers. "They were good troops. They gave me no trouble, unlike others. I can only assume that they discovered intruders in the bunker, and they fired upon them. Should they not have done so?" He looks deeply worried.

"Lieutenant, is it standard procedure for patrols to use lethal force *without* the consent of an officer? If so, that seems ill advised. How many rounds did they fire?"

His eyes dart about the room. "How many? I don't know, sir. We didn't count the remaining rounds in the magazines, nor did we count the spent rounds—except for the American rounds we recovered. Now it seems foolish that we didn't."

Amateurs. Christ. "Can you estimate how many rounds they fired based on your assessment of the damage done to the bunker?"

He stretches his neck. "Well... quite a few rounds must have been fired. Several automatic bursts, at least. There was a lot of damage."

"I see. So, any intruder might have returned fire in self-defense?"

"I don't know general, maybe the Americans fired first, and my men returned fire in their own self-defense! That could've happened."

No, I doubt that. "Think about it, young comrade. If you were armed only with pistols, would you initiate a fight with two soldiers armed with assault rifles?"

He shakes his head. "Probably not."

I smile again. "Yes; probably not. Thank you, comrade. You are dismissed." Poor kid; he's in over his head. Nonetheless, he should have better control of his men.

My next interview is with two warrant officers from the Gleinicke Bridge checkpoint. Both are in their midthirties and have that cocky air of professional noncommissioned officers who believe they know more about soldiering than any officer. They salute lazily when entering the room. I return their salute crisply and motion for them to be seated.

"Okay. Were you both on duty when the American vehicles came through the morning of the seventeenth? On their way toward Potsdam?"

They both nod their heads.

"And how many vehicles went through?"

The short, wiry one answers. "Two. I approached them—not him." He tilts his head in the direction of the taller guard.

"How many personnel were on board? And did you notice anything unusual."

The same guy continues. "Four in each vehicle. Nothing unusual, although eight people and two vehicles means the Americans are up to no good. They either had a big meeting at their Potsdam House, or a mission in the interior."

"Were you both on duty when they returned? What time did they return?"

The talkative one is a tough, professional Soviet soldier with a weathered face and thin moustache. I'd bet a month's salary that he is an "Afgantsy"—a veteran of the war in Afghanistan. He answers. "Yes, we both were on duty, and my partner is the one who approached the vehicles on their return. The two vehicles didn't come through at the same time. They were only in East Germany for a few hours."

That's interesting—just a few hours. We may be getting somewhere.

"What did you see when you approached the vehicles? How much of a time gap was there between the first and second vehicles?"

The tall one speaks for the first time—he's the one who approached the vehicles on their return trip. "The first vehicle's driver was a Green Beret I've seen before many times. He had another Green Beret in the front seat who I've seen a few times. According to the logbook for the seventeenth of April, the second vehicle came through forty minutes after the first one—that's on the return trip. Like he said, they were both together when they came through in the morning. Anyway, I examined both vehicles on their way back. The first vehicle had interesting people in the backseat. There was a young officer sitting behind the driver and he rolled down the window before I requested it, which is a little unusual, but not a big thing."

He said the back seat occupants were interesting. "How were they *interesting*—the people in the back seat?"

"Well, sir, the officer looked very young—almost like a kid that doesn't shave yet. That's unusual for the MLM. The Americans usually are older, more experienced officers. He also talked in a funny way."

Funny way? "Did he speak to you in Russian or English? Do you speak English? What was funny?"

"English? Me? I have a few words. No, he spoke Russian well, but he spoke in an old-fashioned way—his words and his accent were a little odd. He sounded like an aristocrat."

"Did this young officer with the funny accent have reddish hair?" I wonder if the American was Kevin Cattani. He speaks Russian in a formal, almost archaic manner.

The tall guy contemplates the question before answering. "I'm not sure. He had a field cap on. It's possible. He was fair."

"What did he say to you? What did you ask him?"

"Well, sir, I wanted to know if the other passenger was okay. She seemed to be sick."

She? A woman? No one told me there was a woman involved. "The other passenger was a woman?" He nods. "Your comrade here said that eight men came through in the morning."

The wiry guy interrupts me. "No, I said there were eight people; not eight men."

I guess that he did say that. "Was the woman there in the early morning? Why did you think she was sick? Did she look unwell?"

The tall guy continues. "I didn't see her early in the morning but she's in the logbook."

The other guy says, "We don't get women coming through the checkpoint—it's extremely unusual. I saw her in the morning, and she was beautiful. I don't forget someone like that, but I didn't see her on the return trip."

The taller man adds, "When they came through on the return trip, she looked very pale. I could see she was pretty even though she had a hat pulled down over her head."

A beautiful woman on an MLM mission? What the hell are the Americans thinking? "What did you ask the young officer?"

The memory of the woman is clearly distracting the tall guy. "Oh, yes, sir, of course. Well, I wanted to know what was wrong with the woman. The young guy told me that she was fine but that she was overtired because she was jet-lagged. I think he said she had just flown in from Washington. Or maybe it was the driver who told me that. I can't remember."

Washington? "Might she have been injured? Did you see blood?"

The two men look at each other in horror. "Sir, does this have something to do with the two kids who got shot in the bunker?"

How the hell do they know about that? "Men, I cannot comment on such matters. I'm sure you understand. Let's focus on the Americans. Was the pretty woman injured?"

"General, I didn't see any injuries. She was folded into the corner of the seat, and she had that hat pulled down low on her head. She didn't look well. She may have been injured—I never really bought their 'jet lag' story."

"All right, men. What about the second vehicle? Anything

unusual about it?"

The taller man continues. "Not really, sir. The guys in the second vehicle were very nonchalant." He turns to and looks at his partner. "Hey, that weird American major with the Ukrainian name was in the second vehicle. You know, the guy with the spooky blue eyes."

Why is this important? Is this American major important? "Guys, why is it remarkable that the Ukrainian American was in the second vehicle?"

The tall one speaks up. "Oh, that guy is famous. He was at the US Embassy in Moscow for four years and he ran a bunch of crazy-dangerous missions while he was there as an attaché. The American Green Berets told me about him two or three months ago when the major arrived at the MLM. He's supposed to be a real motherfucker—sorry, sir. If they *were* running a big mission on that day—the day you're asking us about, then it would make sense for him to be leading it."

Very interesting. "Comrades, is there anything else you think is important for me to know?

They exchange glances and shake their heads.

"Very well. Did you bring the logbook with you from the bridge?"

The tall guy pulls the logbook from his knapsack. "Here it is, sir. We need to get it back."

"Yes, I just want to read the entries and make notes. You will get it back." I turn the pages of the logbook to 17 April. I find the correct page and run my finger down to the first entry. Good God. There it is. Captain Kevin Cattani, United States Air Force. I find the return entry. There is his name again. The woman was identified as an Army captain. Her name—Lydia Morelli. Well, there you have it. Kevin Cattani, my partner in quelling last year's Able Archer crisis, was on this mission with a woman. Unbelievable. Were Cattani and the woman in the bunker? I contemplate the situation for a few minutes.

The two guards fidget nervously, and the wiry guy says, "Comrade General, I think that's the whole story. What are you going to do now? Did we do something wrong?"

I want to put them at ease. "No, you did nothing wrong. Thank you for the information and for your time today. You have been very helpful." I hand the logbook to the tall guy.

They both rise from their chairs and stand at attention.

I can't let them go that easily. "And thank you for your service in Afghanistan."

The two exchange glances. The wiry one speaks. "General, how did you know? We aren't wearing medals or campaign ribbons."

I allow myself a sly smile. "Why, gentleman, I am a professional intelligence officer. I can tell a combat veteran when I see one."

The smaller one looks at me with curiosity. Then, he smiles slightly, almost imperceptibly. He stands up straighter and salutes—not a snappy salute—but a veteran's casual salute. His tall companion does likewise. They both hold their salutes and wait for me to return them—a sign of deep respect from guys like these.

I stand, smile, and return their salutes. "All right, guys, you're dismissed. Have a drink to my health tonight—and one to your own."

This elicits big, genuine grins from the two soldiers. In unison, they say, "Yes, with pleasure!"

I sit back down as they depart and ponder this extremely odd situation. Why would the Americans send Kevin Cattani back to East Germany after he was nearly killed there by the GRU last fall? It seems careless . . . reckless. On the other hand, if the Americans are still worried about our nuclear posture, especially after the major exercise we just conducted, then maybe it would make sense to send a team into our nuclear command bunker. But to send Cattani? That seems insane after what he went through a few months ago at the hands of Grishin's thugs.

My last task in East Germany is to inspect the bunker, which I do in the late afternoon. It takes over an hour to drive to the location. Once inside, I find that the bunker has been swept clean. I inspect the walls. Clearly, many rounds were fired from automatic rifles to cause such severe damage. My escort points out that none of the locks on the safes have been disturbed in the least. Our most sensitive documents and codes appear to have been unmolested. My guess is that the PRA patrol surprised the intruders before they could break the locks and get at our "family jewels."

I'm wrapping up when I hear heavy footfalls on the metal staircase leading to the main level of the bunker. I look up to see Zhukov, Grishin, and the STASI officer I met this morning. Grishin smugly accosts me. "General, what do you think now that you've examined the American crime scene?"

"Well, let's see, Colonel—I think that a competent team would have treated it like a crime scene by securing it properly and collecting evidence in a timely manner. That's what I think. It's virtually useless to me now. We don't have anything except shell casings and corpses to go on. Not that we'll want to acknowledge the incident to the Americans anyway."

Grishin pushes his red face up to my nose. "The Americans must pay! They cannot be permitted to escape from Soviet justice, Comrade General! You are suspiciously tolerant of their crimes, and you must not let the Yankees off the hook!"

"Look, Colonel, the higher-ups are not going to admit to NATO and its American commander that we let the MLM break into a highly sensitive nuclear command bunker. As far as they are concerned, this incident will be closed once I return to Moscow and report. You've been a GRU officer long enough to understand that much, surely."

Grishin is undeterred. "The Americans cannot be permitted to get away with murder! I will see to it myself if I must and report your suspicious behavior in the process."

"Stand down, Colonel. You have no authority to do anything. You will stand down."

"General, I *will* report this to higher authorities in Moscow—to the Central Committee. Don't think this is the end of it."

"You'll do no such thing. This incident is to be held in a highly classified compartment. If you talk to anyone about it—which would be a violation of your security oath—then I'll make sure you are finished in the GRU."

Grishin mutters, "Crimean peasant." He turns and storms up the stairs followed closely by his STASI shadow. Zhukov grins at me and shakes his head. Christ, Grishin is an ass, but he can cause massive problems for me with the political powers back in Moscow. I have not heard the last of this matter, I am certain of that.

26 April 1984

The following day, I return to Moscow and report to General Ivashutin. He listens closely as I summarize my conclusions. "Comrade General, it is my view that this was an isolated, tragic incident. There are no indications that NATO planned this intrusion as part of a broader RYaN-like attack. Apparently, one of the intruders was injured by our soldiers and the one that was hurt was most likely a woman."

"A woman? Are you certain?" Peter the Great is flummoxed.

Aren't we all? "I cannot be certain, however, the evidence I have collected points to a woman being the individual who was injured in the bunker. We don't know this conclusively, sir, but my interviews support this conclusion."

The old general shakes his head. "Ivan Ivanovich, why on earth would they send a woman on a mission like this one? The danger . . . can you imagine . . . the risk was so very great."

I have a theory. "My speculation is that the woman must have had specialized expertise. I cannot think of any other plausible explanation for her presence."

He gets up from his chair and paces. "And what did these Americans learn? How much damage has been done?"

I trust my conclusions from my inspection of the bunker. "Sir, I don't think they learned a lot that is new to them. They certainly saw our current nuclear alert status since they had access to the map board and that's of some value to them. Our safes, however, were untouched. Even the lockers that were secured with simple locks were not opened. I can only assume that the intruders were surprised by the patrol before they could perform a thorough inspection of the bunker. Perhaps our dead soldiers succeeded in limiting the harm done to the Soviet state by their intervention."

"Yes, yes, Levchenko, I think you may be right. We should decorate the boys posthumously. Of course, their families can never know what happened to them. Can you see to it, Levchenko?"

Secret decorations—another hallmark of the Soviet Union. Why bother? "Yes, sir, I will take care of it all with discretion." What a depressing business. I love my country, but this institutional madness drives me crazy and is a symptom of something dark and dysfunctional.

Before I leave the office, I feel impelled to tell him about Colonel Grishin's threats.

"There is something else, General Ivashutin."

"What is it, Ivan Ivanovich?"

"At the bunker, Colonel Grishin made certain threats. He accused me of coddling the Americans and said he would report my suspicious behavior to the Central Committee. I told him that the facts surrounding the bunker incident are highly classified and must remain secret. Sir, I fear he has no compunction about telling tales to his father and others on the Central Committee."

General Ivashutin grumbles, "Like father, like son. The Grishin family is despicable. But they are also very dangerous. I will take care of this matter, but you must be extremely wary of Colonel Grishin—now and forever."

"Yes, General Ivashutin. Thank you."

I return to my office, shut the door and muse about these recent events. Grishin is a dangerous antagonist and every time I think of his words in the bunker, I get a sharp pain in my stomach. What a bastard.

And, as for the Americans, was it Cattani in that bunker? With a woman? Why would the Americans take such a risk? It must be that they fear us and our capacity and especially our willingness to wage nuclear war. Of course, that's also the reason we fear the Americans. It's an apocalyptic conundrum. This young American is a puzzlement. Obviously, he was acting under orders. I wonder if he objected to them. If I ever do see Kevin Cattani again, I will advise him to stay on his side of the Berlin Wall now and forever.

Map 3: Afghanistan

CHAPTER ELEVEN

A LONELY WAR

General-Major Ivan Levchenko, GRU, Soviet Air Defense Forces
Bagram Air Base, Afghanistan

25 May 1986

*T**he silence of a falling star lights up a purple sky.* Hank Williams captured the melancholy of a lonely lover perfectly and made it universal. *And, as I wonder where you are, I'm so lonesome I could cry.* I first heard American country and western music years ago on Radio Luxembourg broadcasts when I was stationed in Poland. I related to the best songs that address the basic human condition with honesty, authenticity, and poetry.

Tonight, I miss my wife Boyka acutely as I look upward at the stars and the nearly full moon illuminating the midnight sky. It's cold at night here, too cold for late May, it seems to me. I adjust the scarf around my neck to ward off the chill as I walk quickly from my quarters to the communications center that connects Bagram Air Base with Moscow and our forces deployed throughout Afghanistan.

Tonight, the moonlight is strong in the clear sky, and I can see the silent snow-capped mountains in the distance quite vividly. Those massive, disinterested sentinels stand silently over the bleak plain where Bagram Air Base is situated. How many invading armies have those peaks witnessed over the millennia? Afghanistan was an important part of the ancient silk road, making it a crossroads and a battleground for antique empires. It's been ruled by the Persians, Alexander the Great, Arab Muslims, the Mongols, the British, and the Russians. I wonder how many of my officers know that the city of Kandahar in the southern part of the country was laid out by Alexander the Great and is named for the great conqueror. I steal a last glance at the high mountains shimmering in the moonglow as I open the door to the communications building.

My eyes burn from the harsh artificial light inside. I think of the absolute blackness of night in the hills of western Crimea and how it soothed me when I was boy. Boyka likes city lights if they are anywhere but in Moscow. She also loves music but doesn't care for Hank Williams. My wife is a superb classical violinist and a music snob. She insists that I play my country and western records only when she is not in our flat. Boyka especially dislikes Willie Nelson, which is a shame since his *Red Headed Stranger* album is my all-time favorite. Sadly, Willie's singing sends my wife running from the room. I am partial to the western music of the Texas outlaws and the California cowboys. The Nashville-produced country music is too slick and soulless for my taste.

After several failed attempts at connecting me with my wife in Moscow, the radio technician finally has Boyka on the line. The link is predictably weak, but hearing her voice is better than any Willie Nelson record—sorry my red-headed friend. "Hello, Boyka, my love. How are you?"

I hear her sob softly. "I'm so worried, Vanya. The stories we hear in Moscow about the war in Afghanistan are simply awful." The sound of her sad, musical voice makes my eyes tear up.

"Boyka, I'm fine. I'm living on a huge base, with thousands of soldiers around me. I'm completely safe. Say, what do you hear of your family?"

Boyka's family lives in a village on the outskirts of Kiev, and I have read muddled reports about a nuclear accident at the power plant at Chernobyl in northern Ukraine. The site of the incident is not terribly far from where my in-laws live. I am worried about radiation fallout, not to mention a potential reactor meltdown.

"I spoke today with my sister and Oleksandr." Her sister is Oxana, whose husband, Oleksandr Koghut, is an ardent Ukrainian nationalist. "I've invited them to come to Moscow to stay in our flat. I hope that's okay with you. The rumors about nuclear fallout drifting toward Kiev from Chernobyl are terrifying. They'll be safer in Moscow, and I could use some company, too."

Our Moscow flat has a large guest suite. I have no quarrel with my in-laws moving in with Boyka for a while, although I find Oleksandr's radical politics tiresome. My wife is very close to Oxana and if having her sister in Moscow comforts Boyka, then I'm all for it. "Boyka, of course; it's perfectly fine for them to move in. I'd feel better if you had family with you. What word of your parents? Are they going to leave Ukraine?"

There is heavy static on the line. I hope she got my last transmission. "Yes, yes, Vanya, thank you. Oxana will be relieved. Did you ask about my parents just now? It's hard to hear you. Well, you know, they will never leave Kiev. My father—he's a stick in the mud. And the old warrior isn't afraid of a little nuclear meltdown."

This makes me laugh for one of the first times since I arrived in Afghanistan. "Yes, I imagine the brave tank commander refuses to leave his post. After all, he didn't defeat Hitler's hordes by cutting and running!"

The line drops. I don't know if she heard my response. In my frustration I yell at the radio man to get the line back up. The poor boy tries for fifteen minutes but has no luck. It's not his fault and I apologize to him for my outburst. I won't be able to finish my conversation with my wife tonight. My heart hungers for her. I used to think that heartache was just a figure of speech. I now know that it isn't.

Loneliness is an ever-present dull pain for me and most of the Soviet forces in Afghanistan. Russia's latest involvement in this country's seemingly never-ending series of conflicts began in December 1979—and now it is nearly the summer of 1986. The Soviet people are weary of this pointless war against various and sundry Islamic resistance groups that almost no one from St. Petersburg to Vladivostok can identify. The war has been brutal from the outset. Soviet armed forces have destroyed villages, burned farms, laid tens of thousands of mines, terrorized citizens, raped women, and spawned a general militarization of Afghan society. I am determined to ensure that the men under my command refrain from such atrocities and that I get as many of those men home alive as possible. Our Afghan foes are experts at staging devastating ambushes and slaughter our men whenever they have the opportunity. This is a war of no quarter asked and none given.

At the Communist Party Congress in Moscow this past February, General Secretary Mikhail Gorbachev secretly announced that the official policy of the Soviet state is to orchestrate a managed withdrawal of its forces from Afghanistan. Thus far, I'm afraid that there's been more *management* than *withdrawal*. I believe that Gorbachev's heart is in the right place. He became the supreme leader in March of 1985 upon the death of a fossil named Konstantin Chernenko. Gorbachev is a breath of fresh air who wants to improve relations with the United States, limit nuclear arms, and open peace negotiations with the Mujahedin, the term for the collection of Muslim adversaries we face in Afghanistan. Despite his good intentions, Gorbachev is fighting against decades of bureaucratic inertia in Moscow and faces openly hostile reactionaries. Many of my colleagues in the military mistrust him and do not support his policies. Change is difficult, especially in a society as riven with wariness and cynicism toward the government as ours is.

27 May 1986

Bagram Air Base is a perilous, ninety-minute drive from the capital city of Kabul. Soviet vehicles on the main road connecting the two are attacked frequently by Afghan holy warriors—Mujahedin—who plant mines in the roadway or launch rockets at convoys with deadly effect. I've learned that it is safer to fly by helicopter from Bagram to Kabul and that is what I do this morning for my first meeting with the overall Soviet commander in Afghanistan, a young two-star Army general.

I have been in-country since the first of May, having been ordered to the war zone by General of the Army Pyotr Ivashutin, the director general of the GRU. I have never served before in a combat zone. Why would Moscow send me here to lead the entire GRU war effort, including the GRU's special operations forces? General Ivashutin explained it to me with characteristic bluntness. "Levchenko, we all know you have brains and aren't afraid to use them. What we don't know is if you have the balls to lead men in combat and whether you can exercise good judgment when the bullets fly. We're about to find out."

An active war zone seems an odd place for on-the-job training, but I imagine that's the way it's always been—even in Alexander the Great's time. General Ivashutin wants me to do two things here: stop the flow of advanced American weapons to the Mujahedin and help the commander of the 40th Army get our forces safely out of Afghanistan. It's a daunting mission.

And on the seventh day, I suppose, I shall rest.

We know that the hidden hand behind these Mujahedin "holy warriors" is the United States, acting through its ally, Pakistan. Until last year, the Americans provided the rebels very limited support—so little that it was hardly a nuisance. That changed dramatically over the last twelve months. We estimate that the Americans' support to the Mujahedin has increased at least tenfold, mostly consisting of high-quality US weaponry that is killing Soviet troops every day.

We have learned from captured Islamic fighters that they are begging the Americans for their most advanced hand-held surface-to-air missiles, called Stingers. The introduction of such weapons would be calamitous for our air operations. Our attack helicopters and low flying, fixed-wing fighter aircraft are the backbone of our combat advantage over the rebels. Stingers will make those aircraft highly vulnerable to attack, changing the balance of power of the entire conflict. The terrible irony is that the United States, which desperately wants a Soviet withdrawal from Afghanistan, will make a Soviet retreat far more difficult if they supply the Mujahedin with Stingers. I imagine the CIA sees it rather differently.

Command of the 40th Army changed on the final day of April, the day before I arrived in Afghanistan. The new commander is General-Lieutenant Victor Dubynin, who was trained as a tank officer and is a tough, taciturn professional. Dubynin has black hair and a very dark complexion, like a steppe warrior of old. Our first meeting was rather tense. He regarded me with penetrating, brown eyes and remained seated at his large desk, his mouth set in a severe frown. I've never seen anything quite like his face before. The lower half of it looks like an inverted horseshoe when he speaks. I heard in Moscow that Dubynin doesn't like the GRU, and he hates that fact that I command the Spetsnaz special forces units in the theater.

"See here Levchenko, being an expert on the Americans is all well and good, but I need you—your Spetsnaz brigades—to kill the Islamic rebels who are carrying the Americans' weapons across the passes from Pakistan. If you can't do that for me, then I have no use for you." Clearly, I won't have to wonder what Dubynin is thinking. "What do you know about this Commander Ahmad Shah Massoud? The guy they call the 'lion of the Panjshir'?"

I read a good deal about Massoud back in Moscow, but I have no intimate knowledge of the warlord. "General, I know that he's a formidable enemy. I also know that because he was so effective at killing our soldiers, the GRU negotiated a ceasefire with Massoud in the winter of 1983, which held until April 1984. The peace was broken not by the GRU, but by the Afghan regime, which could not abide Massoud living unmolested in the Panjshir Valley. Despite the best efforts of the GRU, the ceasefire failed, and Massoud resumed hostilities with renewed vigor."

Dubynin appraises me carefully. He is reputed to have an incisive intellect and he is surprisingly young to be an army commander. He is only forty-three—three years younger than I am—an example of the youth movement in our defense establishment that also led to my promotion to general officer two years ago.

He doesn't respond to my statement, so I continue. "General Dubynin, Massoud is killing many of our troops and he has become the darling of the CIA since the GRU ceasefire was broken. He leads the so-called Northern Alliance, and the Americans are supplying him with excellent weapons."

The commanding general lights a cigarette and inhales deeply. I'm surprised when he blows large smoke rings into the air above his desk. Smoke rings are a playful gesture for most people, but they seem malevolent escaping from his mouth. "Levchenko, I want you to keep Massoud and the KGB out of my hair. The KGB has teams spread out all over the country, with numbers too few to have any real impact. I have no control over them. They stir up trouble in the hinterlands and get themselves killed or into predicaments that compel me to send troops into the enemy's backyard to bail them out."

His comments about the performance of the KGB in Afghanistan are no surprise to me. "I will work with the KGB to have them coordinate their operations with mine. In fact, I have a meeting with the top KGB man in Kabul later today for that very purpose."

This elicits a gruff response. "Well, do what you can. I hear the KGB has contacts with leaders in many of the key villages. That could be helpful if you can get the KGB bastards to work with you. Remember, I'm relying on the GRU to interdict those weapons that the Americans are sending over the passes and the village elders know how and where the weapons are moved."

I sense that he is finished with me, for now. "Yes, sir, I understand completely. I will demand the KGB assist us more against the Americans."

The general with the upside-down horseshoe mouth nods, indicating that I am dismissed. As I leave him, he is blowing smoke rings toward the stained ceiling.

My command consists of all the intelligence units assigned to our main fighting forces, as well as all the special forces (Spetsnaz) in Afghanistan. Never could I have imagined that I would command such a force. I am not qualified for this job.

I have two Spetsnaz brigades: the 15th Brigade, which is based at Jalalabad near the border with Pakistan, and the 22nd Brigade with its headquarters at Lashkar Gah in Helmand Province in southwestern Afghanistan. Together, the two brigades total about four thousand of the best fighting men in the Soviet armed forces. The main purpose of the 15th Brigade is to disrupt the logistics and supply lines of the Mujahedin, especially those routes carrying CIA-supplied weapons across the Pakistani frontier. We call this border interdiction activity Operation Veil.

My first act is to issue a directive to my troops throughout the country ordering them to abide by Soviet military regulations and laws concerning the treatment of civilians and privately owned property. I also emphasize that anyone who violates this order will be dealt with severely. I don't want my units to engage in the sort of atrocities many of the regular Army detachments have perpetrated.

My new brigades have suffered terrible losses—nearly 140 deaths *per month* over the last twelve months. It's hard to fathom such casualties. Emboldened by the Americans' support, the Mujahedin have even staged raids across the border into the Soviet Union. Those raids aren't militarily significant, but they embarrass Gorbachev and the military leadership in Moscow, and big men in the Kremlin want them stopped.

My executive officer is Major Zhukov—Anatoly Zhukov—the same young officer with the famous military heritage who accompanied me to East Germany two years ago during the bunker incident investigation. He's still a bachelor and he is eager to see action in a war zone. Zhukov is smart, inquisitive, and handsome, and is still engaged to a beautiful fiancée in Moscow from a powerful political family. Zhukov better not string her along for too long, or it will damage his career. I'm surprised that she's tolerated such a long engagement, but I suppose Zhukov is quite a catch himself.

Major Zhukov is with me for my initial meeting with the KBG leadership in Kabul. The chief KGB man is a competent general officer with whom I'm acquainted from Moscow. He and I agree to strengthen communication and tighten the coordination of our activities, especially those related to the illicit arms shipments pouring into the country from Pakistan. It's a productive meeting and I depart hoping that I will have a fruitful relationship with the KGB. Zhukov is especially energized by the meeting and is anxious to work with his KGB counterparts.

After the KGB meeting, Zhukov and I fly to Asadabad, which is located on the border with Pakistan, to visit a GRU Spetsnaz battalion based there. Asadabad is located at one end of the Nawa Pass and is only sixteen kilometers north of the critically important Khyber Pass, the busiest transit point between Pakistan and Afghanistan. Last year, thirty-one Soviet troops were killed in an ambush not far from Asadabad.

28 May 1986

We land at the GRU Spetsnaz base at Asadabad in midafternoon and find the weather quite a contrast with Kabul—very hot and dry. I've already perspired through my uniform shirt when a security escort meets Zhukov and me at the rudimentary runway that serves the Spetsnaz base. I can't help but think that daylight flights such as this one will become extremely hazardous—maybe impossible—if the Americans give the rebels Stinger missiles.

Incongruously, the Spetsnaz battalion headquarters is in an old Anglican church. It's a relic of the British attempt to stabilize Afghanistan in the nineteenth century, a testament to the supreme self-confidence of the British Empire. The church must have been an awesomely impressive building to the local tribes more than a century ago.

Zhukov raises his eyebrows and smiles at me when he sees the Anglican Church. The irony of it all isn't lost on him. The British Army spent decades occupying this area and suffered heavy losses. We are an occupying imperial army, too, although that was not the intention when our first troops landed in Kabul in December 1979. Our intervention was supposed to be brief—just long enough to rid ourselves of the corrupt government in Kabul and to install new, more pliable leadership. Nearly seven years later, the plan for a brief incursion has been overcome by unforeseen civil strife and unexpected Islamic fundamentalist combativeness and we're still here.

The lieutenant colonel commanding the Spetsnaz battalion strides out of the English church to greet us. His uniform is dusty, and he wears a slouch hat pulled down over his eyes. Here is Lieutenant Colonel Vasily Zaitsev, whose impressive biography I read on the plane. He salutes and smiles broadly, his face deeply tanned. "Greetings, General Levchenko. Thank you for visiting us way out here. Your predecessor never managed to find his way to our humble country church."

I chuckle and say, "Colonel Zaitsev, thanks for your warm welcome. I'm pleasantly surprised to see a slice of British culture in this forbidding landscape."

We shake hands. I notice that despite the grime and dust, the colonel's hands are clean. "Sir, you're most welcome. Please, follow me."

The Spetsnaz troops have heavily fortified the old church. The men are used to living in constant danger and these professionals know how to protect themselves. Their patrols take them eastward into the high mountain passes connecting this region with Pakistan. I look up at the towering, snow-capped peaks. There, on the other side of those mountains, are CIA officers who furnish our enemies with weapons that kill our troops and our allies.

Major Zhukov and I sit down with the colonel in his office, which once was the Anglican vicar's private workplace. Zaitsev provides a well-informed situation report. "General, my men are under more pressure from the enemy than at any other time during this war. Since the decision was made at the beginning of this year to curtail major conventional combat operations, the special forces units have borne the brunt of the fighting. In addition, as you know, the Americans have stepped up their support to the Mujahedin to unprecedented levels. It's like we are caught in a vice. The enemy is emboldened by its new weaponry and by the retreat of our motorized rifle divisions into their garrisons. We Spetsnaz are paying the cost in blood."

Zhukov breaks protocol and responds first. "Comrade, would tighter integration with the KGB help your situation? The general has appointed me as his liaison to the KGB and I'd like to help you, if I can."

The GRU colonel looks at Zhukov with sympathetic eyes. "Major, I appreciate your desire to help. Well, yes. The KGB has good access to important tribal leaders in this region. Heretofore, they have been reluctant to share much information with us. Of course, the tribal leaders are friends with us one day and the next day they sell information about us to the rebels. There are no permanent friends in Afghanistan. You'd do well to remember that. But yes—to answer you directly—better access to the KGB's assets wouldn't hurt."

"You see, Colonel, my Major Zhukov is eager to help." I smile at the special operations officer.

The colonel exclaims loudly. "Zhukov! Well, comrade, you have a most famous name. I hope you can provide us the same luck that Marshal Zhukov brought the Red Army during the Great Patriotic War."

I can't resist the opportunity to embarrass Zhukov a bit. "Colonel, young Zhukov here is the famous marshal's great nephew. He's a very promising officer in his own right."

The hard-bitten, Spetsnaz colonel looks at the young major with new eyes. "Indeed! Young Zhukov is welcome to assist us in improving communications with the KGB. I will make introductions for you both with the local KGB major. He's a bit of a prig, but not a bad sort. He'll be impressed that a GRU general and Zhukov's great nephew are making the request. I'll invite him here to dine with us tonight, if that's agreeable with you, General? We have local food here and it's actually very tasty."

CHAPTER TWELVE

THE DAY YOU DIE IS JUST LIKE ANY OTHER

General-Major Ivan Levchenko, GRU, Soviet Air Defense Forces
Asadabad, Afghanistan and surrounding area

29 May 1986

Last night's supper with the local KGB commander was a success, and he seems motivated to improve coordination between our two intelligence services. He is tired of the infighting between the Army and the KGB and wants to be done with it. Zhukov is enthused about working with the KGB and exploiting its contacts with rebel warlords. We agree to visit the KGB outpost tomorrow, some forty kilometers south of the Asadabad Spetsnaz base.

As we depart the Anglican church, the morning air is pleasantly cool, tinged with the sweetness of spring blooms and blessed by a refreshing breeze off the looming mountains. We will travel in a small convoy consisting of two armored personnel carriers and two jeeps. Colonel Zaitsev has sent two mine-clearing tanks ahead of our convoy to sweep the unpaved road of rebel mines. As we drive away, I say a silent prayer that the tank crews do their job thoroughly.

The Spetsnaz captain who oversees my security escort insists that the KBG major, Zhukov, and I ride in one of the armored personnel carriers—and I regret it instantly as we move out. Not only is the vehicle noisy and uncomfortable, but the air inside is rancid, and I feel trapped in its coffin-like interior. Young Zhukov sits across from me and smiles like this is a grand adventure. Unpleasant conditions don't faze him, which is surprising to me considering his pampered upbringing as a Soviet Communist Party princeling—one of the new hereditary elite of Moscow who grow up in comfort and have every societal advantage. Perhaps his famous military heritage has lent him another inheritance—a natural resilience that I find quite admirable.

It takes over ninety uncomfortable minutes for the convoy to cover the forty kilometers to the KGB facility. I decide that I'll ride in a jeep on the return trip later today. At last, we dismount from the clanky APC, and I breathe in deep draughts of fresh air. The mountainsides look very near to us in this place. They are beautiful in the warming sunshine and reflect deep purple and red hues. I must remember that, despite the pristine loveliness of the mountains, they are the bastion of the enemy and contain great dangers.

No general officer from either the GRU or the KGB has visited this isolated outpost in the long years of the Afghan war. We are briefed thoroughly for several hours on the KGB's operations and contacts in the area. Zhukov takes copious notes and looks extremely pleased with himself. His enthusiasm is refreshing, and I find that his positive attitude lifts my own spirits.

We enjoy a late lunch of fresh local food just prior to our departure. Since the enemy owns the night, we must be on our way while there is ample sunlight. I overrule the anxious commander of the security detail and climb into a jeep, rather than an armored vehicle for the return trip to Colonel Zaitsev's base. I had my fill of riding in an APC on the trip down here.

Zhukov and I split up and he rides with several troops in the lead APC. A female nurse, who we met last night, is on her way back to

Russia after serving two years assigned to the KGB outpost. She and her fiancé, a young KGB officer, are in the trailing APC and they will share my flight back to Bagram Air Base tonight. They are to be married in Leningrad. This is a strange place for young people to fall in love with each other, but I am glad they found love to battle the oppressive loneliness and desolation of Afghanistan.

I made the right decision to ride back to Zaitsev's base in the jeep. The afternoon air is delightful, and the warm sun feels comforting on my face. Flowers bloom at the borders of the green spaces where the local farmers cultivate citrus trees bearing oranges, grapefruit, lemons, and limes.

I'm savoring the sweet citrus scents that waft on the soft air when my reverie is ended by the sound of an enormous explosion. The noise deafens me for a few moments, and I cannot tell from which direction it's coming. As my ears clear, I hear frantic shouting and horrifying screams. There are great clouds of dust, and I can see only a few meters in any direction.

My driver pushes me violently out of the vehicle and onto the ground. He falls on top of me with his assault rifle locked and loaded as he scans the area for attackers. Several Spetsnaz troops run by me, and the driver rolls off me. The troops must be coming from the APC at the front of our convoy—Zhukov's APC. Dust burns my eyes. I've never been in combat before, if that's what this is. It's utter chaos and the action seems to be toward the rear. The trailing APC must have been attacked. I squint through the haze and see the armored vehicle ablaze. Did it strike a roadside bomb? Suddenly, it occurs to me that I'm unarmed.

Zhukov is screaming in my ear. "General, are you alright? Are you injured?"

I shout, "No. I think I'm fine."

Zhukov looks around wildly. "I'm going back there to see if they need help."

I am slowly coming to my senses. "Be careful."

Zhukov is gone.

My driver taps my shoulder. "Mount up, sir. Time to go!"

I get up on my knees, which are sore from lying on the hard, baked ground. I clamber into the jeep. Men return from the destroyed APC carrying heavy loads. What the hell are they carrying? The driver said we need to leave now. I hope they hurry. Where is Zhukov?

Two guys climb into the back of my jeep and plop down whatever load they've been lugging. I twist around and see that the burden they have deposited is the nurse—the young woman on her way back to Leningrad to be married. Her eyes are open and the expression on her face is of sudden surprise. It takes me a second to realize that she is dead.

One of the soldiers in the back speaks. "Sorry, General. We searched but we couldn't find her legs."

I reach back to her and touch her forehead. It's still warm. Her skin is warm, but she's dead. I'm appalled by the sight of her, and I decide I will close her eyes to restore her a little dignity. I try. They won't stay closed.

The same guy says, "It's no use. They'll have to be sewn shut to stay closed."

I'm horrified, but I simply nod my head. It occurs to me that this is the reality that these men—and women—deal with out here all the time. This event, however tragic, is routine.

We move out. The men sit in the back with the dead nurse. I ask, "Sergeant, what of the young woman's fiancé—the young KGB officer?"

"Oh, he's gone. Not much left of him, I'm afraid. There was only one survivor. He's in the lead APC now with your major."

That means Zhukov is all right. "Will they attack us—the rebels—while we are on the road? We seem so vulnerable out here."

The sergeant shrugs. "Often, they will set up the real attack by exploding a roadside bomb like that one. If they attack us, then it will happen soon."

We move out with a vicious lurch and race away from the place where the APC was blown up. The road narrows as it goes through a small canyon. I turn around and look anxiously at the sergeant. "Here? Would they attack here?"

He nods with apparent nonchalance. "Could be. Good place for it."

Rifle fire erupts as he finishes his statement. An ambush. Our three remaining vehicles speed through the narrow defile as fast as possible. Bullets ping off my jeep. In an open vehicle, we are completely unprotected. Why didn't I ride in the lead APC with Zhukov?

Miraculously, we exit the little canyon intact. My driver turns around to the trailing jeep and gives a thumbs-up. Due to the towering clouds of dust, I can't make out the APC, even though it's only meters in front of us.

My driver slams on the brakes with such force that I nearly fly through the windshield and the poor nurse's body is pushed forward into the back of my seat.

"Christ, what the hell are you doing?" I hear myself scream at the driver. "Why did you stop?"

Before he can answer, the other jeep comes alongside my door. The Spetsnaz captain on board that jeep yells at me. "The lead APC is gone! They're not responding on the radio."

I think he must be mad, and I yell back at him. "Gone? They were just in front of us. What do you mean?" If the APC is gone, then Zhukov is gone with it.

Our ever-diminishing convoy stops. The captain dismounts and fires his rifle into the air. I still can't see a damn thing with all the dust. A few seconds go by, and another rifle responds with a burst of automatic fire. Who the hell is that? Mujahedin?

I jump out of the jeep, stand beside the captain, and yell, "What's going on? Another ambush?"

He shakes his head. "No. I think the Mujahedin are letting us know they have the APC."

My head feels like it's stuck in a vice. "What happened? It was just fucking there—right in front of us!"

He turns his head and glares at me, his eyes wide with a terror he's trying to resist. "We have to get out of here now! I'll order the drivers to make maximum speed back to Asadabad. We'll be vulnerable to mines, but there are worse fates than mines in Afghanistan."

This can't be happening. My God—young Zhukov.

The remainder of the journey is a crazy race over the rutted track that hardly deserves to be called a road. We are not fired upon again. Immediately upon arriving, the Spetsnaz captain and I rush to the commander's headquarters in the old Anglican Church.

Colonel Zaitsev doesn't look all that surprised when we convey the news of the ill-fated return trip. "How many were in the APC that's gone missing, Captain?"

"Colonel, the three crewmen and five others, including Major Zhukov. It was carrying a wounded guy from the destroyed APC, as well."

Zaitsev rubs his forehead. "General, the odds are not in Zhukov's favor. Everyone who was in the captured APC may be dead by now. The best case is that they are being held by one of the gangs hereabouts to be sold to the highest bidder. The bandits terrorizing these foothills are marginally preferable to the Islamic fundamentalists. Gangs want money. They don't torture and behead their captives. On the other hand, one of the Mujahedin leaders in these parts is famous for skinning his prisoners alive and hanging them from a tree by their wrists until they're dead."

That's reassuring. "What can we do about Zhukov? Anything?"

"General Levchenko, we must wait. If he's still alive, then there's a good chance that we'll be contacted for ransom or a prisoner exchange. He's an officer, and that enhances his value and his chance of survival."

I close my eyes and I try to see Boyka's face, but all I can see is the dead nurse's eyes.

CHAPTER THIRTEEN

THE BLACK TULIPS

General-Major Ivan Levchenko, GRU, Soviet Air Defense Forces
Asadabad, Afghanistan and Bagram Air Base, Afghanistan

29 May 1986

Late that afternoon, I'm back in Zaitsev's office. He opens a half-liter bottle of vodka and fills a glass for each of us. He smiles weakly and proposes a toast to "young Zhukov."

I stare glumly at my glass of vodka and drink it in one gulp. I feel awful—like I'm abandoning Zhukov to a terrible fate. He could be skinned alive by now.

Zaitsev refills my glass and continues. "Sir, I will pursue the Zhukov situation, personally. I think the KGB, with their contacts among the rebels and gangs of thieves, may be our best bet. My money is on the Haqqani family being involved. If anyone will know of the fate of our major, it will be that Haqqani bunch. Nothing happens in these parts without Jalaluddin Haqqani knowing about it."

Zaitsev finishes his drink. "General, I will have your flight delayed until well after nightfall. There are new reports of rebel antiaircraft guns in the hills nearby. They're usually not very accurate, especially at night, but it's better not to take chances. I fear our days of flying around Afghanistan with impunity during daylight are numbered."

He grimaces. I bet he's thinking about how his command is going to function without airpower when the sun is up.

I hate the thought of flying back to Bagram without Zhukov. But there it is. "Yes, I'm sure flying later—after the sun is well and truly down—will be safer. Thank you."

Zaitsev fidgets in his chair and gulps down another drink. "There is one more thing. With your permission, I'd like to send the young woman's body—the dead nurse—to Bagram on your helicopter. And the body of one of my troops who was killed, as well. Otherwise, I don't know when we'll be able to get them to a morgue. The facility we have here is . . . inadequate, I'm afraid."

Jesus, will this nightmare never end? "Yes, Colonel, of course. It's the least I can do for them—for the dead." It's the right thing to do, but I dread flying back to Bagram as the only living passenger.

Zaitsev rises to shake my hand. He fixes his eyes on mine. "Sir, it's been an honor to meet you. I look forward to serving under you. I promise to do my best to find Major Zhukov. Now, if you'll excuse me, I'm going to the flight line to make sure the preparations are underway for your departure."

We shake hands and part ways. I decide to go to the sacristy of the Anglican Church. I'm not certain why, but I feel myself drawn to it. My mother and grandmother were devout followers of the Russian Orthodox faith. I respected their piety, but never shared it. I pause in the vestibule to allow my eyes to adjust to the dimness of the nave. At the altar, I kneel in the gloom and say my prayers for Zhukov, the nurse, and the others lost or missing on this awful day. I may not be religious, but I am a spiritual man, and I believe in the soul of man.

My mind is busy in the darkness. I think of my childhood in Crimea and the day I was told of my father's death and then, years later, of my mother's, making me an orphan when I was a young Air Force Academy cadet far from home. Boyka is my only family now.

One hour after dark, I am on the base's primitive flight line and watch the pilot and copilot perform their preflight inspection of the

M-8 helicopter that will take me back to Bagram. Several of Zaitsev's men load two body bags into the rear of the helicopter. I notice that the zippers on the bags are not fully closed. Have the loaders made an error? I climb aboard and stare at the partially open bags where the men have lain them. "Tell me guys, why don't you close the zippers all the way?"

Two soldiers look at each other. One shrugs, faces me, and says, "General, if you close the zippers, then the bags fill up with gases and explode, especially in warm weather. The dead bodies emit gases that collect in the bags, and then 'boom!' It's nasty."

I nod, sorry that I asked.

I sit as far forward in the cabin as I can—close to the pilots and as far away as possible from our gruesome cargo. Once the aircraft's doors are closed and we are ready to lift off, the stench of violent death nearly overpowers me. I do my best not to wretch. We lift off very rapidly and gain altitude as quickly as possible to avoid the enemy guns lurking somewhere in the darkness of the surrounding hills. As soon as we reach altitude, I unbuckle from my seat and move forward toward the cockpit, taking care not to dislodge my headset cable.

The copilot notices me first and says into the intercom, "Comrade General, do you need something?"

I click my button and respond. "I just want to look out through the cockpit and get a view of the terrain."

I see the two pilots share a knowing glance. The copilot says, "There is a small jump seat here. You can plug your headset into this panel between the pilot and me and ride up here if you wish. I warn you that it's not very comfortable, sir."

I maneuver myself into the jump seat. "No, no, the seat is fine. It's a much better view from up here. Thank you. I'll sit here for the rest of the flight if that's okay with you guys."

The pilot keys his mike. "General, you're welcome to sit there. I know it must stink even worse back in the cabin than it does up here."

Yes, it does. And I prefer to sit next to living humans rather than dead ones.

Thankfully, our flight to Bagram is uneventful. After we land and as the pilots shut down the engines, they chat amiably with each other over the intercom. They joke about tracer rounds that were fired at us during our departure from Asadabad. I was unaware we'd been fired upon, and I think the men have forgotten that I am still plugged into the intercom. Hastily, I take off my headphones and hand them to the copilot.

The pilot jumps out and slides open the door to allow me to disembark. I thank him and shake his hand. Several enlisted men appear out of the darkness and clamber on board. They unload the two body bags from the rear of the cabin and place them on gurneys.

I walk over to where they've lain the bodies. I try to speak in a casual, good-natured tone. "Greetings, comrades. Good evening."

The senior guy amongst them—a warrant officer—sees my shoulder boards and snaps to attention and salutes. "Good evening, General, sir."

He looks drunk. I ask him, "Comrade, do you have information on the . . . victims?"

"Sir, there should be papers attached to their clothing."

I could swear he's reeling a bit. The soldiers handling the body bags look wobbly, too. "Right. Pay close attention, please. The first bag contains a woman's body. She was a nurse. The other one is a Spetsnaz troop. Both were killed by a roadside bomb earlier today. I was there when it happened." God, it seems like it all happened weeks ago. I stop talking. I sound like I am boasting.

The warrant officer in charge of the detail looks at me bleary-eyed. "Yes, sir. We'll take care of them and get them out on the black tulip that leaves tomorrow."

Black tulip? "What's a black tulip?"

The man is most definitely drunk and is trying not to fall over. "Comrade General, the black tulips are cargo planes that transport our dead back home. We place the bodies in zinc caskets and load the caskets into wooden crates that go onto the black tulips."

What a terrible job this young warrant officer must do every day—all these young men. This war will stay with them forever. The sights they have seen . . . good Christ. "Yes, I see, comrade. Look, if you need information on these dead, contact Colonel Zaitsev, who commands the GRU special forces battalion at Asadabad. His name should be easy to remember. It's the same surname as the famous sniper—Zaitsev—from the Great Patriotic War."

He looks mystified. "Sniper, sir? From the Great Patriotic War?"

I feel very old. He doesn't even know one of the most famous heroes of the titanic fight against the Germans. "Yes, Zaitsev was a great hero of the battle of Stalingrad—our most famous sniper of the entire war. Don't worry about it. If you need further information, just contact me—General Ivan Levchenko—at my office here at Bagram—all right?"

"Yes, sir, of course."

I turn and start to walk away but stop. I turn around and walk back to where the men are handling the body bags. "Say there, are you men all drunk? Drunk on duty?"

The young conscripts look terrified and wait for the warrant officer to answer. He stands unsteadily and replies, "Comrade General, the boys stay perpetually drunk. It's the only way they can manage to do the terrible job of handling the bodies. They are surrounded by horrible death all day, every day. Yes, sir, they are drunk. And drunk they will stay."

The conscripted boys look at me with sad, shamed eyes. I don't know whether to be angry or sympathetic. Surely, they have the most agonizing duty to perform. I decide on empathy. "Very well, boys. Carry on. I will pray for you."

As I walk away across the ramp, I hear a young voice call out from behind me. It's one of the conscripts. "God bless you and keep you safe, Comrade General! I will pray to God for your safety."

I raise my right hand in acknowledgment of the young man without turning around. Black tulips. I don't know the origin of the phrase. Nonetheless, the name seems apt—eerily appropriate—a poetic term for something so ugly. Perhaps it's just a sad name conjured up by a drunken enlisted man entrusted with ministering to the dead.

CHAPTER FOURTEEN

AFGANTSY

General-Major Ivan Levchenko, GRU, Soviet Air Defense Forces
Bagram Air Base, Afghanistan

12 June 1986

Today, for the first time in a week, I take a run around Bagram Air Base. I think of Boyka when I run. She's never far from my mind and I imagine what she's doing back in Moscow. I wonder if her brother-in-law Oleksandr is driving her crazy yet. He and Boyka's sister Oxana have been staying in our Moscow flat for about ten days now. I'm glad Oxana is with Boyka. They always have fun together going to museums, concerts, and shopping. I can see the two gorgeous Ukrainian sisters now, walking arm-in-arm across Red Square, laughing and cracking jokes about the elderly morons in the Kremlin. Men's heads will be whipping around to stare at the two great beauties from Kiev.

The past week, I've been traveling a great deal around the country visiting outlying GRU units. It's important for me to get to know my troops and their commanders and for them to know me. There's no substitute for personal engagement and the men appreciate that I make the effort to fly to distant locations, especially since they understand that the Mujahedin have made flying around Afghanistan a rather hazardous enterprise.

It is easy to fall into patterns of behavior here in Afghanistan. Not only am I not running enough, but I am also drinking too much. It is an occupational hazard in Afghanistan. I tell myself that I must get back into the habit of running four days per week and drinking less often. This awful place is wearing on me, however, as is this aching longing for Boyka.

To make matters even less bearable for me, telephone communications with Moscow are terribly unreliable. I write Boyka several letters per week and I had hoped to be able to phone her once per week, but that's proven impossible. I've been in Afghanistan for five weeks now and managed just three partially successful phone calls with her. Today, the communication gods smile upon me, and I'm able to have my longest call yet with my wife.

Her voice—I've never heard her sound so grave before. "Vanya, I'm worried about you. Are you taking care of yourself?"

I want to be honest with her, without causing her undue alarm. "I've been traveling around the country, visiting my units. I must admit that it's hard to stay positive here." I can't say too much, or I'll worry her even more.

As usual, there is a lot of static on the line, and I fear the call will fail at any time. "Vanya, the talk round Moscow about the war is very ... well, pessimistic is a kind word for it. I was shopping with Oxana yesterday and we saw several Afghan War veterans on the street wearing their uniforms, with campaign medals on their chests. Ordinary people yelled at them! Cursed at these poor boys ... saying terrible things about the war and about their 'criminal' behavior and what a waste it all is—can you imagine? And this happened right on the streets of Moscow, only blocks from the Kremlin!"

I hear similar stories from brother officers who go home on

annual leave. They suffer similar abuse and hear ignorant comments about Afghanistan. Many guys can't take the torment from their own countrymen and return to their posts in Afghanistan before their leave is over. "Boyka, it's a shame that those poor boys are treated that way. Most are conscripts who have no choice but to go to Afghanistan and do their duty. It's not their fault that they're Afgantsy. Yet, they are a convenient target when one can't criticize those in charge of things, eh?"

Boyka sighs deeply. "Don't mention those Kremlin blockheads to me." Her voice drips with disgust at our country's leaders. "You're not in danger are you—traveling around the countryside? We hear such stories about bombs on the roads and mines everywhere, and helicopters being shot out of the sky almost every day."

Yes, it's all true. But I can't tell her so. "Boyka, you know how much people exaggerate things. I always have guards with me—I am well protected. And I take care to fly only at night when our aircraft are less vulnerable to the rebels. I'm as safe as a granddad in his easy chair."

She's silent for a moment. "I hope I can rely on you to look after your own safety. How is your young executive officer—Zhukov?"

I've not told her of his disappearance—it would terrify her. "Yes . . . Zhukov. He's on special assignment with our friends in the 'other' service. I can't tell you where he is; however, it's a nice part of the country with lovely orchards." Boyka will know what I mean by our friends in the 'other' service—the KGB.

"Well, Vanya, that's good to hear that he's okay. Will you get someone to replace him; I mean, while he's on assignment?" She's been my wife for such a long time that she knows exactly which questions to ask.

"Yes, love, I've asked General Ivashutin for candidates. After all, I can't be seen carrying my own bags!"

Just then, the line drops with such a *clunk* that I know I've lost her. The communications technician tries to get another line for about twenty minutes, but with no luck. Goddamn it. I miss Boyka in a way I never thought possible.

The more I learn about the history of the 40th Army in this war, the more absurd and fruitless our efforts appear. Just last fall we launched a major operation near the provincial city of Khost, which is very close to the Pakistan border. The target was a Mujahedin base called Zhawar, consisting of a complex of tunnels under the forbidding mountains delineating the border with Pakistan. The first phase of the assault resulted in the destruction of an entire Afghan Army Commando Brigade—our allies. After that disaster, Soviet troops took over the second phase and succeeded in seizing Zhawar, only to find the tunnels abandoned. Our engineers blew up some of the tunnels but had insufficient time to complete the job. We withdrew and the rebels reoccupied Zhawar in a matter of days. The entire campaign was a ridiculous waste of men, a metaphor for the entire war.

Now, we are planning a similar operation. This folly reminds me of the American experience in Vietnam where the Americans seized territory only to abandon it quickly to the Viet Cong or the North Vietnamese regulars. There is no point in fighting wars this way, and I am growing angry and depressed with it all.

20 June 1986

As chief of the GRU here, an important part of my role is to ensure we have adequate intelligence to support numerous operations all over Afghanistan. This morning, I spoke to my senior commanders stationed around the country. Thankfully, communications within Afghanistan—to the major bases, anyway—are more reliable than the links with Moscow. My final call was to Colonel Zaitsev. We discussed intelligence collection requirements for his battalion in support of an upcoming operation across the border into Pakistan. Toward the end of the call, I enquired about Major Zhukov. "Is there any word of Zhukov and the others? Anything at all? It's been three weeks since he was seized." I wait anxiously for him to answer.

"Yes, there is some news. You'll recall that I mentioned the Haqqani network—the important rebel family?"

"Certainly, Colonel. What have you learned?"

"Well, sir, the word is that Zhukov's APC was hijacked by the driver—*our* driver. He was working for the Mujahedin. The driver was a conscript from one of our Muslim republics and was paid to turn over the vehicle to a local gang. I suppose that any passengers on board would have been a bonus."

This sounds promising. "So, Zhukov is being held for ransom? Could he have been sent to the Haqqanis to curry favor? Is that why you mentioned them?"

Even Zaitsev's voice sounds a tiny bit hopeful. "Yes, a Soviet major would be a good prize, especially when the bandits were expecting a crew of conscripts. If the Haqqani bunch have him, then his chance of survival increases significantly."

Now, he *has* raised my spirits. "How can I help?"

"Comrade General, please be patient. These things take time. Months. I assure you that I will stay on top of it and keep you apprised." Zaitsev continues, "General, there are rumors that the Americans are planning to supply the rebels with Stinger surface-to-air missiles. Now, I believe only ten percent of the rumors I hear, but this one about the SAMs is so persistent that I think there must be something to it."

I've read analysis from the GRU in Moscow, based on intercepted American communications and press reports, that Washington wants the Mujahedin to shoot down more of our aircraft. Giving them Stingers, however, would be a major escalation in America's involvement in the war. I'd think the Americans must worry that we'd eventually gain possession of the Stinger technology, if they supply the missiles to the Islamic rebels. Would Washington really risk that? Maybe the CIA is under political pressure to provide advanced SAMs? I can't imagine the Pentagon would be happy about these lawless Mujahedin getting Stingers. These Islamic fighters would sell their mothers to the highest bidder—well, maybe not their mothers—but Stingers, surely.

Later that day, I get a message from GRU headquarters about Zhukov's replacement. My new executive officer will arrive at Bagram tomorrow and it's a man I know all too well—Lieutenant Colonel Mikhail Grishin.

CHAPTER FIFTEEN

STINGERS

General-Major Ivan Levchenko, GRU, Soviet Air Defense Forces
Jalalabad, Afghanistan

20 September 1986

As capable a subordinate as Anatoly Zhukov was, I did not appreciate how good he was until his replacement arrived. Mikhail Grishin has proven to be the epitome of the sniveling, scheming breed of officer that our system at times produces. When I complained to General Ivashutin about my new exec, he told me that Grishin is another test for me. If I can handle him, then Ivashutin says he will know that I will be able to deal with even more dangerous political opponents than Grishin in Moscow. If my future is destined to be filled with people worse than Grishin, then perhaps I should retire now. While I am on the topic of difficult subordinates: Lieutenant Colonel Zaitsev's commanding officer is Colonel Valeri Sidorov, who leads the 15th Spetsnaz Brigade based in Jalalabad. Sidorov's father is a famous senior general officer who runs the General Staff College in Moscow, a powerful position that is very influential with the current and future leaders of the Soviet military. Whereas Zaitsev is a quiet, thoughtful professional whose men respect him for his combination of careful planning and personal fearlessness, Sidorov is driven by personal ambition and a desire to please his father with combat exploits. Sidorov's subordinates know this and are wary of him. So am I.

25 September 1986

The weather is still good in late September, and I fly from Bagram to Jalalabad to check in with Sidorov regarding plans for our fall offensive. With reluctance, I have Grishin traveling with me on the theory that it is best to keep one's enemies close. He hates me with a hot passion. I had his security clearances revoked two years ago when he leaked the story about the American intrusion into the nuclear command bunker in East Germany to his father and other members of the Central Committee. Unfortunately, he was able to get his clearances reinstated by having his father apply pressure in the right places. Grishin is an untrustworthy bastard and a formidable thorn in my side.

For his part, Colonel Sidorov requires closer supervision than my other commanders. He doesn't like my visits, which he regards as amateurish intrusions on his private dominion. I must admit that Sidorov looks like a soldier—like a natural combat leader. He's a big man with ruddy cheeks and moves with a powerful, insistent stride. Sidorov's not a bad officer—he is reputed to be decisive and courageous in battle—but he is not careful with the lives of his men.

Today I've broken my own rule not to fly during daylight hours and Grishin and I fly to Jalalabad in brilliant blue skies. Our Mi-8 helicopter lands uneventfully at the special forces' airfield. I'm safely on the ground again. No American Stingers yet, but the rumors of their imminent deployment persist.

As we walk toward Sidorov's operations center, some instinct tells me to look skyward. I hear the unmistakable rumble of an approaching Mi-24 attack helicopter, no doubt returning to the base from a mission. I stop to admire this vicious looking war machine as it descends to the far side of the airfield. Along with the Su-25 close-air-support fighter, the Mi-24—or Crocodile—is an iconic symbol of our war in Afghanistan. As the Mi-24 prepares to land, I'm blinded temporarily by a terrific flash of light, followed by an explosive roar. The helicopter—this fearsome machine—is falling. It breaks apart as it smashes onto the far ramp. Holy Christ!

Suddenly, emergency vehicles roar out of a hangar just meters from where I'm standing, their sirens blaring. They race across the runway to the crash site. I sprint to the operations center, leaving a stunned Grishin behind. The officer on duty is shouting frantically into his radio phone.

When he hangs up the phone, I yell at him, "Get me a vehicle! Now!"

The young man—a senior lieutenant—sees my shoulder boards and comes to attention. He stutters, "Comrade General, Colonel Sidorov will be here soon. Perhaps you can ride with him?"

"Call Colonel Sidorov and tell him I will wait just outside the door for him. Got it?"

"Yes, sir."

Could this be the work of Stingers? Anti-aircraft guns? God, I hope it was guns and not Stingers. I hurry outside and wait for Sidorov, barely noticing that Grishin has joined me. I can't take my eyes off the burning wreckage on the other side of the airfield. Then, I see a second Mi-24 descending toward the field. It hovers over the wreckage of the wrecked helicopter. I'm blinded by another flash! Then, a crashing boom nearly deafens me. The second helicopter explodes . . . and its wreckage falls and appears to land meters from the first crash site. I feel a sudden spasm of nausea.

A jeep screeches to a halt in front of me; nearly running over my left foot. It's Sidorov. He waves at me to jump in. I crawl in the back, leaving Grishin standing on the ramp. The driver takes off at a mad speed toward the destroyed aircraft. Sidorov points at the sky. A third M-24 is approaching the field. It hovers like the other two until it disappears in a third blinding flash. We're close enough to the far ramp now that we feel the shock wave from the explosion. The third helicopter crashes to the ground. This nightmare must be the work of Stingers. Three helicopters . . . three dead crews.

It occurs to me that I only just landed moments ago. I guess that the Stinger shooters weren't interested in knocking down an unarmed Mi-8 transport helicopter. No. They used their precious weapons on much bigger game and shot down three of our finest combat helicopters in a matter of minutes. This is a pivotal moment in the war, and I am witnessing it.

The driver halts the jeep close enough to the first crash site that the heat we feel from the burning craft is incredible, even from a distance. The smell of burning flesh and fuel is overwhelming.

Sidorov screams at me. "Stingers!"

I nod my head and shout. "Look, Sidorov, you need to get back to the ops center and tell them to divert *all* air traffic from this field. Send everyone to Asadabad. This field isn't safe. We just lost three crews—like that!" I snap my fingers.

Sidorov grabs the driver by the shoulder and yells at him to turn the jeep around. The poor driver's face looks paler than the moon and he is transfixed by the awful crash site. Sidorov shakes him violently and the young man comes to his senses and races like a Formula One driver back to the operations center.

Once we arrive at the ops center, I tell Sidorov, "Get all air traffic diverted to Asadabad. I'll call Zaitsev and warn him about the Stingers. Lieutenant, get me Colonel Zaitsev on the radio. After I finish with him, connect me immediately with the 40th Army commander. Got it?"

The lieutenant stutters again, "The 40th Army commander, sir? The commander?"

What the fuck is wrong with this guy? "Yes, the 40th Army commander, you idiot. Zaitsev first. Now, get on with it!"

"Yes, General."

I explain the situation at Jalalabad to Zaitsev. "Sidorov is diverting aircraft from Jalalabad. You'll need to bed down all aircraft safely and double your perimeter patrols. Get your men and the airfield prepared."

"General, do you think these were Stingers? The Stingers are here?"

"I don't think that any other weapon could have done this. The helicopters were hovering over the airfield—far from the hills surrounding the base. And the accuracy of the attacks ... it doesn't seem possible for guns or other weapons to achieve that kind of accuracy at such a range. It had to be Stingers. Sweep the hills around Asadabad with infantry—don't use your aircraft. Keep all aircraft grounded until further notice."

Zaitsev takes a minute to respond. He is letting it all sink in. "Yes, sir. I understand. We will handle things here. Stay safe, general."

Stay safe, indeed. "Thank you, comrade. You do the same. Out here."

Stingers ... to have the accuracy to shoot down three armored attack helicopters at long range ... what a weapon!

My next call is to my boss—General Dubynin, the 40th Army commander. He understands immediately what the deployment of Stingers inside Afghanistan means. Dubynin may be gruff, but he always listens carefully to my intelligence briefings, and I've been warning about this eventuality since I arrived in May.

"So, Levchenko, the Americans are upping the stakes—that's what you think? Why now, when we are preparing to leave the country?"

I really don't know. I don't have access to our sensitive intelligence on deliberations in Washington. "My intuition is that the Americans don't believe we will withdraw. And I bet their intelligence people are tracking our preparations for additional operations later this year. I shouldn't say more on an open line."

I hear Dubynin grunt. "They don't believe us, eh? The Americans are welcome to this flea-infested sandbox. So, they don't believe we'll withdraw. That's your assessment?"

I don't have enough solid information to make an assessment.

"Sir, I would say my view is informed speculation, rather than an assessment. In any event, it appears that we must assume Stingers will proliferate all over Afghanistan and we must prepare accordingly."

Dubynin grunts and hangs up the phone.

During the night, my nervous pilots fly Grishin and me to Bagram Air Base. When we land, I tell Grishin to go to his quarters and gets some sleep and he offers no objection. My first stop is the communications center to see if there are messages awaiting me from Moscow. I'm surprised to be given an urgent message that I've been summoned back to Moscow by General Ivashutin. In light of today's Stinger attacks, he wants a comprehensive update on the situation in Afghanistan. Clearly, the loss of three Mi-24s—in the space of a few minutes—has gotten Moscow's attention.

So, I'm to return to Moscow to face what? Will there be an inquiry concerning how the GRU was unable to stop delivery of Stingers to the Afghan rebels? I take some comfort that at least I'll be able to see my wife for the first time in months. I'll be out of this ghastly place; if only for a few days. I can't help but contemplate the reception I may receive from Oxana and my brother-in-law, Oleksandr, who are living in our Moscow flat. Both are rabid Ukrainian nationalists who vociferously oppose this war.

I was born and raised in Crimea, which became part of the Ukrainian Soviet Socialist Republic when I was a boy. My family is Russian, and I grew up speaking Russian and attending the local Orthodox Russian church. My earliest years were spent on our tiny family farm in a rural part of the Crimean Peninsula. My mother and grandmother kept chickens and ducks and maintained a vegetable garden. I had no siblings, and my world was limited to a tiny area that had changed little for centuries. My mother bartered our meager produce for milk and other staples with neighboring farmers. I knew no Ukrainian speakers and as far as I was concerned, Crimea was the center of the universe and was as Russian as Moscow.

My father worked as a welder at the repair yard for the Soviet Black Sea Fleet at Sevastopol. Due to the distance from our home in Western Crimea, my father essentially lived at the navy base and only came home for a long weekend about once every other month. When I was six years old, my local school nominated me for an English language program at an elite English school in Sevastopol. I was accepted and my young life was transformed. It was as though I had been released from the cocoon.

I lived apart from my family for the next twelve years. During those school years, I rarely saw my father, even though he was living in the same city. I went home to our farm for six weeks every summer and for the New Year holidays. It was a solitary existence for me, but it put me on the path that led to a career that my parents would not comprehend, had they lived to see it.

After graduating from the immersive English school, I was able to gain an appointment to the prestigious Soviet air force academy, located in Kiev, the capital city of the Ukrainian Republic. By the time I was eighteen and in my first year at the academy, I was fluent in English and, of course, in my native Russian. Before entering the academy and living in Kiev, I'd rarely heard the Ukrainian language spoken and it sounded quite foreign to my ears.

I met my wife during my third year at the academy. We had difficulty communicating since Boyka spoke rudimentary Russian and I spoke no Ukrainian. The sparkling and beautiful Boyka proved to be all the incentive I needed to learn Ukrainian. She, in turn, studied Russian. By the time we married, we could communicate with each other in either Russian or Ukrainian.

I fell in love with Boyka immediately. Her parents became my parents, too, since both of my parents died during my years at the academy. Boyka's sister Oxana is equally gorgeous. Unlike my wife, however, Oxana has always been a political firebrand. She joined a group of Ukrainian nationalists when she was a university student and quickly became one of the leaders of the Ukrainian independence movement after graduation.

Oxana married another Ukrainian radical, Oleksandr Koghut, and the two of them are leading lights in the independence movement. Their politics are not compatible with my career in the Soviet military, to put it mildly. I can sympathize with the Ukrainian desire for freedom, but I could never admit it to anyone, certainly not Oleksandr or Oxana. Perhaps it's because of my English school education, which included reading the works of the Enlightenment philosophers and the founding fathers of the United States, that I am not a doctrinaire Communist. If I'm honest with myself, I'm much more of a Russian nationalist than a Communist. Don't misunderstand me, I believe in the Soviet Union, but I believe in it as a geopolitical necessity, not as an ideological entity.

26 September 1986

My flight to Moscow will depart soon, so I go to my quarters to shower, change, and pack before going to the airfield. When I arrive at the flight operations building, a young officer hails me and tells me that there's a call for me in the communications center from Colonel Zaitsev. I drop my bags at the flight ops counter and rush to the adjacent building that houses the comms center.

Someone hands me headphones and soon I hear Zaitsev's now familiar voice. "General Levchenko, I have some news about Zhukov. The Haqqani group claims that they have him in custody now and they've invited me to meet at a neutral location to discuss his release."

This welcome news seems to confirm that Zhukov is alive. "Colonel, that's excellent news; however, it cannot be safe for you to meet with these scoundrels. They may kidnap *you*! You're a bigger prize than Zhukov."

I hear a muffled chuckle. "Yes, sir, there is always that risk. However, I'm confident that I'll have sufficient security with me to discourage any such action."

I hope he's right. "Yes, yes, of course. You will have thought of all the possible dangers. I wish I could go with you; however, I've been summoned to Moscow. Please contact me through GRU headquarters in Moscow with any developments. Okay?"

"Yes, sir. Of course. I will do my best to keep you informed, given the inherent difficulties in communicating from this godforsaken place. Safe travels."

"Thank you, Zaitsev. I have sent a message to Colonel Sidorov that he is to act in my stead while I am in Moscow. Please call him tonight on my behalf and let him know that he is to make sure that Lieutenant Colonel Grishin does not issue any orders in my name. Understood?"

"Certainly, General Levchenko. I will radio Colonel Sidorov as soon we are finished."

"Send him my compliments and tell him that I mean no disrespect by not calling him directly. My plane is about to depart."

"Yes, sir. I will tell him. Safe travels."

Well, that's it. I will fly to Moscow while my comrades continue to deal with a deadly and treacherous adversary. I board the transport plane and go to the cockpit to talk to the pilots. The aircraft commander says, "General, I understand that your executive officer left earlier tonight for Moscow on the Black Tulip flight and won't be joining us. Is that correct?"

Did he now? "Captain, Colonel Grishin is on another flight to Moscow—that's what you're saying?" I can hear the anger in my voice and the young pilot knows immediately that he has touched a hot stove.

"Yes, comrade General. That is my understanding." He is shaking and I realize that I must calm him down. Grishin's treachery is not his fault and flying out of Bagram with the new Stinger threat to worry about is nerve-racking enough.

"All right. Don't worry about it. I am sure he's going ahead to prepare my return to Moscow. Thank you and let's have an uneventful flight. Shall we?"

"Yes, sir, of course."

I take some comfort in knowing that Grishin won't be able to use my absence from Bagram to create mischief behind my back. But what harm does he have in mind in Moscow? I have no doubt that he will stir up trouble using his father's position on the Central Committee.

PART THREE

The Righteous Arrows of Retribution

I will heap calamities upon them and spend my arrows against them.

—*Deuteronomy 32:33*

CHAPTER SIXTEEN

A MAZE OF HATE

General-Major Ivan Levchenko, GRU, Soviet Air Defense Forces
Moscow, Russia, USSR

27 September 1986

"What are you thinking about?" Boyka says in her soft, melodious voice. I'm spooning her warm, luxurious body. We've made love for the last hour—a blissful, long homecoming session. What *am* I thinking about?

"Young Zhukov, I suppose."

She turns over to face me and puts my right hand on her breast. "Zhukov? After we've been fucking for an hour? I know the war has changed you, but you haven't become a homosexual, have you?" She looks at me, her eyes fierce and accusatory.

"What? Good God, Boyka. Of course not. No."

She grins at me and squeezes my hand—the one holding her breast. "Well, I'm relieved. But, why Zhukov? Is he in trouble? You told me he is on a special assignment."

Goddamn it. I did tell her that on the phone from Bagram. "Well, yes, but he has run into some trouble."

"What kind of trouble?

God knows. "Yes, well . . . we had a problem on a mission and Zhukov was captured."

Boyka sits up in bed with a start. "Captured! He's been captured! When? When did this happen?"

Jesus . . . "It happened several months ago. We think we know who is holding him, and we believe that he's alive. One of my colonels is negotiating his release."

Boyka's face is contorted with anger. "You lied to me! You said he was on special assignment. The truth is that he's been missing all these months. We hear the stories here in Moscow about what happens to our captured troops." She turns her face away from me in shock over the truth of Zhukov's plight and from hurt because of my lie.

"I'm sorry, Boyka. I didn't want to worry you. I should've told you the truth."

She turns sharply to face me. "Worry me? *Worry* me? I'm *terrified*. I can't sleep. I think of you in that awful place with those awful people. You don't understand what it's like to be left behind while you are facing dangers that I can only imagine—and my imagination is quite vivid, I assure you."

I hug her and kiss her long hair. My God. What this war is doing to us.

"The war is changing you, Vanya. I hear it when we talk on the phone. I see it in your face now that you are home. And, to think that you must go back there so soon. It's more than I can handle. I've always supported you in your career and been happy to do so, but this is all too much."

What do I say? She's the only thing in this world that I truly love, and I am hurting her. Afghanistan is an insidious specter menacing our marriage. "I understand, Boyka. I'll have a full home leave in January—I'll be home for thirty days. We'll enjoy the holidays together."

My wife rises, puts on her dressing gown, and goes to the large window next to her dresser. She parts the curtains and gazes through the window. She's a caring, intelligent woman who has followed me to Poland, East Germany, West Germany, and to Moscow, a city she hates. What a musical career she could have enjoyed had it not been for marrying me. She has sacrificed so much for me, while I've done so little for her.

Boyka turns around to face me. "The sky looks like smudged charcoal. The streetlights make the clouds glow so that they look like the photos from Chernobyl. I can smell diesel fuel even though the window is shut. It's early October and it already looks like midwinter in this fucking place. I hate Moscow. My only consolation is that we aren't in Ukraine, living in the shadow of a nuclear catastrophe. You know . . . there's still no real information about the Chernobyl disaster. It's much like the war in Afghanistan. In the absence of facts, the people fear the worst and speculation runs rampant." She pauses. "What time will you leave this morning? Are you going to GRU headquarters today?"

Momentarily, I am awestruck by her. How can this incredible beauty—this brilliant artist—possibly be my wife? I get up from bed. "Yes, and I need to go in right away. I must explain why these American Stinger missiles have been delivered to our enemies. I am probably the one who will get the blame. Also, I won't have time for breakfast with you today. I'll see you all for dinner tonight. Have you made a reservation?"

Boyka's face doesn't register my question, initially. "Oh, yes. A reservation. There's a quiet spot I've found. It's good for conversation. Best of all, no one important ever goes there."

I suppress a smile. "That sounds perfect, Boyka. I spend far too much time with important people."

The familiar drive to GRU headquarters seems surreal to me now after months spent in a war zone. It's disconcerting to observe that life in the capital city is completely normal.

I spend most of the day reading intelligence reports and conferring with GRU analysts. I probe them about how the introduction of Stingers may influence how we conduct operations throughout Afghanistan. I assume that the Americans will supply the Stingers to most of the rebel groups—at least those located along the border with Pakistan. The relations amongst the various native groups are so complex, they are baffling to me. In addition to the CIA's meddling, some of the rebels receive arms from the Chinese, some from Iran, others from Egypt and Saudi Arabia. The confusing political landscape in Afghanistan is a maze of hate.

Late in the afternoon, I meet with the director general of the GRU, General of the Army Pyotr Ivashutin—the legendary long-time head of the GRU. His imposing physical presence and larger-than-life persona make him an intimidating character indeed. He has been the top man at the GRU for two decades. I always enter his lair with trepidation, although I am confident in the conclusions I have made about the situation in Afghanistan.

I stand in front of his desk and salute. "Good day, General Ivashutin, General-Major Levchenko reporting as ordered."

Wordlessly, he bids me to sit. He finishes reading a report before speaking. "Well, Levchenko. How do you find Afghanistan?"

"General, the country is a stew of competing tribes operating against each other on one day and cooperating the next. I call it a 'maze of hate.' The situation is further complicated by the meddling of the CIA, the Pakistan Inter-Services Intelligence Agency, the Chinese, the Iranians, and various Arab states."

Ivashutin's face is swarthy and heavily lined—he looks like an aging outlaw in a John Ford Western film. His gruff voice is a perfect match for his earthy, no-nonsense face. "And, what of our Army? How is morale?"

"Morale is good." This is my honest answer. "Morale is good, and the fighting spirit is high. There exists, however, a deep anxiety over how well the Army's sacrifice is recognized and appreciated by the Soviet people."

Peter the Great grunts. "Yes, I worry about that, too." He pours himself a cup of tea and offers me none. "What about these Stingers? Why couldn't we prevent their introduction? And do they change the nature of the war like so many are telling me? What is your view?"

I'm well prepared for this question, of course. "Sir, it is my view that the introduction of the Stingers, while troubling and dangerous, does not represent a material change in the balance of forces in Afghanistan." I can see from his expression that the general is surprised by my analysis. "Yes, they are formidable weapons. As you know from my reporting, I was at Jalalabad airfield when those first three Mi-24s were shot down by Stingers."

He motions for me to continue.

"General Ivashutin, we've already lost hundreds of aircraft in this war to small arms fire, antiaircraft artillery, and Egyptian-made copies of our own shoulder-fired surface-to-air missiles. It is true that the Stingers are qualitatively much better weapons than anything we have encountered previously. Nonetheless, if we change our tactics and modify our aircraft, then we can deal with this new threat, terrible as it is. I will admit that I had my doubts initially, but I am now convinced we can handle this."

The general swivels his chair so that he can stare out the window at the rainy evening streetscape. All afternoon it's been raining steadily, and a blackish wind has been blowing with some force. Without looking at me—his eyes are fixed on something outside—he says, "How much will this cost—these modifications?" He must be alarmed over how much this stupid war is costing.

"General, I have a team of analysts working with the relevant design bureaus to get their cost estimates on any major modifications for helicopters, fixed-wing transports, and fixed-wing fighters. Each category of aircraft will require different alterations, and I've told the men to determine which modifications can be done in-country and which will require depot-level maintenance back in the USSR. The depot-level mods are likely to be costly."

The general swivels his chair so he can glare at me as he sips his tea. "How long will all this take—this analysis?"

"Comrade General, my priority is on the work we can do in Afghanistan right away, with minimal new equipment. That assessment will be done in two weeks. Our troops are remarkably resilient and creative when it comes to making changes that save lives. The analysis for the depot-level fixes depends on the cooperation of the design bureaus. If I get full cooperation, then it should take one month."

Staring at his teacup, he muses, "Yes, I understand. That is precisely how it was in the Great Patriotic War. Men are fantastically creative when the lives of their comrades are at stake. Such men have no patience with bureaucratic delays. I trust that you, Ivan Ivanovich, are such a man. Give me a list of the design bureaus you need help from. I will call the directors personally."

That's good news. The design bureau chiefs will listen to Peter the Great. "Sir, I assure you that I will act with haste. The fastest thing we can do to save lives is to alter our tactics. I have a separate team back at Bagram working on that problem. I've also called in operational crews from around Afghanistan to provide their expertise. My objective is to make the American weapons as inconsequential as possible, sir."

The general rises from his chair. The interview is ending, and I haven't been fired. "Very well, Levchenko. I believe that you have the proper actions underway. Tomorrow at noon you will make a presentation to Marshal Akhromeyeev and other senior officers at General Staff Headquarters. They will want more detail on recommended tactics and technical modifications. You must be prepared to answer their questions, which can be quite probing at times. Do you understand?"

Having briefed Chief of the General Staff Marshal Ogarkov during the Able Archer crisis in 1983, I know what it's like to brief our country's top military man. However, I don't know Ogarkov's replacement—Marshal of the Soviet Union Sergei Akhromeyeev. "I will be prepared. Shall I draft charts for this presentation?"

The general ponders my question with more care than I think it deserves. "No. I want you to conduct this as a conversation. You're no longer a colonel. You're a general and the top GRU man in the only theater of war this nation has prosecuted since 1945. The marshal will expect you to speak to him as a senior man—a man who has no need of charts and graphs . . . a man who has the details at his fingertips, but who can see the big strategic picture. Do you understand?"

Yes, I believe I do. He's showing great confidence in my ability to allow me to brief the chief of the General Staff. Tomorrow I'd better have my shit together, as the Americans say. "Comrade General, I believe I understand your meaning fully. Thank you for your confidence in me."

This elicits a smirk. "Levchenko, you would not have the job you have in Afghanistan if I had any doubts about your ability."

That's an astonishing vote of confidence from Peter the Great. I salute and say, "Thank you, Comrade General. I'll be prepared."

He turns away from me to gaze once more out the window. What does he see? What is a man of his experience looking for in the bleak, gray, misty evening?

I return to my office and spend longer than I had planned composing notes for the crucial meeting with Marshal Akhromeyeev tomorrow. It's well after 7:00 p.m. when I lock up my papers in a sturdy safe. I call for my driver and order him to take me directly to the small restaurant where Boyka has reserved a table for four. Normally, I would go home and change into civilian clothes first, but there won't be time this evening. I'm certain that by appearing in uniform I will provide my wife's sister and her husband fodder for sarcastic comments at my expense.

The car's tires sizzle on the wet streets like steaks on a white-hot grill as we drive through a cold rain to an old district of Moscow that I don't know well. When my driver parks the car, I see that the restaurant Boyka has chosen is very tiny. It cannot accommodate more than two dozen patrons. I tell my driver, who is also my bodyguard, to come inside and get dinner himself.

The entry door has rounded edges, like the front doors of rural cottages in Ukraine. As I open the door, I find the atmosphere in the restaurant is cozy and filled with the smells of traditional Ukrainian cuisine. I hand my overcoat and scarf to the cloak room attendant. My brother-in-law, Oleksandr, calls out, "Hallo, the conquering hero returned from the wars!" He speaks far too loudly for the small room, and everyone looks up to see who or what has prompted such a disruption. My guess is that Oleksandr has already had several shots of vodka.

"Good evening Oleksandr and thank you for the subtlety of your greeting."

He grins, stands up, and hugs me as I approach the table where Boyka and her sister Oxana are seated. After Oleksandr releases me from his grip, I look at the two beautiful sisters who always seem even more stunning when you see them together. They are seated side by side and look like exotic golden bookends. I bow to Oxana and kiss my wife. "Good evening, my princess."

Oleksandr is quite drunk, and he snickers, "Princess! That's a fine thing for a Bolshevik to call his wife! I may need to report you to the secret police, brother."

I sit down with a sigh. "Do what you must, Oleksandr. Do what you must. Oxana, do you know that I have a shrine dedicated to your sister in my quarters at Bagram Air Base?"

Oxana looks surprised and Boyka pokes me with her elbow. "You do not! You don't have a shrine! That's absurd. You don't have to impress Oxana, you know. Here, drink some of the vodka before our brother-in-law has it all."

I take a healthy swig. "Ah, that's the most relaxed I've been all day. No, but it's true, Oxana . . . about the shrine. In a corner of my quarters, I have arranged several photographs of your sister and a scented handkerchief she gave me when I left Moscow. I decorate Boyka's holy place with pinecones or flowers depending on the season."

Boyka pokes me again and laughs. "You do not. Tell the truth." At least I've made her laugh. I used to have a talent for it.

Everyone is smiling now. The other patrons are watching our table with amusement. I raise my right hand to take an oath. "I swear on Lenin's tomb that I am telling the God's honest truth."

"Aren't you mixing your religions, brother? Lenin and God in the same sentence—imagine!" Oxana laughs.

"Oxana, it's best to have Lenin, God, and all the angels on your side in the Afghanistan War, I assure you. The more holy figures, the merrier." Everyone stops laughing at the mention of the war. "Sorry, I shouldn't have mentioned Afghanistan. Anyway, I'm happy to know that you are safe and sound here in Moscow, well away from those troubles at Chernobyl."

Oxana says in a serious tone, "Yes, we are grateful for your hospitality. We've been away from my parents too long, though. When do you think it will be safe to return to Kiev?"

I have no special insight into what's going on at Chernobyl or how the radiation has affected the rest of Ukraine. What little I know is terrifying, but I attempt to be moderately reassuring. "Oxana, I think the worst of the crisis is past; however, I'm no expert on the situation."

Oleksandr interjects, "Please, can we not talk about Chernobyl tonight? Or Afghanistan? Both topics sicken me. Let's relish the fact that we're all back together and that our brother has returned safely from the combat zone."

He is usually combative—this brother-in-law of mine—but he also has a balanced approach to life's problems that I've always admired. "Yes, Oleksandr is right. I'd like to propose a toast to the two most sexy and beautiful women in Moscow—Madame Levchenka and Madame Koghuta."

We all observe Oleksandr's truce for the rest of the evening and have a lovely meal that evokes memories of a simpler time for all of us. It turns out that the specialty of this restaurant is old fashioned, country-inspired dishes from Western Ukraine, delicious and very appropriate for us. This has been exactly what I needed.

After dinner, I retrieve our coats from the cloakroom and through the window I notice police cars with their emergency lights ablaze on the street just outside the restaurant. Christ, those are MVD cars. What is the Interior Ministry's police force doing in this obscure section of the city?

Two MVD officers crash through the front door and nearly stumble into my bodyguard and me. I am in uniform, which causes them to stop and come to attention. They salute and the fat one says, "My apologies, General. I did not realize you would be here."

"Why are *you* here, comrades?"

"Yes, we are obliged to arrest a Ukrainian traitor—Oleksandr Koghut. We have a warrant."

The wives and my brother-in-law have joined me, and they hear the last statement by the MVD officer. They start to argue but I stop them.

"Everyone, please let me handle this" I tell the fat cop, "Officer, there must be some mistake. Comrade Koghut is my brother-in-law, and he is my houseguest here in Moscow while the Chernobyl problem gets sorted. What is the charge?"

"General, the charge relates to organizing opposition to the Soviet state in favor of an independent Ukraine. I am afraid we will have to take Comrade Koghut with us. Please stand aside, General."

Oxana and Oleksandr know what an arrest by the MVD could mean—jail in Moscow, or a stay in the Gulag, or worse. Oxana's face is contorted with fear.

Boyka says, "Vanya, do something! You outrank these guys."

"Yes, but I have no authority over police actions. Officer, will there be an arraignment tomorrow?"

The fat guy responds, "I doubt it. These things usually take days."

Oleksandr trembles. "Vanko don't let them take me. Help me!"

"Brother, there is nothing I can do. I will visit you tomorrow if I can."

The fat guy pulls Oleksandr's arm, and the other cop pushes my brother-in-law through the door and out into the rainy night. I watch helplessly as he disappears into one of the MVD cars.

28 September 1986

This morning my mind is roiled by thoughts of Oleksandr sitting alone in a jail cell. I know that I must compartmentalize his troubles and focus on my task for today.

I ride with General Ivashutin to our meeting at General Staff headquarters. He reads official papers as we drive, while I review the notes that I made last night and try not to think of my brother-in-law. My mind is distracted, and I must force myself to concentrate on today's critically important meeting.

As we walk under the General Staff building's signature tower, the GRU chief tells me, "You can expect the commanding general of the Ground Forces and the chief marshals of both the Air Force and the Air Defense Forces in the meeting as well as the chief of the general staff. Oh, and your direct boss, the 40th Army commander Viktor Dubynin, has been invited, as well."

Dubynin will be in the meeting—that's a surprise. I swallow hard and reply, "I look forward to gaining the benefit of their experience and guidance."

The old general laughs out loud. "Well said, Levchenko. Well said!"

As we are shown into the chamber, I see that Chief of the General Staff Akhromeyeev's office is decorated to reflect his personality.

He is reported to be a man who is modest of habit and the austere office treatments reflect an asceticism I've never seen before in such a senior officer. I have rarely attended a gathering of such an array of senior officers. The commanders of the nation's Army, Air Force, and Air Defense Forces and the commanding general of the 40th Army sit around a black conference table. I feel out of place and insignificant. General Ivashutin notices my nerves and gives me a confidence-building wink. It's a generous gesture and I appreciate it. Marshal Akhromeyeev is seated at his desk, and he calls the meeting to order with none of the niceties one might normally expect.

General Ivashutin introduces me crisply and gives me the floor.

I'm about to begin when Marshal Akhromeyeev interjects. "General Levchenko, I have the following questions today: firstly, what countermeasures are we undertaking to deal with the new American threat—the Stinger missile system? Secondly, how quickly can such countermeasures be implemented? And thirdly, why have the Americans escalated their support of the Islamic rebels? I trust those questions are clear enough?"

All eyes turn toward me. "Yes, Comrade Marshal. Clear as crystal."

"Very well. Proceed."

"Yes, sir. Thank you, sir. The countermeasures we can undertake to deal with the new Stinger missile threat can be organized into two broad categories: tactics and technologies. Tactics, of course, are easier and quicker to adopt than technology. Many of the tactical changes will be variations on those we've used already to thwart the current threat, which is significant even without the Stingers. Before I go further, I should note that I personally witnessed the very first Stinger attacks at Jalalabad and I was impressed with their accuracy and destructive power. After those attacks, I directed my agents—agents that have infiltrated the Mujahedin—to steal Stingers from the rebels at the earliest opportunity. I'm pleased to report today that we succeeded in getting our hands on two Stingers late last night through those agents." This news elicits murmurs of approval from everyone except Akhromeyeev, who sits in his chair sphinxlike.

I continue, "Comrade Marshal, one measure we can take right away is to have our fighter-bombers fly higher altitude combat air patrols, beyond the range of the Stingers."

My direct boss, General Dubynin, scoffs, "How much higher can they fly? Hell, my ground commanders call the Air Force pilots 'cosmonauts' because they already fly so high as to be nearly useless." He fixes his mouth in that bizarre upside-down horseshoe I've come to know.

"Yes, General Dubynin, I am aware of those concerns and will work with the Air Force to craft tactics that enable them to hit their targets with greater precision from higher altitudes." The chief of the Air Force nods at me approvingly.

Dubynin is unimpressed. "Those airplanes are so high they may as well be in low earth orbit." The Army officers in the room chuckle at this comment, although the unsmiling Air Force and Air Defense Forces leaders are less amused.

Marshal Akhromeyeev asks, "Comrade General Levchenko, how about the helicopters? Aren't they at the greatest risk from this new American threat?"

"Yes, Comrade Marshal, and the helicopter crews will be instructed to fly 'nap of the earth' tactics and use the terrain to mask themselves from the Stingers. As you know, helicopters present a 'hot' target for the infrared sensor of the Stinger. The sensors require a 'cold' background—the sky—as contrast with the hot exhaust of the helicopter to work optimally. We'll have the aircrews fly low against the terrain until they 'pop up' to acquire their targets. Flying low will expose the Mi-24s to small-arms fire; however, the helicopters' armor will provide adequate protection in most cases. Lastly, we will limit daylight flying for both fixed-wing and rotary-wing transport aircraft. Our intelligence indicates that the rebels do not possess night-vision equipment at this point."

Akhromeyeev enquires, "And what of technical measures? What can be done quickly?"

"We are identifying the technical fixes we can make in-country. We can install exhaust baffles on some aircraft in Afghanistan to impede the ability of the Stingers to lock on to our aircraft. Also, I have asked for upgraded flares to be delivered as soon as possible. Those are fixes we can perform in-country. More involved adaptations will require aircraft to be sent to the Soviet Union. We can install infrared beacons that will spoof the Stingers—this can be done quickly, although I don't have a hard estimate yet. The longest-term change is to install upgraded radar systems on our fixed-wing fighters. Better radars will improve time of detection and provide better geolocational data of missile launches."

Akhromeyeev leans across his desk. "Levchenko, why did the Americans introduce Stingers at this point in the war? Why now?"

"Comrade Marshal, my view is that the Americans think we are committed to staying in Afghanistan for the long term. And, that we have cast our eyes toward Baluchistan and aim to seize that area for the purpose of gaining a warm-water port on the Indian Ocean."

The 40th Army commander scoffs, "That's a ridiculous piece of American propaganda. If you buy that nonsense Levchenko, then . . ."

I wait for him to finish his thought, but he lets it hang in the air. "Comrade General, I agree that the notion is ludicrous. Nonetheless, this is widely believed in Washington. Just because we find it ridiculous doesn't mean that Americans don't believe it."

Dubynin responds, "If they believe that crap, then they are more stupid than I thought."

Akhromeyeev gives Dubynin a stern look. He's reputed to dislike coarse language. I look at Peter the Great for guidance and he nods at me, indicating that I should continue.

"In addition to the Baluchistan angle, the Americans want revenge." Akhromeyeev tilts his ear toward me as if to listen more intently. "They want to bleed us. They want retribution for what

Soviet weapons—in the hands of the North Vietnamese—did to the United States in Southeast Asia. The CIA has taken the significant risk of arming these rebels because they—the CIA leaders—want to kill Russians. There is a maze of hate in Afghanistan, and now the United States has entered that maze."

The room is silent for a few moments. At last, Akhromeyev speaks. "They want to bleed us. That's your view? You believe that they have taken this risk to supply Islamic warriors with advanced weaponry simply because they want to kill Russians?"

That's not what I meant. "It's not the *only* reason—many in Washington believe in the Baluchistan theory. Also, there is a congressman from Texas who has marshaled support based on humanitarian concerns over the Afghan refugees living in camps in Pakistan."

Akhromeyev is stunned. "A congressman from Texas? A cowboy?"

"Yes, sir. We know this congressman has visited President Zia in Pakistan and has been to the border area to see the refugee camps on at least one occasion. He's an obscure political figure; however, he's been able to garner support for a much more aggressive policy."

Marshal Akhromeyev folds his hands on the desktop. "General Levchenko, I'm glad you understand these Americans. I certainly don't. Are you aware that General Secretary Gorbachev will be meeting President Reagan soon in Iceland?"

I've heard something about it; however, I have other things on my mind in the war zone. "Yes, Comrade Marshal, I believe the meeting will occur this fall."

"Later this month. All right. Do you have anything else for me?"

I sneak a peek at the GRU director, and he gently shakes his head. "No, Comrade Marshal. That concludes the briefing."

Akhromeyev addresses General Ivashutin. "General, my compliments to the GRU. You have presented a cogent, logical approach to the new threat situation in Afghanistan."

The marshal turns to the 40th Army commander. "General Dubynin, who in the 40th Army has responsibility for interdicting the supply lines for weapons entering Afghanistan from Pakistan?"

Dubynin shoots me a harsh look prior to answering. "There is shared responsibility, Marshal. My airborne and special reconnaissance units work the border region alongside the GRU Spetsnaz brigades."

Akhromeyeev prompts me to respond.

"Comrade Marshal, our forces have interdicted tons of supplies. Nonetheless, the border is lengthy and there are numerous routes through the mountains. We don't have enough men to control the border. When we conduct raids into the border region, we leave behind isolated strong points that must be lightly manned. Our garrisons are too small to conduct meaningful interdiction raids and the men end up spending most of their time defending their outposts from enemy attacks."

Akhromeyeev bows his head in thought for a moment and looks up at me. "Very well. Thank you. I've heard enough. Good day."

Ivashutin and I walk out together. I'm not sure how the meeting went. As we ride back to GRU headquarters, my curiosity gets the better of me. "Sir, how do you think it went?"

He turns his bulky body to face me. "Dubynin isn't a friend. I trust you realize that. I think Marshal Akhromeyeev was satisfied with the meeting. You demonstrated that you understand the issues. The problem is the war itself—the nature of this war. It isn't a fight to the finish. It's a limited war, with limited aims. That's what all of us are struggling with—whether we serve at Bagram or in Moscow. Nothing is clear in this war, including our objectives, and that's a problem. I think your phrase is apt. Afghanistan is a maze of hate and we don't understand it. I just hope we are wise enough to get ourselves out of the maze."

I nod and look out the window at the people navigating the busy city sidewalks.

"Levchenko, tell me why Grishin hates you. His father has a powerful position on the Central Committee and Colonel Grishin has presented him with 'evidence' of your incompetence in the conduct of your duties in Afghanistan. He also asserts that you are disloyal to the USSR and may be an American spy."

I smile ruefully and respond, "Grishin worked for me in West Germany when I commanded the air team at the MLM. The notion of working for a Crimean peasant like me was repugnant to him and he let me know it every day. He also flirted with my wife right in front of me and I finally had him transferred to a post in East Germany. Having to leave the comfort of West Germany for the austerity of the East made him hate me even more. I know he is dangerous and that he spreads lies about me. I was foolish enough to believe that Grishin would be less of a threat here in Moscow than he would be on the loose in Afghanistan. I guess I underestimated him."

"He's a problem, Ivan Ivanovich. While I'm around, I can corral him, but I won't be around forever—even Peter the Great has an expiration date. You will encounter many arrogant asses as you rise in rank, so you better find a way of dealing with them."

"General, I appreciate your support... and your advice. I suppose we all have crosses to bear and Grishin will be one of mine."

"Yes, and don't underestimate Grishin's capacity for mischief. I believe he is behind the arrest of your brother-in-law last night."

So, Peter the Great knows about Oleksandr's plight. And Grishin is the hidden hand behind his arrest by the notorious MVD. "Sir, if I may say so, my brother-in-law's arrest has upset my entire family. Comrade Koghut is a bit of a blowhard, and he does support greater Ukrainian autonomy, but I do not think he is a danger to the state. If I did, I would have reported him myself."

"Levchenko, you would be obligated to report him. You know that." The old General sighs. "Grishin has learned from the best—his old man. Grishin's father is a viper who has flourished in the snake pit that is the Central Committee. Believe me, you will need to be wary of Grishin for the rest of your career. The charges he is making against you are severe. As for your brother-in-law's situation, I will investigate this matter with the MVD. And I want you to stay out of it. Don't put your hand on a hot stove and don't fuck with the MVD. Understood?"

"Yes, General."

"The MVD will try to beat some sense into your brother-in-law. I will see that he is released in a couple of days. Perhaps it is time for this man and his wife to return to Kiev, Ivan Ivanovich."

CHAPTER SEVENTEEN

THE RED-HAIRED MAJOR REAPPEARS

Captain Kevin Cattani, US Air Force Intelligence
The Air Staff, Pentagon, Washington, DC

1 October 1986

It's late morning and my workday is coming to an end. It's a brilliantly sunny autumn day in Washington and inviting rays pour through the tall windows of the Pentagon's "A" Ring, and I feel a pleasant warmth as I walk to my office. The "A" Ring is the innermost of the building's five concentric rings and the windows provide an excellent view of the central courtyard of the Pentagon, which is affectionately known as "ground zero"—a reference to it being the spot where Soviet nuclear warheads will fall in the event of World War III. The lunch counter that sits in its center is known, of course, as the ground zero café.

A couple of hundred feet in front of me, there's a small cluster of people milling about and one of them starts waving his right arm. He's trying to get my attention and calls my name. Who the hell can it be? I'm tempted to turn around and take an alternate route, but there's something familiar about the arm-waver's voice and my curiosity is aroused. As I near the group, I see that the one calling out my name is the Red-haired Major.

He's almost unrecognizable. His clothes are a weird mash-up of battle dress gear and some kind of native garb. Good God. What's he up to now? Maybe I should have turned around.

"Cattani! Cattani! Come over here. Come on. There're some guys I want you to meet."

I stop in front of my old boss. He's with three men who must be Mujahedin officials from Afghanistan, judging by their clothing and overall appearance. The Red-haired Major envelops me in a bear hug. "Cattani, how the hell are you? Jesus, it's good to see you. What the hell are you doing in dress uniform? Are you going to a funeral?"

Laughing, I respond, "No. I'm the morning intelligence briefer. I just briefed the Air Force chief of staff. I have to dress up for him, you know."

The major seems genuinely appalled at my answer. "Christ, Cattani. Who did you piss off to get that shitty job? Why aren't you still in Germany doing real work?"

He's ignoring his guests, if that's what they are. "Sir, are you going to introduce me?"

Shaking his head, he rapidly switches gears. "Oh shit. Yeah, these guys work for Commander Massoud in the Panjshir Valley. You know who he is, right?"

Do I know who he is? Of course, he's the most famous of all the Afghan rebels fighting the Soviets. "Yes, sir, I know about Commander Massoud. It's a great honor to meet you, gentlemen. I'm Captain Kevin Cattani."

The three Afghan men bow and offer me a formal greeting. I can't believe these guys are actually here in the Pentagon. By the look on their faces, neither can they.

The Red-haired Major pulls me aside and says, conspiratorially, "Look, Cattani. I need to deliver these guys to a special office down the hall. Meet me in the main restaurant downstairs in fifteen minutes."

My workday is done, and I am ready to go home. "I'd love to sir, but I really need to lock up my briefing and go home and get some sleep. I have a class at Georgetown tonight."

He looks at me with something approaching horror. He rubs his eyes with balled fists and taunts, "'Waah, waah. I have a class at Georgetown tonight. Waah, waah. I don't think I can meet with you.' Jesus, Cattani. I'll see you downstairs."

"All right, I'll meet you in fifteen minutes. But you're buying lunch or breakfast or whatever this is."

He grins behind his enormous beard, which is heavily flecked with gray. "Okay!"

Downstairs in the cafeteria I get a bowl of soup and sit down at a table with a line of sight to the corridor. I won't be able to miss the older man entering the cafeteria from this vantage point. Naturally, he approaches me from behind instead and grabs me by the shoulders. "Gotcha!" He sits down across from me. "Why the hell are you on the Air Staff with all these Air Force Academy pussies? Why aren't you in Germany doing manly work?"

I'm too tired to argue with him and divert the conversation. "What are you up to these days?"

He puts his right index finger up to his mouth. "Shh. Don't tell anybody, but CIA just made me a two-star general equivalent! Senior Intelligence Service! How about that for a promotion?"

The promotion is huge and a major vote of confidence from the CIA leadership. "I'm happy for you. Good for you, sir. Fantastic!"

He beams. The United States government finally gave him his due for his decades of service and sacrifice. "The best part about it is that I can stay in the field. You won't believe the shit I'm up to. I need to get you read into this program. You'll fucking love it! I need somebody who speaks Russian and can kick some ass. You, my friend, can do both. I could use you. Interested?"

Clearly, those Afghans I just met have something to do with it.

"It's tempting. My girlfriend is going to Georgetown Medical School, and she'll be pissed if I leave her in DC alone."

He's warming to the task of recruiting me and a snitty girlfriend sounds like a weak excuse. "Shit, it ain't forever. Come over for a few months. I bet General Palumbo will agree. You need to get your ass out of here and do some real work before you turn into a pussy like the rest of the guys on the Air Staff. How did you get here anyway?"

I shake my head. "Don't sugarcoat it for me. Just tell me what you think. Well, I had to leave Germany back in . . . when was it? It was late April of '84. You know, after the incident in the bunker."

He nods and says, "Yeah, that deal was a bummer. Have you seen that weak-dick DIA deputy again?"

It occurs to me that I haven't seen the Red-haired Major in two and a half years. "No, thank God. I got a special deal to be a full-time student at Georgetown to get a master's degree in Russian Studies. General Palumbo pushed it through. You know that he's here at the Pentagon now—he's chief of Air Force Intelligence."

The older man looks impressed. "Yeah, I'm glad Palumbo got promoted. He's one of the good guys. And good on ya regarding Georgetown. It ain't Harvard, but hey. When did you start the briefing gig?"

"Well, I finished my master's at the end of August '85 and I came to the Air Staff to be a morning briefer. It's a good job—high visibility—and no one's shooting at me. I'm enrolled at Georgetown in the PhD program—part-time. I guess the Air Force expects me to work for a living."

Rubbing his beard, he replies, "That's a damn good deal you got—getting a master's degree at Georgetown. Of course, the bastards owe you after all the shit you've been through. Well, I've had it good since I retired from the Air Force. The Agency appreciates my talents—obviously. I love what I'm doing, which is more than I can say for you, am I right?"

I enjoy my high-level briefing job, but he won't understand me feeling that way. Some people on the Air Staff derisively call briefers like me "talking dogs." I imagine my old boss feels the same way. I've been doing this for over a year now and I am ready to do something new. "I'm ready for a change, but how would we go about doing this? I mean who do I talk to? I'd have to take a leave of absence from Georgetown. My life is complicated."

He's beaming again. "You don't need to do anything. I'll talk to General Palumbo. I'll grease it with the farm boys at Langley. You're gonna fucking love this shit."

Sandy is going to kill me.

1 October 1986

I get up to go to work at 11:00 p.m. Sandy is just getting home from Georgetown Hospital. She reacts predictably when I tell her about my encounter with my old boss. "You're not *ever* going anywhere again with the Red-haired Major! You understand?" Sandy is exhausted and short-tempered, although she is not one to mince words under any circumstances.

I don't want to sound defensive, but... "It's only for a few months. I realize it's a lot to ask but I'm going crazy at the Pentagon. You're so busy with med school, you won't even notice I've left."

She rolls her eyes theatrically. "Cattani, you can be an idiot for such a smart guy. You can't leave well enough alone, can you? There is some defect in your character. Life is good and you have to go fucking it up."

"Sandy, General Palumbo will probably never approve it, anyway. So, there's nothing to fight about."

Sandy stands in front of me like a defiant samurai. I love that look on her. "Look, Kevin, you are so full of shit, it's oozing out of you. You want to go and if you want to go, then Palumbo will let you go. You're his fair-haired boy." She's probably right, even if that last comment strikes me as a bit racist.

I sigh and say, "Let's not fight about it until there's something to fight about. Okay? I will see General Palumbo in the morning, and he will probably not approve of me leaving the Air Staff." I nearly forget to tell her something important. "Hey, what is your schedule like the next few nights?"

Sandy reviews her schedule in her head and says, "I have a 'relatively' free night tomorrow night. I am in med school, after all. What do you have in mind?"

"I am off the next three days and . . . well . . . my mother called me today."

Sandy looks at me with a new intensity. She knows that communication with my parents is a rare event. "Okay, what did your mother say?"

"My parents are coming to Washington for a wedding this weekend and she asked if we could get together for dinner. They will get here tomorrow afternoon and will stay somewhere in Arlington. Should I call her in the morning and tell her we can meet them tomorrow night?"

Sandy looks at me with a blend of curiosity and apprehension— and anger. "Your parents? You mean after all the time I've known you that I'm finally going to meet your parents and you just drop it into the conversation like it's no big deal?"

I shrug, "In my defense, my mother just called me this afternoon and it was a surprise to me, too." We glare at each other like two cowboys waiting for the other to draw his gun first.

Finally, Sandy says, "Okay. I'll meet your mysterious parents. You and I have lived together in Georgetown for over two years now and your parents live a four-hour drive from here and I've never met them. Don't you think that's weird? Are they mythical? Were you born in a laboratory?"

She is right. It is weird.

"Kevin, I will meet them tomorrow night. I just wonder why it has taken so long." She turns away and goes into the bathroom to get ready for bed.

I walk outside, get in my car, and go to work. On the short drive to the Pentagon, I contemplate how many words exist in the English language that mean catastrophe. I come up with quite a few. I wonder which one will best describe Sandy's first meeting with my parents.

2 October 1986

General Palumbo's executive officer calls my direct line and orders me down to the general's office. Every time I've gone into Palumbo's office, whether here in the Pentagon or in Germany, he's always sitting in the same pose behind his desk. His reading glasses are perched on his nose, his eyes are cast down on paperwork, and he's oblivious to anything else in the world.

I stand in front of his desk. He knows I'm here. I know he knows it. Why doesn't he look up at me? Finally he speaks. "So, Captain, you want to go to Pakistan with the Red-haired Major. Is that right?"

How does he know everything already? Every time I get called to his office, General Palumbo already knows my business. "Well, General, if it's feasible . . . that is, if you think it's a good idea, then maybe I should consider it?"

Palumbo looks at me quizzically, "Either you want to go, or you don't. Which is it?"

I must look like an idiot. "I think it would be good experience for me, sir. It's probably my only chance to actually confront the Soviets in a shooting war."

Palumbo sits back in his chair and looks at the ceiling. "I need you as a briefer. You're my best guy. Don't tell anyone I ever said that. Still, it might be good to have one of our guys over there in Pakistan. The Army has people. I don't. I'd like to have someone on the ground." He is having an internal debate, and I am a spectator.

"Are you and your girl ready for this?"

No. No, we aren't. "Sir, it's only for a few months—right? We should be okay."

Palumbo looks down at his desk and then up at me and shakes his head. He thinks I'm being . . . stupid. "If you go, you need to keep your head on a swivel. Understood? I'll get you briefed on Operation Cyclone. You'll have to go out to Langley for that. Then, you can decide if you still want to do it."

I get home from work late in the morning and call my mother.

"Kevin, we're just about to leave home and drive up to Washington. Where should we meet you for dinner? Your father doesn't want to go to an expensive place."

I hear my father in the background. He tells my mother "Make sure that hotshot doesn't take us someplace for dinner that requires taking out a second mortgage." Christ. Same old shit from him.

"Kevin, your father says—"

"I heard him. I heard him. Where are you staying—exactly?" She tells me and I reply, "I know a couple of good spots near your hotel that aren't pricey. I will meet you at the hotel at six o'clock. Sandy will meet us at the restaurant. She'll come directly from Georgetown."

"Great. I am excited to finally meet your Sandy."

"Does he know that she isn't White?"

My mother whispers into the receiver, "I will try to tell him during the drive today. You know how he is. He still hates the Japanese from his time in the Pacific during the war. He's a little better with the Blacks these days—

"So, you've never told him that Sandy is half Black and half Japanese."

"There's never been a good time. Believe me. I will try today."

Oh my God. This dinner is going to be a disaster. This is why I have kept Sandy from meeting my parents—my father, specifically.

I arrive at the Quality Inn where my parents are staying a few minutes before 6:00 p.m. I am bushed because I was at the Pentagon from 1:00 a.m. until 11:00 this morning. I slept for a few hours this afternoon, went for a short run, and then drove over the Key Bridge to Arlington to this worn-out hotel, which is dwarfed by high-rise buildings housing defense contractors and technology companies. The hotel lobby smells of chlorine from an adjacent indoor pool that must have been quite an attraction when this place opened decades ago. I sit down on an overused sofa where I have a good line of sight on the two lobby elevators and sink deeply into its uncomfortable cushions. I pray that my father will be on good behavior tonight and I hope my mother warned him in advance that Sandy is not a blue-eyed blonde.

I wait for a few minutes and see my parents emerge from an elevator. It is a struggle to extricate myself from the depths of the sofa, but I manage to stand up as my mother rushes across the lobby to hug me.

"Hi, Mom."

"Kevin, it's so good to see you. It's been so long," she gushes as she squeezes me hard.

"Hi, big guy." My father reaches for my right hand, which is pinned against my mother's back. I manage a weak handshake and he releases my hand while my mother continues to hold me with a strength that I did not know she had.

Finally, she lets me go and looks at me. "You look good, Kevin. Is everything okay?"

My father answers before I can. "Why wouldn't he be okay? He's got a cushy job at the Pentagon with the big brass. It's not like he's flying jets off an aircraft carrier during wartime, for Christ's sake."

I shake my head. "I'm fine. We should get going. Sandy will meet us at the restaurant. She's driving over from Georgetown."

"Yeah, so she's going to med school on my nickel, huh? John Q. Taxpayer is paying for her to get a fancy education at Georgetown." My father takes a dim view of anyone who works for the government or who "feeds at the taxpayer trough," including people in the military.

"Oh, Roger, don't get started on all that again." My mother rolls her eyes. She is accustomed to my father's judgmental nature. "Kevin, will you ride with us?"

"No, I'll drive myself and you can follow me." There is no way I am riding with them. I want my own car in case I need to escape.

"But don't drive like it's the Indy 500, Kevin. I don't know my way around here, so don't lose me!" My father doesn't care for my driving style and never misses an opportunity to let me know it. Who does he think I learned it from?

There are several Pines restaurants in the Washington area—the Pines of Rome, the Pines of Florence, and so on. They have a decent mix of rustic southern and northern Italian food, and the prices are modest. We are going to the Pines of Naples, which is close to my parents' hotel. Thankfully, the drive to the Pines is uneventful, and my parents and I arrive at the same time. As I park, I search for but do not see Sandy's car, which is a good thing because I would not want her waiting for us.

The restaurant is crowded but we get a decent table in a corner that is somewhat protected from the din created by the other patrons. Our waiter asks for drink orders. "Let's have a bottle of Montepulciano," I tell him.

"That's too expensive," my father objects.

"I'll pay for it, Dad. Don't worry about it."

My father looks at me harshly. "Really? All right, moneybags. I would've ordered the house Chianti."

Yeah, I am sure you would.

My mother tries to settle the skirmish. "It's all right, Roger. I'm sure Kevin's wine will be delicious."

The waiter disappears and a moment later Sandy arrives.

Sandy looks tired and uncharacteristically disheveled after a long, exhausting day of classes and lab work. Tiredness cannot disguise her beauty, however, and my mother leans over and whispers to me, "Oh my Kevin, she's beautiful."

I nod in agreement, stand up, and kiss Sandy. "Hi, baby."

"Hi." She puts down her purse, smiles at my parents, and remains standing.

My father does not bother to stand up, which strikes me as very rude. I am certain Sandy notices, too. "Let me introduce you to my parents, Catherine and Roger Cattani."

Sandy extends her hand to my mother. "How do you do, Mrs. Cattani."

My mother takes Sandy's hand warmly and says, "I am so glad to meet you—finally. You are lovely! My word!"

"Thank you." Sandy removes her hand from my mother's grip.

She starts to reach across the table to shake my father's hand when he squints at her and says, "What are you?"

Startled, Sandy draws back her hand and replies, "Excuse me?"

"I don't know what you are. Catherine, I had no idea Kevin's girlfriend was . . . whatever she is."

Oh . . . my . . . God. This is the nightmare scenario I feared. I am angry, and I bet Sandy is outraged. I ask, "Dad, what are you saying?"

He shakes his head in disgust while Sandy remains standing. It is an exceptionally awkward moment. Abruptly, Sandy picks up her purse as if she intends to leave. With impeccable timing, the waiter appears with the bottle of wine I ordered, shows me the label, and begins to open it.

My father answers, "Well, I'm just saying that I don't know what the hell she is. Is she a Black or a Oriental or what? I don't know.

I can't tell." He is clearly exasperated and looks around the table for someone to blame. He obviously feels that he has been tricked into coming to dinner under false pretenses. I wonder if my mother even attempted to warn him. My guess is that she did try and that he ignored her and now he is surprised because he did not listen to his wife's counsel.

"Kevin, I think I should leave. You can stay if you want." Sandy glares at me, turns around, and starts to walk across the dining room toward the door.

I look at my father with murder in my eyes. "What the fuck is wrong with you?"

Bewildered, he shakes his head, throws up his hands, and says loudly, "What? What? What are you talking about?"

"You motherfucker." I throw cash on the table for the wine. "Goodnight, Mom. I hope you have a nice weekend."

My mother shakes her head as if she cannot believe what is happening. "You can't leave. I want to see you. We just got here."

Our family tussle is creating quite a scene, and the restaurant manager starts to walk toward the table. I wave at him and indicate that everything is cool and that I am leaving. He nods and goes back to the front of the restaurant.

My father shouts, "Where are you going? Your mother wants to see you. We drove all this way to see you, and this is what you do! Typical! You're a goddamn prima donna. Just go if you are going!"

I lean across the table toward him, trying to resist the urge to strangle my old man. "You have to fuck up everything, don't you! I knew this was a mistake. We can't have a normal meal like a normal family. You've gotta show everybody—especially Sandy—what a fucking, out-of-control racist you are."

"Kevin don't go," my mother sputters. She starts to cry.

"Sorry, Mom." I feel awful for her. I know she was anticipating this dinner with hope, and she was genuinely excited about meeting Sandy. I walk away from the table.

From behind my back, I hear my father yell, "Let him go. He's so goddamn high and mighty. To hell with him."

I rush out of the restaurant and into the parking lot, looking frantically for Sandy's car. It is nowhere to be seen. She is gone. I wonder if she went back to our apartment or back to campus or somewhere to get a drink and decompress. What a fiasco. My father is a trainwreck, and he is an expert at crashing into everyone and everything around him.

CHAPTER EIGHTEEN

THE BEAR WILL GO OVER THE MOUNTAIN

General-Major Ivan Levchenko, GRU, Soviet Air Defense Forces
Moscow, Russia, USSR, and Afghanistan

3 October 1986

My brother-in-law was released by the MVD this morning. I know his freedom is due to General Ivashutin's intervention. I also know that Oleksandr and Oxana must return to Kiev, and I must be the one to tell them. It will be an unpleasant conversation.

As for my return to Afghanistan, it is imminent. President Gorbachev calls Afghanistan "a bleeding wound." It's an apt metaphor. I feel like it's bleeding all over my marriage. Boyka is terribly upset, and she cries openly. I've never seen her so overwrought, and it's soul crushing.

Oxana has prepared dinner for us this evening and I was looking forward to a quiet night in our flat. Unfortunately, our circumstances dictate that this is not to be.

When we sit down to eat, Boyka says, "Afghanistan has changed you and I don't like the change. I need you home with me. Can't you cut your tour short?"

"Boyka's right, Ivanko." Oleksandr offers. "You need to get out of there. Come back to Moscow. Look, brother, choose the harder right instead of the easier wrong."

Sometimes Oleksandr makes my blood boil. He can be an arrogant ass and my boss just got him released from prison avoiding perhaps an even worse fate. "Brother, let me assure you that the harder *right* in my case is to choose to serve in Afghanistan, separated from my wife and in near-constant danger." What does he know of my career? Of the war? He's in no position to lecture.

Oxana unhelpfully adds, "Ivanko, the war is a disaster. Why is it your duty to go to a place no one cares about and kill people no one knows? It's not like you're killing fascists! I can understand serving the country in Germany. But Afghanistan? It makes no sense to me whatsoever."

I hate the Ukrainian nickname Ivanko, and my sister-in-law knows it. Why are they ganging up on me? I understand my service is difficult for them to comprehend. I only wish they wouldn't show their concern by berating me.

"Look, my job is to save the lives of Soviet soldiers. I keep weapons from entering Afghanistan, weapons supplied by our enemies: the Americans. I have been given an important mission to fulfill. My duty is to do the hard thing. I have chosen the *harder right*, not the easier wrong. This is very difficult for me, and all of you are making it harder."

After that, we sit and eat in silence for quite some time.

As we finish the meal, I know I must tell Oleksandr and Oxana to leave Moscow. "Oleksandr, we are happy to have you home safe and sound. I cannot share details, but I will assure you that your release is due to the work of the GRU and its top leadership."

Oleksandr interrupts. "Are you telling me I ought to thank the Soviet GRU for my freedom? I never should have been arrested in the first place. It's an outrage."

Oxana and Boyka nod their vigorous assent to Oleksandr's outburst.

"Allow me to finish, brother." I take a deep breath to give myself the courage to continue. "Your ambitions for Ukrainian independence are viewed in Moscow as treasonous." Oleksandr begins to interrupt again but I wave at him to be silent. "Your overt sentiments and actions are dangerous for you and Oxana and they place me under suspicion for harboring a traitor. This is serious business and those in power will not permit it any longer—certainly not here in Moscow. Therefore, I must tell you that you should return to Kiev as soon as you can make preparations. While I am in Afghanistan, I will not be able to help you as I did in this recent instance. I hope you understand."

Oxana slams her palm on the table with such force that one of the plates falls and crashes on the floor. "We will not be intimidated by the fools in the Kremlin! Oleksandr's arrest was a violation of due process and his human rights. We should stand and fight in Moscow and not return to Kiev with our tails between our legs!"

Oleksandr pats his wife's hand and says, "Our brother is right, Oxana. The Kremlin doesn't care about human rights and due process is whatever they want it to be. I was lucky to be released so quickly and I know it. It is only reasonable for us to return to Kiev. It is safer for you, me, Boyka, and Ivanko. We can continue our activities there and hope for a more propitious time for our goals to be achieved. I admit that I am homesick for Ukraine anyway."

I am pleasantly surprised and impressed with Oleksandr's statement. Oxana begins to protest but he pats her arm, and she quiets down.

Boyka asks me, "How much trouble was Oleksandr in? Was he in danger of being sent to the Gulag?"

I shrug. "My love, it is hard to say. It is important for all of you to know that I have powerful enemies and they will use any weapon they can find to hurt me. Right now, Oleksandr is such a weapon. I wish things weren't like this, but we have to accept reality."

Oleksandr takes a long drink of wine and declares, "It is settled. Oxana and I will return to Kiev as soon as we can get our things together. Thank you for your hospitality here in Moscow." He raises his glass to me, and I reciprocate.

It pains me that the three of us will leave Boyka alone in Moscow, but it cannot be helped.

6 October 1986

My farewell with Boyka is heartbreaking. I assure her I'll be home in January for my annual leave. She punches my shoulders as I hold her. Never has it been so hard for me to leave my beautiful wife. Am I a failure as a husband? What am I doing with my life that it causes her such pain? Despite my brave speeches, leaving Boyka doesn't feel honorable.

Oleksandr insists on driving me to the airport. I just want to be left alone. I assure him my official driver will get me to the plane on time and he shouldn't worry about it, but he brought his own car with him from Kiev, and he insists. I think he secretly wants to take a drive outside of the oppressive environs of Moscow proper. Along the way, Oleksandr whistles along with a popular song playing on the radio that I fail to recognize. The weather is unusually sunny and fine, which puts him in a cheerful mood. I'm glad someone is happy. I grimace at his off-key whistling as we ride along the highway to Sheremetyevo Airport. From the look of it, the highway was repaired recently, and the ride is smooth—unusual for the roads around Moscow.

He stops whistling and turns down the radio volume. "I hope you haven't minded us squatting in your apartment. It has done the sisters good to be together, especially while you are playing Genghis Khan in Afghanistan. We will be on our way by the end of the week." He turns toward me and smiles, his eyes lit by his natural good nature.

I sigh. "Yes, brother, you know I don't want Boyka to be alone. It has been good for her to have company. Unfortunately, you must get out of Moscow for your own safety."

Oleksandr nods in sympathy and agreement. He drives on in silence until pulling up to the terminal entrance. He jumps out of the car, opens the trunk, and pulls out my bags. Oleksandr calls for a porter to assist me. "After all, a general officer cannot be seen carrying his own bags, can he?" He smiles and pulls me toward him in a firm hug. He kisses me three times on the cheeks. "Brother, stay alive. Keep safe and come back home to us in one piece." He pulls away and looks into my eyes. Tears are pouring down his cheeks.

I'm moved, and I thank him in a husky, hoarse voice. I turn my back to him and wave my right hand as I walk into the terminal building. It is a sad ending to my home leave and a premature end to his stay in Moscow. I walk away quickly. I cannot allow Oleksandr to see me crying.

7 October 1986

All too swiftly, I'm back in Afghanistan, confronted by the challenges and horrors of this strange war. President Gorbachev has directed that our withdrawal from the country commence soon with the redeployment of six regiments later this autumn or early in the new year at the latest. Apparently, Gorbachev hopes that once they see evidence of our intention for a general withdrawal, the Americans and Pakistanis will reciprocate by cutting back on their support to the Mujahedin. He seems like a good man, but his thinking in this regard is preposterous and naive. In fact, all the evidence indicates that the Americans are stepping up their weapons transfers along the border with Pakistan, no matter what we do.

8 October 1986

The first full day that I am back at my office at Bagram Air Base, I have an unusual visitor. It's an Afghan woman, a medical doctor, who was a senior official in the national health ministry until the recent change of Afghan presidents. She worked for the Babrak Karmal administration, but Karmal was deposed this past May, having fallen out of favor with the Kremlin and the KGB.

Her name is Anahita Samar. Educated in the United States and in Afghanistan, Dr. Samar is fluent in English and a strenuous advocate for the rights of women. An avowed socialist, she has been a leading voice for social justice in Afghanistan for decades.

"Good morning, Dr. Samar. How can I help you?" I haven't been prebriefed on why she asked for this meeting, but I have been told that she will have an agenda. I am impressed that she made the trip to Bagram from Kabul. It is not particularly easy or safe these days.

Dr. Samar sits across from me at a low table and pours tea from a delicate pot. She hands me a cup and then pours one for herself. It's a very self-confident gesture. "General Levchenko, it has come to my attention that you issued a directive to your troops demanding that they respect the rights of Afghan citizens, especially women. I want to thank you, in person, for your efforts." She speaks English with an American accent—a midwestern accent if I'm not mistaken. She has an elegant coif and expensive-looking clothing that combine to give her an air of sophistication and class. I suppose that being a socialist doesn't mean that one can't present well.

"Thank you, madame, for your kind words. It is a top priority of mine that my men operate within the strictures of the International Law of Armed Conflict. Discipline is essential, especially regarding troops who are in close contact with the civilian population."

She smiles and replies, "It is refreshing to encounter a Soviet officer of such quality. Your English is excellent, sir. How is it that you speak the language so well?"

"Madame, I am a career intelligence officer who has specialized in American affairs for most of my time in uniform. I began English language study when I was only six years old."

Dr. Shamir appears impressed. "Fascinating. So unusual for a senior Soviet officer—a general officer—to be fluent in English."

"If I may ask, where did *you* learn to speak English?"

She laughs slightly and looks at me with great intensity. "I have a nursing degree from Michigan State University in America. Learning English was a prerequisite to entering the program."

"You must have had excellent teachers and have been an outstanding student. How may I help you?"

"Sir, I'd like you to advocate with your superiors on behalf of Afghan civilians, especially women. I suspect that an educated man such as yourself comprehends how life for women has deteriorated in my country over the past decade. Kabul was once a place where a woman could gain a fine education and dress in the latest Western fashion without fear of reprisal. Perhaps one day it will be so again. Until that day, I want to solicit your support for my effort to get all Soviet troops in Afghanistan to adhere to international law. It's fine for your elite Spetsnaz troops and GRU men to get in line, but the problem is with the average Soviet conscripts and their officers. The latter either can't or won't control their men and the former are boys that often don't know any better." Her voice rises dramatically as she makes her case.

During my brief time in the country, I've not met an Afghan woman who is so assertive and so forceful an advocate for a cause. "Madame, I'm sure you realize that men under my direct command will obey me or suffer the consequences. I fear my influence with units outside of my chain of command will be limited. I don't want to mislead you about the extent of my sway in this matter."

She fixes me with her eyes with an almost frightening intensity. Then, she drops her gaze and looks dejected. Even her elegant hairdo looks a bit deflated. I don't want to disappoint such an impressive woman, but I know the 40th Army hierarchy will not take well to a lecture from me about international law. It's simply the way things are. I sense that she's carefully considering her response.

Finally, she says, "I think I understand General. You have internal politics inside the Soviet Army just like any other institution. Perhaps you might sway—I like that word—others by the example you set. Is that possible?"

Frankly, I doubt it. "Madame, I will do my best to honor your request. I agree with you, of course, about the need to protect civilians, especially women and children. I think you already understand as much from the directive I've issued. If my example influences others and if I can push things in a positive direction with the 40th Army, I will do so. You have my assurance."

We both rise and I extend my hand.

She squeezes it tightly in both of hers and says, "I sincerely hope that you will remain safe during your time in my country. I believe you are a good man and that you will do what you can to honor my request. Thank you."

I bow slightly and reply, "You're welcome. And thank you for visiting with me today. I hope it won't be the only time we meet. Goodbye and may God's blessing be upon you on your return trip to Kabul."

She smiles broadly. "Why General Levchenko, you're not a Muslim, are you?"

"No madame, but I do admire Islam's traditions and those of the Orthodox religion, as well."

"Well, I won't say goodbye for I hope to see you again, General. May God's blessing be upon you and keep you safe."

Later that afternoon, one of my junior officers briefs me on the day's intelligence situation throughout the country. I receive these summaries each day before making my daily report to GRU headquarters in Moscow. Today's report contains nothing extraordinary, and the young man finishes and asks if I have any questions. Thinking of none, I thank him and take out a writing pad from the top drawer of my desk. I sense the young officer hovering.

"Is there something else?"

He shuffles his feet nervously and replies, "General, I was handed an urgent report right before I came to your office to brief you."

"Very well, what did it say?"

"It concerns the woman you saw today—Dr. Samar."

"What did it say?"

"It seems her vehicle struck a roadside bomb on the highway to Kabul."

"Is Dr. Samar all right?"

"General Levchenko, the report is preliminary, but it appears that no one in the car survived the blast. I'm afraid Dr. Samar was killed."

"I see." I pick up my pen and stare at it, pointlessly. "Is there anything else?"

"No, General Levchenko."

"See if you can confirm this preliminary report and provide me an update once you do."

"Of course, General Levchenko." The young man pauses and looks down at the floor.

"There's a lesson in this. War is indiscriminate. It kills good and evil alike. Dr. Samar was a force for good. It's important that we support those who have the courage to do good. We can only pray that they outlive the evil ones. You are dismissed."

"Yes, General Levchenko."

The 40th Army plans to intensify its cross-border raids into Pakistan in an attempt to stanch the flow of arms to the Islamic rebels. General Dubynin has ordered his commanders to "take the war to these bastards—even into Pakistan." He wants me to find those "goddamn Stingers" that are shooting down our aircraft at an alarming rate while we await proper countermeasures to be installed. Although I agree that going into Pakistan may make sense tactically, I don't think it will affect the strategic situation. Entering Pakistan also puts us in the same neighborhood as the CIA teams that are supporting the arms transfers to our enemies. We risk a direct confrontation with the Americans.

My KGB colleagues briefed me in Moscow about intercepted Mujahedin communications in the eastern part of Afghanistan. The rebels talk about the Stingers' capabilities, where to get training, and where to get the weapons. They call the Stingers *the righteous arrows of retribution*. Such a poetic phrase! Worthy of Pushkin.

10 October 1986

In his office in the old Anglican mission at Asadabad, Lieutenant Colonel Zaitsev has an ancient and fabulously ornate samovar sitting on a shaky wooden crate behind his desk. He told me on a previous visit that the samovar has been in his family for generations. Today, it's cold in his office and positively frigid outdoors, even though it's only October. The water in the samovar is steaming and emits a warm mist.

I accept a cup of boiling tea while Zaitsev updates me on the situation in his area. "Comrade General, I'll begin with Major Zhukov. The assurances that I've received that he's alive are credible. Unfortunately, assurances of life are all I was able to get from the Haqqani people. I don't know where he is being held or who is holding him. They made vague promises of eventual release, but they refused to share any specifics with me. It's also clear that they know that Zhukov works directly for you—they know that he's a high-value prisoner due to that association, which means they're unlikely to harm him, or release him for now."

"Colonel, tell me, will the new operations ordered by the 40th Army commander affect Zhukov's situation? How will the Islamic groups react when we raid their camps in Pakistan? Shouldn't we do all we can to secure his release *now*, before the raids?"

Zaitsev sips his tea and contemplates how to answer my questions. "Yes, our attacks will raise the stakes for everyone, especially Zhukov. There also is the American factor. We know there are a couple of CIA teams operating just across the Pakistan border, delivering Stingers and monitoring distribution. We also hear that the Americans are now interacting directly with Commander Massoud in the Panjshir Valley—bypassing the Pakistanis. As you know, Massoud is still the most capable of all the Mujahedin leaders. So, you see the Americans are becoming *more* active, even as we withdraw six regiments. I imagine the Americans will be increasingly aggressive in their support of the rebels."

"I see." Zhukov's fate seems bleak. "Zaitsev, you also should know that I heard in Moscow that Gorbachev will propose something big at next month's Central Committee meeting—his intent is to withdraw *everyone* from Afghanistan within one year, or at most, two years."

The colonel reacts calmly. "That is big news but not unexpected. It's strange, isn't it? Here we are about to escalate our attacks, which will get a lot of good men killed, and the bigwigs in Moscow are planning to get the hell out of here as soon as possible! It makes no sense."

I'm sure we're both thinking that no one wants to be the last man killed in Afghanistan. We sit in silence for a moment and contemplate this insanity.

Zaitsev puts down his cup and says, "I've already instructed the troops that since Zhukov is somewhere in these mountains, everyone will need to keep their eyes and ears open for any sign of him. We've also quietly offered a reward for his release through intermediaries. It's risky because don't want the Haqqani gang to know that I am bypassing them."

As usual, Zaitsev speaks like the professional, prudent commander I know him to be.

"Thank you, Colonel. I appreciate all your efforts, including what you've done to locate Zhukov, of course." I pause and regard him. "I'll leave here tonight—after dark."

Zaitsev looks surprised. He'd assumed I would accompany him when his team conducts its cross-border operations. His force will conduct a feint, a maneuver to divert attention from the real assault force, which will be led by Colonel Sidorov.

"I think it's more important for me to accompany Colonel Sidorov and the main strike force. I want to be able to provide direct oversight to Sidorov's men, should that be required. I hope you understand."

My younger colleague nods. "Yes, sir. I understand but I want you to promise me that you'll be careful. Enemy snipers prey on senior officers. We need you alive and in command, General."

I appreciate his vote of confidence more than he realizes. I shake his hand and he grips mine strongly.

Clearing his throat, Zaitsev says, "At least allow me to feed you before you go, sir. The men are preparing quite a feast, I'm told. It should be excellent."

After an outstanding supper of grilled fresh meats and local vegetables, I make my way to the airfield and the helicopter that will fly me through the night to Jalalabad and the command of Colonel Sidorov. I will accompany his force when he enters Pakistan to hunt for Stingers. I tell myself that this operation will be worth its high risk if we can keep at least some of the American Stingers out of the hands of our enemies.

I wonder if we'll encounter one of the CIA teams on the other side of the high mountains and how each side will handle it if we do. The last thing we need is a direct confrontation with armed Americans.

CHAPTER NINETEEN

OPERATION CYCLONE

*Captain Kevin Cattani, US Air Force Intelligence
Langley, Virginia and along the Northwestern Frontier, Pakistan–
Afghan Border*

23 October 1986

It has been three weeks since the disastrous dinner with my parents. Because of what happened with my father that night, Sandy is convinced it would be a mistake for us to get married and that it's best for us to go our separate ways. She decided that I should be the one to move out of our apartment, especially since I am leaving Washington anyway to go "play war" with the Red-haired Major. If I look at our situation objectively, Sandy is right. She is in med school and our apartment is only blocks from the Georgetown campus. I decide to rent a basement suite in a house in McLean, Virginia. The CIA headquarters is a short drive away, and the house is owned by a senior CIA officer who is a friend of the Red-haired Major.

I know that Sandy always feared—even expected—that we might not work in the long run, and my father's prejudice was the last straw. I am depressed over the entire situation. My mother called me shortly after she and my father returned home from Washington.

She asked, "Is everything all right with you and Sandy? She seems like a lovely girl."

I told her the truth. "Sandy and I broke up right after we saw you. Your husband blew up our relationship, but for God's sake don't tell him because that's exactly what he wanted. I'm angry and very unhappy about it, but I am leaving the country soon anyway, so that will help me get on with my life."

There was a long pause on the line and then she said, "Kevin, I'm so sorry. Let me know if there is anything I can do."

"Well, yes there is. Keep him the hell away from me."

"And you're leaving the country? Where are you going?"

"I can't tell you. I never want to see him again and *that* you can tell him. Take care of yourself." I hung up and we have not spoken since then.

I feel completely and utterly unmoored. Sandy is out of my life and my relationship with my family is broken. Work is the only way to maintain my sanity.

One of my favorite lines from the movie *Apocalypse Now* is uttered by Martin Sheen's character, Captain Willard who said, "I wanted a mission and for my sins they gave me one." That is precisely how I feel about going to war with the Red-haired Major. I am ready to get the hell out of the Pentagon and take on a real mission and this is my shot to do it. One of the Red-haired Major's favorite sayings is *If you wear the uniform, then you must show up for every war*. Afghanistan is host to the biggest war in the world right now and I should be there. I think that Captain Willard would be. Goddamn right.

I've spent the better part of October with the CIA preparing to go to Pakistan: getting security indoctrinations, hearing analyst briefings, and performing weapons training. One meeting I attend is a high-level update presented to a United States congressman from Texas, Charlie Wilson, who is the major congressional sponsor of the Cyclone program—the code name for the effort to arm the Afghan Mujahedin. Dr. Bob Gillis, the deputy director of Central Intelligence, attends the briefing and tells me he's happy that I'm joining the program.

The CIA's program director for Cyclone, known only as Michael B, kicks off the session. He presents an overview of our weapons deliveries and the associated logistical and security issues. Congressman Wilson's mantra is *We got to shoot down those helicopters*. Michael B assures the Texas congressman that the Mujahedin have the weapons to shoot down plenty of helicopters.

One of the other briefers is from the Office of Soviet Analysis inside the CIA known as SOVA. This office is part of the CIA's Directorate of Intelligence—the analysis division of the agency. The analysts in SOVA discount Mikhail Gorbachev's public statements about Moscow withdrawing the 40th Army from Afghanistan. They believe that Gorbachev is attempting to sway world opinion and to provide the Soviets leverage in arms control talks with President Reagan. Even Gorbachev's announced withdrawal of six Soviet regiments before Christmas of this year is a ruse, according to the CIA analysts. I think the Agency assessment is wrong; however, the fact is that we simply don't have a good handle on what the Soviets intend to do.

The following day, I have a one-on-one meeting with Michael B. Since Cyclone is his baby, he wants to assess me himself. He thumbs through my personnel file while I sit in a remarkably uncomfortable chair in his small office.

"So, what do you think of our little program, Captain?" I begin to answer, and he cuts me off and continues to review my file. "That was a rhetorical question. No answer required. I do that sometimes. I ask questions you don't need to respond to—okay? Just pay attention and you'll figure it out. I see you managed to pass your polygraph. Good. It's like having your ass dragged through a knothole, isn't it? That poly is probably tougher than anything you'll confront in Pakistan. You passed your medical checks and you've gotten your shots. Are you in shape? You look like you're in shape."

I think this one is a real question, so I answer, "Yes, sir. I'm running six days a week and lifting weights three or four days."

"How fast?"

"Sir?"

He sighs and looks at the ceiling. "Jesus H. Christ. How fast do you run? Look, these aren't trick questions. Shout them out when you know the answers." He seems genuinely angry now.

"I ran a 10K road race last month in thirty minutes and forty-seven seconds."

He looks at me through his glasses. The lenses are so thick his eyeballs seem to float around behind them. "You've run a thirty-minute 10K? Are you shitting me? You must be shitting me."

"I'm not quite in that kind of shape right now."

Michael whistles and laughs, "I guess you won't have any trouble keeping up with my team in Pakistan. Do you understand your mission?"

I know that's not a trick question. "Yes, sir. We're to head north and meet first with Commander Massoud's people and see how our new direct deliveries to him are progressing. Then, we're to head south and audit Stinger deliveries to the Haqqani network and others. We'll be checking the Stingers, specifically, to make sure our master records are accurate. We don't want the Russians getting our Stingers."

Michael nods approvingly. "Yes, you'll be conducting an inventory of the Stingers everywhere you go. This is the most important thing you'll be doing. I want you to account for every weapon system and part. It's like doing the end-of-year inventory at a department store—right? Only a shitload more important!"

"Yes, sir. Copy."

"You guys need to make sure the Russians don't get their hands on any of my Stingers. The GRU will send teams out to steal them—Spetsnaz—you understand? Those are bad dudes and they've been fighting for almost seven years now and they know what they're doing—check?"

"Yes, sir. Check."

"You don't want to fuck with the Spetsnaz."

"Copy."

"I have to tell you that I wasn't too enthused about sending an Air Force guy—a goddamn zoomie—over there. You know what I said? I said, 'Why would we send a fucking zoomie over there?' It's a ground war. That's what I said."

"Yes, sir. I can see that." I'm not about to defend my qualifications. I know that Michael's are impeccable—years of Army Special Forces experience all over the world. Besides, he is probably trying to get a rise out of me with his "zoomie" crap.

He laughs again. "But I think you'll be okay. You've worked with the Red-haired Major before, and he raves about you. That's not normal for him—he thinks everybody is a shit bird, but he says that you fucking walk on water. All right, we're done. Go do something productive."

"Yes, sir. Thanks for your time."

Michael gets in the last word. "My time is your time, but only when I say it is." He laughs and I leave his office. I can hear him guffawing as I walk down the hallway.

1 November 1986

I rendezvous with the Red-haired Major in Islamabad, Pakistan. Of course, he's now in the Senior Intelligence Service and one of the CIA's most senior paramilitary officers, but he'll always be the Red-haired Major to me. It's still hard for me to come to grips with the fact that my old boss is the equivalent of a general officer now.

In the last several months, the United States has delivered some two hundred Stinger missile systems to Pakistan. Most of them are being distributed to the Mujahedin by the Pakistan intelligence service—the ISI. The role of the Red-haired Major's team is to ensure that the precious weapons are not being sold to third parties or otherwise being mishandled in such a way that the Soviet Spetsnaz might get their hands on them.

A Pakistan Air Force helicopter flies our small team—me, the Red-haired Major, and two CIA Special Activities guys named Brad and Phil—to Peshawar and then on to an encampment just east of the Khyber Pass. A helicopter is the ideal way to see this glorious country—a region I've dreamed about seeing since I was a kid reading Rudyard Kipling. It's hard to believe I'm here. It feels like I'm in a Hollywood movie—*The Man Who Would be King*, specifically. Across the mountain from us sits the ancient Afghan city of Jalalabad, on the main road on the western side of the Khyber Pass. A GRU Spetsnaz brigade is based there. The Spetsnaz are tough, battle-hardened troops you want to avoid. It is more than a little weird to think that this formidable force is positioned just over the mountains from us.

Our own camp looks like it's been stitched into the side of a mountain so precariously that it might fall off if the stitches don't hold. Conifers cover the steep hillside above us and the wind roars and swirls ferociously most of the time, sounding like a jet engine when it picks up speed. Newly fallen snow coats our tents and equipment almost every night and the morning frost on the trees gives the place a fairyland, ethereal quality—peaceful and spiritual.

11 November 1986

Over the past ten days, I've been up and down the border region with the Red-haired Major, traveling by helicopter, truck, and on foot. The terrain is as beautiful, rugged, and desolate as I had imagined as a kid reading about exotic places like the Khyber Pass. At this time of year, mornings in the mountains are usually foggy, but some days start with an unbelievably clear sunrise, the sunlight so bright that it reflects off the snow-covered hills in such a powerful way that it's painful to the naked eye.

We've trekked as far north as Commander Massoud's territory, in the mountains adjacent to the Panjshir Valley. The CIA is supplying Massoud's forces with weapons directly. Neither Massoud, nor the CIA, wants to use the Pakistani ISI as middlemen. Massoud also has demanded we provide his forces with more advanced weaponry, including Stingers. To meet the legendary leader, we crossed into Afghanistan, led by a couple of guides.

Massoud himself is Tadjik and the CIA guys on our team—Brad and Phil—both speak Pashto, so we had to hire Tadjik-speaking guides to take us to Massoud's camp. The Tadjik ethnic group lives in the region where the borders of Pakistan, Afghanistan, and the Soviet Union converge. After a lengthy and arduous hike to reach Massoud, we approached his camp just after midnight. One of our interpreters fired a rocket into the inky blackness—a signal to alert Massoud's men to our presence. Massoud's chief of counterintelligence and several of his men emerged from the mountain darkness, searched us, and confirmed our identities. Satisfied that we are not going to blow ourselves up in their midst, the Mujahedin led us to a stone house where we spent the night.

The following morning, we broke bread with Massoud's men. They treated us with the respect traditionally afforded guests—we were the first to wash our hands and eat the traditional dishes from common bowls. I was excited about meeting the legendary Massoud and I awaited his arrival like an impatient, star-struck teenager.

At the appointed hour, Massoud entered our guest house with four bodyguards. Of modest height, the great warrior is dark skinned with a face that exudes intelligence, sincerity, and openness. I was struck by his powerful presence—his charisma evident as he pleaded his case for Stingers. He also voiced his admiration for the Soviet Army, especially the Spetsnaz forces, but had nothing but antipathy for the regime in Kabul. He vowed never to accept a negotiated settlement with the Soviets' puppet government.

The Red-haired Major discovered a soul mate of sorts in Commander Massoud. The big man enthusiastically outlined a plan to provide Massoud's men with Stingers and the requisite training in the shortest amount of time possible. As the discussion concluded, the two senior warriors embraced, with Massoud practically disappearing in a crushing bear hug. Massoud's men exchanged worried glances—fearing that the red-haired man was about to suffocate their leader. They were visibly relieved when the embrace ended.

Suddenly, there was a deafening racket, and everyone looked up to the ceiling. Enemy helicopters! We ran immediately to a nearby bomb shelter. From the safety of the shelter, we heard rockets and cannon fire striking the buildings and ground above us. The hollow thuds were terrifying, but Massoud and his men sat impassively, completely unfazed. I was petrified and expected the ceiling to crash down around us and crush our bodies like insects, but it held firm.

After the attack ended, we scrambled from the shelter to find that the house where we had been meeting minutes earlier was on fire and half of it had collapsed from a direct hit. The Red-haired Major looked at Massoud with a huge smile on his face and roared with laughter like a man possessed by the spirit of an ancient god of war.

That concluded our parley with Massoud. Once night fell, we followed the same rocky trail we traversed the previous night, passing under the gloriously jagged peaks of the high mountains as we made our way back into Pakistan.

15 November 1986

Operation Cyclone has ramped up dramatically during the past year with exponentially more money being appropriated by Congress than in prior years. The money pays for much better weaponry and enables bigger cash payments to various warlords. After leaving Massoud, we trekked southward to inventory the Stingers that have already been distributed.

Today, we are well south of Massoud's area, in a village controlled by the Haqqani network. We've done miles of tromping up and down the mountains on foot and I continue to be amazed at the Red-haired Major's endurance, given that he's in his fifties now. I'm only thirty years old and I'm getting worn out.

Our Mujahedin hosts provide us with a small house to stay in while we conduct our Stinger inventory. As it happens, it was a guy from this very village who shot down the first Soviet aircraft with Stingers—three Mi-24 helicopters attempting to land at Jalalabad. He's a local legend now and we met him last night during our evening meal, where he was honored. A thoughtful, intelligent young man, he and I conversed in Russian for about an hour. I learned that he studied in Leningrad, and we compared notes on that beautiful city.

As I mentioned, the two CIA guys on our team are Pashto speakers. Their black hair and beards make them almost indistinguishable from one another. The older one is named Phil, and he has barely said two sentences since I met him. Brad, the somewhat younger guy, is much more talkative and it seems evident to me that he's still trying to figure out the Red-haired Major. Good luck!

Our temporary lodging is large enough for the four of us to bed down with some degree of privacy, which is a luxury for weary travelers like us. The wind is roaring, strong and cold at this high altitude, and it's good to have the shelter of a house—no matter how simple and austere. It's our first night here and I'm sitting cross-legged on the floor when a couple of local women enter the house with supper—a pot of steaming lamb stew and freshly baked pita bread. The older of the two women serves me a bowl of stew. I am famished and dip a piece of bread into the stew and savor the perfect balance of flavors.

As I eat, the Red-haired Major thunders into the house, trailing a wave of cold mountain air behind him. "Well, kids, ain't this a great hootch? Warm fire, warm food, and cold scotch." He pours himself a healthy glass of whiskey. He takes a deep draught and hands me the bottle.

Brad looks on with disapproval. He has made it clear that he disapproves of imbibing while we are guests in a Muslim country. I have decided that Brad has a bit of the missionary in him. The boss notices the judgmental look and decides to have a little fun at Brad's expense. "So, tell me, newbie, where'd you go to school? Where are you from?"

The younger CIA officer looks up and asks warily, "Why should that matter?"

Oh boy. That was not the correct response to give to the Red-haired Major. "Look, newbie, I'm just trying to get to know my men. It's important for me to know what makes you tick. The human resources guys at Langley have advised me to open up more to my team members . . . to show an interest. Hell, they want me to show more empathy. So, I'm showing you some goddamn empathy. Got it? Now, where the fuck are you from?"

Still suspicious, Brad, a former Green Beret officer, says, "I went to Syracuse University on a lacrosse scholarship. I'm from the south shore of Long Island."

The major's eyes light up. He's having fun now. "Syracuse! You're a fucking Orangeman? That's what you call yourselves—right? Orangemen. What the fuck does that even mean? What's an *Orangeman*, for Christ's sake? You played lacrosse? That's a good game I suppose—if you're a pussy. Are you a pussy, Mr. Orangeman?"

Brad scowls and turns red, which was the boss' hope, of course. He declares, "Lacrosse is a man's game. You gotta be tough to play lacrosse, especially at Syracuse. And I got a full-ride scholarship, too. I come from a working-class family, and it was a big deal for us."

My boss grins at me. "What do you think Cattani? Is lacrosse a game for pussies or men?"

Several of my friends played lacrosse at William and Mary and I used to run with them in the offseason. "Well, my experience is that you have to be tough and talented to play Division One college lacrosse. Syracuse is a legit program—a top program for lacrosse. Brad must've been damn good to get a full ride there."

The older man slaps his hands together. "There you have it. Cattani says you must be good *and* tough and if he thinks so, then that means something to me. I know Kevin doesn't look like it but he's a natural-born killer *and* an excellent judge of character. Ain't that right, Captain Cattani?"

I roll my eyes. I need to get some sleep. "Guys, enjoy yourselves. I'm going to bed. I'll take the little room in the back. Wake me up if you need me."

I get up from the floor and Brad does the same. Phil has already crawled into a side room. For some reason, Brad goes out the front door into the frigid night. Looking at my watch, I see that it's 10:00 p.m. local time. Where could he be going?

I go into the back room and curl up in the corner and close my eyes. I hope I can sleep. Most nights I'm so tired I don't remember my dreams. There are other nights when I have nightmares about Lydia Morelli. Well, not about her exactly, but about our fiasco in the East German bunker. If I am honest with myself, I admit that I do dream about Lydia and the night I turned her down at Bolling Air Force Base.

16 November 1986

I am sleeping relatively peacefully when someone kicks me hard shortly after midnight. I wake up. I'm disoriented for a moment.

"Christ. What time is it?"

Brad stands over me. "Can you get up?"

I roll up to my knees to ease the pain in my stiff lower back. I blink myself awake and ask, "What's going on?"

Brad says in an excited voice, "I went out to talk to a few of the elders after you went to bed." Brad speaks excellent Pashto and can talk to the locals without an interpreter. "They had an interesting story to tell me."

I can barely see him in the dark room. "Okay, what the hell did they tell you?" This guy is irritating me. I need to get some goddamn sleep.

Brad kneels and whispers, "There's a captured Soviet officer being held in the next village—he's a major. None of the fighters around here speak much Russian and they can't talk to him. I think they want to earn brownie points with the United States by letting us talk to him."

This sounds like a bad idea. "Where's our boss?"

Brad shrugs disinterestedly, "I dunno. He wasn't in the house when I got back. I woke up Phil, too."

This is a very bad idea. "Brad, think about it. We're a covert team. The only one who can authorize us to meet with a Soviet officer is . . . hell, I don't even know who has that kind of authority in this situation except the director of Central Intelligence or President Reagan."

Brad is unconvinced. "But think of all the great intel we can get from this guy. The Mujahedin haven't gotten much out of him. You speak good Russian. You should interrogate him."

I hear a familiar laugh—it's the Red-haired Major re-entering the house.

I walk back into the main room of the house with Brad following.

The boss' beard is so thick now, I can barely see his mouth when he speaks. "You won't believe what I just heard from one of the elders who speaks a tiny bit of Russian. The Mujahedin—the Haqqanis—they have a goddamn Soviet officer. They've apparently been holding the son-of-a-bitch for months. He's in the next village over. Can you believe this shit?"

Brad looks at me triumphantly. Gloating, he says, "Yes, sir. We're aware. I interviewed some of the elders myself and they told me the same story. We should talk to this Russian—right?"

The major strokes his beard, deep in thought. "I don't know. I want to interrogate the SOB but we're a covert team. Who has the authority to authorize us to talk to him? Fuck if I know."

I speak up, "Sir, how could we justify blowing our cover here to talk to one Russian. If he's been captured for months, then he probably won't have any good intel anyway. And, if the Soviets pay a ransom to get him back, then he'll be the one with good intel on us."

The older man mulls that over. "Cattani, you have a point. I don't like it, but you have a point. Hey, maybe the guy wants to defect? What if we talked to him because he's a potential defector? That would work, wouldn't it?"

This is nuts. I think we're all going crazy from the altitude in these mountains. "But we don't know if he's a defector. It's too risky."

Unfortunately, the Red-haired Major is warming up to the idea rapidly. "I'm in the goddamn senior intelligence service! If I can't make this decision on my own, then what the fuck is the rank good for? I ask you that, Cattani? Saddle up. We're humping over to the next village, pronto! We're going to talk to our Soviet friend!"

This seems like a very bad idea. Our little team of four, plus a couple of guides, bundle up as best we can to gird ourselves against the midnight coldness and harsh, soaring wind. The chill hits my bones as soon as we leave the small house. This hike is going to suck.

The moon is full, and we have good light on the rocky, steep path that leads to the mountaintop village. My heart rate spikes on the severe slope, and I warm up quickly. Despite my desire for a good night's sleep, I must admit that the scenery is spectacular in the moonlight: tall, jagged peaks, with stars blinking and meteors flashing across the purple sky.

The Red-haired Major walks beside me, huffing and puffing with the effort. He grins under his beard and says between heavy breaths, "Pretty cool—huh? Look at this place! Incredible! I bet this beats the shit out of selling insurance back in Bumfuck, Virginia, doesn't it Cattani?"

Insurance? "I never sold insurance in Virginia or anywhere else."

My old boss is thoroughly enjoying himself. "Yeah. That's my point. That's the beauty of it! You never had to sell insurance because you do unbelievably cool shit like this. It's times like these that make me feel sorry for my old classmates at Harvard. None of them have ever seen the sites we see or meet the crazy fucking people we meet." He waves his left arm in a wide arc. "I mean, look at these mountains. Look at the fucking stars! Have you ever seen anything like this?"

No, I haven't. It is a splendid sight that only a relatively few humans have experienced at this altitude. "It's awesome. Like an alien world." We walk a few more paces up the insanely vertical incline. "Just how far away is this village?"

He gasps for air and responds, "It's a little over one klick. But it's all uphill. Don't tell me you're tired!"

The trail is so steep and potentially treacherous that it takes us the better part of an hour to hike up to the village, which lies on a ledge overlooking a deep canyon. Down below us—way down below—I can see fires in the square of the village where we just departed. Our guides stop about twenty meters from the village wall. They call out a password in the darkness. I hear a faint response. The guides wave us onward, and we walk through a wooden gate into the tiny hamlet.

A local elder greets us and leads us to what appears to be the largest building in the village. We enter and are invited to sit on the floor. A roaring fire warms the room. I huddle in my heavy coat while the elder disappears into a side room.

He reappears in a couple of minutes, accompanied by an elderly woman. The woman speaks to Brad in Pashto, who then relays the message that the elder wishes us to follow them to a different building. Wearily, we stand up and follow the old man and woman outside into the bitter cold. We trudge across a tiny square to a small storage building.

It's noticeably colder inside than the house we just departed. We sit down on the bare, frigid floor. The room is devoid of furniture, rugs, or pillows. I am feeling miserable with fatigue. I look at my watch. It's 1:30 a.m. The old woman plops down next to me and smiles a toothless smile.

Two men in native garb stumble out of a backroom. They sit down on the floor a few feet from us. One of the men has a blended black and blond beard. That must be our Russian. The Red-haired Major nudges me and winks. That is my cue to speak.

I greet the Soviet officer in Russian. "Good evening, sir. Or, should I say, 'good morning'?"

The Russian removes his cap, revealing long, dirty blond hair. He looks at me intently but does not speak.

I continue. "I'm told that you are a Soviet major. I hope you are well. Do you require any medicine? Food?"

My questions elicit a weak smile, and he responds in upper-class Russian. "Good evening. You are Americans? All of you?"

There's no point in lying. "Yes, we are Americans."

He smiles broadly. "I've never met an American before. Do all of you speak Russian so oddly? You sound like a Tsarist officer when you speak." He smiles again and chuckles.

I return the smile. "Yes, I have been told that before. Are you well?"

His face turns serious. "I am well fed. I'm not sick. I haven't been beaten in months. However, I'd love some vodka if you have some. My hosts frown upon strong drink."

The Red-haired Major joins the conversation and says in broken Russian. "I have scotch back in the other building. I'll get you a drink after."

The Russian twists his mouth into a frown. "That sounds like bribery. But a beggar cannot be choosy. Are you CIA?"

I respond, "We're Americans. Let's leave it at that for now. How long have you been a captive?"

The Russian studies me closely and responds, "I was captured in late May. We were ambushed. My driver was a traitor who drove my vehicle into the arms of the enemy. That's how I was captured. My mates in the vehicle were taken away and executed. I've been beaten, interrogated, and shuffled from one group to another. I don't speak Pashto and few of them have any Russian." He seems preternaturally calm and even cocky for a man whose last months must have been a living hell.

"What is your name and rank, sir? Why do you think your life was spared?"

The Russian officer hesitates for a moment and then answers, "I am Major Anatoly Zhukov. Perhaps I was spared so these people can collect a ransom. Who knows?"

Zhukov? The Red-haired Major and I exchange glances. That's a famous name. "I see. Are you related to the famous Marshal Zhukov?"

"Yes. He was my great-uncle. I'm from a military family, you see."

Indeed. "Yes, you're from a very distinguished military family. What is your role in Afghanistan?"

Zhukov closes his eyes. "My role? You mean, my job? Well, what the hell. I'll probably never get home, anyway." He pauses. "I'm the executive officer to the general who commands all GRU units in Afghanistan." He makes this statement with more than a touch of pride.

GRU? A GRU officer? "Thank you, Major Zhukov. And, if you don't mind the question, who is the commanding general of the GRU in Afghanistan?"

He laughs with a touch of bitterness. "My boss? You mean you don't know? I assumed the CIA would know that. Well, all right. He is General-Major Ivan Levchenko."

This news hits me like a grenade. Levchenko! "Major Zhukov, I'm well-acquainted with General Levchenko."

The Russian's mouth drops open in stunned surprise.

I continue in Russian. "I have not seen General Levchenko since the fall of 1983. He's a fine officer. If you are his executive officer, then he will be searching for you."

Zhukov stutters, "You . . . an American . . . you know my general? How can this be? How can he know an American—like you?"

"Don't worry, Major. General Levchenko is no American spy. I'm certain that he is a loyal Soviet officer. He and I worked together at the Military Liaison Mission in East Germany on a very important project back in 1983. I have great professional respect for General Levchenko. He must be working toward your release."

The Red-haired Major sputters in English, "You know this guy's boss?" He strokes his beard. "How can we use that? This could be very interesting."

I switch to English. "Look, we need to help Zhukov. Levchenko saved my life in Potsdam. I'm obligated to return the favor."

"Cattani, think about it. He's GRU. Earlier tonight you didn't even want to talk to him and now you want to rescue his sorry ass? Don't let your personal feelings get in the way."

"Boss, I'm right about this one. Zhukov is GRU. He can be a great source. I know that Levchenko is one of the good guys. General Palumbo knows him and respects him, too. If we can return Zhukov to Levchenko, then we will *gain* leverage. If we can meet with Levchenko himself . . . I mean . . . it'll be a gold mine in terms of what we can learn about Soviet intentions in Afghanistan. That's the prize here. It will be an intelligence coup for us."

The Red-haired Major considers my argument. Zhukov looks at us with great curiosity. I assume that his English is limited if he has any at all. I hope I'm right.

My boss responds. "Well, if we could get a meeting with the chief of the GRU in Afghanistan, that would be a coup. You really think it's feasible?"

"I have an idea. I don't know if we can pull it off, but it's worth a shot. We could buy Zhukov's freedom. Then, we use someone in the Mujahedin to contact the GRU—they must have a means of communicating with the Soviets—maybe via the KGB. You know some of the Mujahedin are playing both sides of the street in this war." I pause to gauge his reaction. It looks like he's interested. "We could demand a meeting with Levchenko to do the exchange—to give Zhukov back to the Soviets."

The Red-haired Major strokes his beard harder. "If we could pull this off . . . but we're not in Germany. There are no established procedures for exchanges like we have in Germany at the Gleinicke Bridge. But still . . ."

"Sir, it's worth a shot. I think we need to try. Look, you know that the analysts at Langley complain we don't have good human intelligence on Soviet intentions in Afghanistan. Who could be a better source than Levchenko—the chief of the GRU in-country?"

"Cattani, I get it. Relax, you've convinced me. This could be a lot of fun!"

I switch back to Russian. "Major Zhukov, I have a proposition for you. Will you cooperate with us if we can secure your freedom and attempt to return you to General Levchenko?"

Zhukov's face registers shock. "Is that really a possibility? My freedom? If you can return me to General Levchenko, then I will tell you on my honor that you will have my full cooperation."

I stand up and encourage Zhukov to do the same. We shake hands. I switch back to English. "Sir, would you mind retrieving your Scotch? I'll stay here with Major Zhukov."

My boss nearly knocks me down as he rushes to give me and Zhukov an enveloping bear hug. "You bet. We'll seal this deal with a drink! But let's go back to the other house. This damn place is freezing."

Zhukov looks stunned at this apparent change in his fortune and smiles like a man reborn.

The Red-haired Major says in his rusty Russian, "Come on, Zhukov, let's drink by a warm fire!"

The old woman, who has not uttered a single word, beckons us to follow her to the other building. We walk briskly through the bone-aching cold across the small square, back to the house with its cozy fireplace.

Once inside, the mysterious woman tends the fire and sits down with remarkable agility in a spot in front of the blaze. Zhukov, my boss, and I bask in the warmth of the fire while we sip scotch. Phil goes to bed and Brad negotiates with the elder for Zhukov's release.

"He wants fifty thousand dollars for the Russian," Brad says, walking over to where the Red-haired Major and I are seated.

"Really, is that all? Well, we'll have to give him a promissory note. I'm not lugging around that much cash." The Red-haired Major shrugs and retrieves a paper and pen from his backpack. He composes a note and hands it to Brad.

Zhukov watches this exchange closely and begins to relax. He must understand English because it's clear that he comprehends what's happening. Back across the room, Brad completes his negotiation with the elder and gives us a thumbs up when he seals the deal for the Russian's release.

With great relief, Zhukov proposes a toast, and my boss and I drink with him. The Russian officer asks in surprisingly good English, "Can we speak English? I can't understand the big guy's Russian very well."

I suppress a smile. My boss replies, "Sure. I know my Russian's a little rusty."

The Russian begins to tell us about his fiancée back in Moscow. Zhukov is worried about her. "She may believe that I'm dead and marry someone else. You must understand that I don't really want to get married, but my fiancée is beautiful, and her father is a senior member of the Central Committee. She's a very good catch and I may not get so lucky again—right? You never know what will happen."

The Red-haired Major likes Zhukov and begins to regale him with a story from the Vietnam War. Zhukov listens intently to the tale of deception, deceit, and bloody battles in Laos and Cambodia. I'm usually riveted by his stories; however, the combination of overall fatigue, scotch, and a warm fire conspire to put me to sleep. It'll be dawn soon. I fall into a deep sleep. In my dreams, I hear helicopter rotors spinning and engines cranking.

Suddenly, someone is shaking me. My boss yells excitedly, "Wake up! Wake up, Cattani! I hear helicopters coming and they're not ours!"

CHAPTER TWENTY

THE BEAR WENT OVER THE MOUNTAIN

General-Major Ivan Levchenko, GRU, Soviet Air Defense Forces
Jalalabad, Afghanistan, and a Village in Pakistan

15 November 1986

Boyka's eyes were the first thing that struck me about her when we met. Russians know the type of eyes I'm talking about. They are sky blue and luminous to the point of translucence and are considered—rightly in my view—as a sign of great beauty. Men are transfixed and captivated by such eyes. I found myself falling in love immediately when I saw her. Of course, most men have the same reaction when they meet her. I've always thought that women with such eyes are the most striking of our Slavic beauties. They clearly have Nordic blood in their lineage. One sees these eyes more often on the streets of Leningrad than in Kiev where my wife was born.

Boyka would be gorgeous even without those eyes. The fact that she has them, combined with all her other physical attributes—beautiful, long blonde hair; classic, high cheekbones; and a lithe, yet voluptuous body—make her a rarity. I think of her while I'm on the flight from Asadabad to Jalalabad. Virtually all helicopter travel is after nightfall now. The entry of the dreaded Stingers into this war has changed the risk of flying, at least until we can get new flares and other equipment to mitigate this threat.

New intelligence, graciously provided by my colleagues in the KGB, maintains that there are as many as six Stinger systems located in a small village in Pakistan just beyond the southeastern edge of the Khyber Pass. That village and its Stingers are the objective of our new mission.

Colonel Sidorov is brave, but he can be careless with the lives of his men. I'd prefer he temper his courage with a dollop of prudence. He has a chronic need to prove his worth to his father, to the Kremlin, to the world, and to himself. Initially, he resisted my directive that all men under my command adhere rigidly to Soviet regulations concerning the treatment of civilians. Eventually, Sidorov implemented my order fully and his men are very well disciplined, which cannot be said for most Soviet troops in Afghanistan.

15 November 1986

I arrive at Jalalabad at 9:00 p.m. and Sidorov greets me on the flight line. He escorts me to his command center, where we will spend the next few hours reviewing his battle plan. I'm determined to leave nothing to chance. This upcoming mission is a high-risk one and it must be planned with great attention to detail. I wonder if Sidorov is up to the careful planning required.

I left Grishin at Bagram Air Base. I can do without his nonsense as we prepare for and execute a risky combat operation in enemy territory.

I also have ordered Lieutenant Colonel Zaitsev's task force to conduct a feint to the north at the same time Sidorov's helicopters cross the Khyber Pass. Zaitsev's helicopters will fly at a higher altitude than Sidorov's, where Pakistan's Air Force will be able to detect them.

This should divert Pakistani attention away from Sidorov's strike force. It is vitally important that we achieve tactical surprise when we swoop down from the mountains on the village containing the Stingers.

Sidorov's senior intelligence officer leads off the briefing. He shows aerial photography of the village, provided by Soviet Air Force reconnaissance, that is detailed and precise. The target village sits at an altitude of about 1,200 meters in a valley surrounded by mountains that aren't especially high by Pakistan's standards. Nothing about the town is exceptional. There is a central square surrounded by typical residential and commercial buildings. No structure is more than two stories in height.

The briefer—he's a major like Zhukov, but that is where the comparison ends—drones on, detailing potential landing zones in the vicinity of the village. He seems rather sleepy and bored, and he mentions nothing about potential air defense threats to our helicopters, which is ridiculous. The mission and our lives will depend on the survivability of our helicopters.

I look at my watch. It's nearing midnight and I'm growing impatient with this guy. "Major, our helicopter assault teams will be vulnerable to ground fire. Are you saying that the air defenses are nothing to worry about? What am I missing?"

The major answers slowly. "Comrade General, we do not believe there will be a threat from Stinger missiles on this mission. The information we have from the KGB is that the Stingers in this village remain sealed in unopened crates. The other air defenses are primitive."

He seems a bit offended that I would question his threat assessment. "All right, Major, the rebels are adept at shooting down our helicopters with anti-aircraft guns, rocket-propelled grenades, and Strella missiles, too. They don't have to use Stingers to kill us. Are you telling me there is no threat from those other weapons?"

Colonel Sidorov jumps into the discussion. "How about that, Major? After all, it will be dawn when we reach the landing zones, with ample light for the enemy to use nonguided weapons."

I stand up, stretch, and look at the men sitting around the conference table. Everyone is tired. Several of the officers look defeated—almost uninterested.

I point out locations on the map. "Look comrades. Here and here are ideal places for the rebels to place heavy machine guns and RPG grenadiers. I was trained as an air defense officer and those are the places where I would put my defenses. I want the attack helicopters to strike those areas first to secure the landing zones." I pause and pick up a photograph. "What's this? Here . . . above the village on a cliffside?" It looks like a small settlement, perched on a ledge of the mountain overlooking the valley. Christ, this hamlet provides overwatch of the main village. "It's an ideal spot for observation and for snipers. From that high ground they can direct fire against our air assault forces. And, as for the distance . . ." I grab a compass and do a quick calculation of the altitude of the tiny settlement compared to the main village. "It is about three hundred and fifty meters higher than the valley floor. It's a bit more than one kilometer in distance from the main village. A sniper team can most certainly reach the village square from that spot. At the very least, they can make us keep our heads down. We need to address this hamlet in our operational plan. Do you agree?"

Sidorov checks my calculations. He grabs his operations officer by the arm. "The general is right. We need to put fire on that hamlet to suppress any potential sniper activity. It is an ideal observation post for the entire valley floor. They'll be able to see our landing zones. We'll lose the element of surprise."

I'm glad I decided to come to Jalalabad in time to adjust this plan. Our assault force will launch in twenty-eight hours. We have time to adjust the attack plan, but just barely.

Sidorov is clearly ruffled. He takes over the briefing. "Comrade General, we will begin the assault with six Mi-24 gunships from Jalalabad. They will conduct preparatory attacks on our two landing zones—here and here." He points to positions on the map just north and south of the main village on the valley floor. "They also will suppress potential enemy air defense positions in the locations you just highlighted. Each of the 'Crocodiles' will have a squad of six assault troops, too."

Good, but not great. I press him further. "There may also be sniper positions carved into the mountainsides that don't show up in the Air Force photos. You need to put fire on those hillsides. Do you have enough aircraft to do this? Do I need to ask for more?"

Sidorov answers testily—he's not accustomed to being second-guessed by anyone, especially a GRU general like me who's never been in combat. "We have enough air support at Jalalabad to handle this operation. We can handle it."

I hope he's right. "Colonel, make sure that we have enough. There is no more important mission than this one anywhere in the theater. We can get more air support from Bagram if need be. I'm leaving it up to you."

He nods vigorously. "Yes, sir."

I turn to Sidorov's air operations officer—a lieutenant colonel. "How many Mi-8s have you assigned to land our troops? How many fully equipped troops can the helicopters carry at this high altitude?"

"Comrade General, the range we must travel is significant and we'll fly over mountain ranges, which are nearly two thousand meters high. Given those factors, each of the four troop-carrying 'Bees' can carry twelve fully armed men and have some room for maneuvering and contingencies. We have two additional Bees dedicated to transporting the Stingers once we locate them. You and Colonel Sidorov will each be aboard one of those helicopters, along with a couple of staff officers and medics. We will have a total of six Mi-8s, four of which will carry assault troops. In addition, as Colonel Sidorov stated, we'll have the six Crocodiles, each with a squad of six aboard."

I do some quick arithmetic in my head. "So, we will have forty-eight assault troops on the Bees and another thirty-six on the

Crocodiles. Do I have that right? Tell me how such a small force can secure this village? What if we encounter a force larger than our own? Remember that we will be on the other side of the mountains. We can't call upon the 40th Army's artillery or motorized infantry to come to our aid should things turn against us. We'll be on our own in enemy country! Can't we pull a couple more Mi-8s to carry two more assault squads?"

Sidorov is becoming more agitated with every question I raise. "Comrade General, we have studied this target for the last ten days. We know where to set up blocking positions to restrict movement in and out of the village. We'll enjoy air superiority. We will be able to bring down overwhelming fire on the rebels from our helicopter gunships. I'm fully satisfied that we have every contingency well in hand."

How the hell can he say that when his goddamn plan didn't even account for that hamlet hovering above the valley. If I had *that* position and sufficient force and firepower, I could obliterate any lightly armed assault group forcing its way into the larger village. I do my best to remain calm. "Colonel, I appreciate the preparation that your team has undertaken to get us to this point. I must point out that your plan did not take into account the strong position on the ledge of that mountain. The enemy can rain fire down on our men from there. I want us to go into this operation with *overwhelming* force. I don't want us to be isolated on the Pakistani side of the mountains and not have enough firepower."

The room goes silent. It appears to me that no one on Sidorov's staff has ever seen him challenged before. He rules his brigade with an iron fist and brooks no dissension. Sidorov examines a couple of the Air Force reconnaissance images, and he won't look up at me.

Finally, I decide to call it a night. We won't get anything more done tonight. "All right, comrades, let's go to bed. It's after oh-two-hundred, Colonel. I want the staff to get busy revising the plan and I want more air support—two more Mi-8s with assault teams. That will give us more firepower on the ground and lift capacity, should we need it. Let's reconvene here tomorrow at noon."

I don't wait for any acknowledgment from Sidorov and his staff. I walk out of the room and go to my quarters where I fall asleep quickly. I don't sleep well. I'm up every hour or so. One of my dreams is about East Germany and the two soldiers killed in the nuclear command bunker by the Americans in the spring of 1984.

16 November 1986

I go for a run in the morning, have breakfast, and join Colonel Sidorov's staff in his operations center at noon. By the look of them, many of the Colonel's staff officers have been up all night. Good. Perhaps they are finally giving this mission its due attention. Sidorov is in a foul mood. His broad face is brooding, and his eyebrows look particularly wild and untamed—furry animals stalking his eyes.

The men wait for Sidorov to speak. "Good day, Comrade General. Based on your recommendations, I have requested two additional Mi-8s. We also have revised the attack plan to account for additional air defense positions around the main village. The initial preparatory attack by the Crocodiles will include an attack on the mountain hamlet that you highlighted in your comments last night. Frankly, I'd like to have fixed-wing support from the Air Force. However, they refuse to conduct operations inside Pakistan. Our Air Force believes that the Pakistan Air Force would detect our fighters and be able to bring their fighter interceptors into the fray in short order. Our airmen are afraid of tangling with the American-made F-16s."

Since May, the Soviet Air Force has lost several Su-22 fighter-bombers and Mig-23s that intruded into Pakistani airspace. All of them were shot down by Pakistan Air Force F-16s. "Colonel Sidorov, I'd also prefer to have fighter support, but we won't get it. The positive thing is that we won't have fighters flying around at altitudes that would make our operation easier to detect. The Pakistani air defense forces are quite competent, and they are more likely to see fighters on their radars than low-flying helicopters."

Sidorov perks up a bit as we discuss the tactical aspects of the plan. "My air chief has instructed his crews to fly nap-of-the-earth profiles over the mountain ranges. Our route of flight is designed to avoid the populated valleys." He turns around and addresses his staff. "Be prepared for a real roller-coaster ride, guys. You need to instruct your troops to secure their equipment and to hold on tight to something."

The air operations officer adds, "The rebels will not anticipate a cross-border, surprise attack. I think that we'll achieve tactical surprise."

He may be correct; however, one should not underestimate this enemy. "Men let's plan for the worst and anticipate that the Mujahedin will be ready for us. Never underestimate the adversary, especially one that is battle-hardened and recently reinforced with Stingers. They are probably feeling very confident these days. Understood?"

The staff officers reply collectively, "Yes, Comrade General."

I decide to leave them to their preparations. Before I depart, I have one final directive for Colonel Sidorov. "Colonel, you and I should meet again in your office this evening for a final check-in."

Sidorov nods, "Yes, sir, of course."

The evening meeting with Sidorov is uneventful. He assures me that he's been drilling his men for this mission for ten days and that they are fit, motivated, and ready. At this point, I have no choice but to trust him. I bid him good night and retire to my modest quarters. I will be up at 0200 to prepare for the mission and I want to try to get a few hours of sleep.

17 November 1986

Surprisingly, I sleep soundly for about six hours. I don't even remember dreaming, which is unusual. I rise and dress in my battle uniform and walk in the cold darkness to the officers' mess for a light breakfast. I have tea and bread with butter while some of the younger officers eat much more heartily. My calmness surprises me. Captains and lieutenants walk up to my table to exchange a few words, and I make casual, friendly remarks to put them at ease. They seem to be heartened by my easygoing manner. I see them smile and joke with each other; I believe they must be thinking *if the general is so calm about a cross-border raid, then I suppose I should relax a bit! How bad could it be?*. Somehow, and I don't know why, I *am* calm. I am the confident, relaxed officer that they see. This must be how Henry V felt and how he was seen by his men on the eve of the battle of Agincourt. We are a band of brothers about to go into combat—me for the first time. I care about the welfare of my troops, but previously that care has been driven by duty and a sense of responsibility. This morning is different. I feel a deep emotion, a great kinship with these young men.

After a few minutes of easy banter with my fellow officers, I sense the tension in the room rise suddenly. Sidorov has arrived. It's shocking to me how fast the atmosphere in the mess changes. What an effect he has on his men. If I am Henry V, then Sidorov is Richard III. As the English bard wrote in Richard III, 'No beast so fierce but knows some touch of pity. But I know none and therefore am no beast.' That describes Sidorov.

I am on one of the two transport-configured Mi-8 Bee helicopters, neither of which carries assault troops. On our return flight, my Bee is to carry the Stinger crates, provided we can locate them. Two of Sidorov's staff officers ride with me, along with several medics. Our fleet of helicopters must be an impressive sight as we soar over the mountains on our way into Pakistan. The pre-dawn sky is clear and ideal for flying. It occurs to me that it's also ideal for spotting a large group of helicopters.

The battle plan calls for the Mi-24s to prepare the landing zones with heavy fire. Two Crocodiles will launch rockets and fire their cannons on each of the two landing zones. A fifth Mi-24 will attack that cliff-hanging hamlet that sits high above the main village. The sixth Crocodile will be held in reserve.

Once the helicopters land at their respective LZs, one squad will establish a blocking position on the north side of the village, and one will do the same south of the town. Each blocking position will have a light machine gun as its primary weapon. The blockers will stop any "leakers"—Mujahedin that are attempting to flee the village and establish firing positions on the hills overlooking our positions. One reinforced squad will proceed to the village from the south and another from the north. Once the troops secure the village, they will conduct a search for the Stingers. I wish we had an extra squad to send up the mountainside to secure that little hamlet that overlooks the valley. But we have the men we have.

The chopper ride across the mountains is incredibly rough. Sidorov predicted it would be stomach-churning and he wasn't exaggerating. I'm glad I had a light breakfast. Two of the staff officers on my Bee throw up their breakfasts as we roller-coaster our way over the mountains. They look miserable and embarrassed. I wink at them and give them a thumbs-up.

At a predetermined point over the mountains, our fleet of helicopters splits into two groups—one will land north of the village and my group will make for the southern LZ. Two Crocodiles lead the way for each group. One Mi-24 flies at the tail of each line of helicopters. The Bees, including mine, hover in a hold position while two Crocodiles proceed to attack each of the LZs. It is quite a complicated aerial ballet orchestrated by Sidorov's air chief.

I can't see much in the weak light of dawn, but the noise made by the Crocodiles' attack on the LZs is deafening. What must it be like to be on the receiving end of such an attack? Our rocket attacks kick up columns of dust and smoke that tower above the valley. It seems like we've achieved surprise. None of the Bees in my group have been fired upon from the ground—yet.

We hover and wait to descend to the LZ. It is terrifying to wait in the air, expecting to be hit at any moment. I see the Bee off the port side of our aircraft take fire from the ground—probably from a light machine gun—white puffs dot its fuselage. Suddenly, our pilot dives for the ground. This wasn't the plan. My Bee was supposed to be the last to land at the LZ. Apparently, my pilot doesn't want to wait his turn and take fire while we are hovering. We drop like an anvil to the ground.

At the last second, the pilot flares our Bee and he lands with surprising gentleness. On the intercom, the pilot tells us to stay on the aircraft. He orders the medics to man the machine guns mounted on each side of the fuselage. My Bee is a sitting duck, albeit somewhat masked by the swirling dust that surrounds us. I'm armed with a pistol. It may as well be a toy gun for all the good it will do me if we are attacked, and I don't know how to operate the Bee's machine guns.

The pilot is on the intercom again, "Comrades, the other two Bees have landed, and their troops are establishing a perimeter. Wait for my command to dismount." Our pilot is only a lieutenant, but he's the aircraft commander. While I am on his helicopter, I must follow his orders, general officer, or not. I don't know if I'm more scared of remaining on board or of climbing out of it into the unknown.

I can feel the blood hammering through my head, which feels like it's about to explode. The two staff officers that were on board just dismounted and I can no longer see them in the orange dust that swirls around our helicopter. Finally, the helicopter pilot speaks into the intercom. "General Levchenko, my copilot will dismount, and he will help you exit. Then, he will guide you to a point of safety. Do you understand?"

His order seems simple enough. "Yes, I understand. Don't worry about me." I try to sound nonchalant, but I am scared as hell to jump out of the helicopter and into unseen danger. The copilot is at the open door and motions for me to hop out of the helicopter. The noise of the engine and whirring blades makes any words unintelligible. I jump out. The copilot and I run low to the ground to avoid the wash from the helicopter blades.

The copilot hands me off to one of Sidorov's staff officers. We run to a position behind a light machine gun. So far, so good. There is so much noise from the helicopters that I don't notice the sound of gunfire until we are in our new position. Then, gunfire is all I can hear. There are hundreds of rounds being exchanged. I cannot see where the enemy is. I know that they must be somewhere off to the north since we are blocking the southern approach to the village. What are these troopers firing at? How do they know where to shoot?

A squad of six troops crawls up to my side. The sergeant in charge looks at me and shouts. "It's a little hot here today, isn't it Comrade General?"

I shout back, "Yes, it is. I hope it cools down."

He laughs and screams above the din, "No! Not me. I love it!" With that he stands up and motions for his men to follow him forward into the fray. I suppose Henry V would have led them into battle.

After a few minutes, the firing dies down a bit and I can hear myself think again. The staff officer who's been assigned to look after me tugs at my elbow, "Let's go, sir. Move forward, but with care."

We crouch and move with darting movements. The smoke and dust are opaque. I feel my lungs ache, and I still can't see much of anything. Suddenly, the young officer pushes me to the ground. "Get down, sir. There are snipers in the village!"

How does he know that? How can he see *anything*? I take his word for it, however, and make myself as small as I possibly can. "Wait here, sir. We have men clearing the village. Stay down. Keep your weapon handy but keep the safety on."

Sure, I'll keep the safety on. I don't want to shoot any of my own men. "Yes, I'll stay here until you give me the sign to move forward."

The staff officer smiles with a gentleness that seems odd for the moment and nods. Just then a bullet strikes against a rock right in front of him. It shatters rock shards, some of which fly up into his face. He grabs at his eyes with both hands and screams in pain. "Goddamn it! I've been hit in the eye. I can't see!"

I crawl closer to him. "Major, I have a first aid kit. Let me look at your eye, please."

He's rolling around on the ground, moaning. His hands cover his eyes and blood is seeping through the fingers of his left hand. That must have been a large-caliber round from a sniper rifle to shatter the rock the way it did. Bad luck. "Major, please let me attend to your eye. Move your hands."

"No, sir. It hurts like a motherfucker! I can't move my hands."

"Let me apply pressure to it. I have a compression bandage."

The young officer drops his hands. His left eye looks horrible. I use a sterile wrapping to clean off some of the blood. Then, I place the compression bandage over his eye and secure it around the crown of his head. "Lie still now. I'll get help. Medic! Medic! Over here!"

I see movement behind us and two troopers crawl to our position. One of them is a medic, thank God. After a brief examination, the troopers pick up the staff officer and rush him back toward the waiting helicopters. I'm glad the major is being helped; however, I'm now alone.

Now, what the hell am I supposed to do? I still can't see what is going on in front of me. I hear shooting, although it is sporadic now. The prudent thing for me to do is wait a bit longer for the village to be cleared. Surely, someone will be sent back to get me. Right? I look at my watch. Should I wait here or go back toward the helicopters? I check my watch again. I will let five minutes go by and then move.

Just before my self-imposed deadline, I see a shape emerge from the smoke. He crawls toward me and says, "Comrade General, Colonel Sidorov sends his compliments and asks that you join him in the village. Follow me and stay as low as you can, sir. The enemy hasn't been completely neutralized."

A few minutes later I'm standing next to Colonel Sidorov. He smiles and shakes my hand, "Well, General, we had a hard fight, didn't we?"

"Colonel, it looks like it. Tell me, how many causalities have we suffered? One of your staff officers was beside me when he was injured."

Sidorov replies, "We don't have a firm count yet. I know for certain that three troopers are dead, and we've had several wounded—maybe ten, including men hurt in the helicopter crash. One of the Bees in your group went down hard and is no longer flyable. Several men were injured when it crashed. We've killed a number of the rebels, but I don't have a count yet."

And what about our main objective? "Colonel, have we located any Stingers?"

Sidorov smiles warmly and answers with enthusiasm. "Yes, sir. We have recovered three Stinger systems in their *original* crates. Our agent told us there were up to six in this village, so the men will continue to search for the remainder."

Three! That's great news. "Well done, Colonel. Will we be able to bring all of them back to Jalalabad?"

"General, I don't know yet. Those we can't take, we'll destroy—I assure you of that, sir."

This is turning out to be a solid operation. Any casualties are terrible, of course, but given the apparent ferocity of the firefight our losses could have been worse. Four troopers struggle by us carrying a large crate—a Stinger crate! One of the men yells, "Colonel, where should we stack the crates? They're very heavy."

Sidorov laughs and tells the young trooper to stack them in the village square. The sun is getting higher, and the air is warming a bit as the smoke dissipates. It's turning into a lovely, sunlit morning and I can see the mountains that surround the valley clearly now. I sit down on a stone stoop in front of a small house that faces the square, protected by a low wall. Troopers carry out additional Stinger crates and stack them in the middle of the square. Stingers! In the flesh and sitting in the sun before me. I feel an incredible sense of elation washing over me.

Sidorov is in the center of the square, close by the stacked crates. I see him gesture at something and then rise on his toes and fall over—hard. Good Christ! Two of the men crouch over him. I stand up and run toward Colonel Sidorov. A young captain screams, "General, get down! Get the fuck down! There's a fucking sniper! Sidorov is hit. Take cover!"

What? A sniper? I stop in my tracks and dive for the dirt. Now I hear the zing of high-caliber rounds. Jesus! I crawl back to the front of the house where I was sitting and lie down behind the low wall. After a minute, I peak over the wall toward where Sidorov fell. He's gone! The men have already moved him out of the line of fire. I can't see where he is. He must be badly wounded. The way he fell . . . was horrible.

The same captain who warned me a few moments ago crawls over to my side. "Comrade General, we think the sniper is in the hamlet up there in the clouds." He points to the tiny village hugging the mountainside. "May I send a Crocodile up there to deal with him?"

Why is he asking me? Because Sidorov is done. Of course. I am in operational command. "Yes, captain. Send it. And, put a squad on the Crocodile to search the hamlet and make sure there aren't more snipers hiding in the rubble up there. Got it?"

"Yes, sir. The Crocodile is too big to land up there. The squad will have to fast rope down into the village."

We need to neutralize whoever is in that tiny village. "Do it. Whatever it takes. How is Colonel Sidorov?"

The young officer responds with a haunted look—a look of resignation. "It looks bad, sir. I doubt he'll survive."

Jesus. "I see. Get that Crocodile airborne immediately. I will take command here. Inform the other officers that this stoop will be my command post. Go!"

"Yes, sir."

He doubts Sidorov will survive. Unlike Sidorov, I am not a

Spetsnaz combat commander. What can I do? As the young officer runs away, I yell after him, "Send over the commander of the helo squadron. I need to talk to him immediately!"

"Yes, sir," he yells back to me, looking over his right shoulder.

Christ. Poor Sidorov. What will I tell his father?

Five minutes later, Sidorov's air chief crawls over to where I am sitting on the stoop, protected somewhat by the stone wall. "Comrade General, I was about to confer with Colonel Sidorov about organizing our dust off. I just saw him, and he's gone. He was shot in the chest, right in the heart. He died almost immediately, according to the men who moved him." The air chief points at his own heart and shakes his head.

Sidorov is dead—brave and impetuous Sidorov with a famous father to live up to.

CHAPTER TWENTY-ONE

SPETSNAZ

Captain Kevin Cattani, US Air Force Intelligence
A Mountain Village near the Khyber Pass, Pakistan

17 November 1986

Our team of four, plus our new "friend" Major Zhukov, runs through the back door of the house. We hear a rapidly approaching helicopter as we scramble up a pile of dirt and debris in the gloomy dawn half-light. All of us fall into a trench, which is the hamlet's only flimsy shelter from attack. In the dawn grayness, I can make out figures huddling together for protection up and down the trench. I hunker down just as a Soviet attack helicopter begins to pulverize the village. I try to cover my ears and my head at the same time. The deafening, brutal onslaught goes on and on. I am reminded that the Red-haired Major likes to say that there is no point in being terrified in combat. Chance rules your fate, so you may as well enjoy the experience.

Now I hear the Soviet helicopter roar right over my head and see the pilot with an astonishing clarity as he manhandles the controls to turn the chopper violently to avoid the cliffside. Suddenly, he swoops down toward the valley and is gone.

I cannot hear anything, but I see the Red-haired Major's lips moving. I think he wants me to get up and out of the trench. He tilts his head and shouts, "Go!" He is the first one to climb out of the trench and I follow, along with Brad, Phil, and Zhukov. The Red-haired Major yells, "Are you all okay? Anyone hit?"

I do a quick check of my limbs. Everyone does the same. It looks like no one on our team caught any shrapnel from the attack, although several of the villagers a few meters up the trench were not so lucky. Brad runs over to them and offers emergency aid while two of the Mujahedin pop out of the trench and scramble to a position that I had not noticed before. It looks like a prepared sniper position dug into the mountainside meters above the trench.

Somewhat callously, the Red-haired Major calls for Brad to leave the injured villagers and come back to the team. He leads us across the village past destroyed houses to the edge of the cliff that overlooks the deep valley. We find a spot next to a shattered wall where we can observe the village far below us. I fish binoculars from one of my pockets and zero the optics on the center of the village. I scan the area just south of the town and see several Soviet helicopters on the ground.

The Red-haired Major looks through his own binoculars and mutters, "Those bastards are after our Stingers. Goddamn it. Michael B will be so pissed." He drops the binoculars and faces me. "See that blocking position south of the town? The Sovs must have another one north of town. The mountainside is shielding it from us."

Zhukov asks me for my binoculars. I hand them to him. He scans the valley, whistles, and whispers, "Spetsnaz."

I switch to Russian and ask him, "How many troops? How many do you think?"

He continues to scan the valley. "Two dozen, maybe? There must be more—a total of sixty men or more."

I tap Zhukov on the shoulder to get my binoculars back. I know I cannot afford to trust him. "We want to return you safely to your side. Do you understand?" He nods. "But we don't want to get killed in the process." He nods again. "I need your assurance that you will follow our lead, okay?"

Zhukov looks conflicted but he nods in assent. He wants to go home, and he sees his own troops tantalizingly close.

The Red-haired Major yells, "They're going into the village and taking fire. They want my Stingers intact. Goddamn it."

I scan the village from south to north. There! Another squad has entered the village from the north. I shout, "They're coming in from the north, too! Look!"

My boss says, "Yeah, they're in a real fight now. Christ."

It is voyeurism to watch combat from a distance like this. We have a God's-eye view of the fighting—of men being shot, wounded, and killed. It reminds me of watching a football game from the top row of a huge stadium where the players are so far away that they look like tiny toys. Of course, in the terrible reality unfolding below us, men are dying on a chilly gray morning.

"Shit!" exclaims the Red-haired Major. "Look! The Sovs have one of the Stingers. Look at the village square. There's one shipping crate in the square and now they're bringing out another one. Goddamn it!"

Zhukov elbows me. I give him my glasses.

The Soviet officer looks intently at the scene in the village below. "Good Christ!" He exclaims. "That looks like Sidorov down there!"

"Who's Sidorov?" I ask.

Zhukov lowers my binoculars. "He's a colonel. He commands the Spetsnaz brigade at Jalalabad. I'm pretty sure that's him down there in the square. He's a very big guy."

He returns my binoculars and I watch the silent movie playing below us. We can hear occasional combat noise, but it is faint and sporadic. Boom! I hear a large-caliber rifle fire from behind us. It must be coming from that sniper position I saw earlier. Can they hit anything in the village at this distance? A successful shot would be a combination of skill and luck.

The Red-haired Major says, "It looks like somebody got hit."

Boom! Another sniper shot. Jesus. Then it hits me. It won't take long for the Soviets to figure out where those shots are coming from. Christ, they'll have to neutralize that sniper position, which means we will come under attack again. My boss comes to the same conclusion and says, "Boys, get ready to scoot. Those bastards will send a gunship up here to take out that sniper. I guess that little, fucked-up trench is our best option."

Brad is scanning the landing zone south of town. He yells, "Guys, there's a helicopter taking off from the LZ. We better get to the trench."

The village elder we met last night grabs my arm and waves wildly, pointing toward a low-lying pile of rubble at the western end of the tiny village. He is saying something and motioning toward the pile. Brad says, "The old man wants us to move that way. He says there's a cellar under the damaged building where we can shelter."

The Red-haired Major hollers, "All right, everybody move to that cellar. Let's go."

Minutes later, we're all inside the damaged building and we scramble down a half-broken ladder to the cellar. I strain my ears to hear the chopper. It seems to take forever for it to climb up to our altitude, but it's just a few minutes.

Abruptly, the deadly helicopter arrives, and we hear it hovering over the village square. There are loud *whooshes* as it launches rockets, undoubtedly aimed at the sniper position. The Mi-24 continues to hover over the hamlet much longer than needed to conduct its attack on the snipers. We all look at each other.

Brad whispers what we all are thinking, "They must be landing troops. The Mi-24 is too big to land here, but they could fast-rope troops onto the square."

We hear the gunship climb off our position.

I nudge Zhukov. "Major, you'll need to call out to the Spetsnaz troops. We need to let them know we're here so they don't shoot up the house and drop grenades on top of us."

The Russian major looks at me curiously. "You need *my* help, now?"

"Look, Major Zhukov, we negotiated your freedom from the Mujahedin. I know your boss—Levchenko. He wouldn't want you to leave us here to die. We're not at war with the Soviet Union."

Zhukov smirks, "You're not at war, but your weapons are killing our men. All right, I will call out to them. Is there a rag I can use as a white flag?"

I translate Zhukov's request into English for our team. Phil replies, "Yeah, I have a scarf that used to be white. It's dirty, but it should work." Phil tosses it to me, and I hand it to Zhukov, who ties the rag to a piece of broken lumber.

The Russian climbs the ladder, holding his makeshift flag of truce. He stops a few rungs from the top and waves the scarf. He calls out, "Comrades! I am Major Zhukov! Major Zhukov! I'm alive. Don't shoot! Do not fire! I am Zhukov!" If there's a response from the Spetsnaz troops, we cannot hear it. Then, I hear a voice call out indistinctly. Zhukov responds, "Comrades, I am Zhukov. I am here! Don't shoot!"

Zhukov climbs out of the cellar entirely. We can't see or hear him any longer. The boss looks at me and shakes his head. He thinks we're toast. We're unarmed and even if we were armed, we couldn't hold off a Spetsnaz team and their gunships. A few grenades dropped into the cellar will kill us all. Suddenly, Zhukov yells down into the cellar. "Cattani! You come up. Alone!"

Stupidly, the first thing I think of is *How does Zhukov know my name?* Of course, he heard the Red-haired Major calling me Cattani last night. "I'm coming up. Make sure they know I'm unarmed."

Zhukov says something to the troopers I can't make out. Then he drops his head into the hole leading to the cellar. "Okay, Cattani. Come up. Raise your hands when you get to the top of the ladder."

I nod at the Red-haired Major, stand up and climb the ladder, not knowing if I will be shot when I get to the top. I crawl out of the hole and stand in the rubble with my arms raised above my head. There are five Spetsnaz troops training their guns on me. Zhukov speaks in Russian and in a calm voice, "Cattani, come over here and stand next to me."

A warrant officer, who seems to be in charge, asks Zhukov, "Who the hell is this guy?"

Zhukov nods at him and says, "He's an American. There is a group of Americans in the cellar—four including this one."

"Americans! Here? What the fuck, Major?"

Zhukov smiles, "Yes, it's confusing but they're unarmed, and they freed me from the rebels. Now, tell me who's in command down in the valley?"

The warrant officer shakes his head and looks at the ground. "Colonel Sidorov. But he was shot by a sniper. I don't know how bad it is."

Zhukov glances in my direction, shakes his head as if to say, "This isn't good," and asks, "Who is in command of the force now?"

The trooper shrugs, "I don't know. I guess the general is."

I have listened without speaking until this point, but I can't hold back now. "General Levchenko is here? I mean in the village—down there?"

The trooper looks at me and raises his gun. "How do you know General Levchenko? How do you know how to speak Russian?"

Zhukov intervenes. "Lower your weapon, please. The general knows this American. Let's get the rest of the Americans out of the cellar. Can the Crocodile pick us up?"

The warrant officer lowers his rifle, but he hasn't taken his eyes off me. "No, Major, we have to hike back down the mountain. Are you well enough to walk?"

"Yes, I'm fine. We'll take the Americans with us. I want the general to interrogate them." Zhukov winks at me to reassure me his intentions are honorable.

The trooper smiles, his yellow teeth bared like a ferocious predator. "Yes, Major. I'll be happy to get off this goddamn mountain, even with Americans as excess baggage."

CHAPTER TWENTY-TWO

DONE AND DUSTED

General-Major Ivan Levchenko, GRU, Soviet Air Defense Forces
A Village in Pakistan

17 November 1986

I am now in command and Sidorov's deputies are counting on me to extricate the task force from this village. The air operations chief stands before me seeking guidance. "General, I can't carry more than two or three Stinger crates out of here on my birds. One of our Bees went down at the southern LZ and it's not flyable. Also, we're up to four dead and thirteen wounded, some severely." The air chief looks at me like he's let me down.

"Colonel, the men are the priority. Absolutely. Any Stingers we can't carry must be destroyed. Understood?"

"Yes, sir."

"Have we heard from the Crocodile that attacked the cliffside—the sniper's position?"

"Not yet, sir. I also sent a squad to that village as you directed. I want to ensure that we have no more trouble from up there."

"Good man. What do you need from me?"

"Your permission to begin the withdrawal. I want to get the

wounded sorted and loaded as soon as possible. I also want your permission to evacuate the northern LZ. I'd like to consolidate my aircraft at the southern LZ. Do you approve?"

"Yes, Colonel, of course. Proceed. Tell the ground team chief to report to me here. I want him to deal with the Stingers and gather the wounded while you consolidate your aircraft. You focus on securing the southern LZ and the helicopters. I don't want you worrying about the Stingers."

He salutes and trots in a low crouch across the town square and disappears around a corner. At least he knows what he's doing. I'll have to rely on the professionalism of the officers—Sidorov's officers—to get us out of here with no more losses.

Another of Sidorov's officers crawls over to me. It is the ground operations chief. "Comrade General, I understand that you are in tactical command now that Colonel Sidorov is dead. What are your orders?"

"Colonel, I am terribly sorry for the loss of Sidorov. He was a brave commander." The lieutenant colonel bows his head like he's in prayer. Sidorov's men may not have loved him, but they respected him. "I need your leadership now more than ever. Understood?"

"Yes, sir, of course."

"Good man. Look, the air chief is consolidating his aircraft at the southern LZ. He's shutting down the northern LZ. Let's get our men moved to the southern LZ as safely and as quickly as possible. The air chief says he can only carry two or three crates now. So, I want you to just load two crates. Destroy the rest. I don't want to press our luck. This mission has already cost us dearly. The wounded are my top priority."

The officer responds, "I'll get the wounded to the southern LZ and secure the perimeter. I fear that a few rebel 'leakers' got out of the village, and they'll pose a threat to our dust off. We simply didn't have enough men to control all the exit points. I'm sorry, General."

I told Sidorov back at Jalalabad that we needed more men.

Hindsight won't help us now. "All right, focus on getting the wounded out first. Then, load up the dead. Load the two Stingers last. Destroy the rest. Now move!"

"Yes, Comrade General."

I almost forgot to ask. "I suppose there's been no sign of Major Zhukov in all this chaos."

"No, General. I'm afraid not."

"Very well. Let's move out quickly."

The lieutenant colonel salutes and is about to step away when the young captain I spoke to earlier comes running up to us in a crouch. He salutes and reports. "Sir, we've observed the squad returning from the mountaintop. They are hiking down as fast as they can. They radioed in that they've neutralized the sniper."

"Excellent. I'd like to see that team as soon as they get off the mountain."

"Yes, sir. There's one more thing. It's odd, but the squad has grown in size. We count an extra five men walking with them."

"Prisoners?"

"General, that's the odd thing. They were ordered not to bother taking prisoners."

"Interesting. Have the squad leader report to me here." Am I missing something? What else should I be doing?

The young officer returns. "Sir, the squad is off the mountain. The squad leader is double-timing it to your position."

I sit down on my stoop and have a long drink of water. I nibble on a biscuit that I took from the officers' mess at Jalalabad early this morning. Breakfast seems like days ago. Henry V! Who was I kidding? My reverie is broken by the appearance of a tough-looking warrant officer who salutes me with a lazy ease. He reports and says, "Comrade General, I was in command of the squad that dropped into the hamlet."

"Yes, comrade. Great work today. I understand you have taken prisoners?"

"Not exactly, sir. Hell, I don't quite know what I've taken."

"I didn't take you for a riddler. Explain."

"Sir, we found a Major Zhukov up there. He's the one you've been looking for—right?"

"Christ! Zhukov! Is he all right? Bring him to me. Immediately!"

"He's getting water with the other guys at the village well. He seems to be okay for a guy who's been held captive. I also captured four Americans up there. Major Zhukov thought you'd want to interrogate them. And here's an odd thing, sir."

"What? What could be stranger than capturing four Americans in this wilderness?"

"Well, sir, one of the Americans claims to know you, Comrade General."

I see Zhukov before he sees me. He rounds the corner onto the village square, and I recognize his confident swagger, even though his strides are shorter than I remember. Zhukov! I never believed I'd see him again, and here he is.

We exchange salutes quickly, perfunctorily. Then, I reach out and embrace my long-lost executive officer. He's so relieved that he's crying in my ear. I whisper. "Welcome, my friend. It seems like a dream to see you."

We break our embrace. "Thank you, General. I've dreamt of this day. I never imagined it would happen. Are you well, sir?"

"Am I well? Of course. I haven't been held captive for half a year. Are you well?"

"Yes, sir; surprisingly."

"What do you need? Tell me quickly. We're heading back to Jalalabad as fast as possible. You'll ride with me on my helicopter."

"Sir, right now I don't need anything. I just want to get back to civilization."

"Yes, yes, of course. Major Zhukov, what do you make of these Americans? What can you tell me?"

"Sir, there are four of them. One is a great, red-bearded bear. He's the leader. I think they are a specialist CIA team that are managing the Stinger transfers. The leader is worried about you capturing Stingers. The one who claims to know you is very young-looking, but the others respect him. He speaks good Russian."

Cattani? "Is his name Cattani?"

"Why, yes." Zhukov squints at me. "So, you do know him?"

I nod and watch the Americans rounding the corner to the square. One is a great hulk of a man with red hair and a massive beard. Two others have dark hair and beards and walk like professional soldiers. The last one is wearing a woolen cap. He is clean-shaven.

The Spetsnaz guarding the Americans salute me. "Comrade General, here are four Americans that were found in the mountain hamlet. They were holding Major Zhukov. The one with the cap claims to know you, General."

"Thank you. Are the Americans armed?"

"No, Comrade General. We searched them and they are unarmed."

"Very well." I approach the one wearing the woolen cap.

He stands up straighter and salutes me in a very crisp fashion and speaks to me in Russian. "Good day, General Levchenko. It is good to see you again and to see that you are well."

Jesus Christ!! It is Cattani! I am as surprised to see him as I was to see Zhukov. How bizarre can this day be? I return his salute. "Captain Cattani. I had not expected to see you in Pakistan. I thought our paths might cross again someday, but not here. Are any of you wounded?"

The red-haired bear shoves Cattani aside and says in broken Russian, "General, I'm the team leader. We're fine."

I answer him in English. "Very well. I want to talk to you about what the hell you're doing in these mountains!"

The red-haired bear pitches his head back and roars, "And, General, we want to talk to you about why the hell *you're* in these mountains."

I point at Cattani and the red bear. "You two, follow me. The rest of you can relax for a few minutes." I walk back to my stone stoop and sit down.

The Americans lean on the wall in front of me. The older man nudges Cattani.

Cattani says, "General Levchenko, we're here to check on the status of weapons that the ISI have delivered to the Mujahedin—nothing more. We ransomed Major Zhukov from the Mujahedin and were going to deliver him back to you even if your Spetsnaz hadn't corralled us up on the mountain."

"I understand. Thank you for helping Major Zhukov. What is your boss' name?"

The huge man says, "General, you don't need to know my name. We can have a nice chat without exchanging phone numbers, can't we?"

I smirk. "All right, I will call you 'red bear.' I don't have much time. Let me ask you guys something." I feel the rage climbing up my belly to my throat. "Why the fuck are you Americans escalating this war at the very time that we are preparing to withdraw from Afghanistan? Don't you see that giving these Islamic fighters Stingers is counterproductive? You want us out of Afghanistan? Well, we want to leave Afghanistan. Your Stingers make that more complicated for us and will delay our departure. Don't you see that?"

Cattani and the red bear exchange looks. The older man says, "General Levchenko, the assessment of the US intelligence community is that you are not withdrawing and that Secretary Gorbachev's pronouncements about a withdrawal are merely propaganda and are designed to strengthen his international standing in upcoming arms control talks."

Just as I thought. I try to contain my rage, but I can't. In my brain, I have the image of Sidorov lying on the ground—dying from the sniper's bullet. "Captain Cattani, you of all people can't believe such bullshit! Jesus Christ! You understand Russians better than those idiot analysts at Langley. Of course we want to get the hell out of Afghanistan. Gorbachev is in his leadership position in large part because he will get us of Afghanistan. You need to get the CIA and President Reagan to understand that Gorbachev is telling you the truth!"

The red bear responds, "General, I get it. But what proof do we have? What can we show them back at Langley?"

Proof? "The proof is in what Gorbachev says in his speeches. He's stating his position in public, for Christ's sake!" I'm exasperated. I think of Sidorov and all of today's dead and wounded. What a waste. "Look, Kevin, you know me. I am *telling* you that the official position of the Soviet Union is to withdraw from Afghanistan in the next twelve to twenty-four months. That's it! Full stop."

Cattani nods sheepishly. "Yes, sir. I get it. But you must understand that American arms shipments won't stop any time soon. Congress won't reverse course easily. The budgets are approved, and the weapons are moving."

I know enough about the sclerotic decision-making apparatus of the American Congress to believe that Cattani is correct. "So, the best we can hope for is no increase in arms shipments. Otherwise, we just have to implement the countermeasures to your Stingers that already are underway."

Both Americans nod their heads a bit glumly.

I continue. "Let me tell you guys something else. You've opened Pandora's box by giving these Islamic warriors advanced weapons. Pick your metaphor, but the genie is out of the bottle now. You can't control these guys, and many are becoming radicalized, and I don't just mean the Afghans. We see this radicalization in our own Islamic Soviet Republics. And, you know who we're fighting in Afghanistan? Lots of Afghans, for sure. But there are others: Arabs from the Gulf States, Egyptians, Chechens, and even Muslims from Yugoslavia. We're seeing a transnational, radicalized Islamic threat. It will touch the Soviet Union even after we leave Afghanistan. It will touch you in America, too. Depend on it."

Cattani looks downcast as I continue. "When you get back to Washington, tell whoever will listen to you what I said here today. That's all I ask. Thank you for recovering Major Zhukov. He's a fine young officer. Oh, and I did your Stinger inventory for you. There were six full systems in this village—all still in their crates. I'll send you my consulting bill in the mail." I stand up and wave at the Spetsnaz officer. It's time to get to the LZ and begin our journey back over the mountains. I tell the red bear, "You're free to go. Captain Cattani, come with me."

Cattani looks at me apprehensively but follows when I walk around the corner of the house. Once we're alone, I say, "What the hell happened in that nuclear command bunker in East Germany back in '84? I know you crossed the Gleinicke Bridge twice that day—into and out of East Germany. We collected casings from American pistols at the scene. Were you there?"

The American looks down at the dusty ground. "General Levchenko, you know that I can't comment on an incident like that."

As I suspected. "What the hell were you thinking? Breaking into that bunker might've pushed the Kremlin over the edge. You knew we were on heightened nuclear alert. It was terribly reckless!"

The taller man looks down at me, directly into my eyes. "Sir, I agree it was reckless—stupidly reckless."

It's good to know that Cattani hasn't lost his good sense. "All right, Kevin. I need to leave. You should get your team the hell out of here now. It won't be any safer for Americans than Russians in this village after today's fight. You understand?"

"Yes, General Levchenko. I'll tell my boss."

"Good. Take care of yourself, Captain."

"Good luck to you, General."

The young American strides away and disappears around the corner of the house. What a horrible day. I hope that Cattani gets out of here safely. The Mujahedin can kill the rest of his team for all I care.

CHAPTER TWENTY-THREE

THE SECRET WARS

Captain Kevin Cattani, US Air Force Intelligence
A Mountain Village near the Khyber Pass, Pakistan

17 November 1986

Suddenly, I feel severe hunger pangs deep in my stomach. We have no food and I know I must ignore the urge to eat, so I take a long drink from my canteen to quell the rumbling. I cannot escape the feeling that today's events have made my entire time in Pakistan a failure. General Levchenko has the Stinger missiles, launchers, and related electronics. He will ship them to the Soviet Union—probably to Ramenskoye Air Base outside of Moscow—where they'll be examined and reverse-engineered by Soviet scientists and engineers. The only bright spot I can think of is that we played a part in getting Major Zhukov back to his compatriots. But that's a humanitarian task and not part of our mission. All-in-all today feels like a major failure.

The Red-haired Major pokes me in the ribs. "They're leaving." He points to our two Spetsnaz guards who have lowered their rifles and are walking across the square away from us and toward the departing Soviet helicopters.

I grunt in response. "What do we do now? Levchenko said we need to get the hell out of here. Where can we go?"

He grins at me through his red mustache and beard. "Don't be in such a rush. Let's go watch the Russkies dust off." How can he be in such a good mood? He acts like he's on vacation and is anxious not to miss the most interesting ride at the amusement park. Doesn't he realize we're in danger? Christ, sometimes he drives me crazy.

The three of us follow our leader, retracing the steps of the Spetsnaz who departed moments earlier. Turning a corner, we are startled to see a helicopter right in front of us take off. It must be carrying the Stingers—it was brought close to the village to facilitate handling the heavy Stinger crates. We watch as another Mi-8 flies off toward the mountains. I assume that one is carrying the wounded and dead. We heard Levchenko make it clear to his officers that he wanted the wounded taken out first.

I wonder if Levchenko himself is on the helicopter that carries the precious Stingers. It wouldn't surprise me. Capturing those missiles is a triumph.

The Red-haired Major shouts over the din of the departing helicopter. "Let's go to the base of that hill. We should be able to see the rest of the choppers take off from the LZ from behind those rocks." He points to a pile of boulders beyond the village wall about two hundred meters away.

I think it would be a wiser move to get away from the village as quickly as possible. But I follow my boss. A bright flash of light blinds me temporarily. An RPG! My eyes adjust and I see the starboard side of the Mi-8 carrying the Stingers explode. The rest of the chopper ignites. I can see figures—men—inside burning alive. What is left of the fuselage smashes into the ground with a thunderclap boom. We are close enough to feel the intense heat and to smell burning flesh and fuel.

The Red-haired Major grabs my left shoulder hard and screams. "Run!"

Run? For a second, I don't understand the order. Then it hits me like a blinding flash of the obvious. The Soviets will hunt down the perpetrators and they won't hesitate to shoot anyone out in the open! That helicopter carried precious Stingers. The Russians will assume that we Americans are to blame. The boss is right. We need to get the hell out of here—now!

The four of us sprint back into the village and run through the square, past Levchenko's impromptu command post, down an alley, and into the northern part of the town. I easily outpace the others and hurdle a stone wall on the town's northern perimeter. I keep running until I reach the site of the LZ that the Soviets had used north of town. Detritus of war is strewn around the site. The others catch up with me and we all lean over with hands on knees to catch our breath. We've just run for about a mile. I don't think it's a record time for me, but it's damn close.

The Red-haired Major is down on one knee, breathing heavily. He manages to sputter, "All right. All right. We need to get to under some kind of goddamn cover. There's a draw about one hundred meters over there to the left. Let's make a run for that. Go!"

We take off at a sprint again. I'm the first to get to the draw and I keep running up the steep incline until I come to a defile that seems like a good hiding spot. Brad and Phil reach me first. Our team leader drags his fifty-something body over to me and tries to catch his breath again.

I speak first to give him time to recover. "So, the Soviets will assume we shot down the helicopter to destroy the Stingers?"

"That's . . . my . . . boy." He sputters through labored breaths. "They . . . knew . . . we . . . didn't want . . . Levchenko . . . to have them."

"And the Soviets will shoot first and ask questions never. Jesus fucking Christ, sir. What do we do now?"

Brad, who's been silent up to this point, offers. "They'll send Mi-24s to try to find us. You know they will."

The major screams at him in utter exasperation. "No shit! That's why we need better cover! Find a place to burrow in. When they come looking for us, we need to look like we're part of the landscape." He's overcome by a coughing jag and shakes his head violently trying to stop the hacking.

Each of us searches the area to find a suitable spot to hide. There are hundreds of boulders and rocks strewn that should offer some concealment. I crawl between a couple of boulders and take several deep breaths. I wonder if Levchenko was on the chopper that blew up. Everyone on board was killed. No one could survive that fireball.

The Red-haired Major is a few meters from me, and he shouts. "Y'all need to look like a goddamn rock. Make sure your jackets are good and dusty. Curl up under them and try to blend in. Pretend you're a fucking rock. It's an old Apache trick."

"Gee, I know you're old sir, but did you really fight in the Apache Wars?" It's Phil. He's picked an odd time to come out of his shell.

The major yells, "Act like a fucking rock. Fucking rocks don't fucking talk. Got it, newbie?"

Phil shuts up. I try to think like a rock. Pretending to be one somehow does not seem good enough.

At last, after minutes of agonizing anticipation, I hear the roar of a helicopter. It is right overhead. If I peek out from under my jacket, I bet I'll see the pilot at his controls. He is hovering. Then he turns the chopper violently several times. When is he going to fire his weapons? A rocket or two down the draw we are in will finish us off. If he fires, I hope he's accurate. I want to be killed outright and not be left to linger in agony on these dreary rocks. Christ. I close my eyes and what I see in my mind's eye is Lydia Morelli's face and bloody hair after our encounter in the Soviet bunker. Why?

Slowly, the chopper moves away, back toward the center of the valley. He sounds like he is hovering over the northern landing zone. Maybe he has finished searching for our location. I squeeze my eyes shut as tightly as I can. If I can't see him, then he can't see me. After a few minutes the chopper returns to hover near our position. He probably assumes that this draw offers the best cover in the area. A deafening burst of cannon shells erupts. They are impacting the ground higher up the draw. I make myself even smaller under my jacket. The thunderous rattle of the cannon fire echoes around the hillside and it is a terrifying noise. I just want to die quickly if I'm going to get killed here today. Now it sounds like the helo is flying back toward the LZ. I think he hovers there briefly and then flies off to the south. Is he really leaving this time? Maybe he is low on fuel. Can we be that lucky?

The Red-haired Major shouts from under his jacket. "Anybody hit? Stay under your cover and check for any shrapnel wounds!"

I check myself from head to toe. No damage. I lift my jacket off my head and look around. Phil is sitting up a few meters away and he gives me a thumbs-up. Then, Brad speaks up. "I think my right shin is cut up but otherwise I'm okay."

The Red-haired Major stands up, shrugging off his jacket. "All right, everybody—stay alert. Looks like we dodged another bullet. Newbie, let me look at your leg." I stand up and join the boss who is standing over Brad. The older man squats down and uses his tactical knife to cut off most of Brad's right pant leg. He examines the wounds and looks Brad in the eye. "It's not too bad, kid. Kevin, hand me Brad's first aid kit. His wound needs cleaning."

I watch as he cleans the wounds on Brad's leg. From what I can see, his leg looks very, very bad. I can see his smashed tibia bone. We have no way to treat a serious wound and Brad's injury needs urgent care. I look away and get out my binoculars and scan the sky for threats. I tell Phil to do the same.

The Red-haired Major declares, "All right, newbie, you're as good as new. Keep still and don't move that leg until I tell you to." The boss stands up and stretches his back, both hands placed just above his hips. "Shit, Cattani, I'm getting too old for this."

I drape the binoculars around my neck. "What's our next move, assuming the Soviets aren't coming back to kill us?"

"Nah, they won't be back. They can't afford to burn up more fuel searching for us, plus they don't want to linger on the Pakistani side of the mountains. We need to get the hell out of Dodge and back to Islamabad. Phil, bring the radio over here. You and I are going to hike up the draw to higher ground and see if we can get a signal. Cattani, you stay here and look after Brad."

The Red-haired Major leans over and whispers in my ear, "His leg is pretty fucked up, but don't tell him. He has plenty of morphine in his kit. Give him a syringe if his pain gets too intense. I'd rather he pass out than go into shock. He needs an emergency room stat to save that leg."

I watch as the boss and Phil gather their things and begin the long hike up the rock-strewn, extremely steep draw. To get a signal they must climb all the way to the top of the ridge, which will take quite a bit of time. Even then, getting a signal will be a crapshoot.

I sit down next to Brad. He looks terrible. "I can give you some morphine now. What do you say? Okay?"

Brad whispers, "My leg is starting to hurt a lot, but I don't want the boss to think I'm a wimp."

"Brad, I am giving you a shot of morphine. It's always better to stay ahead of the pain."

Brad searches my face with watery eyes. He needs the morphine. "Okay. I just don't want to get all loopy."

"It'll be all right." I pull the dose from its case. "Now, lie back and be still." I punch the syringe deep into his left thigh. "You should feel better soon. Let me put your pack under your head. Relax."

Brad nods weakly.

"You'll be all right. I just hope they can get a signal in this damn place. Right?"

Brad closes his eyes and grins a lopsided grin.

He is going to sleep. "Brad, I'm going to look at your dressing and see if it needs to be replaced. Just relax." I pull a clean dressing from Brad's kit. I use my tactical knife to cut off the bloody bandage the boss applied. The wound is very deep, and his tibia bone is a wreck.

He needs serious medical attention soon. Lord knows the true extent of the damage to his leg.

After applying the new dressing, I stand and try to find the two climbers with my binoculars. They are about halfway to the top of the ridge now. They ascended rapidly to get up that high so quickly. They won't stop and try for a signal until they reach the very top.

Concealing myself behind a boulder, I use the binoculars to scan the valley floor from north to south. I don't see any movement. I look back toward the northern perimeter wall of the village. I see a few men walking on our side of the wall. I bet they are looking for us.

The Mujahedin suffered a lot of casualties in this morning's fight, and they will not be happy about being overwhelmed and losing all their Stingers. I just hope they don't vent their frustration on our little team. We are unarmed and completely defenseless. Our best bet is to stay hidden, although the locals obviously know this area much better than we do, and I doubt that they'll miss spotting the Red-haired Major and Phil once they get to the top of the ridge. Maybe they will just leave us alone. Maybe I'm an idiot for indulging in such wishful thinking.

I sit back down and put my binoculars away. Brad is sleeping soundly. Good. It's almost noon now—and we're approaching the warmest part of a cold day. There is very little wind and that is a blessing. We will suffer if we have to sleep in the open tonight. Brad will not survive in these conditions.

For the first time since I got to Pakistan, I think about Sandy. She warned me about taking on this mission. She was blisteringly angry with me. Given my current predicament, her judgment is looking better than mine.

I better get my head back in the game. Grabbing my binoculars, I swing my body around to get a better angle on the slope of the hillside. I settle my elbows on a sawtooth-shaped boulder and scan the ridgeline for the two climbers. This deadly day that began as a gray-sky morning is overcast and there is little contrast between the mocha-colored hillside and the leaden sky. I scan back and forth until I see two tiny black figures on the ridge. I watch them intently so I will not lose sight of them again.

"Russkie?" The questioner is right behind me.

What the hell? I turn around and see a rifle pointed at my face. "No. American. Stingers." I answer in English. I don't speak Pashto and I surmise it would be unwise for me to converse in Russian.

He lowers the barrel to a less threatening position. I sit up straighter and see that there are about a dozen fighters surrounding my position.

"Do you speak English? English?" I ask.

The guy immediately in front of me turns around and surveys his men. They look at him with blank stares. He shakes his head. The answer is no.

I try a different tack. "Islamabad. Americans. Islamabad." I motion toward Brad and jab my thumb into my chest. I point to Brad's injured right leg. "Hurt." I pantomime an injury. The leader seems to understand. He bends down and looks at Brad's leg and grimaces. I point at Brad's injury. "Crocodile! Crocodile!" The fighters murmur. They understand that word and what it means—a fearsome Mi-24 gunship.

The leader asks me something and holds up two fingers. I think he's asking me how many are in my group. I don't think lying is a smart choice. I hold up four fingers. I make a sign of two and make a motion like they are climbing the hill. Immediately, the leader looks up to the ridgeline. I notice for the first time that he has binoculars strung around his neck. He raises them to his eyes and looks at the ridgeline. He must see the Red-haired Major and Phil because he drops the glasses, looks down at me and nods. He holds up two fingers, then four.

I play-act like I'm using a radio to make a call and point up at the ridge. The leader watches me, smiles, and nods. He turns to his men and says something, and they each find a rock to sit on. I guess they plan to wait for my compatriots to return. I may as well take advantage of the situation. I make a motion like I am eating and then look up at the leader with pleading eyes. He smiles and says something to his men that makes them laugh. He tells one of the younger men something. The young fighter produces a pouch with rice cakes and offers them to me. I take two and nod my thanks. I wait a moment and say a prayer before eating. I am not pious, but I decide it is a culturally sensitive thing to do. I feel the eyes of every man watching me.

After eating, I check on Brad, who continues to sleep quietly. His dressing does not need replacing yet. I cover his leg and the rest of him with his jacket and my spare uniform top. During the time we have spent together, I have grown to admire both Phil and Brad for their sturdy professionalism and stolid reliability. They do not fluster easily—in fact, not at all. Although he would never admit it, the Red-haired Major respects them, too.

Phil and Brad look like special operators straight out of central casting. At first, I had difficulty telling them apart since they have similar builds, dark hair, full beards, and tanned complexions. They handle their gear and weapons exactly the same way. The boss teases Brad to the point of harassment but generally leaves Phil alone.

Brad stirs in his sleep and moans. He is in bad shape. I wonder if he will be able to keep his damaged leg or if the doctors will amputate it once we get him to a hospital.

There is nothing for me to do now but wait for the Red-haired Major to return. I check my watch. It is just after 1500. I don't want to doze off, but my exhaustion gets the better of me and my head keeps drooping, my chin hitting my chest. I rouse myself and look at my watch again. It's almost 1600 now. Shit, I must have slept for quite a while. I look around and the Mujahedin fighters continue to sit quietly. Several of them are sleeping. I doze off again.

Someone is pushing my left shoulder and I awaken with a start. It's the Mujahedin leader. He smiles at me and points his long arm up the draw. The Red-haired Major is returning. I stand up and raise my right arm high above my head in greeting. The major reciprocates. He's smiling. That's a good sign.

He walks up to the Mujahedin leader—he instinctively knows who to approach—and bows with his right hand over his heart. Phil says something in Pashto and the leader responds in an even voice. The fighters are all awake now and several finger the trigger guards of their rifles.

"Well, Cattani, I have good news. We're going to be picked up at approximately 1730. How's the newbie doing?"

"Sir, that's great news. Brad's been sleeping since I gave him the morphine. That syringe must contain a hefty dose. I changed his dressing once and it's probably time to check it again."

He grins and nods. "How have your new friends treated you?"

"They gave me some rice cakes once they understood that we're not Russians."

"Good. Phil, tell the leader that we thank him. And that I am grateful that he protected my two men in my absence. Allah's blessing be upon him."

Phil translates the message, which is received with nods and grunts of approval from the group. The leader bows and asks for Allah's blessing on the team.

"Kevin, help me check Brad's leg. Be ready with another shot of morphine. Okay?"

"Yes, sir. I'll stand by with the morphine."

While the big man changes Brad's dressing, the Mujahedin leader watches closely. I can't tell if he's observing to learn a new technique, or to critique the Red-haired Major's ministration to the wound.

Brad stirs and wakes up just as the major is wrapping the new bandage. The CIA man asks, "What's happening? Is everybody okay? I must have drifted off for a while."

The boss smiles at him, "It's okay, Brad. Everybody's okay and we're going to be airlifted out of here in about an hour. We'll get your leg looked after properly back in Islamabad. Kevin is going to give you another shot of morphine before we load you on the chopper so you can sleep on the flight—okay?"

"Yes, sir. Understood."

"Good, good. Look, I guess that lacrosse players must be pretty damn tough, after all. Right, Orangeman?"

Brad smiles and nods weakly. I am happy that the Red-haired Major finally said something nice to him.

The group of Mujahedin fighters stays with us until the Pakistan Air Force helicopter arrives. It sets down on the abandoned Soviet LZ. A machine gunner stands in the open side door of the chopper eyeing the Mujahedin with suspicion. The rebel leader strides to the helicopter and shouts something to the copilot through his partially opened window. Satisfied with the exchange, the rebel leader waves to us to come forward. Two of the Mujahedin fighters help us load Brad on the deck of the chopper after I give him another shot of morphine. We can't get him to a hospital fast enough.

The flight to Islamabad is one of the most turbulent I have ever experienced on a helicopter and that is saying a lot. The Red-haired Major sits with Brad's head cradled in his arms the entire way. He is doing all he can to soothe the wounded man. During a particularly choppy part of the flight, my boss motions for me to crawl over to his side. It is not an easy task with the helicopter pitching and yawing violently. I would rather wait for the chop to calm down, but he is insistent.

After much effort I reach him just as the pilot finally finds some quieter air. The Red-haired Major points at his mouth and I put my left ear close to his lips so I can hear him. He shouts into my ear, "Brad's gone. His heart stopped about fifteen minutes ago. I couldn't do CPR because of the fucking chop. I also figured it wouldn't do him any good."

The news hits me like an electronic shock and I pull away. I watch the Red-haired Major brush the dead man's hair away from

Brad's closed eyes. His face looks peaceful. Brad's wound was bad but not severe enough to be fatal—or at least that is what I had assumed. I sit back and let my head rest against the fuselage and stare into space. Phil gives me a curious look. We seem to be beyond the choppy air, so I crawl over to Phil and I motion for him to bring his ear close to my face. I shout in his ear, "Brad didn't make it. His heart gave out."

Phil pulls away from me in shock just like I did from the Red-haired Major. He shakes his head in disbelief and astonishment. When he looks at Brad's lifeless body, his eyes tear up. Phil turns away and covers his eyes. He and Brad were close—they were in the Special Forces together and they joined the CIA at the same time. I guess you could say that they shared the best years of their lives. Brad's death is a jolt to me, but it must be devastating for Phil. He has lost a brother on this frigid, cruel helicopter ride.

I let my chin bounce off my chest in time with the buffeting of the helicopter and fall asleep. I dream of the dead bodies I saw after the Russian assault this morning. The dead tend to populate my dreams and now I have new recruits. I force myself to wake up. I cannot bear to look at Brad's body for fear that his gray face and outstretched hands will haunt me, too. I think of Brad's family on Long Island. What will Langley tell them about his death?

Maybe I am weak. Men like the Red-haired Major never have such thoughts. I focus on the cold and how tired and hungry I am for proof that I am still alive. Phil is curled up in a tight ball a few feet from me. I hope he is asleep, but I doubt it.

18 November 1986

We finally arrive in Islamabad. The helicopter lands on the emergency pad of a large military hospital. The Red-haired Major escorts Brad's body to the emergency room while Phil and I wait in the visitor" area. We have not had any proper sleep in two days, but neither of us can rest. After a couple of hours, the Red-haired Major finally reappears. "Guys, we have private rooms in the visiting officers quarters, courtesy of the Pakistan Air Force. We all should get a few hours of rest. Kevin, we are expected by the CIA station chief at the embassy at 0900 tomorrow. Phil, I'm sorry about Brad. I know you were close. He was a good man and a fine officer. You will take him home. I am sorry for all this shit."

Phil nods blankly and stares straight forward. He looks almost catatonic.

So much death. I wonder if General Levchenko got out of Pakistan alive or if he was on that helicopter that blew up. I hope he survived. In any event, I will bring his message back to Washington whether anyone wants to hear it or not.

19 November 1986

Phil returns to the States with Brad's body late the following day. He may be excused from the debriefing process in Pakistan, but I am sure he will be grilled back at Langley.

Meanwhile, the Red-haired Major and I are stuck in Islamabad. We debrief with the CIA station chief, who tells us that Michael B will be flying in from Langley to talk to us the following day. The Red-haired Major is worried and confides in me. "Michael is going to have my ass! You'll be fine. You can go back to the Air Force, but I am as screwed as screwed can be thanks to your GRU buddy Levchenko!"

20 November 1986

When Michael B arrives, he wants to know every detail of our journey across western Pakistan and of our brief foray into Afghanistan.

Naturally, he is greatly concerned about Brad's death and the status of the Stingers. He drills in deeply into our encounter with Commander Massoud. When we tell him we were nearly killed in a Soviet air attack with Massoud and his men, he nods and smiles and asks, "Yes, but what is Massoud like?"

We provide him with a full Stinger status report. Michael B focuses mostly on the last part of our mission—when we lost six Stingers to the Soviets. I tell him that all the Stingers in that village were destroyed, either by the Soviets themselves or in the fiery crash of the Mi-8 helicopter. No one can be certain, however, and that makes Michael B very nervous about how to word his report of the event to Langley.

I am more interested in reporting on our interaction with General Levchenko. The general's passionate argument about Moscow's intention to withdraw from Afghanistan falls largely on deaf ears. Even the Red-haired Major is skeptical as I argue strenuously that Levchenko ought to be taken at his word.

At the end of the day, Michael B. chooses to include Levchenko's main points in his report back to headquarters. In my opinion, the Levchenko interview is the most important thing that happened during our sojourn in Pakistan. I pray that he wasn't on that chopper and that I'll get to see him again someday.

27 November 1986

The Red-haired Major and I are assigned a new team of CIA Special Activities guys to accompany us on our rounds of Stinger inspections in the borderlands. We head for the mountains again and there are no incidents on this tour to match our earlier encounters with Commander Massoud and General Levchenko. I sense my boss is rather disappointed by the relative calm; I am grateful, however, for several weeks of respite before I head for home.

21 December 1986

We return to Islamabad and debrief with the station chief. This time our report, like our second tour itself, is fairly routine. There is no drama, and no senior officials travel from Virginia to join the debrief.

I will be back home for the holiday, but the prospect is rather depressing since I will have no one with whom to share the season.. The Red-haired Major joins me on the ramp at the Islamabad airfield a few days before Christmas. I am about to board the plane to begin my long journey back to Washington. My boss and I are both emotional about this parting after all we have been through together. He is doing his damnedest not to lose it. "Well, junior, you did okay out there. I knew you would. And we had some fun, didn't we? Meeting Commander Massoud was a highlight for me!"

I manage an ironic smile. "It was memorable. I'm not sure about the 'fun' part. It's a tragedy that the entire team didn't make it home." Suddenly, I feel tears fill my eyes and I cannot stop them. Are my tears for Brad or for the death and destruction I saw in that village in Pakistan? Or for something deeper that is more personal to me than any of those deaths? Maybe the tears are a response to the seeming futility of our actions in the face of forces much larger than ourselves. Perhaps I am simply emotionally and physically exhausted.

For the first time in my experience, the big man looks lost—truly lost and adrift. He seems genuinely crushed by Brad's death. "I have lost too many men over my career. Hell, Kevin, maybe it is time to put me out to pasture." He shakes his head as if to vanquish such thoughts. "Well, safe travels back to Washington and don't let those fairies on the Air Staff get you down. Remember, you're a warrior and they're just a bunch of fucking bureaucrats! Come here you magnificent bastard." He envelops me in his signature bear hug, sighs from a place deep within, and then turns around quickly and disappears into the night.

CHAPTER TWENTY-FOUR

BREATHING FIRE

General-Major Ivan Levchenko, GRU, Soviet Air Defense Forces
A village in Pakistan and Bagram Air Base, Afghanistan

17 November 1986

I order troopers to load Colonel Sidorov's body onto my helicopter. Four of my wounded men are placed next to his body on the deck. Medics work frantically on the injured—the most seriously wounded of those stricken in today's battle for this miserable village. I'm still awaiting the final count of those killed, but I know it's high.

The medics get the wounded stabilized and attach them securely to the deck and fuselage of the helicopter. The lead medic keys his intercom and tells the pilot that he can take off whenever he's ready. I breathe a sigh of relief. Thank God we're getting out of this hellhole. I wish I had never agreed to this mission. So many men have been killed and far too many wounded for too little gain.

We succeeded in our essential purpose—we found and secured six American-made Stinger missile systems. I don't have enough lift assets to transport all six Stingers, so I had my men destroy four of them and load the remaining two, along with several of the wounded, onto another one of our remaining Mi-8 choppers.

My Mi-24 assault helicopters have taken off already and are providing overwatch for the departure of the transports. We must assume that any rebels who survived this morning's battle have deployed to prepared positions in the rugged terrain outside of the village. They may still be capable of attacking as we lift off.

Finally, my pilot announces that he is ready to launch. I'm anxious to get the wounded to Bagram Air Base where they can receive proper medical care. Unfortunately, we will have to land at the GRU base at Jalalabad to refuel before making for Bagram. The refueling delay could prove fatal for the badly injured.

The large chopper rumbles and growls as it slowly leaves the dusty ground. All the Mi-8s are lifting off almost simultaneously in accordance with my orders. I want the most severely wounded out first, which means my chopper is the first to depart. Following our lead will be the chopper doing double duty, carrying both the Stingers and more wounded. We're about five hundred feet above the valley floor and I watch the second Mi-8 as it struggles to lift off with its heavy cargo. At last, it gets in the air and begins to gain altitude.

I key my intercom and tell the pilot to get to his cruising altitude as quickly as possible. I want my wounded out. Suddenly, I'm blinded by a tremendous flash. We start rocking and rolling wildly. An explosion erupts from the chopper carrying the Stingers! I watch in disbelief as the helicopter crashes and explodes. My chopper shudders from the concussion of the fiery crash. I feel like I'm breathing in fire. I key the intercom and yell at the pilot, "Call one of the Crocodiles and tell him to strafe the hillside! They must have fired from down there."

The pilot keys in, "Yes, sir, but he's already doing it. One of the Crocodiles is pounding the hillside now."

"All right let's get the hell out of here. I want all the transports out of here immediately!"

"Yes, General. I will call the others."

I know the men on that chopper are dead—pilots, medics, crew, and the wounded. And, the precious Stingers have been destroyed, too. The object of our mission today. What a horror today is. I must focus on getting the rest of my men home safely.

Colonel Sidorov's body is close by. At least his death was a clean soldier's death. I suspect that will be little consolation to his family back in Moscow. I watch the medics attempting to calm the wounded, who were jostled severely by the shockwave from the exploding chopper. I nod at them and give them an encouraging thumbs-up. They look back at me with vacant eyes.

One of the Crocodiles streaks by the port side of my chopper. Where the fuck is he going in such a hurry? He's heading northward, back over the village. Is he looking for additional leakers from the village? That would make sense. Or is he chasing after the Americans who supplied the Stingers to the rebels? The Americans won't stand a chance against an attack helicopter. Well, I can't worry about that now. We've got to get to Bagram as soon as possible, or I'll have more body bags to fill.

The flight over the mountainous border between Pakistan and Afghanistan is painfully turbulent. The wounded men suffer from the buffeting as the helicopter dips and rises on the mountain air currents. The medics do all they can to comfort the poor boys. It is awful to hear their pitiful cries.

As I feared, the refueling delay at Jalalabad proves fatal. Two of the four wounded on my Mi-8 Bee die between Jalalabad and our destination of Bagram Air Base. They were pumped up with morphine, which gives them some measure of peace as they expire. Both boys were in their early twenties. When we finally reach Bagram, my chopper is met by two ambulances that rush the surviving wounded to the hospital. We're also met by the base mortuary detail. I stand by and watch them load the bodies of Colonel Sidorov and two of his troopers onto a truck.

I approach the warrant officer leading the mortuary detail. He is drunk and reeking of some vile concoction of home-brew alcohol and God knows what. I yell at him, "Pay attention, comrade! The first body is my Spetsnaz brigade commander, Colonel Sidorov. I want his body and the other dead prepared to be flown to Moscow as soon as possible. When is the next Black Tulip scheduled to depart for home?"

The drunken soldier doesn't bother saluting. The mortuary troops are far too cynical and drunk or stoned on heroin to bother with military customs at this point in the long war. "Yes, sir. I understand. Do you have a dress uniform for the colonel?"

"I'll have fresh uniforms for all the men flown up here tonight from Jalalabad. What about the Tulip?"

"Oh, right. I don't know. I'll have to check the schedule."

"Don't bother. I'll do it. You tend to the fallen."

"Got it, sir. We know our job by now."

I bet you do. "Let me know if you need anything." I walk across the ramp to the base operations center. I need to make some calls. I hope the radio gods will cooperate with me tonight.

The first call I make is to my direct boss, General Dubynin, the commander of the 40th Army here in Afghanistan. I inform him of the death of Colonel Sidorov and tell him that I will provide a full debrief on today's mission tomorrow morning at his office.

"All right, Levchenko. I understand. Make sure you call Sidorov's father personally. I will fly to Bagram before sun-up. You won't need to travel to Kabul. Meet me in my office at Bagram in the morning... let's say about 0800. You can brief me, then." The general's tone is subdued—one might say resigned. That's uncharacteristic of my hard-charging boss. He hangs up abruptly.

My next call proves more difficult. It's one thing to call Kabul from Bagram. It's quite another thing to make a successful call to Moscow, but I must get through to my other boss—General of the Army Pyotr Ivashutin—the head of the GRU. After twenty minutes of trying, the radio technician gets me a line to General Ivashutin. I inform him of Sidorov's death and tell him I will send a classified report on the mission tomorrow through the proper channels. Both of us know the radio link with Moscow is not particularly secure and sensitive information ought not be discussed on it.

"Levchenko, you must call the dead man's father, General Sidorov, tonight. He will want to hear from you directly."

"Yes, sir. He is my next call. It's not one I look forward to making, sir."

"Of course, but you must make it. Don't be wooden with him. Show some emotion—some empathy, but not too much. Understand?"

The director of the GRU is advising me to show *emotion*? "I understand, sir. I will do my best." In fact, I have no idea how to be empathetic but not *too* empathetic.

There is a long pause and I fear that the connection has been lost. At last General Ivashutin speaks. "You'll do well. I have confidence in you." He changes topics abruptly. "When are you scheduled for home leave?"

"In January, sir."

"All right, see me first thing when you get to Moscow. I may have some news for you. Make an appointment with my office once you know the specific dates of your return."

"Yes, sir." What's that all about?

"Goodbye, Levchenko. Good luck."

Now, I must try to reach Colonel Sidorov's father. He is General Colonel Anatoly Sidorov, the commander of the Military Academy of the General Staff. This post is one of the most prestigious in the Soviet military—hell, in the entirety of Soviet society. His son, my dead subordinate, was brave, accomplished, obstinate, and dedicated to winning glory in battle. How well did his father know his son? Did he know that his son would sacrifice his own men—and his own life—to live up to the standards set by his estimable father? How well does any father know his son? The Sidorovs are an old military family. Death in war must be no stranger to them.

The radio technician has less difficulty getting a line to General Sidorov. It's early evening in Moscow and I expect that the general will be leaving the office soon. It's fortunate to get a line so quickly.

The general's executive officer picks up the line. I introduce myself. "Good evening, this is General-Major Ivan Levchenko calling from Bagram Air Base in Afghanistan."

"Yes, sir. May I enquire as to the purpose of your call to General Sidorov?"

"It is an official call of a sensitive nature. I'm afraid I am unable to furnish more detail. Let me assure you, however, it is essential I speak to the general immediately."

"I see. Very well. I will put you through."

The seconds tick by slowly as I wait for General Sidorov to take the call. It is agonizing for me. At last, he picks up the phone. "Levchenko, I gather . . . I fear that this is not a casual call. My son is one of your brigade commanders. Is this call about him?"

I have rehearsed my response to that question for hours. "Yes, Comrade General, the call concerns your son." I take a deep breath and hope that he cannot hear it. "I regret to inform you that your son was killed in action this morning commanding an important and sensitive mission. He led his men with great skill and enormous courage. I am very sorry to convey such sad news."

There is a short pause. "I see. Well, when I heard that you were on the line, I feared the worst. And now I know the worst is true." I can tell that he is covering the phone with his hand. He doesn't want to show me the depth of his grief.

How would I react to such a call if I had a son? "Sir, I am at Bagram Air Base now. I was in action with him when he was struck down. Colonel Sidorov was a great combat leader and had more courage than ten normal men. He will be treated with the great respect he deserves. I will do my best to ensure he is transported to

Moscow at the earliest opportunity. I am very sorry, sir. I personally escorted your son from the battlefield to Bagram."

There is another lengthy pause. I hope the line hasn't dropped. The line crackles and I hear him say, "Thank you, General Levchenko, for your kind words and for escorting him. You saw him fall?" I hear a muffled sob.

"Yes, General Sidorov. I saw him fall."

He collects himself. "I see. So, you were in the thick of the fighting yourself? A general officer on the front line?" He pauses again and says, "You know something, Levchenko? My son told me he wasn't sure about you when you arrived back in May to take overall command. His opinion became more favorably disposed to you in the ensuing months. Much more favorably disposed. And you were with him when he fell. In combat. There is no greater honor than to die for one's country in combat. I am glad you are a courageous man who can appreciate my courageous son. I'm also grateful that you have the courage to call me yourself. Now, I must collect myself and prepare to go home and reveal this horrible news to my wife."

I can feel his heartbreak through the long-distance line, even as he maintains control of his emotions. "Sir, I will accompany your son home, if you wish. If it would make it easier for you and your wife, sir. It would be my honor to do so."

He answers immediately and demurs, "No, no. You have great responsibilities in the war zone to attend to. I want to thank you for your offer. It is appreciated." He pauses for a few seconds before continuing. "Do you know I have another son? He's a lieutenant colonel in the Air Force—a wonderful fighter pilot. He worships—worshipped—his older brother. This will be hardest on him and on my wife. Thank you for your call, General. Forgive me, but I will hang up now."

I cannot relate to the Sidorov family's anguish around the sudden, violent death of their son. I suppose I can as a military man, but not as a family member. I ask the radio technician to call my home number in Moscow. I must talk to my wife. The tech tries to get a line for almost half an hour with no luck. The disappointment in not being able to speak to Boyka hits me very hard. I feel despair for my wife, the Sidorov family, and my country. This is an awful war with no end and no tangible goal. It is all glory and courage and sacrifice without purpose.

I have one more stop to make before I go to my quarters—the base hospital. I must see my wounded men tonight. I order a car from the motorpool to take me to the hospital.

It's a desperate scene in the emergency ward. Several of my men are fighting for their lives. I am told that the others, who are less seriously injured, have been dispatched to the regular ward. The doctors ask me to leave the emergency ward so that I'm not in the way. A nurse escorts me to the ward where the rest of my men are bedded down for the night. I hesitate to go into the ward. I don't want to wake them. The nurse assures me that the men will want to see their commander, and I go in.

I walk into the room and am struck by the harsh medicinal smells. Two young troopers see me first. They say something and a murmur reverberates around the ward. I walk to the center of the room and wave at them awkwardly. Perhaps I should not be here. It feels wrong.

One of the men speaks. "Comrade General Levchenko, thank you for visiting." That breaks the ice. I clear my throat and say, "Well, men, how are they treating you? Any pretty nurses in this place?" Most of the men chuckle softly. "You men performed magnificently today. We accomplished our mission, thanks to all of you. I'm honored to have commanded you today. Let me know if there's anything you need. You made me very proud."

One of the younger guys, whose head is bandaged heavily, asks, "Sir, how many men did we lose?"

Too many. "Ah, we are still getting the final tally, but more than ten of our brothers died today, I'm afraid. You may know that Colonel Sidorov lost his life."

A man with a splinted leg says, "I saw the colonel get shot by a sniper. So, he didn't make it?"

"Sadly, no; he didn't. You should be proud of your commander and of all the men we lost today, as I am proud of you." The young men stare at me in silence. "Look guys, I will put my phone number on this board. This is my direct office line. Have the nurse call me if you need something—anything at all. I will come by to see you about noontime tomorrow. Until then, try to get some sleep." I wave a casual salute at the boys. Most of them struggle to salute me from their beds. This is too much for me. I open the door, and I walk out. I can't see any more tonight. I need to get some sleep if I can.

Back in my quarters, I open a liter of vodka and quaff a couple of big glasses. It will help me get to sleep but not to stay asleep. I have a deep sense of unremitting helplessness when I contemplate the events of this terrible day. I watched my men bleed and die today. For the first time, I was right in the action with them and saw their courage and their fear. The fight was nothing but confusion, dust, death, and the fog of war. Was Henry V's Agincourt experience similar? I suppose so. I know one thing for certain: I'll go see the men in the hospital tomorrow after I brief General Dubynin.

CHAPTER TWENTY-FIVE

HOMELAND

Captain Kevin Cattani, US Air Force Intelligence
Andrews Air Force Base, Maryland

24 December 1986

It is a bitterly cold morning in Maryland, and I pull my scarf tightly around my neck as I walk across the ramp toward Andrews Air Force Base's flight operations building. As cold as the mountains of Pakistan were, somehow this frigid air in Maryland cuts into my bones even more. A northwest wind whips my long hair around. It has been over three months since I had a haircut.

The journey from Pakistan has been so lengthy, I have lost track of the days. The ops building is decorated with Christmas wreaths and its windows festooned with holiday signs.

Sheepishly, I ask one of the guys deplaning with me what the date is.

"Seriously? You don't know?"

"Is it Christmas Day?" My question in response to his question sounds defensive.

He shakes his head in exasperation. "No. Christmas Eve, sir. I mean, come on . . ."

"Okay. Thanks." Christ, it is Christmas Eve, and all of these other guys have people waiting for them. Home for Christmas. They are home for Christmas.

Faces are pressed up against a large window desperately searching for spouses, boyfriends, girlfriends, and parents in the crowd of service people who are walking from the Air Force transport plane. No one is looking or waiting for me.

I always find it weird to come back to the States from overseas—especially when I have been in dangerous places doing dangerous things. It seems especially poignant at this time of year. My reentry into American society is disconcerting and upsetting and I feel like I am returning to a familiar planet from a planet that plays by different rules—a planet that most Americans do not know exists. The sight of Christmas decorations only makes the disorientation more jarring.

Although I am desperate to get out of this cold, I walk right up to the huge window where loved ones wait for their service members. The icy glass separates us. I see a young woman jumping up and down—almost like she's doing jumping jacks. She is so excited about reuniting with her husband or boyfriend after being apart for who knows how long. I walk a few steps farther and I open the door. A harsh blast of Arctic air blows into the building with me. I kick the door shut hard with my right boot.

The small reception room is packed with family and friends. I step back and take a long look at them. The joyous scene makes me feel forlorn, like a deserted ship adrift on a cold, dark sea. I wade through the throng, doing my best not to jostle the exuberant people.

In front of the operations building, I board an Air Force bus that will take me to the Pentagon. The interior of the bus is oppressively hot. I ask the driver to turn down the heat and he tells me the regulator is busted. He has two choices—no heat or too much heat. He has chosen too much. I sit down and doze while the driver makes a couple of stops on his way to the Pentagon. From there, I get a taxi to my new "home" in a rented room in McLean. This homecoming is so gloomy, I think that I probably should have stayed in Pakistan.

Once home, I get in the shower and scrub off the grime from my drawn-out trip. I also knew I lost weight in Pakistan, but now I see how bony I have become. I must have lost fifteen pounds that I did not have to lose.

How do I feel? I feel depressed. I feel like a failure having lost those Stingers to the Soviets and even more so for not being able to save Brad's life. And I worry about Levchenko. Is he dead? I believe what he told us by that village wall in Pakistan. The Soviets are trying to extricate themselves from the quagmire of Afghanistan and our arms shipments to the rebels make their task deadlier and more difficult. And, who knows how those weapons will be used once the Soviets finally withdraw?

26 December 1986

I go to the Pentagon the day after Christmas. On Christmas Day, I went for a long hike in Great Falls, Virginia, but today I need to get back to work. The building is manned by a skeleton crew due to the holiday. The few fellow officers who greet me ask how I enjoyed my three-month "vacation" in a place "far, far away." A few guys kid me about how much weight I lost and my long hair. It is just the usual banter, but it depresses me. It is all so shallow and insipid. None of the younger guys have been in a war zone. I know I cannot return to work here.

I am surprised to get a call from the CIA telling me that Dr. Gillis wants to see me tomorrow in his office at 0730. Gillis himself—deputy director of Central Intelligence Robert Gillis—made the request. He must think I have something important to say if he wants me to meet with him over the holiday break. At least I will have an opportunity to talk to the one man in the intelligence community who can make a difference. I worry that it will be easy for the Agency guys to belittle or downplay what I have to say.

I am about to leave the Pentagon for the day when my phone rings. It is General Doug Flannery. "Hi babes, how're you doing?"

"I'm fine, sir. Where are you? You sound like you're right down the hall—not in Germany."

He laughs and says, "I'm in the Pentagon, in the visiting four-star's office in the chief's suite. I heard you were back from parts unknown. Do you have a minute to stop by and see me? I know it's late in the day and you probably have places to go with it being Christmas season and all."

"Of course, sir. Now?"

"Yeah, now would be good."

"I'll be right there, sir."

When I arrive at the chief's suite, I am directed to the office where General Flannery is working. I knock on the partially opened door and hear his familiar voice call out, "Come."

I open the door and find him leaning back in his chair, smoking a cigarette—of course—and reading a Robert Ludlum novel, of all things.

He looks up. "Babes! Good to see you. Have a seat."

I sit, smile, and look at the general expectantly.

"Damn, Kevin. You're skinny! Are you okay?"

"Yes, sir. I lost some weight climbing mountains in Pakistan."

"I would say you lost some weight! But you're wondering why I called you—right?"

"Sir, it's always great to see you, but yeah."

He shifts in his blue leather chair. "Well, I hear you're going out to CIA tomorrow morning. Is that right?"

"Yes, sir, they want to debrief me on my travels in Pakistan."

He smirks. "I bet they do. Look, I just wanted to tell you how important you are to our Air Force. I don't want the CIA guys stealing you away from us. You're one of us."

I am too far gone with tiredness and depression to be diplomatic in my response. "Sir, I appreciate you saying that, but I'm not a pilot and the Air Force is run by pilots. I love the Air Force but I'm an intel officer." Maybe I shouldn't have been so blunt, but it's how I feel.

General Flannery stares at me for a long, uncomfortable moment. "But you're not like most intel guys—you're an operator—a warrior. I know it. Hell, the chief of staff of the Air Force knows it. You have a good shot at making general officer."

"General, I appreciate the vote of confidence. I'm not planning on doing anything at this point. But I need to think about my future once I get reacclimated to the States."

Flannery grins. "Good. That makes sense. You'll never get rich in the Air Force, but your country needs you."

"Yes, sir. I wouldn't get rich working at CIA either."

Smiling, he replies, "You know people like me are looking out for you, babes. Your Air Force needs you." He looks at his watch. "I better get going. I'm having dinner with the chief at his house tonight. Good luck with the CIA guys tomorrow. I've always got your back, babes."

"Thank you, sir."

27 December 1986

Early the next morning, I make the short drive from my new digs in McLean to CIA Headquarters. It's a gray January day, but not as wickedly cold as it has been since I landed at Andrews.

Once on the CIA campus, I'm lucky to find a visitor's parking spot not far from the main entrance of the headquarters building. I am very familiar with the campus' landmarks and walk past the somewhat eccentric, domed auditorium building known to all as "the bubble," where CIA directors and other senior intelligence officers hold large meetings. A bit closer to the main entrance is a statue of Nathan Hale, the American intelligence operative executed by the British Army during the Revolutionary War, famous for telling the British at his execution, "I regret that I have but one life to give for my country." I pause for a moment before Hale's statue and stare into his youthful face. He was years younger than I am now when he lost his life.

I move on and walk into the main lobby. Carefully, I walk around the famous granite CIA seal. It's disrespectful—bad luck—to walk on the seal. To my right, on the north wall of the lobby, is the Memorial Wall with its stars commemorating those who have died in the service of the Agency, in the service of the United States. I guess Brad's star will be up there soon. I wonder if his family will be allowed to see it.

Michael B. got me a CIA badge before I went to Pakistan, and it enables me to bypass the security desk and go directly through the turnstiles. I am met by a young female officer who escorts me upstairs to a waiting area outside of Dr. Bob Gillis's office. The deputy director has an extensive suite. In his role, Gillis runs CIA on a day-to-day basis and is also the deputy director of the entire intelligence community.

I thank my escort and take a seat. There is a copy of this morning's *Washington Post* on the coffee table in front of me. I pick it up and turn to the editorial pages to a piece on the Soviet war in Afghanistan. How about that! I read it carefully. It is filled with a bunch of crap about the Soviets lusting after a warm water port on the Indian Ocean and the opinion writer predicts that Moscow will invade Baluchistan in the spring. Baluchistan! What a crock of shit. These people inside the Washington Beltway bubble live in a parallel universe.

I'm shaking my head when I notice that Dr. Gillis is standing in front of me. "Hello, Captain. You must be reading the opinion piece about Baluchistan. Am I right?"

Dismissively, I put the paper down, stand up, and say, "Yes, sir. What a crock."

Gillis grins, "My sentiments exactly. Are you ready for our meeting?"

"Yes, sir. I think so."

"I want to talk to you privately in my office before we go into the SCIF with the rest of the gang."

Dr. Gillis leads me to his office, and we sit down on easy chairs around a coffee table. His office is large and furnished beautifully. Having a private meeting with Gillis is a big deal for an obscure junior officer like me.

He pours us each a cup of coffee and says, "Weren't you with the Red-haired Major and that team we sent into Cambodia some years back? It was the mission to get intel on the Khmer Rouge killing fields. I could swear you were part of the team that briefed me down at the Farm after the dust settled. Am I right?" He looks at me with an impish, dimply grin. "As I recall you had quite a fire fight with the Khmer Rouge—right?"

"Yes, sir. That was me and we did have quite a fight. A big fight."

Gillis smiles triumphantly and says, "I thought so." It is evident that he loves his job, and he brings a joyful intensity to it. Dr. Gillis is very young to have risen to such a lofty position—he's only in his early forties. He has had a rapid climb up the ladder. He also seems to have a devilish streak, and the vibe I get from him is that of a whip-smart, mischievous elf.

"I have to ask you something else and I hope you don't mind."

"Okay." What could this be about?

"Well, I heard a story that when you were at the Farm in the paramilitary course you got in trouble over a deer hunting incident. Is that true?"

Oh, no, anything but that old story. "Yes, but it came out all right in the end."

"Did you really draw an automatic grenade launcher from the armory to take on your weekly mandatory deer hunt?"

"Well, yeah. But . . . well, the week prior we'd gone to Fort A. P. Hill to hunt deer and we came up empty. We didn't get liberty that weekend because we didn't kill any deer. Since my class had been checked out on the grenade launcher, I thought I'd use one to frighten the deer—scare them into running into a kill zone where the rest of my team waited. It seemed like a sure way to bag some deer and it worked." This is embarrassing, ancient history.

"And the director of the Farm was so upset with you that he threatened to expel you from the school. Is that right?"

"Yes. It was early on a Saturday morning, and we woke up everyone at Camp Peary and half of the city of Williamsburg, Virginia. I set the fuses on the grenades to detonate in the treetops to get max effect. Honestly, at the time I had no idea how loud exploding trees would be." I stare at the floor gloomily. I hate this story. Telling it makes me feel physically ill.

"And the general in charge of Air Force Intelligence bailed you out? He kept you in school?"

"He called me and demanded an explanation. Once I told him my rationale for doing such a stupid thing, he told me it showed 'great initiative.' He went to bat for me, and I got to complete the program." I look up at Gillis. He's doing his best not to explode with laughter, holding his hand over his mouth like it's a stopper on a bottle.

At last, he giggles and says, "That is the most outlandish story I've ever heard, and I've heard some doozies over the years." He's shaking now and his eyes are tearing up with uncontrolled mirth. Is this story that funny?

Gillis clears his throat and attempts to regain his composure. "So, tell me about yourself, Captain. Where are you from? Where did you go to school?" He's trying his best to suppress gales of laughter.

"Well, sir, I'm from southern Virginia."

"A Virginia boy, eh? So, you're not too far from home—I mean being assigned to the Pentagon. I bet it's a world away from where you grew up, right?"

"Yes, sir. That's an understatement. I went to William and Mary and majored in history, mostly Russian and East Asian history."

Gillis looks stunned. "I graduated from William and Mary. I

majored in history there, too. How did you find yourself in the Air Force?"

"I took the foreign service exam and the CIA exam, too. I got much farther with the Agency than with State. Anyway, this was back during the Carter years and the Agency had to delay bringing in my class of career trainees because of budget problems. I couldn't wait for my class to start—I needed to make money—and a CIA officer at the personnel center advised me to go into intelligence in one of the military services and here I am."

Gillis takes this all in and nods. "Very interesting. I know the Carter years were tough for us from a budgetary standpoint. Did you know that I started my career as an Air Force intelligence officer?"

Now it is my turn to be stunned. "No, sir, I was unaware of that. That's surprising." He was in the Air Force?

He sits back in his chair and chuckles. "Surprising? What, you don't think I'd look good in an Air Force uniform?" He smiles a bit wistfully, as if remembering a distant, younger self. "Unfortunately, and unlike you I suspect, I didn't find my time in the Air Force terribly rewarding. I had to brief Strategic Air Command crews back in my home state of Kansas, and they found nothing I had to say to be of much interest at all! I joined the Air Force to see the world and get out of Kansas, so, of course, they sent me to an air base in Kansas. Your career, however, is something else entirely. You've had a stellar run so far." He grins impishly again. "You're very young to be on the Air Staff, aren't you?"

"I'm younger than most."

"Now, tell me about academics. Are you interested in advanced degrees?"

"I finished my master's degree in Russian Studies last summer. I'm taking classes toward a PhD."

Gillis looks as pleased as if I were his own child. "Terrific. That's terrific. Where are you doing this work?"

"Georgetown, sir."

"Georgetown!" He roars. "I have my PhD in Russian Studies from Georgetown. Did you know that? Why, you're practically my doppelganger—William and Mary, Air Force Intelligence, Georgetown...!"

Gillis smiles, rises, shakes my hand, and says, "I'm glad to see you, a William and Mary man, having such a great career. Let me know if you ever decide to leave the Air Force and want to come to work for us. We'd love to have someone of your caliber—and initiative!" He grins once more. "Of course, since I'm Deputy DCI, you work for me already, don't you?"

"Yes, sir, I do. I'm not sure what I'm going to do next in the Air Force. The thought of sitting in a cubicle at the Pentagon is enough to make my head explode."

He laughs. "Well, don't let that happen. We need good heads like yours. Okay, we have some folks waiting for us in the SCIF and I asked them to come in on a Saturday over the Christmas break so they're probably pretty unhappy with me right now. Let's head over there."

Dr. Gillis leads me out of his office and to a nearby vault door. He opens the cipher lock, and we walk in together. There are three very senior CIA people waiting for us. Dr. Gillis takes a seat at the head of the table. There's an open seat just to his right and I sit there.

Gillis starts the meeting. "Good morning, everyone. I think you all know Captain Kevin Cattani, at least by reputation. Kevin, you know Michael B. And, we also have Barb here, who is the head of the office of Soviet Analysis—SOVA—and Jim who leads the Special Activities Division."

I nod at the CIA leaders. It's quite a constellation of heavy hitters. Jim from Special Activities looks like the ultimate badass, which he ought to be and probably is, given his position. Barb looks like a sophisticated Manhattan socialite, not that I have ever met one before.

Dr. Gillis gets things started. "All right. Captain Cattani has just returned from Pakistan and he's going to give us his assessment of what he saw in the border regions. Captain, you should know that we think the GRU had an agent operating inside one of the tribal groups who was able to bribe his way into getting a couple of Stinger systems. We're not sure when this happened, but it may have been before you and your team began your inventory in the tribal regions."

No shit? That's a kick in the ass if it's true. That would mean that Levchenko already had possession of Stingers prior to the attack on the village that we witnessed. I decide to direct the discussion toward the information most important to me and I ask, "Do you have any information pertaining to General Levchenko?"

Gillis responds, "You mean the GRU commander you met in the village near the Khyber Pass?"

"Yes, that's him."

"Yeah, well, no information but we have a lot of questions *about* him and your encounter with him."

"Okay, I'm happy to tell you everything I know, but do you know if he's alive? You'll recall from my team's report that we weren't sure if General Levchenko was on the Mi-8 helicopter that blew up—the one with the Stingers on board."

Jim, the intimidating chief of the Agency's Special Activities Division, speaks for the first time. "We've asked our contacts in Afghanistan. The bottom line is . . . we don't know. We don't know if Levchenko survived the attack. If he didn't, then we may hear something in Moscow about it."

Gillis takes over. "Kevin, give us a run-down—the highlights from your time over there. We don't get much first-hand intel on the tribal regions. I am especially curious about your meeting with Commander Massoud."

"Sure. Yes, sir." It takes me about fifty minutes to summarize my time in Pakistan. The assembled officials ask a lot of questions about Massoud and the Haqqani network and almost nothing about the Soviets, which strikes me as extremely strange.

At last, the head of SOVA—Barb—asks me about the Soviet assault on the village. She wants details on the Spetsnaz tactics and combat readiness. "Tell me, Captain, what do the Mujahedin think of the Soviets' warfighting capacity—what did they tell you?" Barb asks, an expensive, silver pen in her left hand at the ready.

It wasn't a topic the rebels, except for Massoud, discussed with us. "Well, I would say Commander Massoud has a lot of respect for the Spetsnaz troops. He admires their firepower and their tactical skill. I'm sure you know that the Soviets rotate commanders in and out of Afghanistan much like we did in Vietnam. That means that some hard lessons must be relearned every twelve months or so. The Mujahedin take advantage of that fact. The Spetsnaz units have more continuity in leadership and better leaders than the average Soviet Army units. The fight we witnessed in that village was a demonstration of the high level of proficiency of the Spetsnaz troops."

"Are the Soviets afraid of the Stingers?" Gillis asks.

"They have a lot of respect for them. The Stingers have forced them to make tactical adjustments and technical modifications. General Levchenko was very emotional about the losses the Stingers have caused. He complained that we're supplying Stingers when the Soviets are attempting to withdraw from Afghanistan and that the Stingers make that much more difficult."

Everyone around the conference table smiles and nods approvingly. They don't get it.

"What kind of countermeasures did Levchenko describe?" Barb asks.

"None. He would never share specifics like that with Americans. As I said, he's mighty upset that we're supplying such advanced weapons at a time when the Soviets are preparing to withdraw. He kept stressing that the Stingers represent an escalation of America's involvement in the war at the very time that Gorbachev has ordered the Soviet forces to begin to get out. Levchenko's fundamental point is that our escalation is delaying—even defeating—our own stated goal of getting the Soviets out of Afghanistan." I know I'm piling on, but it's the only way to get their attention.

My comments are met with a silence that freezes the room for a few seconds. Then I see a few eye rolls as my remarks sink in. Everyone turns to the head of the table. How will Gillis respond?

Gillis smiles at me. "Well, Kevin, General Levchenko has an interesting perspective on things, that's for sure. The fact is that we must prevent the Soviets from having long-term control of Afghanistan. We can't permit them to use it as a base of operations to create mischief in Southwest Asia. Whether Baluchistan is part of their plan is open to question, but we cannot risk them driving south toward the Indian Ocean. Surely, you must see that."

Wow. They just don't understand what's going on over there. "Sir, no one 'controls' Afghanistan. Certainly, the Soviets don't. They aren't winning in Afghanistan. They're just bleeding. I believe Levchenko. The Spetsnaz troops I saw in Pakistan are tough and professional, but they are not an all-conquering horde. I'm convinced they want to go home, not invade Baluchistan."

"So, what do you think we should do, Captain?" It's Barb, the Agency's top Soviet analyst. She is scowling at me.

"I would ask, 'What's our objective?' If it's merely to kill Russians, then we should continue our arms deliveries, although I want to make a qualification to that point—in a minute. And if our objective is to induce the Soviets to withdraw, then I'm sure additional arms deliveries will *not* facilitate that goal. And here's my qualification to my earlier statement. I want to stress that there is real risk in flooding the border regions and eastern Afghanistan with weapons. We do not control the actions of the groups getting those weapons. God knows what they'll do with those arms once the Soviets withdraw, but it's unlikely to be good."

Michael B roars, "We have considered that! We have known all along that there is risk in sending Stingers to these guys! You're not telling us anything new!"

Dr. Gillis makes a "T" sign with his hands, signaling time out. "All right, guys. We aren't going to solve this today. Barb, what does

SOVA think of Levchenko's comments and of Gorbachev's apparent, or alleged, desire to withdraw from Afghanistan?"

Barb, an elegantly dressed woman in her fifties, has streaks of silver in her dark hair that amplify her sophisticated air. She must be very good at her job to have risen to be director of the most important analytical office in CIA. "We don't know much about Levchenko. Captain Cattani probably knows him better than anyone else on our side. We know he was with the Soviet MLM in West Germany and has been promoted rapidly. He seems to be a rising star in the GRU. Is he trying to manipulate us? Probably. The question for us to ponder is whether his story about withdrawal is true. Gorbachev has made statements about an intention to withdraw; however, that may well be him angling for advantage in arms control talks."

I raise my hand like I'm in a parochial school classroom. Gillis nods at me.

I take a deep breath. "Ma'am, I do know General Levchenko well, and he was sincere. Let me paint a picture for you. When I talked to him, his men had just finished a bloody fight to secure a village in hostile territory. His on-scene commander had just been shot to death by a Mujahedin sniper. His troops had suffered numerous casualties, including a bunch of KIA, and General Levchenko was focused on getting his wounded evacuated with or without the Stingers that they'd just seized. Believe me, he was in no mood to be manipulative or deceitful. I believe everything he told me that day."

No one comments on my soliloquy.

Gillis clears his throat and asks, "What do you think of Captain Cattani's thoughts, Barb?"

"Sir, he does make a compelling case." Barb shifts in her seat to look at me. "General Levchenko may believe everything he told you that day. We should take his words into consideration. I'm not sure we should change our fundamental assessment of the overall situation in Afghanistan, however."

I guess I have been put in my place.

Dr. Gillis looks at Michael B and asks, "How concerned should I be about arms proliferation in the border regions? We know there are other actors at play in Afghanistan who are not our friends. The Arab fighters, for example. If our advanced weapons fall into their hands, then Captain Cattani's concerns may be well-founded. How worried should I be?"

I can tell that no one in the room wants to answer this question. I'm not touching it. Gillis wasn't asking me, anyway.

Finally, Michael B. says, "It's a risk. There are some real bad hombres over there. We've always known it was a risk."

"Should we back off? Hold back the Stingers for a while?" Gillis asks.

"Congress won't like it, sir. They've voted for bigger budgets for us again this fiscal year. We'll have some tough explaining to do on the Hill if we back off." Michael is visibly uncomfortable with this line of discussion.

Gillis clasps his hands together and looks around the room. No one says anything. "All right. I want an updated risk assessment on Cyclone. I want to focus on the potential fallout of arms deliveries to the rebel groups. Are we creating a monster over there?"

Dr. Gillis looks directly at me. "Your intelligence about General Levchenko is important; however, we can't verify what he told you. That said, it does seem to make sense. We know that Gorbachev inherited this war from his predecessors and that his heart doesn't seem to be in it. Maybe a pause in weapons deliveries is called for but I want that risk assessment first. Michael, coordinate with SOVA and the counter-terrorism people—and anyone else you need to talk to about this situation. Let's recall the Red-haired Major, too. We should talk to him directly. Get him back from Pakistan ASAP, Jim."

Jim, the Special Activities leader, smiles a bright, very white-toothed smile. "He won't be happy about that, sir."

"I know. That's why I want you to deliver the bad news to him, personally," Gillis retorts. "Captain Cattani, thank you for your outstanding service. I wish you luck at the Air Staff."

"Yes, sir," I respond more glumly than I intended.

"Wow, don't sound so thrilled about being back at the Pentagon!" Gillis chuckles. Everyone in the SCIF laughs, the tension broken. "You know you always have a home here at Langley, should you choose to leave the Air Force."

"Yes, sir, thank you. Before we break up . . . can I make a final comment?" I should probably keep my mouth shut but I will never have an opportunity to talk to a group like this again.

"Sure, Kevin. Go ahead." Gillis replies with a look that suggests he thinks I ought to quit while I'm ahead.

"Sir, I want to restate that Levchenko is someone we can trust—certainly on this matter. He really has no reason to mislead us. He convinced me that the Soviets want to withdraw. In fact, I think Levchenko would say that they're desperate to withdraw. I also believe—and so does Levchenko—that there will be a civil war in Afghanistan when Moscow pulls out. Commander Massoud is a fine leader, but he may not prevail in an internal conflict, at least not in the long run. He's Tadjik and that group is a distinct minority in Afghanistan. All of you know that tribal loyalties mean everything in Afghanistan. I also think we should worry more about the foreign fighters—the Arabs, the Chechens, the Balkan Muslims—and the advanced weapons and combat experience they are acquiring in Afghanistan. General Levchenko told me he is troubled about the potential for those groups to influence Muslim radicals in the Soviet Republics with large Islamic populations. Those foreign fighters are gaining experience that they may choose to use against us and our allies, as well as the Soviets. We all know about the law of unintended consequences."

Gillis nods and considers my final remarks. "Interesting." He pauses to jot down a note to himself. "I'd like to hear what the counter-terrorism team has to say about the potential for future trouble with the Islamic fighters. Okay, thanks everybody. Meeting adjourned." Gillis stands and I hear everyone breathe what sounds like an involuntary sigh of relief.

29 December 1986

A couple of days later, General Palumbo returns to the Pentagon, and he asks to see me in his office. "Well, Kevin, has Dr. Gillis recruited you to join CIA?"

"Sir?"

"I bet he put the hard sell on you when you went out to Langley."

"No sir, not really. Well, sort of."

Palumbo harrumphs. "I have some news for you. First, you didn't hear this from me; however, it looks like you will be promoted early. A little birdie told me that you're getting promoted to major—three years early! This is highly unusual, you know. And you can't tell anybody, okay? We're lucky to get even one intelligence officer promoted so early each year and you're it this year."

I'm dumbfounded. "Sir? That's . . . I mean it's a big surprise."

"You understand you can't tell anybody? Not even your girlfriend. Got it?"

I nod. I understand the rules. General Palumbo does not know that Sandy and I have broken up and I am not going to tell him.

"Okay. I have one other thing for you. You know our buddy General Levchenko?"

"Yes, sir. Is he . . . dead?"

"What? Dead? No. He's coming to Washington in February. He's going to be the new senior military attaché at the Soviet Embassy."

"Wow. He's alive. I've been worried that he was killed in Pakistan."

"He got promoted, too. He's going to be a general-lieutenant when he gets to DC. How about that?"

"I'm glad he's alive."

"Me too, Kevin. Me too."

General Palumbo pauses before saying, "What worries me the most are all these weapons we're giving to radicals in Afghanistan. God knows where this will lead." General Palumbo picks up a folder off his desk and starts thumbing through the papers inside. "Okay, Kevin, now get the hell out of my office and go do something productive for your country."

Levchenko's alive! That news is almost enough to restore one's faith. And he is coming here to Washington to be the Soviets' senior military attaché. Perhaps I will have the chance to see General Levchenko again while he is in Washington, although the FBI may take a dim view of someone like me meeting with a senior GRU officer.

As for me, I will be thirty-one years old soon and it is a good time to take stock of my life. Were Sandy and I doomed? She always seemed to think so, or so it seemed to me. I think I need a woman in my life more than she needs a man. I simply do not understand guys that go for years without a woman—without a steady relationship. Some guys can do it. Not me.

Should I resign from the Air Force and go over to CIA? If I believe my own argument—the argument I made to General Flannery—then I probably should. Only the Clandestine Service interests me at CIA. I do not want to be an analyst stuck in a cubicle farm at Langley.

Maybe I should do something entirely different like go to Wall Street. There is nothing tying me to Washington any longer. It would be good to make money. Money buys independence, or so I am told. I have never had any money so I cannot vouch for that contention.

Did I learn anything in Pakistan? I learned that we are bleeding the Soviet Union and that it is being weakened so badly that it could prove fatal to its long-term existence. I think that is why President Gorbachev wants to get the hell out of Afghanistan—he sees that it is a geo-strategic loser for an already faltering USSR. Levchenko sees it, too. Nonetheless, as I told Dr. Gillis and company at the CIA, I fear the unintended consequences of arming Islamic zealots with advanced weapons. So does Levchenko and he is much wiser about such things than I am.

I relearned some other things. When a Russian attack helicopter killed Brad, a dedicated and highly capable CIA officer, I was reminded yet again that good people die in dangerous places in service to an American public that is largely—no—completely ignorant of the sacrifice.

So, I am at a crossroads. Am I a functionary, a missionary, or a princeling? I am no functionary. The missionaries are running the CIA war against the Soviets. As always, the missionaries have good intentions, but will the law of unintended consequences shatter their illusions and defeat us in the long run?

No. I am a princeling and I do the bidding of my betters—for better or worse—in service to my own romanticism, which does not extend to the zealotry of the missionaries. What was Brad? It seems to me that none of my three categories fit him. I think that Brad and Phil represent a fourth archetype—the patriot. They are the silent professionals who do their work with diligence and dedication. How do the patriots differ from the princelings?

We princelings look and act like patriots and it is hard to tell us apart. Neither group possesses the unlimited zeal of the missionaries. Unlike the patriots, however, princelings have a puffed-up view of their own self-worth. We princelings believe that *we* should be in charge. We do not believe that our betters are better than we are, and we want to supplant them and become princes ourselves. Princelings question the direction we receive from on high and worry about the long-term consequences of our country's actions in a way that missionaries do not. We may have been "innocents abroad" once, but no longer.

Princelings can come from very different socio-economic circumstances, but they believe in meritocracy. Ultimately, princelings who turn into princes run the American empire. I shudder to think of an America run by the functionaries or the missionaries.

The two men I respect the most—the Red-haired Major and General Doug Flannery—are princes at this stage of their careers and each recommends a different path for my future. Flannery wants me to remain on my current track in the Air Force and the Red-haired Major wants me to join him at CIA. I do not know what I ought to do, but I have time to decide.

The American rock star Jim Morrison once sang "The future's uncertain and the past is always near." Amen.

EPILOGUE

an excerpt from the private diary of
General Ivan Ivanovich Levchenko

Ivan Levchenko, General-Lieutenant
Moscow, Russian Soviet Socialist Republic, USSR

February 1987

My prize possession during my time in Afghanistan was an English-language copy of William Shakespeare's collected works. I purchased this hefty volume at Foyles Book Shop on Charing Cross Road in London when my wife Boyka and I were in the city over the Christmas holiday in 1982. That wintry week we spent in England was one of the happiest periods in our entire marriage. Reading Shakespeare in my quarters at Bagram Air Base reminded me of that idyll. The Bard transported me back to quiet evenings with Boyka during the wonderful three years we lived in West Germany. In my wartime quarters at Bagram, I kept my beloved Shakespeare on a shelf right next to the precious little shrine I constructed and dedicated to my wife.

As Boyka has said, my experience in Afghanistan changed me. There are warped pieces of my soul that I may never recognize. My sleep is often interrupted by anxious dreams that spin out of control until I force myself to wake up. Perhaps they will dissipate over time. I can hope. After all, "Life's but a walking shadow," according to Macbeth.

Since my days at the English immersion school in Sevastopol, Crimea, I have been fascinated by American culture and history. I must admit, however, that the allure of America has been forever tarnished by my time in Afghanistan. The United States shipped advanced weapons to our enemies and killed scores of my troops. A hard corner of my heart will never forgive or forget what those weapons did to my men and many other Soviet troops in Afghanistan. Even Kevin Cattani, a respected colleague from the Able Archer nuclear war crisis, had a hand in supplying Stingers to the Mujahedin. His involvement still feels to me like a personal betrayal. Surely a man as perceptive as Cattani had to realize how counterproductive the American role has been in Afghanistan—for both of our countries.

I suppose it's a reminder that we are enemies. Provoking the Soviet Union seems to be an American obsession. As an admirer of the United States, it's hard to accept its sometimes wanton behavior in such a perilous age. President Gorbachev calls the early 1980s the most dangerous time in human history because of our potential for global self-annihilation and I think he is correct. As Cassius tells Brutus in Julius Caesar, "Men at some time are masters of their fates: The fault, dear Brutus, is not in our stars, but in ourselves."

Speaking of enemies, Mikhail Grishin has accused me of incompetence and treachery, of harboring a Ukrainian nationalist, and of consorting with American intelligence officers. His father's position on the Communist Party's Central Committee gives Grishin access to power that I cannot claim, and he is exceptionally dangerous because of it. I have managed to fend him off so far, but he remains a grave threat to me, and I have not heard the last of him.

Against my wishes, I will not be returning to Afghanistan. Boyka is happy, of course, but I feel that it's not fair to my men or to me. Why should their leader move on to a new, safe assignment when they are fated to slog it out for God know how long with an irrepressible enemy? The Kremlin leadership stumbled into this war with no clear strategy or concrete set of objectives. They sent troops into a cauldron and then fecklessly left them to boil on their own. After all these years, no one in the leadership has been held responsible for this fiasco. Only the men who served and sacrificed and their families have suffered. Clearly, my men are not masters of their own fates and neither am I. The best I can hope for is to have a positive influence on our leaders and the decisions they make.

I must have hope for the future of mankind, but I fear we are running up a mountain that has no summit. The threat of war—including nuclear war—is ever present, despite recent attempts to lessen the danger through arms control measures. I have learned that one should never underestimate the human potential for miscalculation and hubris.

ACKNOWLEDGMENTS

My wife, Tracy Trencher Morra, once again provided her outstanding story ideas and editing skills to this novel. Her support is invaluable. Phyllis Okon, the wonderful author of bestselling children's and young adult books always provides generous and expert counsel.

My literary agent Nick Mullendore, the president of Vertical Ink, lent his always incisive and heartfelt advice to this endeavor. My Hollywood agent Jon Levin, president of Sustainable Imagination, provided great feedback to me on the television treatment for *The Able Archers*, which influenced me a great deal in polishing the writing of *The Righteous Arrows*. Any deficiencies in the book are my fault and are likely due to me not adhering to the excellent advice of Nick and Jon.

Madeira James and Riley Mack at Xuni.com keep my website and newsletters up-to-date and looking great.

John Koehler and the entire team at Koehler Books continue to support me and produce a great product. The staff support from Koehler is terrific and they are dedicated to improving their work with every book they publish.

I also want to thank the *New York Times* bestselling author Jack Carr, who has been generous with his time and who had me as a guest on his "Danger Close" podcast to discuss *The Able Archers*.

Michael Morell, the career CIA officer who served two stints as acting director of the Agency, has been a great supporter. Michael hosted me on his CBS News Radio program "Intelligence Matters," shortly after the publication of *The Able Archers*. Micheal and his wife have a wonderful bookstore in Middleburg, Virginia. I urge readers to visit Middleburg Books when they are in the Virginia hunt country. I also want to thank Ross Kaminsky for having me on his nationally syndicated radio show on I Heart Radio. I am grateful for all the podcast, radio, and television producers and personalities who had me on their platforms.

Lastly, I want to thank all the book clubs, libraries, universities, and bookstores who have hosted events for me. I especially want to thank my undergraduate alma mater, William and Mary, for its unstinting support. William and Mary's veterans organization, the Society of 1775, and the university's Swem Library have been extremely generous. Kathleen Jabs, who is the university's lead for military and veterans affairs, deserves special thanks for her efforts on my behalf and on behalf of William and Mary's military community everywhere. I also want to thank the Harvard Veterans Alumni Organization for its sponsorship. Many thanks are due to the family and friends who were early readers of *The Righteous Arrows* for their time and advice.

APPENDIX A

BIOGRAPHIES OF THE PROTAGONISTS OF THE ABLE ARCHERS SERIES

Current as of February 1987

Kevin Cattani, United States Air Force Intelligence

Born: Southern Virginia, USA, 1956

Education: BA, College of William and Mary, Williamsburg, Virginia, 1977; MA, Georgetown University, Washington, DC, 1985

US Air Force Training:
- Air Force Officers Training School, 1977, San Antonio, Texas
- Armed Forces Air Intelligence School, 1977–78, Denver, Colorado
- Case Officers Basic Course and Paramilitary Course, CIA, 1978, Williamsburg, Virginia
- Air Force Intelligence officer with a special operations specialty code
- Special Activities Division unit, Tokyo, Japan, 1979–1981

- Chief of Intelligence Analysis, United States Forces, Japan, Yokota Air Base, 1981–1983
- Current Intelligence Briefer, United States Air Forces, Europe, Ramstein Air Base, West Germany, 1983–1984
- Graduate Student, Georgetown University, Washington, DC, 1984–1985
- Current Intelligence Briefer, Headquarters of the United States Air Force, Pentagon, Washington, DC, 1985–1986
- Current rank and assignment: Captain, detailed from the Air Staff to the CIA's Special Activities Division, 1986–1987

Languages (in descending order of proficiency): English, Russian, Japanese

Ethnicity: mixed Italian/Luxembourgish/Irish

Marital status: unmarried

Sports background: college track and cross-country

Ivan Levchenko, Soviet Air Defense Forces/Soviet Military Intelligence (GRU)

Born: Crimea, Ukrainian Soviet Socialist Republic, USSR, 1939

Education:
- English immersion school—grades 1-12, Sevastopol, Crimea, USSR
- BS, Kiev Higher Engineering Radio-Technical College of the Soviet Air Force, Kiev, Ukrainian Soviet Socialist Republic, USSR, 1961

- Military-Diplomatic Academy—a three-year postgraduate school in intelligence and foreign affairs, Moscow, Russian Soviet Socialist Republic, USSR, 1964.

Air Defense Force of the USSR—Soviet Military Intelligence (GRU)
- Beginning in 1964 and through 1980, assignments as a junior and midlevel intelligence officer to units in the Western Military District of the USSR, the Group of Soviet Forces, Poland and the Group of Soviet Forces, Germany (East Germany)
- Senior officer of the Soviet Military Liaison Mission in Frankfurt, West Germany, 1980–1983
- Deputy director and later director for intelligence at the Headquarters of the Red Banner Moscow Air Defense District, Moscow, Russian Soviet Socialist Republic, USSR, 1983–1985
- General-major and commanding general of GRU and Spetsnaz forces assigned to the 40th Army in Soviet-occupied Afghanistan, 1986–1987
- Current rank and assignment: General-lieutenant and Defense Attaché of the USSR to the United States of America, Soviet Embassy, Washington, DC, USA

Languages (in descending order of proficiency): Russian, English, German, Polish

Ethnicity: Russian

Marital status: married to Boyka Levchenka, a Ukrainian-born musician educated at the Tchaikovsky Conservatory, Kiev, Ukrainian Soviet Socialist Republic, USSR

Sports background: college track, cross-country, and boxing

APPENDIX B

A CHRONOLOGY OF THE SOVIET WAR IN AFGHANISTAN

Apr 1978—The Saur Revolution brings a deeply unpopular (with the Afghan population) Communist regime to power in Kabul. A "democratic republic" is declared, aligned with the Communist Party of the Soviet Union.

Apr 1979—Traditional Afghan groups openly rebel throughout the country against the repressive Communist regime. They are known as "holy warriors"—Mujahedin.

Sep 1979—Deep rifts within the Communist regime in Kabul come to a head and the president of the Afghan Democratic Republic, Tariq Aziz, is assassinated in a coup orchestrated by his second in command, Hafizullah Aziz. The coup, unsanctioned by Moscow, angers Soviet leader Leonid Brezhnev. The Kremlin fears Aziz will switch his allegiance to the United States.

Dec 1979—Operation Storm, a combined KGB/GRU attack on Kabul, is launched by the Kremlin to depose Aziz and to install Soviet loyalist Babrak Karmal.

Jan 1980—Some thirty-four nations of the Organization of Islamic Cooperation endorse a resolution condemning the Soviet invasion of Afghanistan and calling for the immediate withdrawal of Soviet forces from the country.

1980—The United States leads a boycott of the Moscow Summer Olympics, largely as a result of the Soviet invasion of Afghanistan. President Jimmy Carter authorizes military assistance for the Afghan Mujahedin in concert with the government of Pakistan. China strongly condemns the invasion along with most member states of the United Nations General Assembly. Anti-Soviet groups rise up throughout Afghanistan, drawing the Soviet military into a protracted war of attrition.

The Soviet Army, made up mostly of conscript soldiers, conducts brutal, scorched-earth attacks against villages, massacres of Afghan civilians, and rape of Afghan women and children. The Soviets use mines extensively in civilian areas to deter civilians from supporting the Mujahedin fighters and to terrorize the population. About 25 percent of the Soviet troops who served in Afghanistan are Ukrainian.

The Soviet occupation has several negative long-term effects: the militarization of Afghan society, the rise of the illicit drug trade, and the rise of the increasingly radicalized Mujahedin as the dominating force in society and the concomitant decline of women's rights.

1985—The number of Soviet troops in Afghanistan is increased to 108,800 and 1985 becomes the bloodiest year of the war for the Kremlin. The Mujahedin also suffer heavy losses, but their numbers are bolstered by a continuing stream of new recruits. The rebels are supported by the United States, China, Saudi Arabia, Pakistan, the United Kingdom, and Egypt. Thousands of volunteers from around the Muslim world converge on Afghanistan. Soviet President Gorbachev begins making policy changes that will lead to the Soviet withdrawal from Afghanistan.

1986—The United States introduces the Stinger man-portable surface-to-air missile into the conflict, providing it to various Mujahedin groups. The Afghan rebels prove adept at using the Stingers to shoot down Soviet aircraft, especially helicopters. Soviet President Gorbachev maintains that the Stingers do not influence his thinking about Afghanistan as much as American economic sanctions do. Mohammed Najibullah succeeds Babrak Karmal as president of Afghanistan.

Jan 87—The Soviet armed forces begin to withdraw from Afghanistan. The official Soviet policy is to turn the fighting over to the Afghan national forces.

Feb 89—The last elements of the Soviet 40th Army depart Afghanistan, a necessary disengagement, but one that tarnishes the reputation of the Soviet Armed Forces. It is a controversial and divisive development among elements of the Soviet national security apparatus. The withdrawal is part of a global change in Soviet foreign policy under President Gorbachev from confrontation to avoidance of conflict.

Apr 92—President Najibullah is overthrown by Mujahedin forces, precipitating a four-year civil war amongst various Afghan factions.

Nov 96—The Taliban emerge victorious after four years of internecine strife and establish an Islamic Republic in Kabul.

APPENDIX C

GLOSSARY OF TERMS

Air Defense Forces of the Soviet Union: one of the USSR's five military services, it was responsible for the missile and air defense of the homeland and forward deployed forces.

Air Force OSI: the Office of Special Investigations—the Air Force's internal counterintelligence and criminal investigative service

APC: armored personnel carrier

Air Staff: Headquarters of the United States Air Force in the Pentagon

CIA: America's Central Intelligence Agency, founded in 1947

DIA: Defense Intelligence Agency, the Pentagon's joint-service intelligence agency

GRU: Soviet Military Intelligence, which also includes special operations units. It reports directly to the General Staff. Russia uses the same organizational name today.

KGB: Soviet Committee for State Security—civilian foreign and domestic intelligence and security agency. Today, the KGB's old functions are split (for the most part) between the SVR—foreign intelligence—and the FSB—domestic intelligence and counterintelligence with some law enforcement responsibilities.

MLM: Military Liaison Mission—after the end of World War II in Europe, the four victorious powers—France, Great Britain, the Soviet Union, and the United States—agreed to establish liaison missions to the headquarters of their respective occupying commands in West Germany and in East Germany. For example, the United States MLM (USMLM) had its headquarters in West Berlin and a forward operating location in Potsdam, East Germany. The USMLM was organized into ground and air teams. The Soviet Union's MLM was situated similarly in Frankfurt, West Germany.

MI6: the United Kingdom's foreign intelligence agency

NATO: the North Atlantic Treaty Organization—the Western alliance founded after World War II to stand as a bulwark against the USSR and its Warsaw Pact allies

NSA: the National Security Agency—America's Signals Intelligence and Cyber intelligence agency

Operation RYaN: the largest Soviet intelligence collection program of the Cold War, designed to ferret out indications of NATO preparations to launch a preemptive nuclear war. Begun by Yuri Andropov in May 1981.

PRA: Permanently Restricted Area—a region in East Germany specified by the Soviet Union as an area strictly prohibited to entry by allied MLM tours

SAD: the CIA's Special Activities Division—the paramilitary arm of the CIA, organized into ground and air segments

SCIF: Secure Compartmented Intelligence (or Information) Facility

STASI: East German secret police, primarily a counterintelligence organization that spied on East Germans and on the Western MLM units and occasionally on the Soviets occupying East Germany.

USAFE: United States Air Forces, Europe

Warsaw Pact: the military alliance led by Moscow that comprised its client states in Eastern Europe, including East Germany. It was the Cold War adversary of the NATO alliance.

Printed in the USA
CPSIA information can be obtained
at www.ICGtesting.com
LVHW091625100224
771270LV00004B/26